Dedi

TO M

Yes, Mom, I'

Acknowledgments

Many thanks to my supportive editor, ELF, for the encouragement, feedback, and shaping the polished work that exists today. Thank you to Rhonda Penders and the amazing staff at The Wild Rose Press.

A heartfelt appreciation for my devoted writers' group who spent endless hours, providing comments as I wrote each chapter, especially Gene, Sandra, Nancy, Pepper, and Jimmy. Over the past two years, we've had many in depth discussions during our virtual meetings. Sometimes I think you know my characters better than I do.

Much gratitude to my community of attentive beta readers: Melissa, Maria, Antoinette, Bob, and Mary Jo.

Thank you to my children, Kevin, Ashley, Brian, and Brooke, for always believing in me.

And last, a special thank you to my number one supporter, my loving husband, Paul. I love you!

He moved closer, his breath warming her face. "I don't want to be a friend. I want more."

Her eyes blurred. "It's only been six months since Mark died."

"Life goes on, Hailey. Mark's gone."

"Six months, Parker." Tears burnt like acid splashing in her eyes. Six months was not nearly enough time to let go.

"I'm sorry. I didn't mean to say it that way." Parker reached over and held her hand. The tenderness in his touch made an instant connection to her heart. She yanked her hand away, ashamed for her heart's betrayal. As she wiped a tear off her cheek, he whispered. "I love you, Hailey. I always have. Somehow life or fate, or whatever it is you want to call it, always got in our way. I kept my distance when you married Mark, but I never stopped loving you." He tightened his grasp on her hand. "Now I feel like an idiot because…I waited too long."

"Parker, please. I'm not sure I even want to get involved with someone again."

"You've become so miserable. You're a strong woman." His face hardened. "Mark wouldn't want you to waste your life grieving. He'd want you to go on—and at least try to be happy." He caressed her cheek with his thumb. "I think deep down, you know it."

Few people had her pegged so well. She bit her lip and whispered, "I do."

Praise for C. Becker

"Saving Euphoria had me flipping pages well into the middle of the night, constantly wondering what was going to happen next. The multiple layers in this story are intricate with 3 POVs, but well done and easy to follow. The characters were enjoyable and C. Becker made it easy to fall in step with their thoughts, really pulling me into the story."

~ Aubrey Grant, author

Saving Euphoria

by

C. Becker

Euphoria Series, Book Two

Saving Euphoria

Cover Art by *Kim Mendoza*

The Wild Rose Press, Inc.
PO Box 708
Adams Basin, NY 14410-0708
Visit us at www.thewildrosepress.com

Publishing History
First Edition, 2022
Trade Paperback ISBN 978-1-5092-4080-7
Digital ISBN 978-1-5092-4081-4

Euphoria Series, Book Two
Published in the United States of America

Chapter One

October 2021

Mark was up to something. Hailey Langley feigned sleep until her husband turned off his alarm and strode into the bathroom.

His latest case consumed his attention.

With a heightened determination to figure it out, she waited for the patter of water against the glass shower door then threw back the bedsheets. He'd been acting strange for the past few weeks. Not really strange. More like secretive. And he was distracted. He'd forgotten about Ethan's high school basketball game earlier in the week, and he hid his cell phone when she walked past him in the living room. Usually his cases didn't trouble him like this.

She scratched her hands and stopped. The tiny scars were barely visible. She hadn't been tempted to scratch in six years. If she'd done something to upset him, he would've told her.

What was he up to?

His briefcase was propped next to his dresser.

Hailey unzipped the front flap and removed two travel brochures on the Hawaiian Islands with a sticky note on the cover—*Buy two plane tickets to Kauai.*

Kauai? Yes! She did a happy dance. They had often talked about vacationing in Hawaii. A tropical island paradise would be a welcome change from the Northern Virginia rat race where they lived. A sudden cloud of guilt dulled her joy. Did she spoil an anniversary surprise?

The shower water stopped.

Uh-oh. She'd better hurry.

When the brochure and notes were back in place, Hailey slid a pair of jeans and a sweater over her thin frame. She had no reason to be insecure. Work had to be the distraction. Brushing her thick mane, she peered at the roots for any gray strands amidst the chestnut coloring. Finished dressing, she hurried downstairs, grinning at her plan. First, she'd put him in a good mood. Mark would be thrilled to have a cooked breakfast with the kids before he left.

Food. It might be a way to a man's heart, but it was also a way to a man's soul.

She sped around the kitchen, cracking eggs into the stainless steel bowl and heating the skillet.

In no time, the bacon sizzled, and the coffee brewed.

As she arranged plates around the table, Ethan moseyed into the room wearing his usual T-shirt and swiped a strip of bacon. "Mmm. What's the occasion?" He reached for another strip.

She swatted his hand. "Leave some for breakfast. I thought we'd eat with Dad today."

Anna stomped through the doorway. "Mom, did you see my social studies book?"

She turned to her daughter, whose bright-hazel eyes and long lashes mimicked her own. "No, where did you leave it?"

The youngster scanned the room. "I don't know."

"Check the stack of papers on the counter." Hailey splashed milk into the bowl and beat the egg mixture.

Mark walked into the chaos as she poured the eggs into the pan. He adjusted his navy tie and planted a tender kiss on her lips. "Smells delicious, honey. I expected you to sleep in today. This is nice."

She smiled and lowered a plate of buttered toast on the table. Anything was nice compared to the bagel he usually grabbed before heading into the District. "My first class isn't until later, but I figured you'd enjoy a big breakfast."

Mark sat next to Ethan and poured a glass of orange juice. "I'll call tonight on my way home. I shouldn't be too late." His eyebrow arched as Anna scurried around the room, lifting papers and banging drawers.

Hailey suppressed a grin and shrugged.

Ethan piled toast on his plate. "Are you going to make basketball practice tonight, Dad?"

Mark frowned. "I wish I could, Ethan. I have some late meetings, so I'll be stuck in traffic."

Anna stooped and peered under the table. "Mom, did you throw it away when you swept the floor?"

Hailey blew a quick breath, lifting the long bangs swooping over her eyes. "Anna. Think. Where did you do your homework?" She set the eggs and plate of bacon on the table. "Come and eat before your breakfast gets cold."

"I put my homework in the social studies book...The dining room!" Anna's eyes widened, and she darted from the room.

Hailey sat and poured a cup of fresh-brewed coffee. "How long is this case going to last?"

"Depends. Another week. Maybe a few months."

She'd worked cases like that. "So then I'll get my old husband back?"

A wry grin spread across his face. "I hope you don't mean 'old' in the sense of my age."

She patted his forearm. He still wore his wedding ring. Fidelity was one piece of the puzzle she'd never have to worry about. "No, but you've been distracted."

"Is it obvious?"

Ethan gulped the juice. "We've all noticed. Even Coach Reynolds asked why you're gone all the time. He needs you to help the guys with layups."

She warmed at the similarity of the two. At fifteen, Ethan was two inches shy of Mark's six-foot stature. They loved working out, although Mark's exercise routine was hit or miss—more miss, the past month. Ethan had a lanky build, much like Mark's when she first met him twenty years ago.

"Found it!" Anna brandished the lost book. She pulled out her chair and scooped scrambled eggs onto her plate.

Glancing at the wall clock, Mark guzzled down the rest of his juice and stood. "I'm late. Gotta go." He tousled Ethan's hair and yanked Anna's braided pigtail. "Have a good day at school, you two."

Hailey walked with him into the living room. "I teach until two o'clock. Let me know about dinner." She took his fall jacket from the closet. "You'd better take this. It's getting colder at night."

He draped the jacket over his briefcase and set it on the floor, then slipped his arms around her waist.

The warmth of his touch sent shivers through her body.

"Last night was nice. Did I ever tell you how lucky I am?"

She gazed into his dreamy blue eyes. "Every night."

He brushed a finger across her cheek. "You're more beautiful than the day I married you. Do you know that?"

She kissed his ear and whispered, "Convince me."

He captured her lips in a fierce kiss. "Don't tempt me or I'll call in sick, and we'll spend the day upstairs."

"I'd love to, but we both have to work." Hailey kissed him back and laughed as he groaned. She glanced at her hands; the desire to scratch diminished. Whatever caused his distraction, it definitely didn't involve her. "Hurry home."

Mark kissed her again, more passionately. When their lips separated, he whispered. "I'm going to be late." He lifted his briefcase, and a business card fell from his jacket.

Hailey picked it up, and her chest tightened. "What's this?"

He snatched the card from her hand before she could read more than the name. "Nothing."

"The Correctional Facility for Women?" Anger rose inside Hailey like a volcano spewing lava as events from six years prior sped through her mind. Colleen Toole was responsible for so many painful memories. Hailey's abduction. Her near-death from Euphoria. Losing Justin. A murder attempt on Mark. "Oh my God. Don't tell me you've been talking to *her*. How could you?"

He hurried out the door. "I'm late. We'll talk about this when I get home."

"Mark Langley—if you contact this woman, don't bother coming home." She swung the door shut with a loud thud and clenched her fists until the nails dug against her palms. "Aargh!" That vindictive woman almost ruined their life. "Damn you, Colleen Toole!"

****

Mark rose from his chair in the private interview room at the Correctional Facility for Women in Baltimore and collected the realtor's listings. He snapped the latches on his briefcase and studied the middle-aged woman seated across from him.

Dressed in a drab slate-gray uniform, Colleen Toole seemed unusually anxious. Even the blue-painted walls, meant to calm prisoners, hadn't helped her disposition.

He'd spent the past two hours trying to convince her turning state's evidence would be the better option. When Colleen refused, Mark showed her the listing of houses on the market.

"Are you sure you won't reconsider?" Mark studied her closer. "If you don't go into witness protection, Mendoza can still find you."

She shook her head. "I won't live that way. I have too few friends to just pick up and disappear."

"I don't agree with your decision, but I understand." His heart sank at how his once-beautiful girlfriend had changed during the six years serving time.

Gray strands of hair curved around her face, and deep lines etched her forehead.

"In eight months, your sentence will be over. I'll have everything arranged, and you'll be flying to your new home in Hawaii."

Colleen glanced at the guard standing with his back to the door, and she gripped the small three-by-five-inch photo in front of her. "I can't shake this feeling something will go wrong."

Mark's work at the Drug Trafficking Agency made him confident. The DTA still sought the drug dealer Manuel de Mendoza for drug manufacturing, distribution, and murder, among other crimes. "I know you're nervous." He leaned in. "But I wish you'd reconsider. You can trust my men. If we can arrest Mendoza, he can't hurt you once you're released."

"I don't trust anyone. You don't know Manuel like I do. He'd find a way to retaliate." She glanced at the guard again. "Somehow I need to make it through eight more months without going crazy." Laying the photo on the table, she wiped a stray tear from her cheek and picked at her unpolished nails, her once-elegant hands now corrupted. "I'm losing precious time."

"Start focusing on your new life. Don't worry about Mendoza."

"But you said your CIA contact knows someone's been asking questions about me. It has to be Manuel. What if he bribes someone here to get information? Or tries to contact me?"

Mark rested his arm against the briefcase. He shouldn't have told her about his concern. "We have Mendoza's house in Colombia under surveillance. He hasn't made contact with anyone here."

"How can you be certain?"

"I trust David. He's the best the CIA has. His team's been monitoring Manuel." Mark tilted his head. "Don't worry. No one can give Manuel the info he wants. Only I know about your secret." He made his voice sound convincing, but even the DTA and CIA couldn't protect against guards leaking information.

Nothing was one hundred percent certain.

Colleen handed him the photograph. "How can I ever thank you? After what I did to you, I'm thankful you're still talking to me."

Mixed emotions from the time they dated blurred with her attempt to kill him and Hailey. He shrugged, blinking away the memory of Colleen trapping him in a building and rigging it to explode. "Don't worry about it. Are you certain you don't want to keep this picture?"

She glanced at the guard waiting near the door. "It's too dangerous if someone sees it."

Mark placed the photo on his planner. She was right. Who knew what would happen if it got into the wrong hands? The picture he had taken four years before always cheered her up. Using a more current photo was too risky. He shoved the planner and photo into his messenger bag.

"You probably won't believe me after everything that's happened, but I only want the best for you. You're a good guy, Mark Langley. You deserve happiness."

"Maybe after you're released and start a new life, you'll find happiness, too." Her sapphire eyes were still bewitching, but they didn't work their magic on him any longer. The sparkle in Hailey's dark-hazel eyes enchanted him. Hailey. She was infuriated when he walked out that morning. He'd have to come up with a convincing explanation when he drove home.

Night was setting in as Mark strode through the parking lot. He unlocked his car, put on his jacket, and slid his cell phone into his front pants pocket. The briefcase and bag landed on the passenger seat. As he drove along the interstate back to Virginia, he pushed the steering wheel control. "Call Hailey." In a moment, she picked up. Was she still upset? "Hi, honey."

"Mark." The sound of her bitter voice justified his decision to protect his family. "When are you coming home?"

"In about an hour. I miss you." He crossed his fingers, hoping his sweet talk would buckle Hailey's anger. "Did you get the roses I sent you?"

"You mean the peace offering? The florist delivered them this afternoon." Her voice became softer, the antagonism melting. "Do you want us to hold dinner?"

His stomach growled. "Better not. It's getting late, and the traffic is still heavy."

"Okay. But we need to talk about this morning."

"We will. Maybe we can stay up a little late tonight after we talk."

She giggled. "Sounds fun."

The laughter soothed his worries.

North of the District, his phone's GPS announced a shortcut to avoid a night-paving project on the highway. He'd merged off an exit onto a state road when the phone rang. Mark pressed the button on his steering wheel. "Hey David, what's up?"

"Did you see Colleen?"

"Just left a few minutes ago. I'm heading home."

"How is she?"

He glanced in the rearview mirror; a sedan loomed with bright halogen lights on high beam. "Nervous. She's still refusing to testify. She thinks Mendoza will retaliate." Mark adjusted his rearview mirror, but the lights blinded him. With one hand, he unzipped his messenger bag and grabbed the glasses he used for nighttime driving.

"There's a good chance he will. If she testified against Manuel and José, the Colombian government could incarcerate father and son for at least a hundred and fifty years."

Mark pushed the glasses higher on the bridge of his nose. "She doesn't want to risk pissing off Manuel."

"He'll be plenty pissed if he finds out what she's hiding. He'll try to stop her."

Mark smirked. "And if it happens, we'll be waiting. Once Mendoza is arrested, my family will be safe."

"You're risking a lot helping her."

"It's the right thing to do."

David sneered. "How can you forgive someone who almost killed your wife?"

Mark could never forget how Hailey almost died from the hallucinogen Euphoria. "It was a long time ago."

"It wasn't that long ago. She almost killed you, too, in the explosion."

"But she didn't."

David scoffed. "The drug she created killed almost fifty people. She's pure evil. Why can't you open your eyes?"

Mark raked his hand through his hair. David hadn't liked Colleen since the day Mark introduced her. "She's changed. I've seen it during—" He lurched forward in his seat, knocking his head against the steering wheel and spilling the contents of his bag onto the floor. "Oh shit."

"What happened?"

The halogen lights shone directly in his field of vision, and he glared in the rearview mirror. "Some asshole ran into me. I've got to go."

"Okay. Call me back."

Mark clicked the connection off and opened his car door.

The driver of a dark-gray sedan stepped toward him.

"Buddy, I'll need your insurance—"

The rough-looking man raised his arms and pointed a gun at Mark.

"What the hell—"

Someone from behind clutched Mark's shoulders and twisted his arms behind his back.

****

The tight cubicle smelled of upholstery and oil. *Dammit! How did I let my guard down?* He was snagged like a wild animal. The two men who rammed into his car had gagged him, duct taped his arms and legs together, and dumped him into the trunk of their sedan. Mark shouted for help during the ride, but the gag muffled the cries. *Think.* Sweat dripped down his forehead as he raised his restrained arms and felt for a trunk release. Nothing. Dammit.

His arm bumped against something hard in his pants pocket. His phone. The goons hadn't confiscated his phone. He maneuvered the cell phone from his pocket and pressed the power button. The light from the phone illuminated shadows in the tight space. He fumbled on the keypad and typed in his password. He pressed a button and redialed his last caller. Come on, dammit. Pick up.

"You decided to call back. What happened with the jerk who ran into you?"

Mark screamed through his gag.

"Hello? Mark? You there?"

He tried making coherent pleas for help.

"Is someone there? Mark?" Click.

The car stopped. He wriggled the phone back into his pocket. *Stay calm.*

The two burly men wrenched him out of the trunk.

Mark steadied himself and considered the men. He could probably overpower them if he had the chance.

They dragged him toward a rundown warehouse where a dark-haired man with a black moustache stood sentry, waving a gun and giving orders in Spanish.

Three men would be much harder to fight off. Who were these goons?

The guard led the way into the building that smelled of cut wood. Old sawmill equipment, forklifts, and lumber filled the room. They slowed their pace at a wall of two-by-four studs stacked to the ceiling. One of the men turned on an overhead light.

The sentry thrust Mark down onto a wobbly wooden stool and ripped off the gag. He was the tallest of the three assailants, maybe six-four, but they all had tanned skin and weathered, dark features. Tattooed on the sentry's inner forearm was a single maple leaf.

The men didn't seem to mind Mark could identify them. If, by some miracle, he got away.

Standing in front of Mark, the sentry cracked his knuckles. "Where is she?"

"What are you talking about?" Mark strained to stretch his fingers bound by the duct tape. The situation couldn't get any worse.

A short bald man with massive biceps and a scar under his cheek punched him in the side.

Mark buckled over.

"The girl. Where are you hiding her?"

Damn. How do they know? Now that Mendoza knew Colleen's secret, he'd stop at nothing to get what he wanted. "I don't know what—" Another punch caught his breath and sucked the air from his lungs. He stayed silent. Maybe David recognized something was wrong.

The captors interrogated him for what seemed like hours. The beatings continued until he spewed the acrid bile juices left in his stomach.

"So you're going to play dumb?"

The bald man stank like he'd bathed in the sewer. "One of us might take a trip to your house and bring back some inspiration. We've been watching your hot-looking bitch." He laughed. "And your two kids."

The blood ran cold inside Mark's veins. Was protecting Colleen worth hurting his family?

"I'll ask you one more time. Don't play fucking games with me." The heavier man with a straggly beard punched him square in the jaw.

Mark's head jerked to the side. When he opened his eyes, rage filled the men's faces. His vision blurred as he scanned the room. There had to be some way to get out. Finally, he forced a gruff whisper. "I'm the only one who knows what you want. If you kill me, you lose everything."

The remark incensed the men more. They took turns beating his head, pummeling his torso, and kicking his legs. Every inch of his body throbbed. Blood dripped down his nose.

He yelped at the next punch. His heart beat in erratic spasms. The pain in his face intensified as his eyes swelled. Why hadn't he been more vigilant? He should have brought his partner. The DTA suspected Mendoza would be desperate and nose around.

"Dammit! Where is she?" The sentry's voice dripped with disdain.

The bearded man turned to the sentry. "Should we get his wife and kids? That'll make him talk."

The sentry gnashed his teeth. "No, I'll deal with them later." His stare bored into his captive, and he spit in Mark's face. "Talk, dammit! Where are you hiding the girl?"

He swallowed hard, too weak to think. Hailey and the kids knew nothing. The sentry's foul breath constricted his stomach, and bile rose again in his throat. This was a battle until the end. Holding out on the information was his last hope to lure Mendoza into the U.S. *Don't ruin the agency's plan to capture this bastard.*

The sentry squeezed Mark's jaw.

God, his teeth were going to pop out of their sockets. How was he going to survive this? The room spun around him. *Dear God, keep my family safe.*

The shorter man tramped away and returned a few minutes later, carrying a red container.

Gas. The smell was unmistakable. Sweat dropped from Mark's forehead as the man splashed the contents on the floor.

The sentry sneered. "This is your last chance."

He fought to hang onto consciousness. Thoughts of Hailey, Ethan, and Anna flooded his mind as blackness overtook him.

Chapter Two

January 2022

Manuel de Mendoza stared out the window of the helicopter as the pilot zoomed toward his father's training camp. The mere idea of meeting José made Manuel's head pound like a machine gun firing.

The pilot turned. "Shall I wait for you after I land, *señor*?"

Manuel nodded and gazed out the window once more. "I shouldn't be long." Though accustomed to the constant demands of his family's drug business, his mind was elsewhere. *Un cerdo*. That's what he was. A worthless scumbag. Why had he jilted his beautiful Bella? What kind of a man left a girlfriend scorned and alone to face the legal consequences of their crimes? Did Bella think about him as often as he thought of her?

She would be free from prison in less than a year. In the States she was known as Colleen Toole, but he preferred to call her Bella because of her stunning beauty. Would she want to see him? His heart twisted at his cowardice. Up to this point, he'd kept his distance. No doubt, the authorities had been on alert. They'd open any letter mailed from Colombia, listen in on any cellular communication. Surely, considering the shocking news he'd learned four months ago, Bella still had feelings for him.

The pilot waved a hand in front of Manuel's face. "*Señor* Mendoza, we're here." He had landed about one hundred yards from the training camp.

Manuel blinked away the memories of Bella.

The world in Colombia was different from the States. Palm trees and sugar cane plants grew amid the dense jungle bushes, bordering the camp where a group of peasants gathered, stacking crates next to a makeshift tent. Two men with assault rifles trained a small group of young men.

The camp was one of several *Fuerzas Armadas Revolucionarias de Colombia* (FARC) territories throughout Colombia where commanders organized their dissidents.

His father, José, ran a tight clandestine operation on the western terrain near Antioquia. José's preoccupation with the training camp kept his attention directed away from Manuel's affairs. His father had spent weeks away from the Mendoza estate, working drills with the new FARC fighters in the field.

Rage raised his blood pressure, and his chest muscles tightened; even now, Manuel was afraid of the man. He preferred to keep his distance from the camp, away from his father's vicious temper. He'd seen too many atrocities. Kidnappings. Rapes. Summary executions. The harsh violence still gave him sweat-soaked nightmares. The only involvement he wanted with the family's organization was overseeing the production of coca plants. He respected all of the aspects of the family business—cultivating the plant, manufacturing cocaine, and distributing the drug to other countries.

"*Señor*? Can you hear me?"

How long had the pilot tried to get his attention? Manuel nodded and stepped off the chopper. He held his breath against the stench of decaying plants as he tramped on the jungle floor. In the sultry environment, his clothes clung to his skin, a situation made more insufferable by his thick, heavy hiking boots.

The cicadas buzzed around him as he pulled back a handful of bushy palm fronds and took in the campground activity.

At least twenty men dressed in fatigues, black helmets, and boots up to the knee circled the area, performing warm-up exercises. The few soldiers who hadn't strapped their guns across their chest and backs held their weapons ready in position.

Manuel grimaced. Had he actually joined this activity in his younger days?

Behind a stack of crates, José talked to a man dressed in dark olive camouflage. Except for his father's gray hair, Manuel mirrored the man's physical features—his height, dark eyes, chiseled jaw, and muscular physique. The physical traits were where the similarities ended. His father was like a stranger.

Manuel made his way to José.

The man speaking to José eyed Manuel and departed.

"Papà."

Turning, José coughed. "*Hijueputa!* You've decided to join us?"

The derision never stopped. Manuel pointed to the weaponry around the camp. "You know I don't agree with this."

His father's expression hardened. "Then why the hell did you come?"

"Mamà read about the latest assassinations of Yohan and Hader and she's worried about you. You've been gone for two weeks."

José coughed again. "I told her I was needed in the city."

"She doesn't believe you. Smart woman." He studied the soldiers José was training. "I'll never understand why you hide this from her."

"Why should I tell her? She spends all her time at the orphanage."

"She's your wife. Besides, Mamà's more clever than you think."

José gestured at the soldiers making bombs. "I don't need the fucking lecture. Especially if you refuse to help. It's a damn shame I get more respect from these men than I get from my own son."

Manuel clenched his fist. *Maybe because you've never treated me like a son.* He turned, but his father's hand clasped his shoulders.

"Did the latest shipment go out?"

He smirked. Maybe his father didn't know everything after all. "I thought you would have been privy to the information."

"What the hell are you talking about?"

"Your spies report on everything I do." Manuel waited for a denial, hoping his allegation wasn't true.

"Because you keep everything from me. Did the shipment leave last night for Honduras?"

Manuel glanced toward the rebels. "The authorities confiscated the shipment shortly after it left the dock."

José rubbed a hand over his graying beard. "*Maldita sea*! I needed the fucking funds for more ammunition."

What a quagmire. His father was too old to lead a revolution. In the weeks following the peace agreement, Manuel's optimism that the government would improve the lives of impoverished Colombians diminished. It'd been more than five years, and the rural areas around his home were still without water, electricity, and roads. How could the government expect farmers to stop harvesting coca leaves, yet not distribute the promised cash payments or supply replacement crops?

Frustration flowed through him at the lack of access to education and basic needs. When the neighboring towns disarmed, new hostile groups formed, gathering weapons. Manuel and his family had no choice but to protect what was rightfully theirs. Cocaine trafficking continued as a lucrative family business. "I ordered another shipment, but acres of our coca plants are withered. As soon as the cocaine is packaged, I will call Alej."

José coughed again, more forcefully. "Damn this new government. The paraquat spray killed off half of our crops—and continues to ruin our health. Whoever survived the pandemic will die from the spray."

"*Bixa aparra* is heartier than coca. I can order a shipment of Euphoria sent out anytime."

"*Maldición!* You and your damn plant. Wasn't it enough you killed thirty-eight people when you smuggled the shrub back here? Why do you waste time on it?"

"I shouldn't have rushed the drug. The problem with Euphoria is fixed." Would he ever regain the respect of his father, friends, and countrymen after the catastrophic incident? "I have to go. Call Mamà when you get near phone service."

C. Becker

"Wait." José wiped his forehead with his sleeve. "I have bad news." He waved to an older man with a dark moustache who was standing near the young rebels. "Daniel, over here."

Daniel passed his gun to a subordinate and stepped toward them. His knotted black hair was in dire need of a trim. He was one of José's most trusted confidants. No doubt José used him to train new recruits.

José hacked up a mouthful of phlegm and spit. Throughout the region, the herbicide had caused coughing and wheezing. "Last week Daniel came to the house. He found something—with the computer files."

Manuel lifted his brow. "Oh?" The insult stung. *Papà should have asked me to update files on the computer.*

"Do you remember I told you something strange was happening when the FARC leaders began supporting the peace treaty? When I said someone influenced them?"

Manuel groaned. "Not again." His father's paranoia grew worse every day. "What are you getting at?"

"When Daniel backed up the computer records, he noticed a file had been opened remotely from an unknown device."

"Which file?"

Daniel fidgeted. "The one containing the FARC contacts."

Fuck. The day just got worse. Not only did the file contain the FARC contacts, but it also contained a spreadsheet listing contacts for the drug networks.

A spark flashed in José's eyes. "I told you someone had gotten to those men. You thought I was crazy. I bet

20

the government blackmailed them or offered them immunity in exchange for support. It's the only reason my allies would have agreed to the treaty." He glared. "I *didn't* lose my mind."

Manuel suppressed a retort. Papà had lost his sanity long before this happened. "Dammit. How did someone break into our files? Weren't they encrypted?"

Daniel shifted his stance. "I encrypted them when I added them on a cloud server so you could access them in the States. Someone found the passwords and got inside. That's the only way those files could be opened." His tone was accusing.

Manuel clenched his jaw. "I didn't share the password or leave it lying around. Perhaps you don't know your job as well as you should. Is there any other way the passwords could have been compromised?"

"I don't know."

"Were any other files opened?"

Daniel shook his head. "I'm not sure yet."

"Dammit. My father trusted you." Manuel held a hand to his head as pain pounded against his skull. He shouldn't have come today. Wherever his father was, a headache followed. "When was the file opened?"

Sweat beaded on Daniel's face. "Maybe a month before the first peace treaty was proposed."

That was six years ago. The same year Manuel left his home in Washington and flew back to Colombia. When he deserted Bella and let her take the rap for Euphoria. "Can you tell who opened the file?"

Daniel scratched his head. "I ran a check and located the IP address at an ISP in the States—Buffalo Creek, Wyoming."

Manuel blinked hard. "The States? Are you sure?"

"Yes."

Had Bella discovered the password and opened the file? Sometimes he had found her in his bedroom office after they made love. She had plenty of opportunities to access his computer. And she was definitely cunning. Had she betrayed him? No. If Bella had intended on ruining him, she could have disclosed a lot more damaging evidence than this. Manuel rubbed his temple. There was that night when those two SCA agents broke into his office. The night of his dinner party when he promoted Euphoria to the prominent political leaders and businessmen around the world. Could they have downloaded his files before his security captured the female agent?

José glowered. "What the fuck is in Buffalo Creek, Wyoming?"

Manuel shrugged. "I have no idea. I had no business dealings in Wyoming."

"Maybe the American *puta* betrayed you? What's her name?...Colleen Toole." José's voice dripped with hatred.

Manuel clenched his fists so tight his palms became numb. How did José know about Bella? Being around his father was difficult enough, considering what he did to Selena. Now José was targeting Bella. "She's not a whore! She was in jail at the time the file was opened. It couldn't have been her." He shut his eyes, trying to convince himself. It wasn't just sex. Their bond had been real. Bella wouldn't betray him.

"Then who accessed the damn files? I can tell by the look on your face you know something."

Manuel lowered his head. "There were two agents from the Special Crimes Agency who broke into my mansion in the States. Hailey Langley and Tom Parker. It's possible one of them opened the files."

"*Maldición*! No wonder we can't get the damn shipments out. The authorities have our contacts." José pivoted toward Daniel. "I want to know if they accessed our files. No one makes a fool out of me. No one!"

"I'll get right on it, sir, but it will take time to track down."

"Don't bother." José reached on the ground next to his leg and picked up a heavy automatic. "You've done enough damage."

The man opened his mouth as José fired.

Daniel's body spasmed, and he stumbled backward, blood oozing from the hole in his chest.

A metallic smell filled the air.

Men glanced at them and then went on like nothing had happened.

José sneered at the body and gestured for a soldier to remove it.

Manuel had an uneasy feeling his father might point the weapon at him someday. Who would be next? His headache pounded harder. Was Bella's secret safe from this maniac?

Chapter Three

April 4, 2022, Fairfax, Virginia

Hailey leaned forward, peering through the foggy darkness. *This window defroster is useless.* The rain dripping down the windows paralleled the tears in her soul. How much more sadness could she take? She steered the car to an empty space, parking next to a blue car with bold white POLICE letters on the side. With a long sigh, she opened the door and stepped onto the sidewalk. She clicked her key remote to lock the door. *What am I forgetting? My purse.* She unlocked the car door and grabbed her purse from the center console. Garnering strength, she trudged toward the entrance and opened the glass door.

The station streamed with officers directing rough-looking men and women through the waiting room.

A female officer escorted a tall red-haired woman dressed in a provocative dress, heavy eyeliner, and red lipstick past the information desk.

A bearded man in handcuffs gave a hard stare, ogling Hailey up and down.

Hailey turned, trying to ignore the commands and retorts tossed back and forth between the man and the police officer. She wiped her sweaty palms against her slacks as she approached an older clean-shaven man in uniform at the main desk.

He spoke without looking up from his computer. "Can I help you?"

Hailey turned. She shouldn't be here.

"Ma'am?" He regarded her now, as if she was dumbstruck.

She scratched her hand. "Um, I got a call my son was picked up and taken here."

"Name?" His voice was as stern as his hard expression.

"Hailey Langley."

"No, your son's name."

"Oh sorry. Uh, Ethan. Ethan Langley. He's only fifteen."

The man's expression changed from firmness to a sympathetic frown. "Let me check." He typed some information into the computer and squinted at the screen. "Ah, here he is. Vandalism. Do you have a lawyer, or do you want the court to appoint one?"

She flinched. "What? Vandalism? No. Don't appoint one…I'll call a lawyer."

"Okay. I'll start the paperwork to release him. Have your lawyer bring a statement in."

"Is he charged?"

"We'll talk to the owner of the store to see if he wants to press charges."

"How long will it take?" Anna wasn't used to staying by herself for long periods.

The officer surveyed the receiving area. "We're busy this evening. Maybe an hour." He shook his head. "Sorry, ma'am."

She rubbed her forehead. *Get a grip. What would Mark do?*

Someone hurried past and halted. "Hailey?"

She gazed at a tall man dressed in a gray suit. "Parker? What are you doing here?"

"I could ask you the same thing."

Hailey blinked back tears, grateful for the familiar face. His deep husky voice had an uncanny knack of soothing her nerves. "Ethan's here. I'm waiting to see him."

Parker slid a hand under her elbow and guided her away from the desk. "Let me see what's going on. Give me a few minutes." He strode up to the desk. The two men exchanged words, and the desk officer showed him a clipboard. Parker glanced at Hailey and shifted back to the officer again.

She stepped into the waiting area and sat in a chair near a wall. The urge to sob pulled at her.

At last, Parker met her. "They're processing his paperwork now. Ethan will have to meet with a lawyer and go to an arraignment later next week."

She stood, wringing her hands. "Can I see him?"

"They'll bring him out after they process the info." His voice softened. "I can stay a few minutes. Do you mind having company while you wait?"

She pointed to the seat beside her. "That would be great. Thank you."

They sat, and he studied her face. "Did they tell you what happened?"

"Not too much. Someone called from the station and said Ethan was arrested. When I got here, the officer said he'd been picked up for vandalism."

"A couple of kids threw a rock through the window of an electronics store. The police caught Ethan. They brought in another boy, too." Parker's eyes narrowed. "I'm surprised about Ethan."

"He's been going through a rough time lately." She paused, afraid to go on.

He nodded and touched her hand. "I'm sorry about Mark."

"I got your card."

"I tried calling a few times, but I wasn't sure you'd feel like talking. He was a good man. Are you doing okay?"

How did "okay" feel anymore? "Some days are easier than others. This obviously isn't one of them." She waited as another criminal in handcuffs shuffled past. "How long have you been working here? I thought you were still in Chicago."

"I'm on a special assignment. Moved here about four months ago."

"And you never contacted me?"

He frowned. "I didn't know if you'd see me, under the circumstances."

Parker made a valid argument. The last time she'd seen him, he left without saying good-bye. She forced a small smile. "Well, I'm glad to see you now."

"What's going on with Ethan?"

"I wish I knew. Ever since Mark's been gone, Ethan's changed. The counselor at school even contacted me about his grades." She raised her hands in the air. "Now he's hanging out with a new set of friends."

"The friends seem like they're trouble."

"What do you think will happen?"

He scratched his chin. "That depends. Do you have a lawyer?"

"We had a lawyer when Mark and I made our wills, but it's been years."

He reached into his pocket and removed a business card and pen. "I'll write down the name of a lawyer you might want to call. He's done many juvenile cases." Parker handed her the card and held her hand.

The reassuring security of his touch warmed her.

"What exactly happened with Mark?"

Her vision blurred. She cried every time she thought about the tragedy.

Parker gently squeezed her hand. "It's okay. We don't have to talk about it."

How many times had she reiterated the few details she knew about Mark's death? She mustered some inner strength. "He was working a case, and the building ignited. The place was engulfed in flames by the time the fire department came."

"Oh, Hailey, how horrible. I'm so sorry."

They conversed the next twenty minutes about Ethan and the usual protocol for juvenile arrests.

The sergeant at the front desk stood. "Hey, Parker. The Langley kid will be out shortly."

****

Butterflies swarmed in her stomach when an officer escorted her son into the room.

Ethan stood there in his ripped jeans and T-shirt, looking upset and frightened. He eyed her through his long bangs.

Hailey wiped the tears pooling under her eyes and hugged him as if he'd been gone for five years.

Ethan pushed her away. "Mom. Stop it!"

Parker stepped beside her. "Ethan. Show some respect to your mother."

Scowling, Ethan turned to Hailey. "Who the hell is he?"

"He's a friend." She hugged him again. His clothes reeked of grease, sweat, and skunk.

The officer escorting Ethan handed her a clipboard with some papers attached. "Once you sign these papers, your son is free to go. Have your lawyer bring in your son's statement before the arraignment."

"Yes, officer." Her voice quivered.

At the end of the hall, an officer escorted another teen and spoke to a man with thick black hair and brown skin. The man appeared to be around her age.

The teen had sometimes talked to Ethan when she picked him up after school. Jake—that was his name.

Jake and Ethan made eye contact but said nothing.

Parker waited as she signed the papers at the desk. "Are you able to drive home, or can I call someone? You still look upset."

As she considered the offer, a young policeman hauled in a thin middle-aged man in handcuffs who spit on the floor and tossed around the F-bomb like WWIII was beginning. She glanced at Ethan, helpless to shield him from this pandemonium. "No, I'm okay to drive. It's better I'm alone with Ethan when I start yelling."

A woman seated behind a reception desk stood and covered the handset. "Parker, phone call. Walt is on the line. Do you want to take it or send it to voicemail?"

Parker hesitated.

How was this stranger once her closest friend? That was years ago. Life went on. She nodded and adjusted the purse strap over her shoulder. "Go ahead. It was great seeing you." Turning to Ethan, she pointed to the door. "Let's go home."

So many emotions swirled around her head as they walked to the car. How could she love this boy and want to shake some sense into him at the same time? "Are you okay?"

Ethan's lip quivered, and he nodded. With his long hair and grease-stained shirt, he seemed like a complete stranger.

She opened her door. "What happened?"

"I don't know."

"Well, you better figure it out because when we get home, we're going to have a long talk."

He groaned.

During the ride home, Hailey did her best to calm the shaking in her hands. How did other parents deal with this situation? She should have realized he was hanging out with the wrong people.

At ten minutes before midnight, she navigated the car into the driveway.

Ethan opened the passenger door and sprinted toward the house.

Hailey turned off the ignition and opened her car door. "Ethan!" Leaning over the seat, she grabbed her purse from the console. "Ethan, wait! We need to talk about tonight."

The front door slammed.

She held in her anger as she marched into the house.

Anna rushed down the stairs, clad in her pink flannel pajamas. "Mom, what happened? Ethan ran in here crying."

She couldn't stop shaking. "He's had a tough night. I'll tell you about it later. Go back to bed." Following Anna, she climbed the stairs and trudged to her son's room at the end of the hallway.

Loud music blared from inside his room.

"Ethan?" When he didn't answer, she pounded her fist hard against the door. "Ethan. Let me in. We have to talk."

The music stopped, and the door opened.

Ethan fell backward onto the bed. As he stared at the ceiling, a tear rolled down his cheek. "Go away."

Every fiber in her heart splintered as she gazed at her son. This was once her baby, the beautiful child who brought happiness and joy. Not some vandal. He wasn't a criminal. With careful steps, she approached the bed and sat. "Tell me what happened."

"Nothing happened."

"We need to talk about this."

With his sleeve, he brushed his eyes. "It was nothing, Mom. We were just fooling around."

She shook her head. "I don't consider throwing rocks through a store window as fooling around. You know better."

He shrugged.

"Which of your so-called 'friends' suggested to break the window?"

"It doesn't matter."

"It *does* matter. Was this your idea?"

"No."

"But you went along with it?"

He paused. "I didn't want to, but they're older, and Zac had the car."

"Who's Zac? I thought you were with Jake."

"Zac is Jake's cousin. I've told you about him. They live with Jake's stepdad. While we rode in the car, Zac's friend Chase said he wanted a new TV. So Zac stopped the car, and they got out."

"A new TV? In the middle of the ride?"

31

He exhaled. "I didn't know what he was talking about either. They ran to the electronics store up the street. Zac stayed on lookout while Chase found a stone and smashed the window. Then the store alarm started blaring. Chase and Zac ran into an alley, but Jake and I were still in the car. We got out and ran in different directions. A cop picked Jake and me up. Zac and Chase must have gotten away."

"Why didn't you try to stop Chase from throwing the stone?"

"I told you, Mom. He's older. Twenty-three. I wasn't going to tell him what to do. He'd beat me up. Besides, I didn't know what was happening until it was too late."

"You're lucky you weren't killed tonight. I don't want you hanging around those boys anymore. They're nothing but trouble."

Ethan sat and tossed a pillow from the bed. "That's not fair."

"Why are you defending them?"

"Jake's my best friend. He's the only friend I hang out with anymore."

"Friend? Friends don't try to get each other arrested."

"Jake doesn't do that."

"His cousin is a bad influence, and Chase sounds like a hoodlum."

"But Mom—"

"No buts. I want your cell phone." She extended her arm and waited.

Standing, he stomped his feet. "I need my phone."

"Not for the next two weeks, you don't. Hand it over. Now!"

Red streaked down his face and neck as he glared. His tousled long hair gave him a frenzied appearance.

"Fine." He slapped his cell phone in her hand. "But you can't make me stop seeing my friends."

"Not seeing your friends will be the least of your worries after I'm done grounding you. Do you realize you could have a record now?" A twinge of shame stabbed her chest as her voice continued to rise. Ethan needed comfort, not her censure. "This could follow you the rest of your life."

"Will I have to go to juvie?" Ethan's face paled.

"I hope not. I'll call tomorrow morning and find a lawyer to handle your case before the hearing. We'll know more then." What could she say to make him understand the gravity of his actions? "Can't you see how serious this is? I don't know what you were thinking." She stepped to the door. "You're not to leave this house for two weeks, except for school."

"Two weeks?"

Her temper surpassed her desire to stay calm. "Yes. You can do your homework. Your grades are horrible. And I want you to think about what you did tonight. What would your dad say?" The pain in his face made her pause.

"Mom! Stop it, okay? Don't scream at me!" His eyes teared. "Leave me alone!"

Hailey tramped down the hall and grabbed the railing at the top of the stairs until her anger subsided and the wave of dizziness passed. Scenes like tonight's weren't helping her anxiety. She'd spent years parenting him and had never lost control like this. Heaven help her. In all her years as a mother, she never imagined she'd be having this conversation.

Chapter Four

Beep. Beep. Beep.

"No!" It was too early. Hailey slapped her hand on the cell phone and snoozed. She'd taken two anti-anxiety pills the previous night before she climbed into bed. Sleep without pills was impossible lately. Too many nightmares of Mark in the fire. Why was her whole life hit with one crapstorm after another? She inhaled the scent on the other bed pillow and rose.

In the shower, the hot water pounded on her skin. This was her safe haven. No kids around to hear her sobs. The water diluted the tears. As the mini-meltdown ended, she shampooed her hair. *The kids need me to be strong.* She dressed and checked out her pencil skirt and lavender top in the mirror. At least on the outside, she appeared normal.

She grabbed her purse and went downstairs into the small study off the living room. Turning on the computer, she searched her purse and found the card with the name Parker had written. Donald Greene. A few listings appeared on the screen when she typed in his name.

When Hailey called, a receptionist with a pleasant voice answered and offered a morning consultation time.

Hailey took the nine-thirty appointment and cringed when the receptionist quoted her the fee.

Although his hourly rate was teeth grinding, with twenty years of experience in handling juvenile cases, Mr. Greene sounded like a good choice.

Glancing up at the wall clock, she texted her teaching assistant, Zhang.

—I have a family emergency this morning. Are you available to give the Bio 101 quiz at 10 AM?—

Zhang texted back immediately. *—No problem—*

Satisfied, she phoned her department head. After explaining the situation and getting approval, she texted Zhang. *—Thanks. The quiz is in my office. Elizabeth will help you if you have any trouble finding it.—*

She hurried to the kitchen and pulled out the griddle. Ethan could use a fresh start with a cooked breakfast.

Anna meandered into the kitchen dressed in stylish jeans and a floral blouse and plopped her backpack on the floor. Then she started packing her lunch. "Morning."

Anna's perky presence brought a smile to Hailey's face. They were alike in so many ways. Style, looks, interests. Soon, her daughter would be as tall as Hailey.

When Hailey scooped the last slices of French toast from the skillet, she turned off the flame. "You can start eating. I'll get Ethan."

Hailey called for him from the living room and stepped back into the kitchen.

Anna stuffed her lunch bag in her backpack and zipped it before sitting in her chair. "What's going on with Ethan? I heard you fighting last night."

Loud footfalls stomped down the stairs.

Hailey pulled the juice carton from the fridge and whispered, "I'll tell you later."

Ethan shuffled into the kitchen, his shoulder-length hair wet from a shower. He wore the same ripped jeans he'd had on the previous day, but the blue polo shirt was clean.

Hailey waited. Would he say anything about the previous night?

He made eye contact and slid into his seat.

Anna poured syrup onto her French toast and glanced up periodically. When she finished eating, she grabbed her math book from the backpack. "I have a test. I'll study in the living room."

Hailey washed dishes until Ethan finished eating. "I found a lawyer in town who's willing to meet with us." She turned and faced him. "Hopefully, he'll take your case. He has an opening this morning. I'll pick you up at nine."

Ethan's face flushed red. "Nine? Why can't we go after school?"

"I checked, but he's in court the rest of the day."

He stood and stomped into the living room.

When the kids left, she climbed the stairs and searched Ethan's dresser drawers. If he was hanging around troublemakers, he might be getting into other types of trouble. There were too many stories in the news about kids and drugs; prescription drugs were free game for teens trying to experiment. She'd have to keep her anxiety medication in her purse, just in case.

When she arrived at the high school, she buzzed at the front entrance and headed down the hallway.

The guidance counselor greeted her outside the office. "Good morning, Mrs. Langley. How's Ethan?"

If she only knew about last night. "Hanging in there."

The woman stepped closer. "I've tried helping, but he doesn't tell me much. Ethan said you're taking him to a professional counselor?"

Hailey nodded. "I'm taking both kids. I thought someone experienced in grieving might get him to open up more." *Talking to a psychiatrist helped me as a teenager.*

A few minutes later, Ethan arrived, dragging his feet.

Hailey did her best to act cheerful, but he seemed more down than he had in a long time. During the drive to Greene's law office in Fairfax Station, she wasn't surprised Ethan was still giving her the silent treatment.

She parked next to a smart parking meter, and they walked to a small office in the historic district.

The secretary took their names and pointed them to the reception area. "Mr. Greene will be with you shortly."

Ethan fidgeted, browsing through a car magazine, while Hailey checked her phone for messages. She was replying to an email when a tall, gray-haired man around sixty years old appeared at the doorway.

The thin man adjusted the wire-rim glasses on his nose. "Mrs. Langley? And you must be Ethan." He shook their hands. "I'm Donald Greene."

Hailey liked him immediately. The grip on his handshake was strong, like he was in control.

He led them to his office and motioned for them to sit in the chairs across from his desk. Stacked behind him was an assortment of law books. A few folders lay neatly arranged on his desk beside a computer keyboard. He sat in his leather chair and gripped a pen and tablet. "Now Ethan, tell me what's going on."

Hailey listened as her son explained the details behind the previous night's arrest.

Mr. Greene took notes and nodded, asking questions, clarifying obscure points.

The lawyer had shown remarkable professionalism in speaking with them; his knowledge about Ethan's type of case reassured her. By the end of the session, she relaxed a bit.

"I'll file the report, and we'll wait to appear before the judge. We'll meet with the judge in his chambers, and he'll make a ruling. Usually for first-time offenses like this, the judge will be more lenient. You'll possibly pay restitution. Do some service hours." He tightened his smile as Ethan groaned. "I'll let you know when the court date is scheduled."

When the meeting ended, Hailey dropped Ethan off at school and drove to the university ten miles down the road.

Her office was unlocked when she arrived. Liz had to be close by.

Space was tight, and the university didn't have enough room for adjunct professors to have their own office. Hailey lowered her purse next to the desk and unpacked her attaché case.

Normally she welcomed conversation with the other woman, often chitchatting for hours about their families, but today she wasn't in the mood. It was just as well Liz wasn't there. She powered on the computer and replied to emails from anxious students regarding study guides for the upcoming finals.

"Hailey, are you cancelling your afternoon class, too?"

"Huh?" She lifted her head.

Elizabeth Shoemaker stood next to the desk, staring. The fifty-year-old woman pointed at the wall clock. "Your class starts in five minutes."

"Oh shit!" Hailey grabbed her graded biochem tests from the desk. "Thanks. I must have zoned out."

"Don't forget your lecture notes." Liz reached over and handed Hailey a stack of papers next to the keyboard. "Rough night?"

Hailey surveyed her desk. She'd deal with the clutter later. "It's not what you think."

****

Traffic crawled on the way home. Hailey couldn't stop thinking about the previous evening. Ethan didn't hang out with many friends anymore. He talked about Jake the most; the boy already had a driver's license—and his own truck. Ethan's other friends had stopped coming around after Mark died. Anna had handled Mark's death a little easier.

When Hailey arrived home an hour later, Ethan was lounging on the couch playing a video game, eating a bowl of corn chips and salsa. He didn't look up as she slipped off her shoes.

"Where's Anna?"

He shrugged.

"How was school?"

"Fine."

She stared, tempted to rip the electronic game from his hands. "Anything happen?"

"No."

"Was Jake there?"

"No."

She crossed her arms. "How about a little cooperation here, Ethan? I'm trying to help you, and you're giving me the cold shoulder. We need to find a way to put all this behind us."

"Sorry." He let out a huff and glanced at his watch. "Jake didn't show up today. I need to see him and Zac tonight."

"You're grounded."

He scowled. "But Zac wants to talk about last night."

She browsed through the mail sitting on the end table. "No. You're stuck here for two weeks. Besides, Mr. Greene advised you against talking to those boys."

"Mom!" He threw his controller on the cushion. "You're being ridiculous. Jake is in all my classes. He sits next to me in history."

Ethan made a valid point. "Then stay away from Zac and Chase."

Standing, he kicked the sofa. "You can't keep me home like I'm a prisoner."

"If you don't watch it, you will be. How do you even know Zac wants to talk to you?" She shifted her hands to her waist. "You don't have your phone."

"I saw him when I got off the bus. As if you even care."

"Watch your tone. I can make you *feel* like this home is worse than a prison."

"You're unbelievable." He stomped up the stairs, passing Anna on the way down.

"He's been grumpy ever since he came home last night." Anna shook her head and stepped to the front door, collecting her shoes. "Mrs. Rogers texted to ask me to babysit this afternoon. She needs someone to play with Sam and Rose while she works."

"Did you finish your homework?"

"I didn't have any today." The young teen leaned over and tied her sneakers. "Rose got a new dollhouse. Sam said they've been playing in the secret playroom all week." When she stood, the corners of her mouth turned down. "I wish we had a secret room."

"We had the option to use the bonus space behind the bedroom closet as a study or secret room. All of the neighborhood houses had similar floorplans."

"Why didn't you do that?"

"We couldn't afford it. Your dad and I were on a tight budget when we wrote the contract on this house." Hailey sighed. In hindsight, putting drywall over the space wasted square footage.

"You should see Mrs. Rogers's study, Mom. It's like a real office. I wish you could telework from home."

"Me, too." Hailey nodded. "Take the path behind the house and text me when you get there. Dinner's at six."

Anna hugged her. "Thanks, Mom. Love you."

Hailey climbed the stairs and changed into comfy sweats and a T-shirt. What to make for dinner? There was still some chicken in the fridge to use before it expired. Would Ethan even bother coming down to eat?

Chicken parmesan and mashed potatoes sounded good. She started breading the chicken. While she boiled water for the potatoes, the phone rang.

Hailey set down the peeler. "Hello?"

"Hi, Hailey. It's Parker."

His warm voice melted away her frustration.

"I took a chance you still had the same cell phone number. I wanted to check on you. I didn't like having to leave so abruptly last night."

She smiled. It was nice to know someone cared. "Thanks. I understand. We're doing okay."

"Did you get a lawyer for Ethan?"

"I contacted the guy from Fairfax Station. You can tell he's done these types of cases before. Ethan liked him. Thanks for recommending him."

"I'm glad he's working out." Parker paused. "Hey, listen. We didn't have a lot of time to catch up yesterday. Would you like to go out sometime so we could talk more?"

"Ah…" Hailey's mind wandered to her son. With everything going on, she should stay at home and watch him. She frowned. Now she was acting like a probation officer instead of a mother.

"It's not a date. We could go out to eat. Just dinner between friends. I don't have many of those anymore."

She rubbed her temples. "It's not that. I don't want to leave Ethan alone. I've grounded him for two weeks."

"I could come to your place if it's easier."

She considered the alternative. Parker had always been a good friend. Although she had her network of friends at the university and in the neighborhood, close friendships were hard to nurture after Mark died. Maybe it would be all right to leave. Get away. Show Ethan she trusted him. "I guess it'll be okay to go out."

"Cool." His voice brightened. "How about tomorrow night?"

She checked the calendar on the kitchen wall. "The kids have a counseling session at three, but later in the evening will be fine."

"I'll pick you up around six?"

"Okay. See you then."

****

After the kids had gone upstairs to bed, Hailey relaxed on the sofa, massaging her hands as she watched the news. The tingling in her hands was more pronounced.

She jumped at the loud ring of the phone.

Dr. Bruce Hanover's name appeared on caller ID.

"Hello?"

"Hailey, how y'all doing?"

She'd never tire of her friend's upbeat Texan accent. "Bruce, don't tell me you're working."

"It's not quitting time yet. It's only nine-thirty. I had a free minute and thought I'd check in. See how you and the kids were getting along."

After her own father had passed away, Bruce had been like a father. "We're doing okay. Better than the last time we talked." Normally, she avoided this conversation. Unless someone experienced her nightmare, no one would understand the pain. But Bruce had endured deep losses in his life. "It's been a process. We're still in denial."

"It'll take time."

Hailey pressed a finger against her eyelid. *Don't cry.* "What's new with you? Let me guess. You finally decided to retire, and you're calling to invite me to your retirement party?"

"Funny."

Sooner or later, she'd talk him into retiring. "How's your research?"

"Slow." His voice lost enthusiasm.

"Uh-oh. What's wrong?"

"I'm stumped."

"What invention are you working on this time?"

"Skin regeneration."

"Rebuilding skin?"

"Something like that. The flowers in *Bixa aparra* have properties similar to other herbal medicines on the market, but this is even more promising. Like the skin healing properties in purple coneflower and chamomile."

Bixa aparra. The Euphoria plant.

A shiver ran down her spine. Would she ever feel calm hearing the plant's name? An image of Manuel de Mendoza flashed across her mind. "I thought the plant was extinct."

"Not yet. When I went to med school, my colleague and I each stole a sapling from our classmate Chuck Moulin." Bruce laughed. "Chuck never realized what we did. A.C.'s plant died, but I grew mine as a hobby. Now the plant's dying."

"Why?"

"I'm not sure. It's been healthy for fifty years. Last month, the leaves started turning yellow."

"I've never seen what *Bixa aparra* looks like."

"Hold on. I'll text you a picture from two months ago when it was in full bloom."

"Could the plant be too old?"

"It's possible. I never started saplings. Didn't think the plant was too useful. Now I've discovered there's uses other than the Euphoria drug. Okay, the text should be going through now."

Her phone pinged, and she studied the picture as Bruce continued.

"I got a government grant to study skin regeneration, so I need to keep the shrub alive and gather more flowers."

Hailey studied the bushy plant. Wow, it towered over Bruce. "Are you watering it enough? Plants from the Amazon must use a lot of water."

"I keep it in a tropical environment."

She enlarged a section of the bold pink and yellow flowers on her screen. "This is magnificent. How many blooms are on this plant?"

"Lots. It blooms every six months. Two months ago, I collected about fifty of them. It was quite a project. Any contact on my skin would have killed me."

She winced. "How did you learn that?"

"A shaman warned Chuck."

"You really think it can regenerate skin?"

"I do. But I have to boil the petals to inactivate a chemical in the oil or find a way to precipitate out the toxic chemical first."

"How do you harvest them?"

"Wearing thick latex gloves. Chuck mentioned the aborigines boiled the flowers in a cauldron until it formed a thick paste. If you ever want an exciting research job, I could use an associate."

She laughed. "You tell me that all the time."

"Because I mean it. You have research skills. We'd make a marvelous team."

"I'll think about it." The project sounded too hazardous. "Hey, you'll never guess who I saw the other day."

"Who?"

"Parker."

"Parker? What's he doing on the East Coast?"

"He's working at the police department in a neighboring county."

"I thought he liked Chicago. Why did he move?"

Good question. She'd have to ask him. "I don't know."

A high-pitched beep chirped in the background.

"Jumping lizards. I've got to run. My timer's beeping. Say hello to Parker for me."

"Okay."

"Promise me you'll consider what I said—I could use you as a research associate."

"I promise I'll think about it."

Chapter Five

"Call, dammit."

Manuel stared at the phone in the study of the family's mansion. How hard could it be for his contact in the States to find one person? Four weeks left. He had no room for error.

He crossed another day off the desk calendar. Tightening the grip on his pen, he jotted down more tasks and concentrated harder.

A firm knock rattled the door, and José strode into the room. "You're here. Camila told me you left."

Manuel nodded and laid down the pen. "I had a few matters to attend to before I went to the facility." Why was Mamà the only person who wasn't disappointed in him?

He swiveled his chair toward the window and studied a monkey climbing a Chaca tree.

The little simian leaned on the branch and batted at a butterfly flapping around his head.

A kaleidoscope of brown butterflies emerged from the foliage, and Manuel's heart turned cold at the sign of bad luck. He spun back to José and gestured to the empty chair across his desk. "What do you want, Papà? I thought you'd be at the camp again."

José stepped into the sitting area instead and relaxed in the high-back leather chair. "The training and drills are going according to schedule. On my way there last week, I flew to the laboratory and spoke to Lionel. Why didn't you tell me another worker died?"

How dare his father check up on him? Dammit. His researchers needed to keep him abreast of problems. "I'll check into it when I fly to Sierra Nevada de Santa Marta this weekend."

"Hijueputa." José's lip curled. "Lionel said you haven't visited the lab in weeks."

Manuel tensed. With José spending the majority of time training new recruits, the financial success of the family business depended on Manuel's dealings. "I've been busy. I said I'll check on the facility."

Inwardly, he groaned. The project was becoming as much a bad omen as the dark butterflies habituating the Amazon Rainforest. Fleeing the United States had cost him everything. After the government had frozen his accounts and assets, the banks in Virginia repossessed his house. The Mendoza estate was scraping bottom. If the researchers could make Euphoria as successful as cocaine, his family would regain the dependable cash flow they needed.

"You're wasting money on this goose chase."

He met his father's gaze. "It's not a goose chase. We've propagated enough plants to extend the research and increase production of Euphoria. The greenhouse is full of seedlings, and we have shrubs all along the mountainside."

José stood from his chair and scoffed. "When will you get it through your stubborn skull? I'll never allow you to sell Euphoria again. Your foolish scheme killed everyone we sold the drug to."

"How long are you going to hold that mishap over my head? It was six years ago."

"People are still dying. Your plan of hiring scientists to research *Bixa aparra* has resulted in nothing but angst. New wonder drug—*mi culo*!" José slapped a hand against his ass. "Stick to our main staple. Coca leaves."

Manuel paced the floor. His father was wrong about the venture. He'd smuggled small shipments of Euphoria out of the country, and no one had died yet. The drug was an auxiliary means to make money if the government's attempts to destroy the coca plant succeeded. He scratched his beard. "Euphoria is my project. I have a strong feeling about it."

"Fuck your feelings. Over two dozen workers have died this year harvesting the plant. When they brush against the blossoms, their skin bleeds and turns black. You claim Euphoria is similar to cocaine? We've never had deaths like this harvesting coca leaves."

Manuel pressed his lips tight. Hadn't Colleen mentioned years ago there were special medicinal properties to the flower? He needed her now more than ever. "The team's discovery is relatively new. The shrub saplings are flourishing. Give them time."

He'd hired more researchers to work on the project. One older researcher from Peru had prior experience with the shrub, having worked with the Amazon aborigines.

Manuel consented to their request to test the drug for migraine pharmaceuticals and stress treatments, but he kept the researchers' theories from his father. Until the results were more definitive, he wasn't ready to publicize the plant's powers—no matter how many more lives he sacrificed. The finding could earn back his respect—and replenish his bank account.

Manuel considered the two Leal frescos hanging on the wall across his Darina wooden desk. Artwork by Sorolla, El Greco, and Miró lined the walls with the other Spanish Masters. He missed the freedom to indulge in frivolous extravagances since he returned from the States. Each time he traveled, he collected another sculpture, another piece of art or furniture. Sadly, they were the only treasures he had left. He thumbed a marble sculpture of a horse purchased in Italy and licked his lips. He still had one gem to bring home. Hopefully two.

José squared his back and glared. "The five scientists I hired from Peru and India are making progress. We can't lose them."

"If we do, I'll find more."

"It's costing me a fucking fortune." José strode across the room to the built-in bar. "What did your American girlfriend do to the drug to keep it from being so toxic?" His voice dripped with contempt each time he mentioned Bella.

"I don't know." Manuel should have questioned Bella more in the evenings instead of bedding her.

Blood rushed to his loins at the memory. Damn her. Even now she distracted him. Could he get the information from the other researcher, Bruce Hanover? No. The American was too smart to be duped twice.

"*Hijueputa!*" José slammed his hand on the desk.

Manuel flinched, but his father didn't seem to notice. Would he ever stop tensing around the man?

"Six years we've worked on this revolutionary new drug, but we have nothing to show for it."

"You're wrong." A surge of confidence flowed through Manuel. "We've never focused our time on this plant. The high from Euphoria is just as intense if not better than what comes from cocaine. But instead of producing it, you force us to place our resources on other priorities."

A vessel on José's neck pulsated. "Focus on coca production. The big money is still in cocaine."

"Not if the government continues to wipe out our crops. The fields sprayed with herbicide are ruined. The coca plant is being wiped out. So far, only *Bixa aparra* is resistant to the herbicide."

José scowled. "That's even more reason to fund the Resistance. The government isn't working for the people. They're bending over backward helping the U.S. eradicate drugs. How does the Colombian government expect its citizens to thrive? The poor in the rural areas continue to get poorer."

He ambled over to the granite cocktail table and studied a sculpture of a woman by Antonio Caro.

The artwork reminded Manuel of Bella.

Stepping to the bar, José poured a glass of rum and then sat in a gold-threaded Louis XV armchair. "Any news on our shipments while I was in the mountains?"

Manuel poured a glass of scotch and inhaled the disinfectant aroma of the cresol. He swallowed the drink and sat in a matching chair next to José. "The authorities confiscated another cocaine shipment two nights ago. Luis confirmed it." He tensed. Wait for it...

"That's the third shipment this month!" José's white knuckles protruded when he raised his fists in the air. "*Maldición*! Because of your carelessness, they know all our contacts. The SCA *puta* is costing us millions. Tell Luis to speed up production and send another shipment to the Caribbean."

"The villagers are already pushing cocaine's full yield."

"Then push harder. I need the capital to supply the Resistance with weapons. The *Ejército del Pueblo* never should have bargained with the government. They surrendered most of their weapons, and yet poverty and inequality prevail."

"I'll tell Luis."

José stared out the window where the monkey hung from a branch and swatted at the dark moths. "Tomorrow I'm meeting the Resistance in Bogota. Call Felipe, Nicholas, and Luis and set up a meeting for when I return. I want to find out why the latest shipments to the Caribbean aren't making it to the States." He marched to the door. "And tell Kellan to cut down the bush outside. It's attracting black moths. We don't need any bad luck around the house."

Chapter Six

Hailey was cutting a kaiser roll when Ethan strode into the kitchen.

He yanked the box of cereal from his sister's grasp and claimed his seat. "Why's your hair so flat today, Anna? Forget to shower?"

Anna fingered her chestnut-brown hair. "I used a straightener." She twisted to look at Hailey and gnawed on her fingernail. "Mom?"

Hailey plucked the box from Ethan's hand and passed it back. "Straight hair is the new style."

The nit-picking never stopped, but at least Ethan wasn't sulking around the house. Was he up to something? It was hard to tell what was going on in his mind.

After Ethan headed to the bus stop, Anna lingered and winked. "I think Ethan's in a better mood today." Then she hugged Hailey and opened the front door. "I'll see you after school."

Hailey gathered her attaché case and locked the door. She walked past the overgrown lawn to her car and sneezed. Allergy season had begun. The grass needed cutting a week ago, but the man at the repair shop hadn't called to say the mower was repaired. She started the engine and headed to the university.

The cramped office wasn't as elaborate as other faculty workplaces on campus, but it was large enough to equip Hailey and her officemate each with a desk, two chairs, and filing cabinet.

Hailey reserved Friday mornings for student appointments and dedicated the rest of the morning to prepare for lectures. On this particular day, her three appointments had finished by ten-thirty, and her mind wandered to Parker's phone call. Why was he reaching out now, after moving to town months ago? *Stop thinking about it.* If Parker had wanted to see her sooner, he would have.

A sad cloud hovered over her. Losing Mark still made her feel hollow.

Stay focused. She plucked a binder from the shelf and glanced at her officemate's tidy desk.

Ten years Hailey's senior, Liz was so organized and driven, she could have been a top CEO for a huge conglomerate or a city council member like her husband—she even had the expensive wardrobe for it.

Hailey opened the binder and recorded the latest bio quiz results.

"Somebody must be having a terrific day."

Hailey lifted her head toward her officemate standing in the doorway. "Why do you say that?"

Grinning, Liz folded her arms across her cobalt-blue silk blouse. "I heard you humming from down the hall."

"Really?" Hailey's cheeks warmed. She glanced down at her casual cotton shirt, a stark contrast to Liz's stylish outfit.

The brunette-haired woman nodded and stepped closer to the desk. "Yes, it's a nice change. I was worried about you yesterday. You seemed flustered. Is everything okay?"

"Ethan was picked up by the police."

Liz's smile faded. "Oh no. What happened?"

Hailey laid the binder on the desk and gave Liz the details.

"Did the police find the two older boys who broke the window?"

"I'm not sure. Ethan said they have prior records. And they're over eighteen. I hired a lawyer yesterday to represent Ethan."

Liz primped her pixie-style hair. "He's had a tough time since your husband passed, hasn't he?"

The tears came at the most inopportune times. Hailey slid the binder back on the shelf. "I knew his job was dangerous and there was always a possibility...but I never imagined we would really lose him." She sniffled. "The kids are going through their own emotions. Ethan said his old friends don't understand what he's going through."

Liz squeezed Hailey's hand.

Her skin was soft, and she had meticulously manicured nails. After Ethan and Anna were out of school, Hailey would have time for these luxuries, too.

"Don't be too hard on him. Is he still seeing a counselor?"

Hailey nodded. "I take the kids every week, but he doesn't open up much."

"Give him time. Peter and Hunter acted out the same way when they were around Ethan's age. After George started gambling, our world turned upside down. It took years to pay off his debt."

"At least your sons grew out of the rebellious stage. I don't know about Ethan. He's been a bear without his phone."

"Taking phones away from kids is the same as cutting off their lifeline with their friends."

Hailey valued any advice she could get. "How did you discipline your kids?"

Liz shrugged. "Hunter and Peter are older now. They didn't have as many electronic devices as kids have nowadays. The most important thing is to stay firm." Liz tugged at the hem of her silk blouse and gave a sympathetic smile. "Your son will get his act together before long. You're a good role model." She glanced at her Italian designer watch. "I have to get to my micro lab. We're doing spore stains today."

Hailey leaned back in her chair. She definitely wasn't in the running to win a mother-of-the-year award. Other parents had it as hard, if not harder. If Liz was able to bring her family together after their upheaval, Hailey could do the same.

Liz's advice carried Hailey through the afternoon. After preparing for the Biology II and Biochem afternoon lectures, she pulled a spinach walnut salad from her insulated lunch bag and checked her voicemail. The counselor's secretary had called to confirm the kids' three o'clock appointment. With so much going on, Hailey had forgotten.

****

The counselor opened her door at four.

Hailey stood as Anna and Ethan each grabbed a lollipop from the container on the counter. "How did the session go?"

Dr. Moyer handed a chart to the receptionist and smiled at Hailey. "We're making progress."

As Ethan and Anna piled into the car, Hailey's cell beeped a reminder for the dinner with Parker. She glanced at the time. If she didn't hit traffic, she'd have time to make the kids a quick meal before he came.

At six o'clock, she opened the door to Parker.

He stood with his hands shoved in denim jeans, and he wore a dark-green polo shirt. Gray peppered his dark hair, and deep wrinkles encircled his eyes.

She hadn't noticed those details at the police station—but then she'd had other things on her mind. Once, he'd meant the world to her. His gentle gray eyes still fascinated her.

"Hi. You look nice."

His husky voice put her at ease. "Thanks."

Good, her decision to dress casual in dark jeans and a flowing blouse was a wise choice. Dressy, but not overdone. Oh God, he was staring at her. She raked her fingers through her hair. Although she had considered getting her hair shortened to the fashionable style Liz wore, a commitment cut was costly to maintain.

Parker stepped into the foyer entrance. "The place is the same as I remember."

Hailey took a hard look at the room.

The cracks on the ceiling needed patching. The walls needed paint, and the faded carpet needed replacing.

The furnishings were old, but she could never throw away Mark's favorite recliner. Or the end table where he stacked the daily newspaper. Or the family pictures hanging on the wall.

Ethan sprawled on the couch playing a video game. He eyed Parker and tightened his lips.

Please don't let Ethan cause a scene. When Hailey had told the kids she was going out to eat, they both vocalized their opposition.

"Parker, you remember my son?"

Parker nodded. "Hi, Ethan."

Scowling, Ethan turned back to the screen.

The snub was like a kick in Hailey's gut. Her son knew better.

Anna pranced in from the kitchen holding a half-eaten bagel.

Hailey clutched her sweater on the rocking chair. "Tom Parker, this is my daughter, Anna. She's my youngest."

Anna waved. "Hi."

Parker shook her hand. "Hello, Anna. How old are you?"

She straightened. "Thirteen."

"You look so much like your mother."

Hailey glowed. No one could deny her daughter had inherited Mark's extroverted personality, but Anna had Hailey's wavy hair, hazel eyes, and high cheekbones. She looked more like Hailey with each passing year.

Anna blushed. "Everyone tells us that, Mr. Parker."

He chuckled. "Please, call me Parker. I never use my first name."

"Okay." Anna turned to Hailey. "Mom, can I go to the park to play with Sam after dinner?"

Hailey nodded. "Don't stay out past eight."

"I won't." She chewed on a fingernail. "I have English homework to do anyway."

"Text me when you get home. The spaghetti is warming on the stove. Remember to turn off the burner."

Anna leaned against the sofa. "Okay. By the way, my bathroom sink's still dripping."

"I'll look at it this weekend." The housework never ended. "Parker, we should go."

As they climbed down the porch steps, Parker held out his key remote and unlocked the car. "Do you want me to take a look at the faucet?"

She chortled. "You were never the mechanical type. Don't worry. I'll fix it. There's always something breaking in the house. First, it was the washing machine. Then the lawn mower—and now this." She took in the yard and shook her head. The small engine repair shop still hadn't called.

Parker walked her to the red sports car parked behind her car, opened the door, and waited while she climbed into the passenger seat. As he backed out of the driveway, he pointed to her car. "Why don't you park in the garage?"

The garage was like a vault, safely storing another painful memory.

She scratched her arm. "Mark's car's in there."

"I didn't realize you kept his car."

"To be honest, I wasn't sure I wanted to. Mark's supervisor had it towed here after Mark died, but I haven't driven it yet."

He braked the car at a stop sign and glanced at her. "Then why are you keeping it?"

There were occasions she had to go into the garage to fetch the lawn mower or gardening tools, but she never stayed long. Too many memories of Mark flooded back.

"The car's paid off. Ethan will be sixteen in another two months. He'll need a car when he starts driving."

Would she ever be able to sit in that car again?

At a traffic light, Parker drummed his fingers against the steering wheel. "It's hard to imagine he's old enough to drive. I still remember when Justin got his permit."

She ached to hear more stories about Justin's childhood. Had enough time passed for Parker to talk about his son? Or did Parker feel as sad over losing Justin as she did losing Mark? "It's amazing how quickly kids grow up. Even Anna's getting older. She started babysitting now that she's thirteen."

He glanced at her and returned his gaze to the traffic. "Do you ever think about going back to work at the Special Crimes Agency? I'm sure Stefan would hire you again."

"I went back part-time for a while after we finished the Euphoria case. The work at the SCA was mostly research with a few traveling assignments. It was hard leaving the kids. If I were to go back again, I'd need to commit to working full-time to keep up my skills. I still practice at the firing range when the kids are at school." Hailey allowed a half-hearted smile, grateful to be part of the agency's tight-knit family. "Stefan and his son Erik visited after the fire. The other agents called. They still treat me like family."

Parker grinned. "Once you're part of the SCA, you belong for life."

Forty minutes later, they entered Georgetown.

Parker found an open underground parking garage, and they walked a block to Fabrons, a charming restaurant in the heart of the city.

He opened the front door and followed her into the white painted-brick building where the staff moved around carrying trays of food above their heads.

The aroma of steak and seafood whetted her appetite.

The host escorted them to a table in the corner of the room overlooking the Potomac River and Key Bridge.

Oh, she'd forgotten how beautiful the lights sparkled on the river.

Parker pulled out her chair and then sat across from her.

A young server approached and passed them dinner and beverage menus. "Would you like a sample of our wine?"

Parker's gaze met hers, questioning.

Hailey shook her head. She couldn't mix alcohol with her medication.

He passed back the beverage menu. "Not tonight, thanks. I'll have a coke, please. Hailey?"

"Iced tea is fine, thanks. Decaf."

When the server stepped away, Hailey browsed the menu. "That girl can't be a day over fifteen. They all look so young now." She fished her phone from the purse. "Speaking of kids, I should text Anna and check in. I worry about those two together. Ethan has a terrible habit of teasing her."

A few minutes later, the server delivered the beverages. She set a basket of warm breadsticks on the table and jotted down their order.

Parker reached for a breadstick and passed Hailey the basket. "So tell me, what have you been up to the past few years?"

A chill ran through her. She rubbed her hands over her arms and glanced around at the tables teeming with customers. "I've kept busy. The kids' activities filled my free time. Now that Mark's gone, I'm constantly taking the kids places. I signed us up for some Jeet Kune Do classes two months ago." She paused when he snickered. "Don't laugh. I was building skills before we stopped. The classes were intense. Or maybe I'm getting older."

Parker raised a hand in front of him. "If you say so. Why did you stop going?"

"It was too time-consuming. Anna's involved in dancing, and up until a while ago, Ethan was on the basketball team. Between teaching, helping kids with homework, and driving them around, I don't have much time." She grabbed a breadstick and bit into it.

"How's Anna handling Mark's death?"

"She's trying to keep busy. If she's not at dance or student council, she's hanging out at a friend's house. Anna doesn't like to think about her dad being gone."

"I hadn't thought of it like that. I complained to Grace when she became too involved in activities."

"I think the tendency is natural. In their own ways, Anna and Ethan are escaping." They were all escaping.

"Other than Ethan's run-in last week, how's he been coping?"

Hailey reached for her drink. Ethan rarely expressed his feelings. "His grades are dropping. He's lost all motivation to succeed in school." She rubbed her arms. "A year ago, he wanted to go into law enforcement, like Mark. Now he's ruined his chance."

"You don't know that yet. Besides, his record could be cleared when he's eighteen. Have you talked to the guidance counselor?"

"The guidance counselor *and* a highly paid counselor. I take both kids for counseling once a week."

He chewed on another breadstick. "That's smart."

"Mark's mother, Peggy, recommended it. She was a teacher before she retired and knew about families coping with death. I didn't want to admit the kids were having grieving issues, but she cornered me one evening and pointed out how withdrawn Anna had become. She also said Ethan was transforming into a different boy."

His brow arched. "Was she right?"

"Yes." She closed her eyes. Peggy's conversation replayed in her mind. *They need their mother.* "I was too caught up with my own emotions to notice. The kids don't complain too much about going to counseling."

The attendant served their entrees.

Hailey couldn't wait to taste the stuffed crab. "Mmm, this smells delicious. I can't remember the last time I've gone out to eat." She sampled a bite and smacked her lips. When had food tasted this good?

"Is the counseling helping?" Parker cut into his Porterhouse and chewed the steak.

"A little. Maybe. I keep hoping something will get us out of our funk."

"It sounds like you're doing the best you can."

Hailey sipped her iced tea. "It isn't enough."

"Do *you* see anyone?"

He didn't need to know about the psychiatrist. "The kids' counselor asked me to schedule a few sessions, but I haven't gone."

"Why not?"

Why did she need counseling when she wasn't ready to admit Mark was really gone? Her cheeks heated. "You know I hate seeing therapists."

He chuckled. "You *were* always wary about them."

"Counselors represent sadness and despair. I had my share of them after my parents died. I can't justify spending more money toward another counseling fee when I'm handling my own life just fine." Her words tasted bitter as soon as she spoke them. Fine was a huge overstatement. "I joined a support group. It's helped. I've met some nice people."

She tasted more of the entree. "Did you join any support group after Justin died?"

He bowed his head. "I should have. I was too stubborn to admit I needed someone to talk to. I think that's why Grace gave up on us."

"Don't be too hard on yourself."

When she finished her steamed broccoli, she lowered her fork. "Do you still talk to Grace?"

"Not too often. We tried making a go of our marriage after Justin passed away, but it didn't last. We were incompatible."

She wished she could erase the sadness in his face. "I'm sorry."

He guzzled his coke. "It's fine. Grace is doing okay. Four years ago, she met a man at one of her counseling meetings, and they married. Now she's a proud mother of twins."

"Twins? Bet she has her hands full."

The server cleared the table and poured two cups of coffee. "Any room for dessert?"

Hailey shook her head, but Parker stretched back in his chair. "I think you can twist my arm." He placed a dessert order with two spoons and an extra plate. He glanced at his watch. "I should have asked for an earlier reservation time."

She scanned the room. The crowd was thinning. "We're fine. I don't work Saturdays."

The lines deepened on his forehead. "Where do you work?"

Hailey picked up her cup and swallowed the coffee. "I teach at the university—in the biology department. When I started my doctorate degree in biochemistry four years ago, I applied for and accepted a graduate-assistant position at the university. After I completed my degree, I was hired full-time. It's only a temporary position, but it's renewable, so I hope I can either get hired again for next fall or get a permanent position somewhere. It would be nice to get tenure someday…What's so funny? You don't think I can teach?" His contagious laugh lifted her mood.

"It's not that." He raised his hands in front of his chest. "Don't take this the wrong way. I know you love staying at home with the kids, but they're getting older, and you're the type of person who needs to stay busy."

"Hmm. Maybe."

"What courses are you teaching?"

"A couple of Bio I and II classes and an Intro to Biochemistry. Fortunately, the students seem to like me. I miss working in research, though. My NIH career was years ago, but I did some interesting experiments for my doctorate studies. Maybe someday I'll find a position where I can do that again."

He drank his coffee. "You can become another Bruce Hanover."

"Hardly." She chuckled. In truth, Parker couldn't have paid her a bigger compliment. "He called last night. Wanted to know if I'd help with his research."

"Why don't you take him up on his offer?"

Hailey scratched her neck. "He's too far away. Someday, when the kids are grown, I'll think about it. For now, teaching helps pay the bills."

"Didn't Mark have life insurance?"

She hesitated. Did she really want to get into the probing questions tonight? "His life insurance has been one big headache after another."

His brows knitted together. "What do you mean?"

Maybe Parker could help her. Or would he think she was crazy? "I can't get Mark's death certificate." Trembling, she lifted the glass, the ice cubes rattling against the side.

"Why not?"

"The medical examiner couldn't confirm the remains."

He flinched. "Why not?"

Tears clouded her vision. "The body was burned beyond recognition." She leaned in closer, lowering her voice. "Just between you and me, I think something fishy is going on."

His eyes widened. "You think Mark's alive?"

"Maybe…No." She shook her head. Was she crazy? "I don't know what to think."

"Come on, Hailey. If Mark was alive, he'd be here with *you* right now."

She shouldn't have brought up the subject. Talking to Parker made her hopes seem like a far-fetched wish.

He whispered, "My, God. You're serious, aren't you? Do you think he wasn't in the building?"

"I don't know what to think. David said—"

His eyebrows raised. "David?"

"David Smith. Remember him? He helped find Mark's missing coworker a few years ago."

"The CIA guy?"

The chair creaked as she nodded. "David said Mark called him that night on the drive home. They were discussing a case when Mark hung up. Twenty minutes later, Mark called him back, but all David caught was high-pitched yelps."

"Was he sure it was Mark?"

"Mark's name was on caller ID. David was suspicious, so he called Mark's supervisor, Owen, at the DTA and had Mark's phone traced. They tracked the signal to a warehouse in Maryland. When David and the authorities arrived, the place was engulfed in flames."

She struggled. Talking about the fire, thinking about the excruciating agony Mark had suffered, seared pain through her mind. "After the fire department extinguished the fire, they found Mark's phone and charred remains."

"So they *did* find his remains."

Rotating the drinking glass in front of her, she fought to maintain control. "The fire marshal found remnants of *someone's* bones."

"Didn't they run DNA tests? Dental records?"

"The place was stacked full of lumber. The fire's extreme temperature burnt everything beyond recognition. The fire marshal said the fire cremated the body."

"I'm so sorry, Hailey."

"Without a body, I have to wait years to declare Mark dead. I called his supervisor at the DTA to help me search for Mark in case the body in the warehouse wasn't his, but Owen referred me to the agency's trauma counselors."

Parker scoffed. "Owen's an ass. What did David say about your theory?"

"He said the phone's GPS was still pinging when he arrived, and there was no way Mark walked out of the place. The marshal found remnants of Mark's phone in the ashes. That's all I know. No one tells me anything. They treat me like I have no brain. I called Stefan, but he said the SCA didn't have jurisdiction over the case." Hailey shrugged. "The whole situation is surreal."

"This is the reason you think Mark's still alive?"

Her rationale now seemed silly. "I know the remains were probably his." Her eyes blurred, and she patted her chest. "My head gets that he's gone, but my heart isn't ready to let him go yet."

"So you're living in limbo."

The pity on Parker's face was unmistakable.

"Other than the support group, do you talk to anyone?"

She dabbed her eyes with a napkin. "David checks on us Friday evenings. He was close to Mark's family. He thinks he owes it to Mark to make sure we're doing okay."

"*Are* you doing okay?"

"Yes. Luckily, we paid off the mortgage last year, so my job covers most of the bills. I can dip into Mark's retirement fund if I need to, but I won't until I know the truth about his death."

"Do you honestly believe something deceitful is going on?"

She carefully considered her reply. Parker was her only hope. They had been partners once. She could trust him. "My heart tells me something's not right."

"Did the police find anything?"

"Not that I know of. There was nothing in the newspapers. The DTA won't tell me why Mark was in the building or why he was a target. David's been working on the case, too. He's as frustrated over this as I am."

"The truth has to surface." Parker reached across the table and held her hand.

The warm touch felt comforting.

"Why don't you work at the SCA again? It would be easier to investigate."

"I'm not ready."

"What's holding you back? The kids are older now. I thought you always liked the work."

"I did...I do. But..." She shrugged. "Stefan would never agree to it."

"Sure he would."

"I already asked him to let me investigate Mark's death. He said I was too emotionally involved to think clearly."

"Investigate his death on your own time while you're working other cases. Stefan wouldn't have to know. You'd have access to computer records. You could talk to other agencies—use all the SCA's resources."

"No. It's too much time away. It would be unfair to the kids for me to leave on a mission every few weeks." An image of her sneaking into the Kremlin flashed through her mind. Was that daredevil still lurking inside her? "Besides, what if something happened to me?" In the next vision, gunshots blasted at her. She covered her mouth. "They'd have no one. It's better I stay close to home."

"But you were a talented agent. You have strong instincts. Don't you miss it?"

"Yeah, I miss it. Stopping the bad guys never gets old." She clenched her hand. "I'd love to hunt down the bastard who did this to Mark, but I can't do it on my own. I need a partner to bounce off ideas—like you."

The server brought a double-decker brownie sundae covered in hot fudge sauce. "Let me know if you need anything else." She folded the bill and placed it on the table.

Parker divided the brownie and ice cream onto the extra plate and scooped up the dessert with his fork. "This tastes delicious. You'd better help me."

Hailey grabbed her fork and sampled the treat. Since Mark had died, everything tasted bland. "Will you please consider helping me? If we worked together, I know we could find out what happened to Mark."

"I'll give it some thought. For now, just take things day-to-day."

"That's funny. Bruce said the same thing yesterday."

Ice cream fell from his spoon. "Is he still in Atlanta?"

She nodded. "He's the same old Bruce. Researching twenty-four seven."

"No doubt trying to discover the world's next biomedical secret."

Hailey explained Bruce's research grant for *Bixa aparra* studies. "I don't know why he's trying to save the plant. I'll never forget how Euphoria killed Justin."

"Neither will I." Parker scratched his head. "But wouldn't it be ironic if Bruce discovered some wonder drug from the plant that could help people?"

She scooped up more ice cream. "I suppose. I wish Bruce didn't work so hard. He could've retired ten years ago."

"For as long as I've known him, he's worked as if he had something to prove. Leaving the SCA had to have been a hard blow." He finished the last bite of brownie and laid down his spoon.

"It was." She smoothed the napkin on her lap. "What about you? What made you want to leave Chicago?"

"I'm investigating a drug case." He shrugged. "I needed a change anyway."

"I wish you had called to let me know you were here."

"I didn't know if you wanted to see me again. I took off in a rush last time."

She crossed her arms. "I was angry at you for that. But once I learned it was because Justin died, it made sense."

Tears pooled in his eyes. "Six years, Hailey. It still hurts."

She rubbed his hand, her vision blurring. "I know it does. I can never thank you enough for adopting Justin. I wasn't able to provide for him like you and Grace did."

"I miss him so much." He clenched his hand and banged his fist on the table. "God, what I wouldn't do to have him back."

She turned her head a moment, keeping her composure. "Our son was a gift. I truly believe that…Just like Mark. Losing Mark makes me think about Justin even more."

"Do your kids know about Justin?"

She shook her head. One of her biggest regrets. "I plan to tell them someday. I know they'll ask a lot of questions." She closed her eyes. "I'm not ready to tell them about my past."

Parker withdrew his credit card. "You'll know when the time is right." His gaze lingered on Hailey for a long moment. "Thanks for a nice night. I can't remember the last time I had such a good meal—or such wonderful company."

****

It was after ten-thirty when Parker drove Hailey back home. Taking slow steps, they strolled to the front door.

In the darkness, Hailey fumbled for the keys in her purse. "I should've asked the kids to leave the porch light on."

Parker took out his cell phone and switched on the flashlight. He picked up a box by the door. "Looks like you got mail."

"Thanks. I was expecting this." She took the box and fished her keys from the bag.

"I had a really nice time. Thank you." He held her hand and squeezed it gently. "Do you mind if I call you again?"

"I'd like that. I had a great time, too." She'd forgotten what fun conversation was. "Thank you for tonight."

He waited as she switched on the porch light and went inside.

The house was dark except for the lamp lit in the living room.

Thank you, Anna! Hailey tugged back the living room curtain.

Parker paused on the porch step, looking at the night sky, and whistled. He ambled to the car and backed down the driveway.

She followed his movements. Yawning, she locked the door and opened the package. *Good.* Her prescription had finally arrived. Even though packages arrived a day late sometimes, mail order was more convenient than standing in line to pick up a prescription. She tucked the bottle into her purse and climbed the stairs. Better to keep her bag with her. After Ethan's last caper, he might sample some of her pills, too. Dear God. When did she stop trusting her son?

In the hallway, she peeked into Anna's bedroom at the sweet girl curled up in the bed. Hailey tiptoed down the hall, pausing at Ethan's door, and tapped gently. When he didn't answer, she opened the door. The dresser lamp cast shadows on the comforter, still neatly pulled over the bed pillows. She stepped backward, her stomach buckling like a horse had kicked her.

I'm going to kill him!

Clenching her fists, Hailey raced down the hall to Anna's room and switched on the lamp. She dropped her purse and nudged her daughter's shoulder. "Anna?"

Anna blinked. "Mom? What's wrong?"

"Do you know where Ethan went?"

"He headed out after you left." Anna sat back against the pillow. "He said he'd be back before you came home."

"Where was he going?"

Anna shrugged. "I don't know."

An engine rumbled in the driveway and a door shut.

Hailey rushed downstairs.

Ethan stepped inside the foyer. He paused and winced when he saw her.

"Where were you?" Hailey barely recognized her shrill voice.

"Nowhere." He tramped to the stairs, placing his hand on the banister.

"Don't play smart with me. I was worried sick."

He scowled. "Oh my God, Mom. Lay off."

"You know you're not supposed to go anywhere when you're grounded." She reached over and jerked off his baseball cap. "And no hats in the house." She studied the green and brown stains smudged over a company logo. "Where did you get this?"

"It doesn't matter." He grabbed the hat and stomped up the stairs, storming down the hallway.

Every stamp of his foot wedged a stake deeper in her heart. She resisted the urge to call him. She had to be the worst mother in the world. Heaven help her, but she was too exhausted to battle Ethan at that moment and tell her son that she loved him.

Chapter Seven

Hailey calmed down and crawled into bed. Ethan's stunt, coupled with memories of Mark's death, foiled any chance of pleasant dreams.

When the digital clock read 5:30 AM, she turned her head and inhaled the earthy scent of Mark's vacant pillow.

Walking to the dresser, she fished inside her purse and removed the bottle of pills, her lifeline during the past six months. The need to take them pressed her more lately.

In the bathroom, she swallowed another pill. She frowned in the mirror at the dark circles under her eyes. She desperately needed sleep. The psychiatrist had warned the medication could make her drowsy, but she wasn't sleeping better. She returned to bed and tried breathing techniques.

When her alarm buzzed at eight, she was grateful to have slept a little. It was the weekend, and Ethan was safe. At least for now. She'd have to figure out a mature way to handle him and his defiant attitude.

Reaching across the nightstand, Hailey grabbed her cell. Her sister-in-law had texted.

—*Planning the summer schedule. What date is best for the kids to visit this summer?*—

Hailey typed a text back to Laura. —*Anytime after June 3 will work. They can't wait to see their cousins.*

How's your mom and dad? Are they driving home today?—

She laid the phone next to the empty pillow and caressed an index finger over Mark's face in their wedding photo. Hailey closed her eyes. At least in her memory she could still see him.

She dragged into the bathroom and showered. Another Saturday. Another mundane weekend to catch up on house cleaning, laundry, and yardwork.

The house was quiet as she dressed in capris and a cotton tunic. The kids liked to sleep in on weekends, and after last night, she wouldn't be surprised if they slept all afternoon. She tugged the sheets over the bed and finished tidying the room.

Downstairs in the study, she logged onto the computer and paid the utility bills.

When she finished, Hailey stepped into the living room where her daughter was lying on the couch, chatting on the phone.

Anna waved to Hailey and lowered her voice.

Hailey returned a wave, smiling at the giddy conversation regarding a boy. She'd never told the kids about her ultrasensitive ear implants, a perk from her work as an SCA agent. Mark had known about the device Bruce Hanover designed to regain her hearing, and he was careful what he said around her. Once, the hearing implant's GPS feature had been used to save her life.

Hailey opened the front door and found the newspaper hidden in the grass. She'd find a way to cut the overgrown lawn even if she had to use hand clippers. In the kitchen, she unfolded the front page and began reading.

An hour later, laundry was in the washing machine, and she was vacuuming the carpet.

Ethan shuffled downstairs wearing his torn jeans and the baseball cap from the previous night.

Hailey studied him. "How'd you sleep?"

He plopped on the couch. "All right."

"We need to talk about last night."

"Mom, I don't need another lecture." He glanced at his watch. "I gotta go."

"You're not going anywhere."

The doorbell buzzed.

"This place sucks." Ethan headed her off on the path and opened the front door. "Hi, David, what's up?" He brushed past the burly man and hurried down the porch steps.

"Come back! You're still grounded," she called after him.

Ethan gave her a dismissive wave and raced across the driveway to a rundown truck waiting at the mailbox. He leaped inside the open passenger door, and the vehicle peeled down the street.

David grimaced. "Do I even want to know what that was about?"

She forced a tight-lipped smile and opened the door wider. "Probably not. Come in."

Somehow, David's visits eased the chaos at the house. Since the fire, he stopped by every week, usually on Friday evenings. At first, she viewed his visits as an intrusion, but she had grown accustomed to his help and buoyant personality.

"No one was home yesterday when I came by. I hoped you didn't fly off to Aruba without me." He gave a fake pout.

His sense of humor remained as constant as his charm.

"I didn't think you'd want to bask in the sun, so we went without you." She smiled at the quick comeback. If Mark were alive, would they have gone on their Hawaiian vacation yet?

"Promise you'll take me if you go again."

"Deal." It was one promise she could keep. "Actually, I forgot you were coming. Anna and I were out. Ethan should've been here, but he went AWOL." She led him to the living room. "Can I make you some coffee?"

"No, thanks. I already stopped for breakfast. What's going on with Ethan?"

She pointed to the recliner. "Have a seat. It's a long story."

When she had filled him in on the past few days, David scratched his chin. "What happens next?"

"Ethan will have a hearing with the judge. The storeowner will give the police the video surveillance to use as evidence."

David shook his head. "I'm surprised at Ethan."

Hailey massaged her forehead. "These friends he's hanging out with are bad news."

"Sounds like it. Is he doing better in school?"

"Not really. He's getting Cs and Ds."

"Do you want me to talk to him?"

Would Ethan listen? "I don't think it would do any good."

The lines on David's forehead carved deeper. "The boy's got to get his act together. His behavior's going to land him in jail if he doesn't shape up."

"That's what Parker said."

He tilted his head. "Parker?"

"Tom Parker. He was a friend when I lived in Texas." *He adopted my firstborn son.* Would Mark have mentioned Justin to David?

"I remember the name. He worked with Mark on the Mendoza case, right? Wasn't he your partner at the SCA?"

Her face heated. Of course Mark would have confided in David about her former career. "Yes."

"He had the boy who died from the Euphoria drug."

Hailey closed her eyes. David had an excellent memory. Such a sad way to sum up her son's short life.

"What's he doing in town?"

"He transferred to the police department where Ethan was taken to the other night."

David's eyebrow arched. "Is that right?"

"I know. Strange coincidence. But he was a godsend at the station. Last night we caught up over dinner."

"You had a date?"

"No." The heat ran up her neck. "Not a date. He's just a friend."

David frowned.

His expressions were easy to read. "Really, I'm not ready to move on yet. Mark's only been gone for six months." She wiped a tear from her eye and squeezed his hand. "I know you miss him, too."

He pulled a handkerchief from his pocket and wiped his nose. "Once you have a best friend like Mark, it's hard to let go."

Although he and Mark were the same age, David looked older, his blond hair now gray and receded.

Sniffling, he paced to the window. "What's going on with the grass? It looks like a jungle out there."

Grimacing, she repositioned a pillow on the sofa. "The mower is still in the shop."

"What's it been? Three weeks now?"

She sighed. "I don't know what's taking the man so long to fix it."

"You should have had Adam or me look at it."

"You have a full-time job, and I hate to bother Mark's dad, especially after his heart attack."

"Has Adam had any more chest pains?"

"Not since last month, thank goodness." She held back a grin, jesting. "The bathroom sink needs a plumber if you want something to do."

His eyes widened like a deer seeing headlights. "Pipes and I don't get along." He exaggerated a scary face. "I'm a better mechanic. Mark's dad taught me everything I know about cars and engines."

"I wish Ethan would take a keener interest in fixing things. He does nothing but play video games."

"He needs a job so he can start making money and pay for those video games. Speaking of money, do you need any help paying the lawyer?"

"I told you I can't accept any of your money. So far I'm making ends meet."

"The money you get from the university isn't a lot."

"David, I appreciate your offer. Things are tight, but I'm handling it."

"How?"

"I've cashed in some of our stocks."

He shifted in his chair. "That should be for your retirement."

"It's for emergencies. And it helped catch me up on the bills. You shouldn't feel the need to help me."

"Mark would offer the same if he were in my shoes."

The kind words tugged at her heart. "You're a special guy. How is it a girl never snatched you up?"

"I never found anyone who looked at me the way you looked at Mark." He shrugged. "I think selfishly, I'm holding out for that type of special relationship."

David was right. Mark was her lifeline. It wasn't right to end the connection yet. David's visits were always bittersweet. "I hope you find it someday because you're going to make one terrific husband."

"Maybe when we get to Aruba."

An uneasy silence blanketed the room. She could feel Mark's presence. Did David feel it too?

He clapped his hands together. "It's quiet today. Where's Anna?"

"She went to a friend's house to work on a school project."

"She's quite the social butterfly."

Hailey chuckled. Her children were moving on without her. At least Anna didn't cause her any trouble.

His phone beeped, and he read the message. "I have to go. Do you need anything before I leave?"

She shook her head. "Just the bathroom sink fixed."

"If you get desperate, I'll look at it, but I can't guarantee there won't be a flood."

Hailey laughed. "I'll fix it myself. Mark told me stories about your plumbing fiascos at college."

Chapter Eight

Mark pushed the weight of his body onto the forearm crutches and kept his focus on the blonde nurse at the end of the room. The tiled path to the goal line stretched out like an endless highway in front of him. He envisioned Hailey cheering next to the perky nurse. If his wife were here, his life would be complete. He made two steps. *Not bad for a dead man.*

Steadying himself, he leaned against a crutch and wiped the sweat beading on his forehead. *Lift the left leg.* In quick waves, pain rippled from his toes to his spine. His knee buckled, and he dropped toward the floor. "Dammit!" The skin tightened, squeezing more pain, and he collapsed.

The physical therapist standing beside him buffered him from completely falling.

Kit leaned over and held his arm as he reached for the crutch. "You're pushing yourself too hard, Mark. Tomorrow we'll go back to the walker until you get stronger." She nodded at the nurse standing five yards away. "Faith, I think we're done for the day."

He lobbed the crutch to the side, and it bounced off the wall. "No! I *have* to keep working."

Faith stepped toward them and lightly patted Mark's hand. She smelled of a flowery perfume Hailey used. "Mark. You've had a long day. I'll help you back in your chair."

"No, dammit! I want to keep walking." He swung his elbow, blocking Faith and Kit's extended arms.

"Hey, buddy. Causing trouble?"

Mark turned at the deep voice behind him. His best friend leaned in the doorway. Today was not the day for David's jovial attitude. "Where have you been? I waited up all night for you."

"Better late than never." David moved toward him and handed Mark's crutch to Kit. "I'll take it from here."

Kit's tense face relaxed. "Thank you, Mr. Smith."

Faith retrieved the other crutch, and the two women hurried out the door.

Mark scoffed. "Where did you find them? They never work me hard enough."

"They came highly recommended by the burn center. You need a competent outpatient rehab program to continue your treatment. This place offers everything you need to get back on your feet again."

Mark scanned the room. David had rented a two-bedroom apartment in a guarded assisted-living development and converted the space into a makeshift rehab room, complete with a patient bed, motorized chair, walkway, and stairs for therapy. *David should've let me die in the fire.* "The therapy is useless."

"I disagree. You've only been away from the burn center for two months. You're lucky you were discharged from the hospital in Texas so quickly."

"But this is hopeless. I still can't walk."

"You had two broken legs. Kit said your rehab is progressing well. Your range of motion is improving, and you're getting stronger." David pulled the walker closer. "Don't rush it. Stay with the walker until you're stronger. You can't keep taking your frustrations out on them."

Mark pointed to the wheelchair. "They don't know shit. They keep holding me back."

David helped him ease into the chair. "They don't want to overwork you."

"They're pissing me off."

"It's not their fault you're here."

Mark struggled to keep his composure. Why was David always right? He stared at his hand, fitted with a custom-made compression glove. "God, I hate this."

"Me, too. How's the pain today?"

"Horrible." He wheeled the chair to the bed. "Last night I waited for you. Why didn't you call?"

David dragged a chair closer and sat. "Hailey wasn't home yesterday. So I went back to the office."

Mark narrowed his eyes. "What's wrong with Hailey?"

"What makes you think something's wrong?"

"I can tell by your face."

David sighed. "Ethan got picked up the other night for vandalism."

Mark clenched his hands, but his left fist barely tightened. "Dammit! Ethan?"

"Yeah. Hailey has her hands full."

Mark pressed his hand against his forehead, and he winced. Few places didn't hurt where he touched. "What happened?"

When David had filled him in on the details, Mark closed his eyes. "This is my fault."

"Hailey hired a lawyer, and they're handling it, but Ethan's really been acting out lately. Talking back. Leaving the house."

Mark leaned his head against the headrest. "Dammit. I should be there."

"There's nothing we can do. You and Owen wanted it this way. I told you from the beginning I didn't approve of this plan."

He scowled. "Oh, give me a break. I never intended *this*."

"What did you expect after we faked your death? That Hailey and the kids would live happily ever after tripping through a field of daisies? They're in pain, Mark. They hurt from losing you." David's eyes closed. "The boy lost his father. He's suffering, and he won't or can't share his pain. Anna avoids the house, and Hailey's at wits' end trying to keep the family together."

Mark clenched his jaw, his frustration mounting to a new level.

David tugged his sleeve. "Do you want to tell Owen the plan's over?"

He met David's stare. "And then what? Expect Hailey to run to me with open arms?" He pointed at the clear mask on his face used to minimize scarring. He still couldn't bring himself to look at his reflection in the mirror. "Look at me. I'm a freak. And a cripple. Even if I could walk, she couldn't see past these grotesque scars."

"You don't give her enough credit."

Mark spit. "And you're living in a dream world. I'm repulsive."

"Hailey would be thrilled to learn you're alive."

"For how long? Until she stops feeling sorry for me?"

"She loves you."

"And I love her." Mark's voice cracked. "That's why I can't do this to her."

"You're making excuses." David's lips tightened. "I hate being in this position. I get Owen didn't want Hailey to know you survived, but I don't like it."

"It's the best way to bring Mendoza to the States and arrest him."

"If word gets out Owen and I made everyone believe you're dead so we could track down Mendoza, a lot of heads are going to roll."

"Bullshit! This is the DTA and CIA we're talking about. The government does questionable things every day, and it never goes anywhere. The end justifies the means. Isn't that the motto?"

"I'm just saying we can all lose our jobs and most likely go to jail."

"We won't go to jail if we catch Mendoza. He's wanted by every agency in the country, not to mention in fifty other countries around the world."

David got up and paced. "There's a lot at risk. All our asses are on the line."

Mark lowered his left hand on his lap, the disfigurement like a permanent retribution. "I know that. There's no way I can ever pay you back for everything you've done."

"I'm not asking for you to pay me back."

"Then what do you want from me? It might have been deceitful when Owen and I set up contingency plans in case something went wrong, but I won't apologize for what I've done. If I stay dead, we maintain the element of surprise. I have no regrets. Besides, Hailey would have mourned twice if she'd seen me and I died later."

"Right, but you're not dying. The doctors said the chance of bacterial infections has diminished. The protein metabolism from the trauma is stabilizing now, and your immune system is strengthening. You're not going to die. At least not anytime soon."

All the medical lingo still made his head spin. Mark crossed his arms and flinched. Would he ever get used to the pain? "I can't let Hailey know I'm alive. Her life is at stake."

"You're making excuses again."

"Dammit! Hailey doesn't know anything about Colleen's secret. If I stay dead, Mendoza will leave her alone."

"Bullshit. There's no guarantee."

"I know how Mendoza thinks. If he knows I'm alive, his goons will harm Hailey and the kids to force me to talk. This is the only way to keep them safe."

"Mendoza's under surveillance in Colombia."

"Your surveillance isn't foolproof." A chill ran down his back. "As long as Mendoza's out there, I have to play dead. You said yourself he's been in contact with someone here. Hailey can't know I'm alive until we have him in custody."

David sat in the chair again. "If that's what you want. But we have another problem on our hands."

"What?"

"Tom Parker's in town."

Mark jerked his head. "Parker? Shit! What the hell is he doing here?"

David shrugged. "I don't know. Hailey said he took a job transfer, but my gut tells me it's something more."

Chapter Nine

"We'll be landing soon, *señor* Manuel." The pilot glanced through dark glasses at the gauges and flipped a switch on the control panel.

Manuel nodded, enjoying the view from his seat in the cockpit. He never tired of the Sierra Nevada de Santa Marta's mountains; the lush, tall palma de cera and encenillo trees reaching up to the clouds could still take his breath away. Since he was a young boy, his father had taken him to the family property nestled in the western portion of Colombia near the Venezuelan border and the Caribbean Sea.

An older, dark-skinned man in a white lab coat waited below the helicopter.

Juan David Rey's punctuality didn't disappoint Manuel. The lead scientist from Brazil ran a tight crew and seemed excited when Manuel called, apprising him of the visit.

When the landing skid made contact, the pilot jotted notes on a clipboard. "I'll return later this evening. Your father needs supplies delivered to the camp."

Manuel unbuckled his belt and stooped, fighting his way through the strong gusts of the helicopter blades.

Juan stepped forward and shook his hand. "*Señor* Mendoza."

Manuel slapped the man's shoulder. "Juan, you look well. I hear there's been a lot going on recently. Give me a tour and catch me up."

****

Throughout the morning, Juan drove Manuel around the property in his jeep. The three-hundred-acre grounds, which belonged to Manuel's maternal grandparents before they passed, consisted of four dark-green stucco buildings with corrugated roofing tiles situated at two thousand meters elevation. The tallest structure housed the researchers' offices and blocked the view of the smaller buildings where a crew produced cocaine.

As Juan drove past the workers harvesting the crop in the coca fields, Manuel pointed to a structure made of clear glass walls. "The greenhouse was a useful addition."

"Building it was Lionel's idea. He needed it to grow more *Bixa aparra* saplings. The younger plants are dense in bixine. It's easier to harvest."

"Bixine?"

Juan slowed the jeep. "It's a chemical found in *Bixa aparra's* roots. It alters the mind."

"As in a drug?"

"Yes."

First Euphoria, now bixine. "How many drugs are in this damn plant?"

"Several. We haven't studied them all yet." Juan parked the jeep.

When they had walked the grounds, Juan led him to the upper offices in the main building where a woman with curly black hair sat at a computer. "Do you remember Paula?"

Manuel regarded the woman's high cheekbones and sultry eyes. He had approved hiring Paula Bhatt two years ago. She reminded him of Bella. Not in physical appearance, as Paula was a native from India, but both women were intelligent and poised. Unfortunately, despite Paula's extensive experience in pharmaceuticals, the woman lacked grit. Manuel deliberated hard before hiring her, but there was a warmth in her smile that evoked his former lover. He extended his hand, savoring her orchid-scented perfume. "Indeed. How are you?" Her warm skin was as soft as Bella's.

"Good, thank you."

Paula's smile stirred his loins.

She led them to a room where a table was set with three place settings. "I took the pleasure of ordering a lunch here in Juan's office. I hope you don't mind."

Manuel stepped to the table. "Not at all." Did she know how alluring she was?

From his seat, Manuel waited as the staff served sancocho—a thick soup, and a dish of white rice. The aroma of lamb, potatoes, and corn filled the air. He savored the taste of the robust stew. "I'm happy to see the greenhouse is flourishing. I hoped to see Lionel today."

Juan sipped water from his glass. "He had to pick up supplies this morning. He should be back soon."

"He's made progress with Euphoria?" Manuel leaned forward, optimistic about his new researcher.

"Lionel's been concentrating more on *Bixa aparra's* cellular properties. He's also researching methods for leaf extraction, working on a way to increase Euphoria's production. He was overjoyed to see it growing in the valley. Until he came here from Peru, Lionel assumed the plant was extinct." Juan raised his glass to Manuel. "I told him we wouldn't have the plant if you hadn't shipped it back from the U.S."

Paula stirred sugar in her tea. "How did the shrub end up here—"

"Don't ask." Manuel waved his hand. "I'll tell you about it next time when I can stay longer." *And spend the night with you.*

Juan poured oil on his salad. "Since Lionel has been heading Euphoria production, Paula and I are focusing on bixine."

"You mentioned bixine when we toured the greenhouse. Tell me more."

"Bixine affects the memory, but we haven't completed studies using different concentrations. In his youth, Lionel traveled through the Amazon and saw a shaman make a broth from the root." Juan glanced at Paula. "We both tried it."

Paula nodded and lowered her fork. "It was like I had dementia. Thankfully, the effects are reversible."

"Can we sell it like cocaine?"

Her smile turned. "No."

Manuel frowned. "Then why are you wasting your time?"

"Bixine may lead to a new pharmaceutical or something bigger."

Manuel scrubbed his beard. Bella had alluded to the same possibilities. "I'm not following."

Paula wiped her mouth with a napkin. "We believe the drug would make a useful psychological weapon."

Manuel hid his surprise. "Go on."

"Foreign governments might be interested. They can use the drug to alter people's mental clarity. Render soldiers useless for following orders." Juan passed Manuel the lamb. "Limit their concentration, especially on the frontline. We could run experiments on the Resistance soldiers to determine the correct dosing."

When Manuel said nothing, Paula's eyebrow arched. "Your father seemed interested."

He pressed his lips together. "I told you not to tell my father about our research."

Paula dropped the napkin. "I'm sorry. I mentioned it when he was here a few months ago."

"Months ago? And you never said anything?"

"You haven't been here. It slipped out."

"I don't tolerate slips. If you expect to keep working here, remember that." There was an awkward silence as Paula fidgeted with her salad. "What did my father say?"

"He wanted to take samples of bixine powder with him." Paula's hands shook. "And he asked us to form bixine into pills."

Manuel narrowed his eyes. "Tell me you didn't do it."

Paula's fork fell in a loud clink against the plate.

"Dammit! How much did you give him?"

"Five pounds of powder...and three hundred pills, fashioned in three different designs." Her voice quavered. "I told *señor* Mendoza we haven't done studies, but he threatened to end our research."

"Has he asked for more?"

"Last week. He needed another hundred pills—twice as concentrated. I got the impression he's messing with someone's mind."

"My father doesn't play mind games. He kills people."

Paula guzzled some water. "He hinted a slow painful death is more satisfying in this circumstance."

"If my father asks you for bixine again, tell him 'no.' Understand?"

"Yes, *señor*—"

"And contact me immediately. This is my project. I'll be damned if he interferes."

Juan glanced toward Paula. "As you wish, *señor*."

Manuel picked up his fork again. "What's this I hear about a researcher dying recently?"

Juan gulped his coffee. "Mateo. He was hired last year. We warned him the blooms were dangerous, but he was overzealous. The petal's oil absorbed through the skin, and necrosis set in." He winced. "Mateo's death was gruesome."

"Spare me the details." Was he in for another disappointment with this plant? Something inside told him to continue. He'd invested too much time and money. Manuel reached for the dish of sliced avocados. "After we eat, I want to see the shrubs in the valley."

Chapter Ten

"Dammit!" Hailey banged a wrench against the bathroom drainpipe. For the past hour, she'd contorted like a pretzel, jammed in the tiny cupboard, trying to tighten the fitting. If only she had a wider wrench to clasp around the pipe.

The doorbell rang in two quick chimes.

She wiped the sweat from her forehead and descended the stairs.

A tall, tanned man dressed in a flannel shirt and grass-stained jeans stood at the door, wringing his baseball cap. He was the man who was at the police department the other night—the brawny guy walking beside Jake.

Ethan and Jake stood behind him.

"Hello?"

"Mrs. Langley?"

"Yes…What's going on?" She stared at Ethan. Had he done something again?

"I'm Santino Ruiz—Jake's dad. I want to apologize for my kids' behavior the other night. And for involving Ethan."

Hailey struggled to respond. "Your apology's a little late."

He frowned. "I'm sorry. I didn't get the whole story until I drove Jake home. Ethan earned money on a landscaping job last night to replace the store window.

He said leaving the house caused a lot of trouble, so I wanted to explain."

Why hadn't she considered reparations? She turned to her son. "Why didn't you tell me?"

Santino massaged his neck. "It's my fault. I told the boys making amends is best kept quiet. Yesterday they mowed grass and trimmed until long after dark. Then they cleaned the warehouse. This morning we called Mr. Holland, the owner of the store. The boys apologized and installed the window."

Hailey tried not to stare at the tattoos lining his right arm. Ethan had never let on. "What did Mr. Holland say?"

Santino scratched the stubble on his chin. "He was glad to have his window replaced, but I think he was happier the boys expressed regret."

A broad smile spread across Ethan's face. "He said he won't press charges, Mom."

Santino nodded. "Mr. Holland said the security video from the store showed Ethan and Jake weren't around the boys who threw the rock. I didn't see the video, but I'd bet Zac and Chase were caught on it."

Hailey felt like she could breathe again. "I...I don't know what to say."

"The boys will have to work another week to finish paying off the window." Santino shifted his stance. "The decision is up to the judge, but at least the kids learned a lesson about taking responsibility and making things right. If I could get hold of Zac and Chase, I'd make them pay for the window, too." He placed the cap back on his head. "I'm sorry this whole thing had to happen. Zac has a habit of drawing Jake into his shenanigans."

Ethan's eyes brightened. "Since Mr. Holland's not pressing charges, am I still grounded?"

Was he serious? After the week he put her through? "Yes, you're still grounded."

"Why?"

"You showed poor judgement."

"Dad wouldn't be this hard on me."

She allowed a small smile. "He would have been tougher."

"Dude, that sucks." Jake scowled.

He looked nothing like Santino. His blond, curly hair touched his shoulders, and he wore a studded earring in each ear. No wonder Ethan wanted his ears pierced.

Hailey reconsidered. Ethan went out in an effort to right a wrong. "I'll meet you halfway. I'll give you back your cell phone—but you're still grounded after school. We're going to have a long discussion later about your attitude."

Ethan stepped forward. "Okay. But can I show Jake my video game for a few minutes?"

She nodded.

Ethan rushed past, Jake following close behind.

"Boys and their video games." Santino shook his head. "Jake told me about Ethan's father. I'm sorry. It's hard being a single parent. My wife ran off two years ago." Deep lines carved his tanned forehead.

The man must have battled a lot in his day. "I had no idea."

"I married Janet seven years ago. Jake is her kid. After New Year's, she hooked up with another guy and left town. Jake had nowhere to go, so he stayed with me."

"I had no idea. What about Zac?"

He shook his head. "Zac's a whole 'nother story. He's Jake's stepbrother from Janet's second marriage. The boy's a hellion on wheels. Takes after his old man. Been picked up by the police a few times. I haven't seen hide nor hair of him since the other night."

She took so much for granted. "I'm sorry."

"He'll hide out for a few weeks until he thinks it's safe." His eyes darkened. "What else could I do? I figured if they had a male adult to guide their life, maybe they'd keep out of trouble." He frowned. "I guess I ain't done a good job."

Gosh, her judgement of him had been way off. "Don't be so hard on yourself. By making these boys earn money for the window and teaching them how to install it, I think that's good parenting, Mr. Ruiz."

"Please. Call me Santino." His cheeks reddened. "I guess the trick is to set rules and don't slack off."

She was beginning to like this man. "I feel like I'm losing my mind trying to enforce my rules."

He removed his hat again and wrung it with his hands. "Don't give up. Ethan seems like a great kid. I'm sorry for the trouble."

"Thank you."

He leaned against the doorway, as if he were hesitant to leave.

Oddly, she was reluctant to end the conversation, too.

Finally, he straightened. "I best let you get back to what you were doing."

"I was in the middle of trying to fix a leaky pipe. You wouldn't happen to know anything about plumbing, would you?"

His face brightened. "Actually, I do. I'm a contractor for the repair shop on Maple Ave."

"Henderson's Home Repair?"

"Yep, that's the one. I have my plumber's license. Frank hires me out to do small jobs for his customers. I also own a landscaping business." He nodded and pointed to his truck. On the door was a sign promoting Ruiz Landscaping. "I can look at your pipe if you'd like. I have a toolbox in my trunk."

"If it's not any trouble." This man was too good to be true. Hailey cringed at the high grass as Santino cut across the lawn.

Fifteen minutes later, he had tightened the pipe, and Hailey had placed the toilet brush back under the sink. She followed him downstairs. "I can't thank you enough. I've never bought a pipe wrench. No wonder I couldn't tighten the fitting."

"Your crescent wrench never would have worked." Santino laughed.

He had a nice laugh. "Can I offer you something to drink? Soda, coffee, tea?"

His biceps bulged through his shirtsleeves. "Iced tea, if you're having some, too."

She raised two fingers in the air. "Two teas coming up."

During the next fifteen minutes, Santino filled her in about the boys' experience replacing the window. He gave another hearty laugh. "Ethan and Jake didn't set the edge in flush. For a minute, I thought we'd have to buy another damn window."

"I'm glad you showed them how to install it. I wish Ethan would get a job to keep him busy instead of those video games he plays."

"How old is he?"

"He'll be sixteen in a few months."

Santino rubbed his jaw. "With Zac ducking out of sight, I could use another hand. If Ethan's willing, and if you agree, I'd be happy to hire him. He'd need his working papers, though."

"I can ask him. Where does he get these papers?"

"You can fill it out online." He guzzled down the rest of his drink and pulled out his cell. "I'll text Jake to come downstairs." When Santino finished the message, he stood. "Thank you for the iced tea and conversation. I'm sorry we stayed so long."

Hailey led him to the door. "You're fine. My support group doesn't meet until seven."

"Support group?"

"It's a bereavement group—for people who have suffered a loss in their life. We meet at the church on the corner of Longview and Elm." She lowered her voice. "You're welcome to go sometime if you'd like to talk about your wife leaving."

He stepped backward. "I've never been much for groups."

"I felt the same way, but this one has helped—and it's free." Would he agree to come?

"You make a good point. I'll think about it."

Chapter Eleven

At 4:00 AM an engine revved outside the bedroom window.

Manuel rose from the bed and watched José's car drive down the lane. Papà was sneaking off again. Groaning, he returned to bed. Between the pressures from his father's guerilla movement and his project in the mountains, he rarely slept anymore.

By the time dawn ignited the sky, he had managed two hours of sleep.

In the kitchen, he grabbed a cornmeal-and-cheese biscuit left on a platter and poured a cup of coffee. He carried the breakfast tray to the study and sat at his desk. Sliding the burner phone from his pocket, he peered at the blank screen and cursed.

His first message had appeared eight months earlier when he opened his mail and found a disposable cell phone inside a package. Manuel turned on the phone, surprised by a text.

—*I have news about Colleen Toole.*—

News on Bella? Was she all right? He texted back. —*Who are you?*—

A reply came within minutes. —*Someone who knows about your American girlfriend. Can't risk our phones being wiretapped. Dispose of it after today. There are more arriving shortly.*—

—*What do you want?*—

—$50K. I'll send the information after you transfer the money.—

—You're crazy.—

—Maybe, but you'll want to know what I have to tell you.—

—How can I trust you?—

—Wire $25K to my bank account, and I'll tell you half of what I know.—

The contact texted Manuel the account information. When the transfer had come through, Manuel received another text.

—Colleen Toole is in the Maryland Correctional Facility for Women—

He clenched the phone. *— I paid you $25,000 for that, you asshole? I know where she is.—*

—She delivered a baby five years ago.—

Manuel collapsed in his chair.

—Your baby.—

—How do I know you're telling the truth?—

—I am. Send me $25K more, and I'll give you the birthdate.—

Irritation filled Manuel at the juvenile games the sender played. A baby? Was it possible Bella was pregnant when she went to jail? Images of their lovemaking danced in his mind. They'd been hit-and-miss with birth control. He hadn't always used protection. Did she dutifully take her birth control pills? It was possible he got her pregnant. Actually, quite possible.

—Boy or girl? And that's part of the original 25K—

—Girl—

—Where is she?—

—No location yet. I need money to investigate.—

He had added the contact to his payroll. Each week Manuel received updates, but the contact hadn't found Manuel's daughter.

Another message was due today. He typed on the keypad. *—What's the status?—*

Like his contact, Manuel kept the messages short and ambiguous. It was hard to know whom to trust, especially for a mission as critical as this.

"There you are." His mother's silvery voice resonated from the hall. Camila strolled into the room, dressed in slacks and a cashmere sweater.

"Good morning, Mamà." He shoved the phone into his pocket and greeted her with a light kiss on the cheek. "Did you need me?"

She adjusted the emerald bracelet circling her arm. "Do you know where your father is? I wanted to speak to him before I left for the orphanage."

Manuel held back a grin. José de Mendoza did not answer to anyone, least of all his wife. "I'm not sure what his plans were. He took off before dawn."

"I'm worried, Mano. I think he's involved in a revolution again." Small lines formed around her mouth as she frowned.

Her instinct was always dead-on but delayed.

"The peace treaty was signed years ago, Mamà."

"Yes, but he didn't favor it. José wants a new president. He's vocal about the government's attempts to reduce the coca plants. Has he said anything to you?"

"Papà doesn't tell me much." He hid his uneasiness over the falsehood; he was no different from his father.

"José noticed you've been distracted." She glanced out the window and turned when a simian peeked in.

"Did you hear Julian Duarte was assassinated last night?"

One of Papà's closest allies before Duarte surrendered his weapons.

Manuel nodded. "His son contacted me this morning. He's the fifth ex-FARC leader killed."

"I need to warn José."

The phone vibrated in his pocket. Finally! News from his contact. How would his mother react to his big announcement?

Camila eyed him. "Do you want to talk about it?"

"Not yet." He brushed a kiss on her cheek. "I have to leave. Soon, I'll tell you everything."

Chapter Twelve

Hailey wiggled her fingers. The numbness was more prominent this morning.

She gazed at the contents on Mark's dresser. Loose quarters Mark had saved for the car wash were scattered on assorted receipts and fast-food gift cards.

Keeping physical mementos didn't fill the void in her heart. The room would never be complete without his presence. She had saved everything exactly the way Mark had left it. Even the thought of giving his clothes away made her weepy. Oftentimes, she would open one of his dresser drawers, take out an undershirt, and inhale the scent of motor oil and grease. Remnants from working on cars in his dad's garage.

She steeled herself for the day. Grocery shopping was top on the list. What else could she do with the kids? Her in-laws were still in New Jersey. Coping with Mark's absence was toughest on Sundays. Ever since the kids were young, Mark had designated Sunday as Family Fun Day. Attending baseball games and touring sites in the D.C. area were family favorites.

The birds chirping outside her bedroom window beckoned her to begin the day.

Hailey tossed back the covers and accepted the song-filled invitation. She'd let the kids sleep while she shopped. Without the junk food the kids tossed in the cart, she might keep the bill low.

During the drive across town, she drifted out of focus as the car traveled down the divided highway. *How did I get here?* She rubbed her eyes. If she didn't start feeling better soon, she'd call the doctor.

As Hailey walked through the cereal aisle, she passed Rita Brown, the woman in charge of the support group. "I guess we both wanted an early start today."

Rita lowered a box of corn flakes into her cart. "We missed you last night."

Busted. When the small engine repair shop didn't call, Hailey stormed into the garage and grabbed the trimmer, tackling the lawn with the weed eater. Now the grass was choppier than before. "Yesterday wasn't a good day."

Rita gave a kind smile. "I hope to see you next week."

When Hailey checked out, her phone pinged.

Parker sent a message. *—Any plans for the afternoon?—*

She texted back. *—Not yet, but I'm open to ideas.—*

It was nice having someone to lean on. Sure, David tried, but her relationship with him was different; he was Mark's best friend.

—How about the amusement park? I've never been to Adventure Horizon.—

She hesitated. The park was only a forty-minute drive away, but tickets were so expensive.

Another message followed. *—My treat. You and the kids could use something fun to do.—*

Fun. They needed that. Anna and Ethan had been living under a dark thundercloud.

—Okay. I'll ask them.—

An hour later when Parker arrived at the house, Hailey and Anna had already packed a bag of sunscreen, towels, snacks, and extra clothes. Humor flickered in Parker's eyes as he pointed to the bags. "This outing is only for a day."

Hailey smiled. She had been doing that more lately. "The kids packed their swimwear for the waterpark section. The temperature's going to be in the eighties today."

"Is Ethan coming?"

"Yes." Hailey pushed from her mind the heated argument she had earlier with her son. "He can't resist amusement parks. He and Mark used to ride the Laser Lobster all the time." How could memories that brought so much happiness cause such heartache? Would Mark approve of them having fun with Parker?

Wearing basketball shorts and metallic sunglasses, Ethan plodded down the stairs.

Parker waved. "Hi, Ethan."

Ethan's face tensed. "What's up?"

If Parker noticed the awkwardness, he didn't show it. "Just hanging low today." He picked up the cooler and bag of clothes. "Who's ready for some fun?"

****

The afternoon was a blur. Hailey started unwinding as the Wild Whip-it Rollercoaster threw her up against Parker.

Even Ethan warmed up to him after braving Spindle, the wildest roller coaster in the park.

She waited for Parker and the kids at the Roaring Amazon Rapids exit. Water oozed from their clothes like a melting popsicle on a hot summer day. Hailey couldn't hide her laughter.

Anna squealed and grabbed a towel from the bag, wiping her arms as water dripped from her long hair. "Mom, we're drenched."

Hailey laughed. "The sign warned you'd get wet."

They stopped for dinner at one of the air-conditioned park restaurants. Ethan and Anna finished their hamburger and fries in a flash, then they hurried back to the waterpark.

Parker grinned as they ran off. "Who would have thought a day at the park would make us laugh so much?" He swiped a fry from Hailey's plate. "I think I'm growing on Ethan."

She nodded, stopping herself from telling Parker about Ethan's resistance about coming to the park. Her son needed to be around as many positive role models as possible.

"He's slow to trust people. Today's been a nice change." Hailey dipped a fry in ketchup. "Here"—she gestured at the pile of potato sticks—"I'm finished."

Parker munched on the fries. "Ethan reminds me a lot of Justin. He's almost the age Justin was before he died." The bright gray flecks in his eyes darkened. "I wish I would've spent more time with him."

Hailey squeezed his hand. "It's hard working full-time and staying involved in your child's life. Mark regretted it, too." She finished her water bottle and beheld the room; the crowd was thinning. "Why were you interrogating Ethan about Chase and Zac?"

"What do you mean?" His eyes narrowed. "I just asked if Ethan had seen them."

"It sure seemed like an interrogation." She leaned her elbows on the table. "I know you, Parker. What's going on?"

He stuttered. "I'm trying to see the type of kids Ethan hangs out with. Maybe if I'd been more involved with Justin's life, he'd still be alive."

Hailey studied him. Was he hiding something? It was hard to tell. "Don't worry about Ethan. He has a good head on his shoulders. I can take care of him."

"And who takes care of you?"

Silly question. "I take care of myself."

"What happens if you get sick and need help?"

"Uh…David's offered to help with the kids."

"Do Mark's parents help out? Give you a weekend off?"

"Peggy and Adam are getting older. They offer to have the kids sleep over, but those days are rarer to find. Ethan and Anna have too many activities. I can't expect Mark's parents to drive the kids around."

"I imagine Mark's death impacted his parents hard."

"It did. They need my help—especially now since Adam's health is declining. He and Peggy both got sick with coronavirus last year. Adam was in the hospital for two weeks."

The lines creased on Parker's forehead. "How long has Mark's father been in poor health?"

"Adam had his first heart attack a few months after Justin died. Mark and I were in Wyoming when it happened."

"Wyoming?"

Although her recent memories were difficult to recall, this distant memory was clearer. "We were on a family vacation at a quiet resort in Buffalo Creek. Mark wanted a remote place in the middle of nowhere to fish with the kids. I had started working at the SCA and had research to do, so it was a perfect getaway. One night I was working on the computer when Mark's mom called and told us Adam was in the ER." Hailey shivered. She'd never forget the helpless panic in Peggy's voice. "We flew back to Virginia immediately. After I saw how much care Adam needed, I quit the SCA."

"You just gave it all up?"

"Yep. Mark's parents mean the world to me. They're the only parents I've known in years."

"Did you miss your job?"

"Sure. Don't get me wrong—it was hard to leave the agency. Especially since I was in the early stages of digging up dirt on Mendoza."

"What kind of dirt?"

She lowered her voice. "Do you remember downloading files on a flash drive when we broke into Mendoza's office?"

"Yes."

"Stefan delegated me to examine the files."

"What was in them?"

"A list of passwords and links to his father's files. Most files were encrypted, but the one I could open had José Mendoza's contacts for the revolt in Colombia." She grinned at the surprise grin forming on Parker's face.

His eyebrows raised. "FARC?"

She nodded, impressed at his awareness of the Revolutionary Armed Forces of Colombia. "When I was at the resort, I passed on the copied files to Stefan. Before I quit the agency, our agents had already started working with the Colombian government to contact the FARC members and persuade them to a revised peace deal. Many were offered immunity."

Parker whistled. "You helped set that in motion?"

She lowered her gaze as heat traveled up her neck. She had to admit, the discovery was significant. "Can you imagine the anger Manuel and his father must have felt over the betrayal?"

Parker smirked and leaned back in his seat. "José never knew what hit him."

"The Colombian government didn't offer José immunity. He's responsible for murdering hundreds of people. The government wants to nab him for being a rebel leader. Now, José is forming a new dissident group to rebel against the peace treaty." Hailey paused. "You were responsible for this victory, too."

"Would you have stayed on the case if Mark's father hadn't suffered a heart attack?"

"Probably. But I can't dwell on what ifs. Stefan assigned the case to another agent."

Parker shrugged. "It's a good thing you left. José and Manuel might seek revenge. How's Mark's dad now?"

She frowned. "His health's not the best. Mark's death has taken a terrible toll on both his parents."

"Do you see them much?"

"Usually on the weekends. Mark's sister Laura and I are still close. She got divorced last year. Francine and I talk occasionally, but she's in Arizona so I don't see her as often."

Parker collected the napkins and empty cups and threw away the trash. "I thought about what we discussed the other night."

She followed him outside. "About looking into Mark's death?"

"Yes."

"And?"

"I'll make some calls and see what I can find out."

She clapped her hands. "Thank you!"

"But—I need to know everything about Mark's activities leading up to that day."

She swallowed the lump building in her throat. Her final argument with Mark was no one's business. "I told you everything. I swear."

They found Anna and Ethan standing in line for their favorite roller coaster.

Hailey muffled a yawn. "We should think about heading back. The kids have school in the morning. And we both have work."

Parker folded the amusement park map and tucked it in his pocket. "Okay, sleeping beauty. Home it is."

****

The chatter in the car ride home seemed like old times.

As the kids rehashed their favorite rides, Anna stretched her arm toward Hailey. "My fingers look like prunes from the water rides."

Ethan's voice equaled her excitement. "I thought the girl ahead of us on the Free Floatin' Rollercoaster was going to hurl when we turned upside down."

Back home, Ethan grabbed the damp swimwear and raced Anna to the house. He unlocked the door using the hidden key and darted inside with his sister.

Parker helped Hailey carry the cooler to the porch.

How would she tell Parker good night? This wasn't a date. Why did she suddenly feel awkward?

Turning, she faced him. "I had a nice time today. The kids did, too. Thank you." She grabbed the bag in Parker's hand, dropping her purse.

Lipstick, comb, cell phone, a pen, and other items spilled across the porch floor.

Parker reached down and picked up the contents. "Here you are."

"Thanks." She took the items, but he clung to the bottle of pills.

He held it up to the porch light. "You're taking anti-anxiety medication?"

She snatched the bottle from his hands. Why was she ashamed? Many people took anti-anxiety medication. "Not that it's any of your business, Mr. Nosy, but they help me sleep at night."

"Grace used them after Justin died."

His dark gray eyes were more intense than she remembered.

"I enjoyed today." He leaned closer. "Can I see you this week? Maybe dinner again?"

His warm breath brushed her face and she inhaled. She had always felt at ease with his fresh scent. Clean. Safe. Being around Parker was a nice distraction. "Okay, but I'd rather stay here—in case Ethan leaves again."

A glint in his eyes sparkled. "How's Tuesday?"

Hailey smiled. "Works for me."

He pushed back a loose tendril of hair behind her ear. "I'll call you."

The warmth of his touch stirred nerve endings on her skin.

She waited while he started his car and drove off. Was this relationship heading past friendship? When she was younger, she relied on Parker a lot, trusted him completely. Was she reading too much into his magnetic gaze? His touches?

No. Nothing would happen. Sure, his interest flattered her, but it was too soon to move on.

She stepped inside the house and patted her purse. Tonight would be another restless night unless she calmed her nerves.

Chapter Thirteen

Nothing felt right. Mark rotated his wheelchair away from the oak table where he'd eaten a bowl of bland chicken-and-rice soup. He laid an outdated magazine on the counter and lifted the family photo. Guilt weighed on him every time he stared at the picture. His body was mending, but the progress wasn't fast enough.

In the morning, when he asked the physical therapists to let him do extra walking, they declined and warned he was pushing himself too hard.

He waited until they took off, and he continued the therapy, falling twice. When he was satisfied with his progress, he sat back in his medical recliner and crossed his arms. His entire body ached. Damn the stupid therapists. He didn't need them.

A knock drummed on the door.

As Mark turned his head, a sharp pain streaked down his neck. "David."

"Feeling any better today?" His bright smile could lessen anyone's misery.

Mark frowned. "I'm still not advancing fast enough."

David lightly patted Mark's shoulder. "I talked to Kit. She said you worked all morning. Don't be hard on yourself. If you saw the rough shape you were in six months ago, you wouldn't feel this way."

"If you say so." Mark rubbed his beard. He rarely shaved; the razor stung the patchy scars.

"I'd call your progress significant, considering you spent months in the burn unit, undergoing hydrotherapy and those painful stretching therapies."

Mark stared at his scarred limbs. It seemed like ages since the doctor confirmed he was medically stable.

The physical therapy continued to be extensive and intense. Therapists used splints to position his hand and legs. Compression wraps helped ease the pain from the skin moving. Stretching exercises were a constant obsession. Even everyday movements of brushing his teeth and dressing seemed like monumental feats.

David sat next to him. "When I dragged you from the fire, I thought you were a goner."

Mark huffed. "You remind me of that a lot."

Memories were still scattered. The thugs' punches had pulverized his body. Gasoline fumes assaulted him. His mind had blocked out the men's faces, but in his dreams, their voices still heckled him. The last recollection he had was of lying on the grass. The smell of burnt flesh scared him as his pained body spasmed. David pleaded, *"Stay with me, Mark. Help's coming."*

Mark blinked hard. He couldn't run from the flashbacks.

He massaged the itchy scars on his thickened skin. "Are you sure only two men died in the fire? There were three."

David nodded. "Positive. Owen cornered a man on fire near the rear of the building, but the man stopped breathing before he confessed anything. There was one set of remains inside—the set Hailey believes is yours."

Mark's hands shook from the memory, and he picked up a newspaper from the table. Why did articles only focus on the negative? "The damn bastards should have all burned up and gone to hell!" He flung the paper on the floor and started finger stretches. "Any leads on the one who got away?"

"No." David placed his palm over Mark's fingers and held pressure, stretching the skin over the knuckles. "Why the questions? You said you never wanted to talk about that night."

"I'm worried about Hailey. Has she asked any more questions?"

"Not lately. The last time was when Owen towed your car to the house. She guessed the DTA searched the car, but she didn't suspect any bodywork on the crumpled bumper. I have to admit, having the other man's remains burn beyond recognition was a fluke. She believes it was you."

Would he ever get past hurting the love of his life? Was his sacrifice worth the pain he caused? The hunt for Mendoza needed to be resolved soon. "Did you check on Colleen this week?"

"Last night." David released Mark's palm.

Mark straightened his fingers. "When's her release?"

"In four weeks."

"She's still refusing the relocation program?"

"She wants to do things her way." David repeated the stretching exercise, moving down Mark's fingers to the next knuckles.

"Colleen should've turned state's evidence against Mendoza before the baby was born. The prison in West Virginia was one of the few in this area that allowed a pregnant woman to room with a baby after delivery. If she had testified, she would've gotten a reduced sentence and been released before the baby had to leave." Mark shook his head in disgust. "But no. She had to backpedal and piss off the judge."

"I don't think Colleen believed the judge would separate her and the baby."

"She didn't. Now she's afraid Mendoza will bribe someone to get to her daughter."

David released his hold on Mark's fingers. "Maybe she plans to move to Colombia."

Mark straightened his fingers again. David never trusted Colleen. "In other words, you think she's still the same selfish, spoiled woman she's always been?"

"I would have used bitch in there." David's eyebrow arched.

He waited as David continued the stretching. The exercises were time-consuming, but Mark had plenty of time. "Colleen's showed positive changes over the past six years. Responsibility will do that to a person. How did she act when you saw her last night?"

"Nervous."

Mark started his thumb exercises, stretching his thumb to his pinky.

One assailant was still out there. Why couldn't he recall the man's description? In a few weeks, the nightmare would be over, and his family would be safe. Unfortunately, he'd feel the effects from his deception for a lifetime.

When the exercises were completed, David stood. "I should head back to work."

"Have I ever thanked you for being such a good friend?" Mark's lips quivered.

C. Becker

"Never." David's eyes were damp.

"Have you found anything on Parker yet?"

"I haven't had time."

Mark scowled. "Then bring me a damn laptop, and I'll investigate—" He paused when David grinned. "What's so funny?"

David advanced to the door and turned. "It's about time you get your fight back."

****

Hailey eased into a tempo run as the school bus drove down the street. After living nearly fifteen years in the community, she could navigate the paths with her eyes closed.

She ignored the pressure developing in her chest and let the peacefulness surround her as she loped through the neighborhoods. The liquid motion gave her time to think. She reminisced about specific cases she worked during her early career at the SCA, many of them with Parker. The trip to Beijing where she met foreign dignitaries from China. The meeting with the Prime Minister in Russia after the espionage investigation in Lisbon. Gosh, she missed those days.

"Good morning, Hailey."

She stopped and waved to Joyce Rogers who was watering flowers with a garden hose. The woman's wavy golden hair reminded Hailey of a young Doris Day. "Hi, Joyce."

Joyce shut off the valve. "It's a nice day to exercise."

Hailey stretched a calf muscle. "Running clears my mind. Lately, I've had a hard time concentrating."

"That's understandable, considering all you've been through." Joyce wiped the sweat from her brow.

"God, it's hot. Even in the morning, I can't beat the heat."

"Spring's a horrible time for my allergies, too." She admired Joyce's colorful tulip beds. "Anna enjoys babysitting your girls."

Joyce pulled weeds from a flower box. "Anna does well playing games with them. We haven't found any kids Rose's age for her to play with since we moved here."

"Anna mentioned Rose isn't in school this year?"

"Oliver and I felt it might be easier on Rose's separation anxiety if she waited until next fall."

Anxiety troubled Hailey even now. "Even though Anna is two years older than Samantha, she talks about her all the time."

"Same here. I'm glad Sam has a best friend. I didn't feel close to anyone until I was in college." Joyce turned off the spigot and rolled the hose. "My sorority sister helped me get through some tough days when my mom died of cancer. We'd do anything for each other."

Hailey understood the special connection; Parker helped her through some difficult months after her parents died. "Do you still keep in touch?"

"When we can. You know how life goes." Joyce gathered her garden gloves and pruning shears. "I hope Sam and Anna will stay friends after we move."

"Are you leaving?"

"The girls and I are going to live with my dad in Boston while Oliver's deployed in Syria. We're waiting on his orders."

"We'll have to make sure they video chat. I saw Rose playing outside a few weeks ago. She's growing taller."

Joyce grinned. "They're both growing like weeds." Her cell phone rang, and she plucked it from her pocket. "I'm sorry—it's work, I need to take this. We'll catch up later."

When Hailey arrived home, she finished her cooldown routine and sat on the porch steps, overlooking the bushy grass and blooming azaleas. Rose wasn't the only one growing like a weed. *Should I call the repair shop and threaten to buy a new lawn mower?*

Hailey sneezed as she unlocked the door and stepped inside the house. After a string of sneezes, she grabbed a tissue and blew her nose. She swallowed an antihistamine and jumped into the shower.

Downstairs, she opened a yogurt in the kitchen. Her cell phone chimed.

—Are you still free for dinner tomorrow night?—

She warmed at Parker's interest. This sort of seemed like old times. *—Definitely—*

—6:30 ok?—

—Sure—

Though the pressure in her chest still hurt, the achiness from the previous night was gone. Was her improved mood from the morning run or the anti-anxiety pills kicking in? She filled her water bottle and drove to work.

****

Hailey registered many blank stares during the amino acid structure review with her 11 AM biochem class. She ambled back to the office and searched her computer files for the final exam study guide. A knock tapped on the door. Her graduate assistant stood in the doorway. "Zhang, come in."

The second-year Master's student brushed the long bangs from his eyes. "Hi, Dr. Langley. Can you clarify a few questions before I set up today's lab?"

"Of course. Let me grab my notes." She shuffled the clutter of papers on her desk until she found the packet. "Today should be a fun lab. Determining sugar content in different pancake syrups. Make sure the students calibrate the spectrophotometer with deionized water as their blank…"

At 2:10 PM, she opened the bottom desk drawer and removed her lunch. She took a bite of her tuna sandwich and turned on the cell phone. The screen flashed two messages.

Anna: —*I'm playing with Sam after school.*—

Ethan: —*Call me when you get a chance.*—

She pressed in his number. "Ethan, is anything wrong?"

"No. Yeah. Can I go to Moonie's?"

She suppressed a scream. "Are you kidding? I heard about the shenanigans at that hangout. Besides, you're grounded."

"I need to see them. They're mad I didn't meet them the other night."

"Who's they?"

"Zac and Chase."

The names kicked her in the gut. "Stay away from them."

"They want to know what I said to the cops. They want Jake and me to take the blame."

Could the situation get any more absurd? "I bet they do. Why should you take the rap?"

"Oh my God, Mom. Don't you get it? It's my first offense. Zac and Chase have records. They're over eighteen. They'll go to jail if the police find out they did it."

She leaned back in her chair. "They *should* go to jail. Maybe you'd find some decent friends then. Besides, Mr. Holland already turned in the tape. You weren't in the video. Those two boys were."

"Geez, Mom. I have no other friends. Don't you see that?" He disconnected the call.

The tremor of his voice concerned her. She hated them for bullying him. She texted back. *—Mr. Greene advised you to stay away from those boys. We'll discuss this tonight.—*

Liz strode into the office and dropped her attaché case on the floor. "What an exhausting day!" Sitting, she placed papers in a neat pile on the desk and twisted off the cap on her mineral water. "How was the support group Saturday night? George's city council meeting ran late, and we were stuck in traffic after our dinner at the marina."

"I didn't make it either. With the chaos surrounding Ethan, I wasn't in the mood."

"I plan to go this Saturday." Liz drank some water. "The group's been a lifesaver for me, especially after George sucked us down a black hole with his gambling."

"At least you didn't let it destroy your family."

"You find ways to survive." Liz plucked an apple from her lunch bag. "How was your weekend?"

"Productive. The kids and I went to an amusement park yesterday."

"How nice. Did you get your lawn mower fixed?"

"Dang. I meant to check on it. Mark and his dad could have built a new engine by now."

"How's Ethan?"

"The seriousness of his arrest is hitting him. But every time I think his attitude is improving, he says something nasty to Anna."

Liz shook her head. "Hormones. Raising teens is a different ballgame from raising children."

"I'm realizing that." Hailey glanced at her watch and placed her lunch bag in the bottom drawer. "I'd better get to class."

Liz tossed the apple core in the trashcan. "Did Zhang ever find you?"

"I saw him earlier." She grabbed her lecture notes and rushed toward the door.

"Aren't you forgetting something?" Liz pointed to the lanyard and keys on Hailey's desk.

Heat flowing to her cheeks, Hailey hurried into the room and looped the lanyard around her neck. "Thanks. I'd forget my head if it wasn't attached."

Chapter Fourteen

Manuel pushed the duvet off his chest and sulked at the empty pillow on the king-sized bed. He hadn't had a meaningful companion since Bella; he had no desire for a lasting relationship with someone other than her. The previous night he visited one of the brothels his father owned. There was an endless supply of whores for one-night trysts.

He rubbed a hand over his chin. His skin still smelled of the *puta*'s perfume. Selena used the same fragrance. His flesh would swell when he caressed Selena's long legs and took in her scent. How many men had she slept with now? His blood boiled at the thought of Papà selling her for a profit. Why did he send her away? Women were meant to be cherished. Made love to. Have babies.

The longer he brooded over Selena, the tighter his fists squeezed. He'd have no part of selling women. Paying them money for occasional sex was one thing, selling them as property was unacceptable.

He sat in bed and closed his eyes. Why were memories becoming harder to recall? Selena had been a virgin when he met her. She was younger than he was, but they had fallen in love instantly. He'd run his hands through her dark-brown hair, gazing into her coffee-colored eyes while he lay in bed with his arms around her after making love. She understood his brokenness.

He understood hers. He had planned to have a family with her—until José sold her.

From the window of his private wing, Manuel peered at the trucks lining the lot by the conservatory. Men dressed in camouflage gathered around the cobblestone walkway. The forces must be starting to convene. He steeled himself for the morning's meeting.

After he showered and dressed, Manuel headed to the dining room.

The *cocinero* had already arranged a small plate of beans and rice. Luna smiled and poured the fresh-brewed coffee. "*Buenos días, señor Manuel.* Can I prepare you anything else?"

He sipped the coffee, savoring the dark, rich flavor. "Did my mother have breakfast yet?"

"*Si, señor.* She left an hour ago."

He frowned. Even at Camila's advancing age of sixty-five, she still frequented the orphanage daily. In the past five years, the number of children left behind without parents had increased threefold. Mamà had to realize the Mendoza family was responsible for a large number of those orphans. Dissident guerillas, kidnappings, and drugs were rampant in the village.

Manuel checked his phone. Damn. Still nothing. He had a lot to sort out before he could tell his parents about his secret.

He was a father. Just thinking about his daughter gave him hope for a new beginning.

A child excited him. And scared him.

What would his parents say?

His mother would love her, he had no doubt. But his father? Manuel sighed. Papà's reaction was only half of the problem.

Manuel still didn't know where the child was located. He gave her a name, though. Katia. The name meant pure. Just like the love he had for Bella. He checked the burner phone again and strode to his father's office.

When he stepped inside the meeting room, José was pacing the marble floor, arms clasped behind his back. A pang of regret pinched Manuel at the man's anxiety. Euphoria and the new drug from *Bixa aparra* would solve the money dilemma for his father's resistance.

Felipe and Nicolas waited on the leather couch, and Luis sat in a chair across from José's desk.

Manuel greeted them, his nod quicker with Luis.

"The meeting was scheduled for nine o'clock. No?" José's voice had the familiar tenor of authority.

"I'm expecting a message from the States."

José scoffed and faced the group. "We lost another shipment yesterday." He whirled around and pointed a finger in front of Felipe's face. "One of your men got caught landing at Mexico's docks. *Maldición*! That's four fucking shipments foiled in two weeks."

Felipe tapped his foot against the floor. "The authorities seem to know where to target. I'll get another order ready."

José lowered his hand to his pocket and withdrew a semi-automatic pistol. "Don't bother."

Felipe's face turned whiter than cocaine.

José pulled the trigger and delivered a bullet to the man's forehead.

Manuel's stomach lodged in his throat. He'd never get used to the violence. His father never winced—the despicable, selfish beast.

José aimed the gun at Nicholas and laughed as the color drained from the man's face. "Make sure the next shipment makes it."

The heavy man squirmed like he had snakes in his ass. "It will."

"I won't tolerate another mishap, or your family will pay."

Nicholas swallowed hard. "Understood."

"You two can go." José gestured toward the door. "Luis, I want the report on all available men and weapons by this afternoon. And send someone to clear out this mess."

Maintaining a stoic expression, Luis nodded.

When the two men had fled, José ambled to the wet bar and poured a bourbon. He held up the glass and swallowed the drink. "Damn government agencies. They're getting wiser about detecting our contacts and routes."

"We can go elsewhere."

José's face twisted in disgust as he clanked his glass against the counter. "The U.S. has the biggest markets."

"Why waste time assembling men for a coup?"

"You idiot! Our government is working against us. The new administration is focused on curbing drug trafficking, not profiting from it."

"You are one of the wealthiest men in Colombia. You have property and money. You have businesses set up around the world to launder money. What more do you want?"

José glared. "Power. It trumps everything."

Manuel stared as his father marched out of the room. He'd wait another day before questioning him about bixine. His insides reeled as he stared at the blood oozing from the body on the carpet. José was a heartless bastard. His father always was.

He stepped to the window and searched for black moths. There had to be some moths flying around the bushes. As a boy, their ominous presence bothered him until his mother told him the moths were a sign of protection against his father's stern temper. For years, Manuel believed the fabricated tale and enjoyed his mother's loving protection.

But the security ended the week before his eighth birthday. Camila wasn't home to protect him from José's wrath. She found Manuel hiding in his bedroom closet. After she nursed him back to health, she assigned a bodyguard in case José tried hurting him again.

Manuel closed his eyes, and memories of Antonio raced across his memory. Manuel would do anything to have his loyal confidant back.

Chapter Fifteen

Hailey braked at a red light on the drive home. It was only Tuesday, but the days were blurring together. Anna had ballet practice after school, and Parker was coming for dinner. At least it wasn't Hailey's day to carpool. A car honked, and she gripped the steering wheel tighter as the car sped past and the driver made a rude gesture. How long had the light been green? She rubbed her eyes. The late nights must be catching up with her.

She pulled into the driveway next to a white truck and blinked hard. Was she at the correct address? Her yard could pass for a botanical garden.

Santino sat on a riding mower, cutting the shaggy grass.

Ethan and Jake trimmed bushes near the right side of the house.

She grabbed her purse and attaché bag and ambled over to Santino.

A bright smile spread across his face when he veered in her direction. He cut the engine and tipped his baseball cap in a nod. "Good afternoon."

His deep voice melted her heart.

"What's this all about?" She breathed in the smell of fresh-cut grass.

Santino removed his cap and wiped the sweat beading on his forehead as he let out a hearty laugh.

"Ethan told Jake you used a weed eater to cut the grass the other night."

Her cheeks heated. "It seemed like a good idea at the time."

"The shop still hasn't fixed your mower?"

"No."

"I finished work early today. Decided we'd surprise you. I figured anyone desperate enough to use a weed eater wouldn't object."

"I don't know what to say. You must think I'm a nutcase."

He grinned. "Trust me. The thought never entered my mind."

His gaze lingered, mesmerizing her.

"I like how resourceful you are."

Was he flirting with her? She scratched her neck and studied him. He'd shaved since Saturday, making his cheekbones more defined. "It's hot out. Can I get you something to drink?"

He rubbed his sleeve against his cheek and gave her a wide smile.

He had nice teeth, too.

"That would be great, thanks."

"Is water okay?"

"Anything will be fine."

Ignoring the tickle in her nose, she climbed the porch steps and sneezed. Her grass allergies would be especially bothersome today.

In the kitchen, she took two antihistamines and poured water into glasses.

When she stepped outside, Santino was sitting on the top porch step. Hailey passed him a glass from the tray. "Here you go. I'll take these to the boys."

His tanned skin made his teeth look whiter. He was a lean man. Muscular. His tattooed arms and biceps were well-defined. The man had to frequent the gym.

"Thanks." He picked up a second glass. "I'll save one for you."

As if dancing, she glided across the grass. Life was good. The thick, plush lawn was soft beneath her shoes.

When she returned, Santino motioned to the empty spot next to him and handed her a glass. "Can you join me for a minute?"

"Sure." She ignored his sweaty clothes. "I can't thank you enough."

They chatted for a while, sipping their drinks, while Ethan and Jake mowed the side yard.

Hailey pointed to her son. "It's nice seeing Ethan in a chipper mood—and working. He used to help Mark all the time."

"Work keeps kids out of trouble."

"I talked to Ethan about working for you. He agreed."

"He told me today. Since Ethan's only fifteen, he'll have some restrictions on his hours." Santino placed his empty glass on the tray. "This is a nice place you have."

"Thank you. Mark and I bought the property years ago. The builder used the same floorplan throughout the neighborhood to keep the price down, but he preserved the trees."

"I like the privacy."

She finished her drink and stood, her fingers tingling as she set the glass on the tray. "The developer installed a walking path behind the wooded properties. Anna takes it to see her friends." She fell silent. "Mark and I planned to live here forever."

His brown eyes captured her attention. Was it sadness she saw?

"I never met your husband, but he was a lucky man to have you."

Heat flowed up her neck. His face blurred. The sun must be getting to her. "It's…very nice…of you to—" She clutched his sleeve and struggled for the right words.

"Are you okay?"

A loud buzzing in her ears muffled Santino's voice. "I feel like I'm in a centrifuge." She held her head, and her legs weakened.

Santino caught her and carried her inside. He laid Hailey on the couch and pulled out his phone. "I'll call 9-1-1."

She shook her head. "Please, no ambulance. I'll be okay in a minute."

He hesitated. "Would you rather rest in your bed?"

"This is fine." She shifted to a sitting position, wavered, and slumped over.

"Dammit! You're going to fall. Where's your bedroom?"

His words became lost in the darkness enveloping her. She mumbled, "Upstairs, on right."

Santino wrapped his arms around Hailey and carried her up the stairs.

She felt like a bird in flight; the landing was smooth as he lowered her gently to the bed.

A soft blanket spread over her, and she tugged it to her neck. Finally, the dizziness and ringing subsided. She opened her eyes.

The uneasiness on Santino's face made her second-guess the seriousness of the fainting spell.

He placed a cold washcloth on her forehead. "Here. This should help. Are you sure you don't want me to call an ambulance?"

"I'm sure." She massaged her forehead. "Thanks for the washcloth. You make a good Florence Nightingale."

He blushed. "My ex-wife was a nurse. Are you feeling any better?"

"Yes. I just lost my balance for a minute."

Santino studied her, as if he were responsible for her well-being.

His watch beeped.

"Damn. I have a delivery coming. Stay here. I'll have Ethan check on you." He smoothed the blanket over her. "If you need anything, Ethan can text me."

She faked a smile, but inside she was trembling. "Thanks. I'll be fine."

He turned in the doorway. "Get some rest."

Hailey shut her eyes and nestled under the covers.

****

A soft knock woke her. Why was she in bed? It was too dark to be morning.

She glanced at her clock. 6:25 PM.

Memories of her collapse became clearer.

"Mom?" The door creaked, and Anna crept inside, carrying a tray. "Ethan said you fainted. Are you feeling any better?"

Hailey nodded and propped her shoulders against the pillow. "I hope I'm not coming down with something."

Anna laid the tray on the bed. "Maybe you'll feel better if you eat. I made grilled cheese and chicken noodle soup."

The aroma of melted cheese stirred her appetite. "Smells scrumptious. Thank you, honey."

Anna pointed at the purse on the nightstand. "The phone's in here in case you need to call the doctor."

The doorbell rang downstairs.

"I'll see who it is." Anna disappeared into the hall.

With her hearing implants, Hailey listened to the voices down below and smoothed her hair. How did Parker find out?

Shoes padded on the carpet, and he appeared in the doorway, concern written over his face. Mark used to look at her like that.

She gave a small wave. "Hi."

He loosened his tie and sat on the bed beside her. "What happened?"

"I was outside, and everything started spinning."

"How are you feeling now?"

"Fine. Whatever it was passed."

He held her hand. "I'll take you to an urgent care."

"And say what? That I was dizzy. I was probably out in the heat too long."

"The doctor can still check you out."

"No. I'm fine." Didn't he remember her aversion to doctors? "Why are you here?"

"I was going to order dinner. We agreed on 6:30?"

She leaned back into the pillow. How could she have forgotten? "I'm sorry."

"Don't be. We can do it another time." He placed his palm on her forehead. "You don't feel hot. Are you sure you don't want to see a doctor?"

"I'll be fine." She narrowed her eyes at his loose tie and rolled-up dress sleeves. "You look tired. Did you have a hard day?"

"More like frustrating."

"Want to talk about it?"

"Not tonight."

She picked up a sandwich and tore it down the center. "Anna made grilled cheese. Here." She savored the buttery bread. "Did you find out anything about Mark?"

"Not yet. I made some calls, but no one's gotten back to me."

"Any leads on the case you're investigating on drugs coming through the area?"

Parker shook his head. "The Mexican drug cartel has a lot of contacts in town. As soon as we find one, five more pop up." He brushed a stray hair from her face. "Enough about work. I'll stay here until you fall asleep."

****

The medicine took the edge off the pain. Mark managed to sleep an hour in the afternoon before the therapist came for the stretching exercises. In his chair, he browsed the newspaper, noted the day, and tossed it onto the table. Damn! Three more days. He lived for Friday. David could condense an entire week of Hailey and the kids' activities into a brief hour.

Mark closed his eyes. If his family only knew how much he missed them. Loved them. Needed them.

Using his walker, he moved to the bathroom. *Look in the mirror, you coward.* As he turned on the light, another image from the fire flashed across his mind. Trembling, he grabbed onto the counter and breathed slowly until the episode passed. He raised his chin and shriveled at his reflection in the transparent burn mask. Could Hailey ever love him again? His eyes were the same. Hailey often drank in his blue eyes. Dreamy blue eyes, she had called them.

Mark rotated his neck and considered his hair. He almost looked normal. If he could go the rest of his existence with half a face, he might have a chance at an ordinary life. How would his lips feel to Hailey? The counselors reminded him positive body image was more than physical attributes. Easy for them to say. The left side of his torso was a carpet of scars. Most of his burned skin was now thick and dark pink in color. He could barely grasp a fork in his hand. Hell, he couldn't walk steady without a walker and even then, it set his nerve endings on fire.

Would he be able to accept his kids' stares? Deal with the longing if Hailey refused to make love again? If she touched him, how could he tell if the touch was a tender caress or in sympathy? Would she even want to take him back? He had dragged her and the kids through so much pain! In one quick moment, he had lost everything. The fire not only destroyed his life, it wrecked Hailey's life. His entire family's life. And David's life. He stared at his reflection again. *Congratulations, you asshole. You have successfully fucked up the life of everyone who cares about you.*

A tap knocked on the door, and David appeared in the hall. "Hey, I'm glad you're here."

Mark turned. "Where would I go?"

David laid a black case on the kitchen table and stepped beside him into the living room. "I thought I was the wise guy." He settled on the sofa beside Mark's chair. "I got home from work early. Wanted to bring you a laptop. Compliments of Owen." He pointed to the bag on the table. "You look tired."

Tired was a polite description. Mark studied David's haggard face. "You don't look any better."

"Rough day?" David removed his jacket and hung it over the armrest.

"I didn't sleep much."

"Where's Faith?"

"She had to leave early."

David arched an eyebrow. "She said you threw her out."

"If you knew the answer, why did you ask?"

"Testing your mood. Did you tell her you had a hard time sleeping?"

"She gave me some pain meds. I need more."

"We're not going there again. You were becoming dependent on them. I didn't get you this far to have you slide downhill and ruin your life." David paused. "We're on the same team. What's bothering you today?"

Mark frowned. He had to control his irritability. Faith and David didn't deserve this treatment. "I've fucked up your life."

"Oh, so you're the reason I'm the way I am."

"I'm being serious. I'll never be able to repay you—"

David raised his hand. "Whoa. Hold it right there, buddy. We're friends. Best friends. And friends help each other."

"You've given up your life to help me."

"I'm a bachelor. I spend my Friday evenings talking with Hailey and you. No big deal. I have more free time than six married men."

Mark wiped his eye. How could he properly thank a man who sat beside him in the hospital as he cried out

137

in pain, begging to die? "I can never pay you back for everything you've done."

"I never asked you to. Just be thankful Grandma Catherine willed me a lot of money when she died. Her marrying the old oil tycoon paid off for us. It covered all my flights between Texas and Virginia when I hopped planes and checked up on you and Hailey." David grabbed the newspaper on the side table and scanned the front page. "Guess I'm not in the headlines today." Standing, he crumpled the paper and tossed it across the room into a garbage can. "Three points."

"You should have tried it sitting down."

"Wise guy." David sat again. "If you want to hand out praise, give Owen credit for pulling strings to get you into the burn unit at the SCA. He also rented this apartment and arranged for the therapy and private nurses you balk about constantly."

"I wonder if it was the same complex in Austin where Hailey stayed as a patient."

"It is. I read about it when I ran her background check." David whistled. "The facility has so many covert activities going on, it puts the CIA to shame." He gazed at Mark. "Enough shoptalk. Are we good, or are you going to spend the day complaining how you're indebted to me for the rest of your life?"

"We're good. Thank you." Mark grasped David's hand. "You're the best."

"I know." David grinned. "Now tell me, did you stretch this evening?"

He shook his head. "It hurts too much. I told Faith to skip the treatments tonight."

David moved closer to Mark's left side. "I know the stretching is painful, but you have to do it. I'll help you." Mark glared, but David held firm. "It's critical you stretch. Loosen the tissue. Prevent contractures."

"Spare me the lecture. I know the drill."

With great care, David moved him into the stretching exercises, beginning with chest and neck movements, shifting to the shoulders, elbows, and hands. When they finished, David pushed the walker into reach. "I'll help you get into bed before I head out. Brittany should be here at eleven." He beamed as Mark stepped across the room. "Your stride is smoother."

Mark chuckled. He'd noticed the improvements, too. "Maybe all this therapy shit is making a difference." The snug pressure garment on his torso tightened as he sat, and he grimaced. "I had another nightmare last night."

David secured the splint under Mark's wrist. "Brittany called me. She found you curled up in bed again, crying. Still images from the fire?"

"Yeah. I hear the goons' voices heckling me, but I can't see them. Then my clothes catch on fire, and everything goes black."

"You'll remember when you're ready." David lifted Mark's legs onto the mattress.

Mark tensed. "It would be quicker if you'd tell me. Have you heard from Hailey?"

"Not since last weekend."

"I guess no news is good news." Mark eased his back onto the pillow as his friend slid smaller pillows under the legs.

"Try not to give the nurses and therapists a hard time. You've had a lot more outbursts lately."

When the door closed behind his friend, Mark gazed at the photo David had taken of Hailey and the kids during Anna's birthday party. He wiped a tear and braced for another night tormented with nightmares. Tomorrow, he'd research Tom Parker. Something brought Hailey's former partner to town. That something had better not be Hailey.

Chapter Sixteen

Sunlight penetrated through the blinds, waking Hailey. The events of the previous evening flooded her. When did Parker leave? She had a faint memory of him pulling a heavy blanket over her shoulders at midnight.

She tested her feet on the ground. The tingling sensation was gone, but her legs wobbled on the way to the bathroom. Teaching class would be a struggle, but the department head had issued a stern warning about too many sick days.

Ethan checked on her before he headed to the bus stop. "Mr. Greene left a voicemail last night."

Anna set a tray with oatmeal and a slice of wheat toast on the nightstand. "Feel better, Mom. I'll lock the front door when I leave."

The cooked oatmeal smelled too delicious to resist, and Hailey forced herself to eat.

Deciding against a shower, she dressed in a knee-length floral dress and pushed a comb through her hair. As she laid the comb on the counter, the bottle of anti-anxiety medication tipped over, spilling four pills. It couldn't hurt to take another one. During the night, she had swallowed one. Or was it two? She poured three pills back and downed the remaining one in her hand.

Hailey carried the half-eaten food and tray downstairs and stepped into the kitchen. Her cell pinged.

—It's Santino. Are you feeling any better?—

Darn. She had forgotten to text. *—A little. I'm sorry I didn't call you back last night.—*

—Don't be sorry. I'm mowing at Sunnydale Ridge. I can stop by if you need anything.—

—I'm on my way to work. Can I text later?—

—Sure. Let me know if you need anything.—

At noon, Hailey opened her office door.

Liz sat, working on the computer, her eyes puffy and red. She pointed at a folder in Hailey's wall file. "Zhang dropped off the list of broken and missing glassware."

"Great. I need to charge the items to the student accounts." Hailey hesitated. "Are you all right?"

Liz wiped her nose. "I'm fine. Just tired."

She didn't look fine. Hailey should've been more sensitive of Liz's issues, instead of letting her own problems consume her. Liz had a full life, juggling a career, family, and husband with a gambling problem.

Liz removed a container of veggies from her lunch bag. "Zhang said you weren't feeling well?"

Hailey set her purse and attaché case on the desk. "I fainted yesterday afternoon and was in bed until this morning."

"You poor thing. Are you feeling better?"

"Now I am. I think it was a twenty-four-hour bug."

"You can always call if you need me."

"Thanks. I called the doctor this morning. He thinks the dizziness is a side effect of my anti-anxiety medication. He prescribed something new." Hailey sat in her chair. "Just my luck. The refill for my other prescription came in the mail this weekend. The pills are so expensive."

"How long will it take until you get the new medicine?"

"Usually a day or two. The pharmacy sends a text alert when they mail it, although lately, the packages arrive a day later than they estimate."

Liz chuckled. "That's the mail for you." She opened a water bottle and sipped. "Hopefully, you can rest after finals."

"Maybe. But then summer classes kick in."

"Are the kids still going to your sister-in-law's house in New Jersey?"

Hailey nodded. "They've been looking forward to this visit for months. The house has been so disruptive lately."

Liz nibbled on a celery stick. "Don't forget you need a break, too."

Hailey searched inside her attaché case. "Oh shoot."

"What's wrong?"

"I forgot my lunch in the car." She looped the purse around her shoulder. "Be back in a jiffy."

****

Parker texted sometime during Hailey's afternoon lectures. —*Feeling any better?*—

She messaged back on her way to the car. —*Yes*—

—*Can I stop over?*—

She shouldn't encourage him, not when she was still mourning Mark. —*Not tonight. I'm hitting the bed early.*—

—*All right. What about tomorrow? 6:30? I'll take you and the kids out to dinner.*—

She shouldn't overanalyze things. It was only a date. —*OK. Thanks.*—

143

When she arrived home, Anna was lying on the couch with a book open across her lap. Hailey slipped off her shoes. "How was school?"

Her daughter flashed an anxious smile. "Bad. I have two pages of math problems and a science test to study for."

A minute later, Ethan strode through the front door and pitched his backpack, just like Mark did when he tossed his briefcase after work. "Feeling better, Mom?"

"A little." Her voicemail chimed, and she fished the phone from her purse.

Ethan stepped into the kitchen and opened the fridge. "When's dinner? I'm starved."

"I haven't thought about dinner yet." She relaxed on the sofa and listened to the message. "Mr. Greene's assistant called. Your hearing is scheduled for next Wednesday."

Ethan came back into the living room. "So soon?"

"Don't worry. Whatever happens, we'll get through it together." She plucked a pillow from the sofa and held it against her chest. "Anything else go on today?"

Anna closed her book and slid next to her. "Mrs. Kingston gave us a pop quiz."

Hailey faked an exaggerated grimace. "Oh boy. Social studies. How'd you do?"

"100%!"

"Way to go!" Hailey passed a high-five.

"My teacher told me if I study hard, I can go to any college in the country."

"That's true." College, already? Gosh, it was too early to think about those decisions.

"I want to go to Harvard. Sam's mom went there."

"That's an impressive goal. Keep up the good grades." Hailey ruffled Ethan's hair. "How was your day?"

"The counselor helped me fill out the paperwork for Santino." He slid a paper from his pocket. "You need to sign these before I can start working."

Hailey warmed at his excitement. "I'll look at it after dinner."

The doorbell chimed, and she opened the door. "Joyce. What a surprise."

The neighbor passed Hailey a baking tin covered in aluminum foil. "At the bus stop this morning, Anna mentioned you were sick. I thought you might appreciate a lasagna dinner."

"Thank you." Hailey accepted the pan, still hot from the oven. The room filled with the aroma of cooked noodles and tomato sauce. "You shouldn't have gone to so much trouble."

Joyce waved her hand. "It was nothing. I was making one for my family tonight. Are you feeling better?"

"I am. Can you come in for a few minutes?"

"Just for a few."

Hailey passed the dish to Anna. "Honey, can you take this into the kitchen?"

Anna sniffed the lasagna. "Mmm. This smells delicious, Mrs. Rogers."

"It's Sam's favorite." Joyce glanced around the room as Anna walked into the kitchen. "Do you need anything?"

"I appreciate the offer, but I'm okay. Mark was always good about taking care of things when I was sick."

Joyce pointed at a family portrait on the wall. "Your husband seemed like a nice man."

"Did you ever meet him?"

There was a long pause as Joyce regarded the picture. "Just once."

"Oh?"

"Oliver and I met him at the realty company when we were house hunting last fall. The one by the movie theater? *True Living Realty.*"

"What was Mark doing there?"

Joyce hesitated. "I have no idea. But when he overheard I needed a kid-friendly place, he recommended this neighborhood. He raved about the schools and fine arts programs."

"Mark never mentioned it."

"He knew all the safe areas around town. Thought our girls would get along. He was right." Joyce smiled at Anna, returning from the kitchen. "I should go. I told the girls I wouldn't be long."

Hailey stood at the window rubbing her temples as Joyce hurried down the sidewalk. Had Mark mentioned a case involving a realtor? Her brain hurt too much to make sense of it.

****

The lasagna was a hit; they each had a hefty helping, and there was plenty left over for another night. After Hailey put the dishes away, she helped Ethan complete the work-permit paperwork, and then folded laundry upstairs.

At nine, Anna collected her pile of folded clothes. "Dinner was delicious tonight." She hugged Hailey and sauntered down the hall.

Hailey agreed. Mark would have loved—

Mark's gone. She needed to accept it. She had a strong support group offering to help. Peggy and Adam. Her neighbors. David. Santino.

Even Parker. What was the chance he'd show up again after six years?

Hailey slipped into her nightgown and brushed her hair.

Parker was still easy on the eyes. Had a reserved quietness. Their past ran deep.

She opened her purse and checked her cell phone. The technician from the repair shop left a voicemail. The mower was ready for pick-up. She chuckled at the irony.

Hailey opened her medication and shook a few pills into her palm. Dr. Thomkin thought the new beta-blocker medicine would have fewer side effects. She could only hope. The order would arrive in a few days. She swallowed one pill, dropping the others back into the bottle, and then she slid under the sheets, praying for a restful night's sleep. Joyce's comment replayed in her mind. *We met at the realty company.* Hailey rotated onto her side and scratched her hand. Why had Mark talked to a realtor?

Chapter Seventeen

Mark ignored the sweat dripping from his forehead. *Move faster.* Pain pricked his legs as he shuffled in baby steps across the floor.

He eased into the medical recliner at the kitchen table and inched back against the cushion. Who would have thought using a cane would be such a significant accomplishment? When Kit took off after lunch, she had warned him about overdoing the exercises.

Ignoring the itchy sensation on his palm, Mark held his breath, slowly stretching his fingers. *If you want to get home, you have to work through the pain.*

He stared at the laptop David had left on the table. It was his portal to the outside world. He opened the lid and waited as the computer booted.

Sleep the previous night had been impossible. He supposed the nightmares couldn't get any worse, but each time he drifted off, another disturbing image woke him. Parker laughing with Hailey. Holding her. Kissing her. Mark lowered his hands to the keyboard and typed. T-O-M-P-A-R-K-E-R. He held his breath and waited.

Within seconds, internet articles containing Parker's name filled the page.

Mark leaned closer, clicking on the story dated March 16, 2019:

"Chicago Police Officer Placed on Administrative Leave Pending Investigation"

A picture of Parker in his uniform filled the top portion of the article. Mark began reading:

A Chicago police officer is on paid administrative leave after allegedly assaulting a drug suspect during an arrest on March 14.

The status of Officer Tom Parker, 43, is pending and will be determined after an investigation is finalized. Wendell Hautz faces charges of drug possession with intent to distribute. Following Hautz's arrest, he was taken to Chicago General where he is in critical condition.

As he scrolled the page and continued to read, someone tapped his shoulder. Suddenly the sentry from the abandoned building was beating him. Mark swung his arm in defense.

"Hey, buddy. It's only me." David rubbed his chest.

Mark lowered his fist. "Shit! I'm sorry, are you okay?"

"I'm fine."

"You scared the hell out of me."

"I knocked. When you didn't answer, I let myself in." David laid a paper bag and soda cup on the table. "Thought you might like some fast food tonight."

The smell of fried grease tickled his nose. His hand trembled as he peeked inside the bag and pulled out a cheeseburger and fries. Did David notice his nervousness? "Thanks."

"I figured going off your diet once in a while won't hurt. Kit said therapy was rough today."

"Every day is rough."

David pointed at the computer screen. "Researching Tom Parker, I see."

"We were right to be apprehensive." Mark opened the cheeseburger. "Pull up a seat."

When he had finished showing David the articles, they sat in silence. Mark swallowed the last french fry and tapped his fingers on the table. "Hailey should know."

David rose and stepped to the window overlooking the common area. "We should think this through."

"Why? Parker killed a man. I don't want him hanging around my wife."

David turned. "Come on. The guy was a drug dealer. You roughed up the same sleazeball when you questioned him about Euphoria."

"But that's different. I didn't kill him…You have to tell Hailey."

"I disagree. There's something more to this story. If I tell Hailey, she might get defensive and ask questions. I don't want to open a can of worms that will morph into rattlesnakes."

Mark scratched his arm, his anxiety exacerbating the itchiness. "Parker was dismissed from the force. What more do you need?"

"There's nothing about the rookie who rode with him. Where's his statement?"

"Why are you fighting me on this?"

"I have a feeling there's more to Parker's story than what we just read."

"But—"

"Listen. Hailey seems to be coping better. I think Parker's responsible for the change." David paused. "I know you're upset, but the last thing we need is Parker sticking his nose in the Mendoza case. Let it ride until Colleen gets out of prison."

It might be too late if he waited. "Will you at least call your contacts in Chicago and ask what happened?"

"I will." David stood. "Let's do your exercises before you settle into bed."

When the night nurse arrived later that evening, Mark sulked in the darkness. Had he really expected Hailey wouldn't move on? Would she forgive him when the ordeal was over, or would she choose Parker?

He felt the left side of the pressure garment covering his torso where the flames had charred his skin. Owen and David should have let him die in the fire.

****

Mark breathed in the gasoline vapors. His heart pounded like a rocket launching; swollen eyes blurred his vision. A deep voice laughed behind him. The heat spread every direction, feeding on the spilled fuel. A man screamed. Was it Mark's own voice? He twisted away, but the fire spread up his leg, latching on to his torso. The fire licked his chest and neck and singed his hair.

"Mark!"

David shouted, fighting his way closer, as bullets sprayed the building. He heaved Mark to the floor, chair and all, rolling him until the flames smothered.

Mark's body rippled in pain.

"Stay with me, buddy!" David's cries blended with Mark's shrieks as David cut the ropes around Mark's arms and carried him out of the fiery building.

"Mark? Wake up. It's okay."

He opened his eyes and blinked.

Brittany leaned over him, patting a damp washcloth on his forehead. "Shhh. You had another nightmare. You're safe."

Holding his hand, the night nurse sat beside him, comforting him until he stopped crying.

Mark turned his head and stared out the window into the darkness, his soul waiting for exhaustion to overtake him. God, when would the nightmares end?

Chapter Eighteen

Manuel finished reviewing the bank records and drummed his fingers on the desk. The contact in the States emptied his account faster than drain cleaner. What was the man doing with the money Manuel deposited into the overseas bank account each week? He sighed. There was no other viable alternative. Any tidbit of information could be critical in locating his daughter.

The contact had hired two private investigators to support the search, but they hadn't located any foster-care records. Did Bella even put his name on Katia's birth certificate?

By a stroke of luck, the contact also agreed to transport cocaine shipments on the eastern seaboard. Already, the Mendoza narcosub had successfully transferred five shipments; the last three shipments carried Euphoria. At least some money was finally coming in.

His father's hacking cough echoed in the hallway.

Manuel logged out of the computer and cleared his desk.

"I've searched all over for you." José exuded warmth like a guard directing an execution.

Manuel scowled. "I've been here all day."

If the taunt irritated José, he didn't show it. "How was your trip to the lab this week?"

"Educational." Manuel clenched his fist. "I learned you commissioned multiple orders of bixine pills." He leaned back in his chair, studying his father's reaction.

Glowering, José lifted his chin. "I wanted to verify bixine was as good as Juan boasts."

"You had no right to interfere in my project. The researchers are still studying the effects."

José scoffed. "I have my own test subjects."

Manuel blinked. "Who?"

"It doesn't matter."

"Who are you giving the pills to, Papà?"

"The American *puta*."

"Who?"

"The SCA agent."

"Hailey Langley?"

José nodded. "I traced her to Buffalo Creek, Wyoming. She's the *perra* who betrayed us. The *puta* needs to be taught a lesson."

"Why don't you just order a hit on her?"

"This is sweeter." José licked his lips. "With low doses of bixine, she'll think she's losing her mind—like you suspected of me." He paused and picked up a photo of Camila with a group of orphans. "In higher doses, blackouts occur—with permanent memory loss."

Manuel waited as his father set down the photo. "Who else are you giving the drug to?"

José stared at the photo and remained quiet.

Manuel pounded his fist on the desk. "Dammit! I'm in charge of this lab. If you're experimenting with bixine, I need to know. I won't have the government targeting our fields."

Scarlet streaked down José's neck. He threw the picture frame on the floor, shattering the glass.

"*Maldición*! This is my house." José met Manuel's gaze, challenging him.

Manuel bolted from his chair. "Mamà's family would disagree."

José's eye twitched. "*Hijueputa*! The property became mine when I married your Mamà."

"I doubt *el abuelo* would approve your schemes." Manuel strode to the window and glanced at the bare spot where the Chaca tree had been cut down. He shouldn't let his father get to him. What had his grandfather been thinking, agreeing to his parents' marriage? "Carlos mentioned you met with two Syrians yesterday. Why are you entertaining their company?"

"Al-Qaeda has shown interest in supporting the Resistance."

He turned. "You're willing to sell your soul for their help?"

"They have power, influence, and trade."

"We don't need them. What cocaine doesn't provide in capital, Euphoria will."

José snickered. "It already has."

"What do you mean?"

A malicious glint lit in his eyes. "I've begun to exploit every avenue of your precious plant."

"Dammit. What have you done?"

"Let's just say bixine powder is easily dissolved in food." José smirked. "Especially tea. Next, I'll use it on the military. Everyone's vulnerable."

His father was a crazed man. "You're messing with people's minds."

"Other countries have used drugs to manipulate their citizens. You're aware of the reports the American CIA did experiments with LSD, yes?"

"Do you hear yourself? You're doing this because you want to overthrow the government?"

José coughed and shook his fist. "I'm not the only one upset over what is happening here. Many guerrilla groups sided with me until the president convinced them to support the peace deal."

"Your allies agreed to the treaty. Why can't you and the other revolutionists do the same?"

"Someone got to them." José squared his shoulders. "And now they're being executed for their actions. The spineless cretins only surrendered after they were given immunity."

Manuel closed his eyes; there was no use in arguing when Papà acted this way.

"It's time to convene with the ex-FARC groups. I contacted the leaders in Medellín. They'll notify the others in Venezuela." José strode to the bar and poured some bourbon in a glass. "Nicholas and Luis are strategizing the attacks. I want you there."

Manuel sneered. "Why do you keep Luis around?"

"He's a fine man."

"I don't trust him."

José smirked and swallowed the bourbon. "He was almost your brother-in-law."

"But you stopped the wedding. He must want revenge."

"You worry too much. Luis is devoted to the mission." José laid the glassware on the bar, and a devious glint sparkled in his eye. "After your fling with the American *puta*, I'd thought you'd be over Selena by now."

The blood heated in Manuel's cheeks. How could he forget his first love? The orchid scent of Selena's silky skin stirred his loins when they made love. In José's eyes, Selena was nothing more than a lower-class daughter of a taxi driver.

José's glass clinked on the table. "Luis has never given me reason to doubt his loyalty. Even after I shipped Selena away, he remained faithful to the cause. Unlike others I know." His eyes burned into Manuel, and then he marched out the door.

Sitting in his chair, Manuel pounded on his desk. The old man drove away everyone Manuel loved. Selena would have made a stunning bride. He'd never forget the night before his wedding when José kidnapped Selena, sold her as a prostitute, and smuggled her out to the Caribbean. Did Selena cry for him at night when she was forced to fuck someone else?

Selena and Bella. He had loved them both. Was he destined to live a solitary life? If he played his cards right, he could still have it all. The wife and the family.

The burner phone vibrated.

He yanked the phone from his pocket and read the screen.

—*Release is in five weeks.*—

Manuel studied the calendar and hurled it onto the floor. If only Mark Langley had given up the child's location before he died.

He stood and paced the room. Travel to the States was risky, but could he entrust a stranger to carry out the kidnapping?

Chapter Nineteen

A horn beeped when Hailey steered the car into the driveway, and she glanced in the rearview mirror.

Santino's truck sputtered as he parked behind her.

Ethan opened the passenger door and ran to her car, sweat dripping down his forehead. "Hi, Mom."

"How was work?"

With the back of his hand, he wiped his brow. "Fine. We mulched and planted flowers by the mall."

"I'm glad it's working out." A week ago, she doubted Ethan's attitude would change.

"Can Jake come in a minute? He wants to try out Demolition Derby."

She glanced in the mirror again. Jake sat in the cab next to Santino. "Doesn't Santino have to get home?"

"He said he'd wait five minutes. Please? I don't think Jake has many video games."

Since when did a demo take only a few minutes? Ethan was becoming his outgoing self again. She'd use the time and talk to Santino. "Okay. Five minutes."

Ethan waved at the truck. "Come on."

Jake scooted out and slammed the door. Both boys sprinted into the house.

Hailey reached across the seat and picked up her belongings. When she turned, Santino had already gotten out of the truck and opened her door.

"Need any help?"

"I'm okay. Thanks."

He wiped a hand across his grass-stained muscle shirt and closed the door. "How are you feeling? For real?" His gaze dipped lower as he studied her.

Hailey splayed a hand across her chest. She should have realized his attraction to her sooner. Only Mark ogled her like that. "I'm feeling better. Honest."

The furrow between his brows deepened. "No more dizzy spells?"

She tried not to stare at his brawny arms, but the anchor tattooed on his right shoulder caught her interest. Was he in the Navy? "Better. I'm not as shaky." What was the sense of telling him the truth? "How did Ethan do on his first day?"

"Good. He's a hard worker. Willing to learn. And he listens to instructions."

"I'm glad. His father would be proud." She pointed at the grass. "The yard still looks great. The shop left a message yesterday. My mower is ready."

He chuckled. "Took long enough. Do you want me to pick it up?"

"Thanks, but my father-in-law will bring it here Monday."

"If you need it sooner, let me know."

"I will." She paused, surprised at how easy it was to talk to him. "Say, would you like to stay for dinner? It's the least I can do to thank you for mowing the yard the other day."

Santino removed his tattered baseball cap and ran a finger over the lettering. "You don't have to thank me."

"It would be nothing fancy. Just some leftovers." He probably didn't get many decent meals. Or maybe he did.

A broad grin spread across his face. "That would be mighty kind of you."

She strode with him into the house. "We'll talk in the kitchen while I heat up dinner."

The leftover lasagna was more than enough food. She preheated the oven and placed the lasagna pan and garlic bread on the rack.

Anna stepped into the kitchen as Hailey removed five glasses from the cupboard shelf. "Mom, when's dinner?"

"Soon. Can you help?" While Hailey prepared a salad, Santino and Anna set the table. When the timer beeped, the room smelled like an Italian brick oven.

Anna called Ethan and Jake downstairs, and the group settled in their seats.

As Ethan grabbed a slice of garlic bread, the doorbell rang. "I'll get it." He returned a moment later. "Mom, it's for you."

"Who is it?"

Ethan made a funny expression, wiggling his eyebrows.

Hailey removed her oven mitt and stepped to the door.

Parker stood on the porch, his brow furrowed. "Am I early? We agreed on 6:30."

"Pardon?"

"We were going out to eat tonight."

She slapped her forehead and stepped onto the porch. "Oh crap. I'm so sorry, I forgot."

"What do you mean, you forgot?" His tone was harsh. "I texted yesterday—and today—to remind you."

The last thing she needed was a lecture. "I know. But Ethan started working with Santino today, and he came home all excited. I got distracted. I invited Santino and Jake to stay, to thank them for mowing the grass." She rubbed her hands; the numbness was more noticeable today. "I feel awful."

His silence reprimanded her like a stern, old-fashioned schoolteacher.

Ethan came to the door, eyes twinkling at her predicament. "Mom, are you coming? I'm starved."

"I'll be right there." Hailey waited until Ethan closed the door. "Please eat with us. I'll introduce you to Santino."

"I don't want to crash your party."

Party? Was he jealous? "It's a dinner—and I want you here."

"Go back to your visitors. I'm sorry I intruded." He whirled around and stepped down.

"Parker. Wait."

He shoved his hands into his pockets. "Enjoy your dinner."

"Please don't be mad." How could she make him understand?

"I'm sorry to have bothered you. Good night."

"Parker."

He got in his car and backed down the driveway.

As she stepped across the porch, Santino opened the door. "Is everything okay?"

She forced a polite smile. "Everything's fine. Let's eat."

****

After dinner, Ethan, Anna, and Jake worked on homework in the living room while Hailey and Santino cleared the table. When Hailey loaded the dishwasher, a glass slipped from her hands and crashed onto the floor.

Santino picked up a glass shard and dropped it, wiping a finger on his shirt. "Damn!"

Hailey grabbed a handful of paper towels. "Here. Let me see."

Blood ran down his finger as he held out his hand.

"You might need stitches."

"Nah." Santino wrapped a paper towel around his finger. "It isn't deep."

"Are you sure?"

"I learned a few things living with a nurse. Janet was always on me about tetanus shots. Trust me, I'll live." He leaned against the counter. "Are you feeling okay?"

She blinked. "Yes, why?"

"It seemed like something was bothering you earlier. Was it the guy who came before dinner? I'm sorry if I ruined your evening."

Her heart fluttered. "No, it's my fault." She finished wiping the counters and explained the mix-up. "How did I forget Parker was coming?"

Santino placed a hand on her shoulder.

Hailey moved away. He was showing kindness, but only Mark touched her that way. She struggled against giving him any mixed signals. "I had a nice time tonight."

"Me, too." His gaze lowered to her breasts. "What do you say if we go out sometime? Grab a burger and beer?"

In another lifetime his dark brown eyes would have charmed her. She fidgeted with her hands. "I don't know."

"Is it your husband? Do you feel you're not ready?"

How could she explain she hoped Mark was alive? "I'm sorry. Right now, my life's full, taking care of the kids. What I'd appreciate, though, is your friendship."

He nodded. "Friendship it is. I felt lost when Janet left me. You'll know when it's time."

"That's what Rita says."

"Who?"

"The woman who leads the support group I attend." The loneliness in his eyes moved her. "Are you sure you won't come sometime? Saturday night is the next meeting. Seven o'clock."

"I'll think about it." Santino's gaze lingered. "Do you mind if I ask you a personal question?"

"Depends."

"You talk about your husband as if you're in limbo. How did he die?"

"There was a fire." Her voice quavered, and she turned away, starting the dishwasher.

"I'm sorry. I assumed he had been sick."

"No. He died in an abandoned lumber mill in Crayfield."

"In Maryland? What was he doing way up there?"

The question had tortured her mind a million times. "I don't know. He was working on a case."

"Your husband never told you what he was doing?"

"No." She hung the dishtowel over the dish rack. "He didn't talk about his work."

"Maybe he mentioned something, and you forgot."

Hailey shrugged. Anything was possible.

****

After Santino and Jake took off, Anna patted the cushion. "Mom, can you sit with me?"

163

The next hour, Hailey snuggled beside her daughter, watching a sitcom on TV while Ethan worked on homework. At ten o'clock, when the kids went upstairs, Hailey sipped hot tea and stretched her fingers as she relaxed on the recliner. The numbness was becoming more of a problem. That glass slipped right out of her hands earlier.

The incident with Parker bothered her, and he deserved an apology. If he was going to help her find out what happened to Mark, she needed to pull herself together. Hailey also couldn't ignore the other matters weighing on her mind. Joyce's encounter with Mark. The questions about his work. She moaned. How many secrets had Mark kept from her?

Chapter Twenty

The lot was almost full when Hailey turned in at the precinct. She parked in an open space near Parker's car and lowered the window, letting the light breeze cool her skin. It was the end of May, but the hot, humid days already felt like summer.

She glanced at the console clock. 3:57 PM. Parker had mentioned his shift ended at four. She hadn't been this nervous since she stalked assailants. What was it about Parker that made her lose all sense of reason? He was one of the good guys. Like Mark. At one time, she had liked Parker—a lot. Something about him still attracted her. She shook her head. Was she even ready to move on from Mark?

The phone buzzed in her purse. A text from David lit up the screen:

—Plan to stop over this evening. Will you be home?—

Between Parker's dinner invitations, Santino's handyman help, and David's close eye, her social life had never been so full. Too bad none of them was whom she really wanted. Her fingers skated across the keypad as she responded to David's text.

—Yes. I'll pick up pizza. I'll treat you and get anchovies.—

She licked her lips. After filling David's stomach with food, she'd question him again about Mark. There had to be something more to Mark's death. Or was she grasping for any strand of hope to keep him alive?

She tapped her fingers on the steering wheel. 3:59 PM. Her apology should be in person. If he refused to talk, she'd slide back in her car and drive away without too much embarrassment.

Small groups of officers filtered out of the building. Two minutes after four, Parker pushed through the front door, walking with a confident stride.

Mumbling a quick prayer, she stepped out and moved toward him.

When he met her gaze, his back straightened.

Her knees melted as she waved. Darn! She was acting like a giddy middle-schooler. "Hi."

"Hello." His gruff words were growled, cold and distant.

He wasn't making this easy. "I'm sorry about yesterday."

"No apology necessary. I shouldn't have made it such a big deal."

"You had every reason to be angry with me."

Parker put his hand on his car handle and turned. "How could you forget?"

Hailey rested her back against his car door. He'd have to push her aside. "I forget everything lately." She tilted her head at his dubious expression. "It's not only you. I forget the kids' counseling sessions. My keys. My lunch. Everything. Trust me. I'm more frustrated than you. Something weird is going on. I'm having issues with my hands and feet going numb. My chest hurts, and I've been getting a lot of headaches."

"Have you told a doctor?" Concern mingled in his deep voice.

"My psychologist thinks it's a side effect from my medication."

"Then he should prescribe you another medicine."

"He did. I'm waiting for the new prescription to come." She stepped toward him. "Let me make it up to you. Have dinner at my house—Sunday afternoon. I don't want you angry with me."

He thrust a hand into his front pants pocket. "I wasn't angry with you."

"Then why were you upset?"

"I was pissed at myself."

She blinked as Parker tunneled a hand through his hair. He was nervous, too. "You're not making any sense."

"You don't get it, do you?"

"Get what?"

His lips tightened to a thin line. "Never mind."

"Parker, what's going on with you?"

He hesitated. "You want to know the real reason I didn't call you after Mark passed away?"

Part of her wanted to run. "Why?"

His eyes darkened. "I wanted to give you time."

"What are you saying?"

He walked a few feet away, putting a moat of distance between them. The other cars had disappeared, and all that remained was Parker and her.

When he turned again, chills spread through her body.

"I care for you, Hailey. Deep down you must know how I feel. I've always liked you." Parker rotated back toward the precinct building for a moment. "I was afraid I'd do something stupid you weren't ready for. So I did the honorable thing. Gave you time to mourn before…before asking you out." He shook his head. "Now, you're with this Santino guy, and I'm too late. Again." He raised his hands in the air. "The story of my life."

A heavy weight of thick air pressed against her on all sides. Why was everything so difficult lately? "I'm not seeing Santino. He's a friend. Just like us."

He moved closer, his breath warming her face. "I don't want to be a friend. I want more."

Her eyes blurred. "It's only been six months since Mark died."

"Life goes on, Hailey. Mark's gone."

"Six months, Parker." Tears burnt like acid splashing in her eyes. Six months was not nearly enough time to let go.

"I'm sorry. I didn't mean to say it that way." Parker reached over and held her hand.

The tenderness in his touch made an instant connection to her heart. Ashamed at her heart's betrayal, she yanked her hand away and wiped a tear off her cheek.

He held her hand again and whispered. "I love you, Hailey. I always have. Somehow, life or fate, or whatever it is you want to call it, got in our way. I kept my distance when you married Mark, but I never stopped loving you." He tightened his grasp on her hand. "Now I feel like an idiot because I waited too long."

"Parker, please. I'm not sure I even *want* to get involved with someone again."

"You've become so miserable. You're a strong woman." His face hardened. "Mark wouldn't want you to waste your life grieving. He'd want you to go on—

and at least try to be happy." He caressed her cheek with his thumb. "I think deep down, you know it."

Few people had her pegged so well. She bit her lip, "I do."

"You deserve joy in your life again."

"I'm…I'm scared to go on without him."

"I know, but you owe it to yourself. To Mark. To the kids."

She sniffled. "What if I'm never ready?"

"You will be. It just takes time." He wrapped an arm around her shoulders and drew her closer. "I'll wait as long as it takes."

****

"What do you mean Hailey invited another man to dinner?" Mark straightened in his chair. For the past ten minutes, he'd listened as David recounted the night's dinner with Hailey and the kids.

Despite how much progress Mark made in his therapy, he had so little control over his life.

"It's no big deal. Just pizza."

"That's dinner two nights in a row."

"Hailey only invited Santino because he dropped Ethan off after work."

"That's another thing. Why didn't you tell me Ethan got a job?" He pointed to the walker. "I need to walk."

David slid the upright walker closer and helped him stand.

"I didn't think it was noteworthy. Ethan's getting older. Work will be good for him."

"I'm sure Santino agrees." Mark frowned and paced on the living room carpet. "How often does he come over?"

"Almost every day. He picks Ethan up after school. I told you about Santino before. The guy mowed Hailey's lawn last week."

"Yeah, the same guy who fixed the faucet. Do you think he has a thing for Hailey?"

David shrugged. "Hard to tell. Hailey treats him like a friend." He strode to the fridge and grabbed two water bottles. "I'd be more worried about Parker putting the moves on her. He's popping in for dinner Sunday."

Mark scowled. What he wouldn't give to go back in time and relive the past year. "Why do you say things to annoy me?" He opened and closed his fist. Strange. The action didn't feel tight.

"It's the best motivator to make you want to get better." David untwisted the bottle cap and passed Mark the bottle. "If you don't believe me, look how good you're walking."

Mark gulped a long drink. His life was falling apart, but he could control his progress. His walking *had* improved in the past week; he had even asked Faith to bring back his crutches. A cane would follow. Walking unaided was only half his concern; he still had to catch Mendoza and ensure his own family's safety. "What's going on with the case?"

David stepped into the living room and stared out the window. "Colleen's set to be released in four weeks. She's been quiet since your death."

"She should've turned state's evidence when we initially set it up. Colleen and her daughter won't be completely safe unless they get a new identity."

"She wants to do things her way." David turned. "With you gone, Colleen doesn't trust anyone. She's lost all hope." He guzzled half the water bottle. "Her one priority is to keep her daughter away from Mendoza. When Colleen's released, she'll petition the court for permanent custody and leave town."

"She's lucky her best friend agreed to take guardianship." Mark pushed his walker closer to David. "There's more, isn't there?"

David nodded. "Owen called. Someone hacked into the Child Welfare Agency's database."

"Dammit!" Mark lifted the walker in the air and slammed it onto the floor. "The bastards are getting bolder."

"We anticipated that." David laid the water bottle on the end table. "Good thing we blacked out information from the custody records."

Mark's walker guided him faster around the room. "Mendoza's not an idiot. Once he learns his child isn't in foster care, he'll figure out someone has custody."

"Then he'll still find nothing."

How could David remain so calm? "Any other news on Mendoza?"

"He's in Colombia. The portable satellites and drones we set up are monitoring his home. At this point, I'm more concerned about José. He's the wild card."

"No telling what either man is capable of."

David glanced at his watch. "It's getting late."

"Before you leave, can you help me stretch?" Mark eased back on his chair. David propped Mark's legs on a pillow and massaged the length of thickened tissue.

Mark pushed through the discomfort. "What did you find on Parker?"

"Not much more than what we read. After Wendell Hautz died, Parker resigned."

"He must have really done a number on the man. Did Parker use a body-camera?"

"He did, but Hautz ripped it off in the scuffle. Only the initial two minutes of the confrontation were recorded."

"What about his partner?"

"He was a rookie. Forgot to turn on his camera. Doesn't matter. Parker admitted to beating Hautz unconscious."

"I can't believe Parker would lose control. I thought he was a decent man. He raised Hailey's son— and risked his life once to save mine."

David rubbed Mark's other leg. "The guys at the Chicago PD kept a tight lip when I called. Not even his partner would talk."

Mark winced.

David eased up on the massage. "Does this hurt?"

"No. The damn pressure garment's uncomfortable." Mark readjusted in the chair. The discomfort was as bothersome as the new itchy skin.

"Let's stop for the night. I'll help you settle into bed."

Mark led the way into his bedroom. "How did Parker get hired here?"

"He didn't. He's working undercover."

"For who?"

David shrugged.

Mark tensed. "Hailey needs to know."

"Not yet."

"What if he loses control again? He could hurt her and the kids."

"Mark, stop being patronizing. Admit it. You're not worried that he'll hurt Hailey. You're jealous.

Parker hasn't shown any signs of violence since he moved here. He's a perfect distraction—and he can help keep your family safe. I can't be at your house twenty-four seven."

Why did David have to be so blunt? "Get Owen to assign more coverage."

"He won't unless Mendoza's in the U.S. Until Mendoza makes a move, Parker is going to be our new best friend."

Chapter Twenty-One

"Mom! I'm late!"

Hailey was mopping the floor when Ethan raced into the kitchen. She blocked him from crashing into the cranberry muffins cooling on the counter. "Whoa! Floor's wet."

Exaggerating careful steps, he pulled a box from the freezer and popped two waffles into the toaster. "Sorry. Santino's picking me up early."

She leaned the mop handle against the wall. "I forgot you're working today. I had plans to take you and Anna to see your grandparents this afternoon." She poured grape juice in a glass and slid the drink to his place at the table.

Ethan tossed the hot waffles onto a plate and grabbed the syrup from the pantry. Smothering the waffles in syrup, he shoved a huge bite in his mouth. "Can't make it. Are we still going to Aunt Laura's house this summer? I have to let Santino know when I'm gone."

The doorbell chimed.

Ethan stuffed the rest of the waffle into his mouth, garbling his words. "He's here."

Hailey stood. "I'll talk to him while you finish eating. Try not to choke."

In the foyer, she opened the door. "Good morn—"

Santino's face was crimson.

"What's wrong?"

"Your detective friend—he's what's wrong."

"Parker?"

Santino wrung the cap in his hand. "He's snooping around my business."

"What? Are you sure?"

"Yes, I'm sure. Frank Henderson, the man I get supplies from, said a Detective Tom Parker stopped by his hardware store asking questions. The woman who does my billing told me Parker poked his nose around the office, asking about my permits. He even questioned her about Zac and Jake."

Hailey shook her head. "I'm sorry. I had no idea."

"Where does he get off going around half-cocked? I should report him for harassment."

"I'll talk to him." Was Parker being overprotective, or did he have cause to investigate Santino?

"Coming!" Ethan rushed out the door, carrying a paper lunch bag. "Bye, Mom."

When Ethan landed on the last porch step, Santino adjusted his cap. "I'm sorry to vent like this. It's not your fault. Jake and I enjoyed eating here this week."

"We liked having you."

With Santino's mood, this probably wasn't the best time to mention tonight's bereavement group meeting.

He cleared his throat. "I'd appreciate it if you'd tell Detective Parker to leave me the hell alone. Pardon my language. I don't want my reputation ruined because he has a vendetta."

When Santino drove away, she picked up a package propped next to the door. The new prescription had finally arrived. If the rest of her day was anything like this morning, she'd need the medicine soon. Hailey hurried to the kitchen, grabbed her cell, and pressed Parker's number.

He answered on the second ring. "Hi."

"Why are you questioning people about Santino Ruiz?" She grabbed a pen from the drawer and clicked it while she waited.

After a long pause, he spoke. "Don't be angry."

"Of course I'm angry. When I asked you to help me find out what happened to Mark, I didn't mean to investigate everyone I know."

"I wanted to make sure he was legit."

She gripped the pen tighter. "I don't need you to protect me."

"Do you know he has a past?"

"So what! I have a past. So do you."

"His wife left him."

"I know." Click. Click.

"Did he tell you those two boys living with him have arrest records? The older one was picked up twice already for dealing drugs and assault. They aren't even his kids."

"I know that, too." She jammed the pen into a pack of sticky notes. "Leave the man alone. Let me get to know Santino and make up my own mind. He's already told me about his life. He served in the Navy for five years and his ex-wife was a nurse. I don't need a police report to tell me who I can be friends with. He's trying to help Jake and Zac, and he's good to Ethan. Don't make life harder for him." *And for me.*

"Okay."

The pen snapped, the cap flying in mid-air.

Hailey followed the cap's trajectory. "You shouldn't—wait. What?"

"You're right. It's not my place."

"You can say that again."

"I won't, but do me a favor. Don't give him your complete trust. Trust no one, Hailey."

She ended the call and collected the broken pen pieces. Her life was as shattered as the busted pen. Why didn't Parker understand she was trying to hold her life together?

She had too much housework to do to let Parker ruin her day. Hailey climbed the stairs and stopped at Anna's room.

Her daughter was lying on the bed with a photo album. "What are you doing, Anna?"

"Looking at pictures of Dad and us."

Hailey sat beside her, and they perused the pages together.

When they had finished, Anna sprang from the bed. "Can I go to Sam's house for a while?"

"You see her all the time. I never see you."

Tears glossed Anna's eyes.

Hailey hugged her. "Honey, what's wrong?"

"I thought you wanted it that way."

She smoothed Anna's hair. "Why wouldn't I want you around?"

"You're sad all the time. Ethan said we should give you space."

A chill rippled down her spine. Had the kids seen through her facade? "Why?"

Tears streamed down Anna's cheeks. "He said you need to get over Daddy dying."

"What on earth made your brother say that?"

Anna's bottom lip quivered. "You act like you don't want us around."

She winced. "What are you talking about?"

"You never want to do anything with us. We never spend time together anymore."

Hailey's mind raced to find one example to disprove Anna. "We went to the amusement park Sunday."

"Only because Parker suggested it."

"But—" Hailey scratched her neck. She *had* been distant. The times she asked about their day, she only half-listened. "Honey, I'm so sorry."

"We want to help you, but we don't know how." Anna sniffled and wiped her cheek. "I miss Dad, too.*"*

Hailey drew her closer, breathing in Anna's flowery-scented hair. "I know you do. Don't worry about me. I'm the parent. It's my job to take care of you."

Anna gnawed on her fingernail. "I want you to get better. Please don't send me away."

"I'd never send you away."

"Some parents leave their kids."

Was she referring to Zac's mother? "Did Ethan tell you that?"

Anna hesitated. "No."

"I promise I'll never send you away. Let me start making things right again. Let's bake a pie before we drive to Grandpa and Grandma's house."

Anna jumped off the bed. "Can we make blueberry pie? It's Grandpa's favorite."

****

Hailey steered the car into her in-laws' driveway and leaned back in the seat. Something about Peggy and Adam's house made her feel at peace. Mark's spirit was everywhere.

When Adam opened the kitchen door, his eyes widened at the pie in Hailey's hands. "Let me help you." He inhaled. "Mmm. Blueberry. You sure know how to keep an old man happy." He laid the pie on the counter and yanked Anna's ponytail. "How's my favorite thirteen-year-old?"

Anna grinned. "Good. Where's Grandma?"

He pointed toward the living room. "On the deck."

Hailey smiled as Anna scrambled out the patio door, and then she turned to Adam. "How was your trip?"

"It went too fast. I wish Laura lived closer, especially now since the divorce. Her kids didn't stop talking about Ethan and Anna the entire time." Adam ran his finger over the baked filling and licked his finger, like Mark used to do.

She dragged a chair from the table and sat. "When did you get back?"

"Yesterday morning." Adam sat across from Hailey. "I had a cardiologist's appointment in the afternoon."

"What did the doctor say?"

He slapped his chest. "Running like a smooth engine."

Hailey chuckled. "Speaking of engines, can we still pick up the mower Monday?"

"I can, but don't you teach class?"

She shook her head. "It's the day before finals. No classes."

"Perfect timing. How's the car running?"

She tapped her knuckles against the wooden table. "Good, but I need an oil change soon."

"I can do that."

"But your heart—"

"My ticker's running fine. I ran my shop for years. I can change your oil with my eyes closed. I'll haul the mower on my truck bed and drop you off. Then I'll have the afternoon to change the oil *and* the transmission fluid."

She started to object, but he raised his hand. "I need an excuse to get out of the house. Peggy has a whole 'honey do' list."

"If you insist. But Anna and I will bake you something."

He reached over and patted her shoulder. "Deal."

****

When Hailey and Anna returned home, Ethan was on the sofa, eating a muffin.

Hailey settled next to him. "How was work?"

Ethan wadded the muffin paper into a ball. "Good. We finished early, but Santino paid me for a full day. He said I can work again Tuesday after school—unless it rains."

"How was his mood?"

"He's still pissed off at Zac and Chase for leaving him during the busy season, but other than that he seemed fine. He let me use a trimmer."

"I'm glad you had a good day, but I'm deducting your allowance if you use foul language again. Your father would never allow it." Fighting the urge to scratch, Hailey rubbed her palms along her shorts. Lately, thoughts of Mark consumed her more than usual. "Let's eat dinner early. My support group meets at seven. Anyone want to help?"

Ethan propped his feet on the coffee table. "Not me. My shoulders are sore."

"Whiner." Anna threw a pillow at him. "It's pity-party time!"

Ethan grinned and hurled it back.

Hailey laughed, trying to remember the last time they had a pillow fight. She grabbed two pillows and joined in.

****

The support group gathered in an empty church classroom. Hailey sat in the last row and listened as the leader, Rita Brown, spoke to an older woman who had lost her husband to cancer a year earlier. At 6:58 PM, Liz strode into the room and sat next to her. "We both made it."

When Rita started the meeting, her gaze shifted to the door. "We have another guest."

Santino stood at the door, dressed in khaki pants and a clean polo shirt. "Am I too late?"

Rita extended an inviting smile. "Your timing's perfect. Please, come in."

Relief settled in Hailey. Santino was willing to seek support from his ex-wife leaving. Like a proud hen, she pointed to the empty chair on her right. When he sat, she whispered, "I'm glad you came."

His cheeks reddened. "I figured it couldn't hurt."

When the meeting opened to discussion, Hailey thought twice about opening up. It was hard to talk to a room full of strangers. "Sometimes I think I'm handling my husband's death okay, but then something sets me back. I want things to be normal again…whatever that is."

Liz twisted her wedding ring around her finger. "I had to create a new normal. When I learned about my husband's gambling problems, I thought I was being punished. Looking back, I grew stronger. Now he has a good job and is a city councilmember. I didn't know what I was capable of until I was tested."

An elderly man wiped his glasses. He had begun coming to the meetings after his wife passed away from cancer. "Meredith told me not to grieve when she passed. She said I better grab life by the damn horns and enjoy the beating until the good Lord called me home."

Tears stung Hailey's eyes. How lucky Meredith and her husband were to share her end together. Life cheated Hailey.

After the meeting, she strolled with Santino in the parking lot. Calmness blanketed her as they conversed. "I'm glad you came."

"Me, too."

"Do you think you'll come again?"

Santino sighed. "I don't know if I belong."

"What are you talking about? Of course you do."

He shook his head. "Janet didn't die. She screwed another man and left me with two boys. I miss her, though. We were close—told each other everything. Shared our dreams and our secrets." He removed a handkerchief and blew his nose. They stopped at Hailey's car. "I'm sorry I yelled this morning."

"You had reason to be mad."

"I shouldn't have taken my mood out on you."

Hailey opened the car door.

His honesty was refreshing. If Mark was alive, he and Santino might have been friends.

Chapter Twenty-Two

Manuel strode near the orphanage in town where his mother spent her days.

Activities inside the ancient stone structure flourished once his mother began volunteering twenty-five years ago. The Colombian government provided teachers and educational supplies; local companies and wealthy families donated food and clothing. No one would believe Mamà's demure demeanor hid a cunning woman capable of blackmailing the most honest politician. The once-dreary place now sang with children's lighthearted laughter.

Even Manuel had taught the orphans while he attended the university. Throughout the town, villagers spoke of his mother's kindness.

The fuchi game stole his attention. He and his bodyguard, Antonio, had kicked a similar version of the hacky sack game in the States. Older boys nearby played Manuel's favorite childhood game of rana, a ring-toss activity involving throwing disks in a frog's mouth.

Manuel strolled past a vendor selling toys. He stopped and bought a basketful of ragdolls, spinning tops, and puzzles. Beckoning to an older girl on the street, he handed her the items and tipped her in Colombian pesos. "Take these to *señora* Mendoza in the orphanage."

At one time, Manuel never would have helped young penniless peasants. He stared at the children playing. Was Katia homeless like the orphans across the street? Dammit! Where had Bella hidden her?

A little girl in pigtails played on the teeter-totter.

Did Katia look like her? Did his daughter have Bella's blonde hair? Sapphire-blue eyes? Manuel hadn't a clue, didn't even know her real name. Hell, he didn't even know what kind of father he would be. Bella had robbed him of the opportunity. But he'd make it up to the girl. When he found Katia, he'd buy her the best clothes, the best shoes, the best toys, and the best schools. He would show off his prized possession to the world; she was his last link to Bella.

Stealing Katia was vile, but Bella had kept secret the knowledge of his daughter for over five years. Guilt bedeviled him. Was this karma for treating Bella so poorly? Why had he returned to Colombia without her? Manuel shook his head. *You know why.*

He turned down the street to a row of dilapidated buildings bordering the town. After he finished high school, the violence in his life worsened so much he had few happy memories of his youth left. His soul weighed on him like a tombstone. His two lost loves hurt as if they had died.

"Deceitful opportunistic bitches."

He shuddered at Papà's cruel words. Manuel would never understand why his mother stayed with the bitter man. When they first married, Camila—Mamà, worked countless hours ministering to the poor. While Papà hardened, she attended mass at the Catholic Church each morning before helping the orphans. She wasn't a deceitful bitch—she was a saint.

Selena wasn't a *puta* either. And neither was Bella. Why was Papà opposed to Manuel's happiness? After Selena, Manuel had hoped for a second chance at love—and he found Bella. The stars had aligned once again, and then he deserted her. Could he win Bella back? Convince her to move to Colombia by blackmailing her with their child? They could live together as a family, away from his father. He glanced back at the orphanage playground.

Moving across the street, Manuel stepped onto the stone patio of a quaint two-story restaurant with its painted flower boxes under the oversized windows. He selected an empty table, and a young *señorita* passed him a menu.

His order of *aguapanela* and a plate of *buñuelos* arrived within minutes. He picked up a fritter and swallowed it perfunctorily without registering the taste.

Would Bella forgive him? He shook his head. Too much time had passed. God, he was an asshole. Sooner or later, he'd have to come to terms with the reason he'd left Bella. The guilt he carried aggrieved him as much as how he had hurt her.

Footfalls tapped behind him. "Mano."

He lifted his head and smiled at the beautiful older woman. *"Buenos días, Mamá."* The brown bag she held smelled of fried doughnuts.

A young girl dressed in a cotton T-shirt and shorts clutched Camila's free hand.

The wrinkles around his mother's eyes disappeared when she smiled. "I'm surprised to see you in town so early."

Manuel glanced at the girl who was staring at him with wide, dark brown eyes. She looked to be around ten-years old. He shifted his gaze to Camila. "I got an early start today. I'm waiting on a call."

"Does this have anything to do with the big secret you've been alluding to?"

"Yes. But I can't talk about it yet."

Her eyebrow lifted. "Can you give me a hint?"

"Soon, Mamá."

"Very well. Can you spare a few minutes to talk?"

"Certainly." He gestured to an empty seat across the table.

Camila gave the girl the paper bag. "Take this back to the orphanage and give it to Katrina. I'll come back in a few minutes." She waited as the girl raced down the street, then sat in the chair across from him. "The poor child had a night terror. She insists monsters are trying to break into the girls' rooms." She shook her head. Her russet-colored hair had turned shades of dark gray, and age spots dotted her tanned skin.

It was difficult to see her aging. *Should I tell her about Katia?* No. The timing wasn't right. He motioned toward the fritters. "Do you want one?"

"No, thanks." She stretched her arm, blocking the food. "I'm worried about you. Did José do something again?"

"No, Mamá. Surprisingly, this has nothing to do with Papà."

Camila waved at the server and ordered a cup of coffee. "I wish you'd stop this grudge."

He munched on another fritter. "It's a little late to erase all my childhood memories."

"Can you at least try to forgive the man?" Her eyes darkened. "He's your father. He cares for you."

"He has an odd way of showing it."

"Someday when you have a child of your own, you'll understand the love a parent has."

"I would never strike anyone the way he beat me." He swallowed hard. Would he turn into his father? Was his daughter in danger?

"One day you might have children. I had hoped the woman you planned to bring home when you lived in the States could turn into something serious. What happened between you two?"

Manuel winced at the memory of the lab when he last saw Bella. He had grabbed her arm tightly—out of anger. Too tight. His eyes blurred as he remembered the ugly black-and-blue prints his fingers left on her arms. "Do you think I'm destined to become like Papà?"

Confusion and darkness filled her eyes, and then understanding set in. "Oh, Mano, don't tell me you hurt her."

He massaged his temples. He had kissed Bella's arm, wishing the bruises away. His worst fear had come true. Manuel had become his father. "I was angry at Bella for something she did. Leaving her was the only way I could keep her safe—from me."

"Did you explain that to her?"

He shook his head. "I couldn't face her."

"You need to apologize."

"Why would she forgive me? I deserted her."

Camila reached across the table and held his hand. "Explain what happened."

"It's too late. It's been six years."

She shrugged. "If she loves you, she'll understand."

Was his mother telling him something? Had Papà hurt Mamà? He searched his mother's eyes.

Her gaze became distant and then her face twisted, revealing her answer.

I thought I was the only one. "Dammit! He hurt you, too? I should have stopped him. I'm no different than Papà."

"Nonsense. You were a child. José hasn't hurt me since he struck you."

"Why do you stay with him? You don't need him."

"The property is mine because I stay married to your father. Tata arranged the terms in a prenuptial agreement when he willed me the land."

Manuel scratched his cheek. So this was the reason she stayed. Society still frowned on women landowners. José married her—used her—to gain status and wealth. "Your grandfather shouldn't have placed you in that situation."

"Tata wanted to guarantee the land stayed in the family. If José abandons, divorces, or shames me, the family estate transfers to me." She smiled. "It becomes yours—if you have an heir."

Mine? Manuel concealed his surprise. "You never mentioned that before."

"I didn't want to put pressure on you."

"Is Papà aware of this stipulation?" A chill ran down Manuel's spine. Is this why he sent Selena away? To prevent an heir?

As if she could read his mind, Camila patted his hand. "You're wrong about your father. I know he's a harsh man, but I've grown to love José." Her expression was stern. "Don't you dare look at me like that. José's changed. He visits the orphanage once a week, and he plays games with the children. He even brings supplies."

The server brought the coffee and laid creamer on the table.

Camila sipped the coffee. "*Gracias*."

Papà was spending time at the orphanage? With his busy schedule? Manuel waited until the server walked away. "What kind of supplies?"

"Clothes…beans…rice…tea…"

"Tea? You get plenty of tea from donors."

"José brings it for the older girls. He claims his tea has fewer pesticides."

"What about the boys?"

"He brings coffee for them." Camila sipped more coffee. "Trust me. José is trying to be better. He's even found jobs for the girls."

"What do you mean?"

"He takes them into the city and helps them find work. Many of them have left the orphanage."

"Why would he help them when his responsibilities keep him busy?"

Camila lowered the coffee cup. "I don't know, but the girls must be thriving. They don't return." She shrugged. "I'd be lying if I said I didn't miss them, but they're starting their own lives."

What was Papà up to? "Is he helping the boys find jobs?"

"Just the older girls. José thinks boys should join the resistance. He said I can't expect the girls to stay in the orphanage forever."

Manuel frowned. "How many girls have found work?"

"Eight in the past two weeks." Camila glanced at her watch and stood. "I have to get back. Promise me you'll try to get along better with your father."

"We'll see."

"Mano, if you expect Bella to forgive, you need to practice forgiveness, too."

Camila kissed him and left.

He remained at the table, pondering over the conversation. His father was up to something. Why would Papà find jobs for those girls?

Manuel's thoughts shifted to Selena, and his breathing stopped. The fucking bastard. José hadn't turned a new leaf by bringing the orphanage supplies. He was using tea leaves and bixine to drug the girls. *Hijueputa*! That's how he was getting money to fund his revolution. The latest cocaine shipments had been confiscated, but sex trafficking would bring in the money they needed.

The realization convulsed Manuel's body like a seizure. His father couldn't stoop any lower. Was Katia's life in jeopardy if Manuel brought her here?

Chapter Twenty-Three

Hailey stretched her arms above the pillow and opened her eyes. The previous night's meeting still contented her, and she slept well, without taking any pills before bed.

Thunder roared in the distance.

The forecasted rainstorms would force the kids to stay in the house today. When the kids were smaller, Mark would put together a puzzle. Now his death was a puzzle.

She reached for her phone on the nightstand and texted Parker.

—*See you this afternoon.*—

Smiling, she laid the phone on the bed. Fate had to have brought Parker back into her life. With his law-enforcement background, he had the means to help find out what happened to Mark.

After showering, Hailey hummed as she dressed and applied make-up. She studied her reflection in the mirror. The scar on her cheek had faded and didn't cause concern anymore. It was odd how she had worried Mark would think differently of her. A soft-rose lipstick added the perfect amount of color, and she smacked her lips together. She hadn't spent so much time on her appearance since Mark was alive.

Downstairs, she stepped to the sofa where Ethan was reading a book, his legs dangling over the armrest.

"I guess I'm the sleepyhead today. What are you working on?"

"Trig. I have a quiz tomorrow."

She smiled, but inside she shouted, "Hallelujah!" Finally, he was getting his act together. "Need any help?"

He punched some numbers in the calculator. "Maybe later."

Anna sat on the carpet, coloring a design in one of Hailey's stress-relieving coloring books. "You look nice today, Mom."

"Thanks." Life suddenly felt brighter. "I'm in the mood for a big breakfast. French toast and bacon. Who's hungry?"

"Me!" Anna jammed the colored pencils in the box. "I'll get the cinnamon."

****

At two o'clock, the doorbell rang.

Hailey scratched her hands as she stepped to the foyer. Would Mark approve? Didn't she deserve some happiness?

She opened the door.

Parker's polo shirt was soaked, but the downpour didn't mask the amber scent of his aftershave.

"Come in—why didn't you bring an umbrella?"

"It flipped backward and broke." Parker shook the rain from his hair like a wet dog shaking after a bath. He stepped inside the house and handed her a box of candy. "I hope you still like caramels."

"Thank you." Her cheeks heated as she held the box. Parker remembered her fondness for caramel, but nothing could replace how Mark touched her heart when he brought her roses.

While a stuffed chicken roasted in the oven, Anna pulled out some board games from the closet. "Anyone want to play?" She turned. "Where's Ethan?"

Hailey climbed the stairs and found Ethan listening to music on his bed. She nudged his shoulder and waited as he removed an earbud. "Anna has some games. Are you interested?"

Ethan shook his head.

"Parker's here. Can you socialize a little?"

He scowled. "Why did you invite him?"

She had anticipated his resistance. "Parker's my friend, and he brings some normalcy back to this house."

"This house will never be normal without Dad."

She sat beside him. "True, but I'd like to believe he'd want us to move on. He loved you."

Ethan squeezed his eyes shut. "I miss him."

"I know. I do, too. But we have to find a way to go on living."

"How?"

"Dad's here with us. In our hearts." She pointed to her chest. "I'm not asking you to forget your father, but he'd want you to be happy." She tousled his hair. "Why don't you come down when you're ready?"

Thirty minutes later, Ethan joined them in the living room.

Anna opened her favorite game and passed out fake money. "I want to be the shoe."

The game progressed, and Hailey rolled doubles for the third time. "Not again. I don't even have enough money to bail myself out of jail." She slid her marker along the board to the corner while Ethan faked a police siren.

"It's the third time you've landed in jail, Mom." Laughing, Anna shook the dice. "Did you ever know anyone who went to jail?"

Hailey's body turned cold. The fight she had about Colleen Toole the day Mark died seemed insignificant now.

"Mom?"

"I knew one person, but it was years ago." Hailey forced her attention on the game. She'd forget about Colleen—for now.

****

"Compliments to both chefs. This is one of the most delicious dinners I've ever eaten." Parker grinned at Hailey and Anna. He scooped extra potatoes onto his plate and passed Ethan the dish. "Might as well finish it."

The interaction between Ethan and Parker had improved, especially after they discussed baseball and predicted how the Nats would perform. Did Parker miss having a son to talk to as much as Ethan missed Mark?

Parker grabbed the water pitcher and refilled his glass. "What do you want to do when you get out of school, Ethan?"

Ethan shrugged. "I don't know yet. I like doing what Santino does. He gets to set his own schedule."

Parker frowned. "Unfortunately, not all jobs let you do that."

"You can if you're your own boss. Santino takes off when he wants. He and Jake are fishing today." Ethan peered out the dining room window. "At least they planned to. It's been raining all day."

Anna laid down her fork. "Do you have any kids, Parker?"

He gulped some water. "I had a son. He died when he was seventeen."

Hailey tensed, willing Parker to keep her secret. Would the kids ask questions?

Anna rested her arms on the table. "How did he die?"

He glanced at Hailey, and his gaze shifted back to Anna, who stared wide-eyed. "He died from using drugs."

Anna gasped. "What drug?"

"It doesn't matter." Parker frowned. "All drugs are dangerous."

Ethan ate the last of his stuffing. "Everyone at school uses drugs."

"Not everyone." Hailey pressed her lips together. *It better* not *be everyone.*

Ethan nodded and emptied his glass. "Just about everyone. And a lot of kids vape."

"Still? I thought that ended after all the health problems were reported."

"Whether they vape or shoot up or inhale, people are playing a risky game with their lives." Parker wiped a tear pooling below his eye. "It's better never to start. I wish to God my son never tried drugs. I told him countless times to stay away, but he did it anyway."

To Hailey's astonishment, Anna reached over and patted his hand. "I'm sorry. I didn't mean to upset you."

Hailey stood. "Anna, why don't you help me serve the dessert?"

When they had cleared the table, Hailey loaded the dishwasher.

"Anna, would you please take the garbage cans out to the street?"

"I hate taking the trash out. It's Ethan's turn."

"Your brother went upstairs to study."

Anna pouted. "I have homework, too."

Parker stepped forward. "I can do it."

"No. It's the kids' job." Hailey gave Anna a hard look.

"What if I help you?" Parker lifted the trash bag from the can. "We'll get it done faster."

Anna huffed and led the way to the garage. "Okay, but next time Ethan has to do the trash three times in a row."

Hailey turned to Parker and mouthed silently, "Thank you."

By the time they returned, Hailey had finished wiping the counters.

Anna added a new bag into the trashcan and hugged Hailey. "I'll finish my homework upstairs. Good night."

Hailey motioned Parker toward the living room. "Coffee?"

Navy specks flickered in his gray eyes. "Sounds perfect."

When she brought out two mugs of coffee, he was sitting on the sofa, flipping through the TV channels. She passed Parker a mug and sat beside him. "Thanks for helping Anna with the trash. That's the one chore she complains about. She hates the smell." Hailey held her cup and breathed in the malty aroma.

"I think we can cut her some slack. It sounds like she helped a lot with dinner." His voice became distant. "Sometimes I wonder where Justin would be if he were still alive." Parker traced his finger along the cup's rim. "He'd be out of college now."

It didn't seem possible her son could be that old. "I'm sure he misses you, too."

"I don't think I loved anyone as much as Justin." He stared into his mug. "He had his stubborn moments though, especially when I taught him how to drive."

She leaned against the cushion. "Ethan gets his permit in a few months."

Parker picked up a coaster and set his cup on the end table. "I'd be happy to help with driving lessons."

"Thanks. David offered, too." She sipped the coffee, careful not to burn her tongue.

"I saw the car in the garage when we wheeled out the trashcan. The battery's probably dead."

She curled her fingers tighter around the cup. *I wish Mark could charge it.* "I'll keep it in mind."

"Thank you again for dinner. Home-cooked meals are a rarity these days. I enjoyed the food—and the company." His gaze lingered.

She bowed her head and set her cup on the side table. "Have you found anything out about the fire?"

"Not yet."

Why couldn't Parker appreciate she needed closure? "I know you think I'm being foolish, but I don't understand how Mark ended up in a deserted building in Maryland when he phoned to say he was on his way home."

"I'll check into it this week." Parker held her hand. "How did David know where Mark was?"

She closed her eyes. "He was talking to Mark about a case and the call disconnected. David became suspicious and asked Owen to trace Mark's cell phone. I didn't know anything had happened until the police cars were outside, and David knocked on the door."

"Can you write down everything you remember? Ask David why Mark was at that particular location and about the case they were discussing."

"Okay. But there's something else. I had forgotten about it until today."

"What is it?"

"The morning Mark died, he dropped a card that had the name of a prison on it—a woman's prison."

He stared a moment. "You think he saw Mendoza's girlfriend?"

Hailey nodded. Her stomach twisted in knots just thinking about the possibility.

"Why would Mark be in communication with her? She tried to kill him."

"I wondered the same thing."

"Maybe Colleen's lawyer contacted him? Or a parole officer?"

"I wish I had asked someone about it after Mark died, but there was so much going on. Today, when Anna brought up the subject of jail, I thought about Colleen. Maybe she knows something."

"You want to see her, don't you?"

She nodded. "I want to know if Mark contacted her."

"Do you know where she's serving time?"

"I think the judge sentenced her to a facility in West Virginia."

"I'll make some calls."

The weight on her shoulders became lighter. "Thanks, Parker."

"I have a confession." His gaze made her nervous. "I'm doing this for us. So you can find closure. Maybe then you'll give us a chance."

"Parker—"

"Shh. Don't say anything." He leaned over and captured her mouth in a hungry kiss.

Panicking, she pulled away.

"I should go." He gave her hand a gentle squeeze. "I'll let you know what I find out."

Hailey waited on the porch as he drove away. She touched her lips. The kiss had stirred something inside her. Twice before they had kissed, but this was different. More intense. Was she ready to move on? Spending the day with Parker made her feel alive again.

She closed the door and turned the deadbolt. It was a shame the night had to end. Life almost felt normal again.

Almost. Ethan's court hearing was still coming up. Every time she mentioned it, he grew quiet. Would she be able to handle the aftermath if the judge sent him to juvie? Mr. Greene had felt confident the video would exonerate Ethan, but backup support couldn't hurt.

She sat on the sofa and searched her cell phone contacts, passing over Parker's name. After that hot kiss, she couldn't call him. She needed support, not a distraction. Finally, she pressed a button.

David answered on the second ring. "Hailey? Is everything okay?"

"Everything's fine. It's sad you think something's wrong every time I call."

"I'm sorry. It's a reflexive reaction. What's going on?"

"Ethan's court hearing is scheduled for Wednesday morning at ten. I know it's short notice, but I was wondering if you could come with us? Give moral support?"

David cleared his throat. "Sure. I'll rearrange my schedule."

"Thanks. We'll meet you there. I'll text you the details."

She disconnected the call and went upstairs to her bedroom. Tomorrow she'd make a list of questions to ask David about Mark.

As she dressed in her nightgown, images of Mark and Colleen spun around her mind. She opened the medicine that had arrived the previous day, and she read the directions.

Take one to two pills twice a day as needed.

Did she really need them? What a silly question.

She shook a few pills in her palm. They looked like the last prescription. Milky white, but oval instead of round. She studied the label again. It was impossible to keep up with the antidepressants on the market. Dr. Thomkin told her this beta-blocker had fewer side effects.

Hailey swallowed one pill and poured the others back in the bottle. Tomorrow was another big day, and she couldn't risk a sleepless night.

In bed, she imagined Mark lying with her. A tear rolled down her cheek as she gazed at her wedding picture. She kissed her fingers and pressed them against his face.

Chapter Twenty-Four

Damn. Mark growled at the computer screen and pushed the keyboard. His Internet research resulted in a long string of dead ends. Leveraging his gloved hands against the table, he gripped the cane and paced the floor. Lately, his best thinking happened while he walked. God knew he had plenty of opportunities. He gazed out the window at the landscaped courtyard as suspicion ran through his bones. What the hell was Tom Parker hiding?

Last night, his nightmares bounced from Hailey and the kids, to the fire, and then to Colleen and Mendoza. Daybreak snuck in sometime before Faith arrived at seven. After she helped him dress and run through the series of stretching exercises, Mark stayed busy researching on the computer.

A light tap played a rhythm on the door, and he jumped. *Calm down. It's only David.* Mark leaned against his cane. "Come in."

David stepped inside the apartment with the usual cheery smile extending across his face. "A cane? Looking good."

A warm pleasure flowed through Mark. The extra efforts were becoming apparent. "What's up? I thought you worked today."

"I do, but Owen called."

"What did he want?"

"He's worried about you, said you wanted access to Tom Parker's files?"

Feigning disinterest, Mark resisted a smirk. He must have struck a nerve if his supervisor had contacted David already. "I want to find out what Parker's hiding."

"The investigators closed the case."

"But—"

David followed him in the living room. "It's over. Parker resigned."

Mark grunted. "Then why didn't he face charges? How did he get hired here?"

"I don't know."

"What if he gets violent with Hailey or the kids?" Mark paced across the room.

"Do you hear yourself? You're acting like a jealous boyfriend."

"I'm not a boyfriend. I'm a *husband*. I don't want Parker around my wife."

David shook his head. "It's not your decision."

Mark stopped and faced the window. "Is he putting the moves on her yet?"

"I'm not getting that vibe."

Parker wanted her once before. "Will you at least tell Hailey that Parker killed a man?"

"He's a cop. I'm sure Hailey's shot people, too. Just like you and me." David sat on the sofa. "Why don't you sit? You're wearing a path through the carpet."

"I'd rather walk."

"Suit yourself, but I'm not paying to install new carpet. Where's Faith?"

"She had to leave."

David became quiet. "Hailey called last night."

Mark stopped walking. "What's wrong?"

"She asked if I'd go to Ethan's court appearance Wednesday."

"She didn't ask Parker?" His words tasted bitter.

David shrugged. "Maybe he was busy. I told her I'd go."

Mark lowered his gaze. "I wish I could be there."

"I know, buddy." David picked up a paper next to the keyboard. "What's this? You're researching skin regeneration?"

Mark reached for the article, but David held it from his reach. "It might help my scars."

David read the article. "The report says this stem cell therapy hasn't been approved yet." He frowned. "Why are you worrying about this? We've made sure you have the best care."

Mark pointed to his transparent burn mask. "Yeah, I'm supposed to be happy I have at least another year in this." He squeezed his fingers until his skin tightened in the glove. "There has to be something out there."

"The doctors at the burn center used the most current therapies."

"Those treatments were six months ago. Every day new cures are found. Stem cell-based skin substitutes are—"

"Not approved by the FDA yet."

"But—"

"Stop. I know where this is heading. If the doctors think you're a candidate for more treatments, we'll be the first to know."

The front door opened, and Kit stepped inside the apartment.

David handed Mark the article. "I have to go to work. Focus on your rehab, and let me worry about everything else."

Mark slid the article under the keyboard. "Don't forget to warn Hailey about Parker."

****

Hailey parked beside her father-in-law's truck and opened the car door. "Sorry I'm late."

Adam sat on the porch, tying the laces of his work boots. "Did the kids get off to school?"

She grabbed her purse from the seat console. "They only hurled a few insults at each other before they took off. Did Mark pick on Laura and Francine when they were kids?"

"Not too much. He was younger, so he was more annoyed when they doted on him." He plucked the keys from his pocket. "Let's get this show on the road."

An hour later, Adam unloaded the mower off the cargo bed and latched the tailgate.

Hailey pushed the grass cutter into her yard. "Thanks for your help today, Dad. Can I make you breakfast before you leave?"

Adam wiped the sweat from his forehead. For a moment, he looked like he might accept the offer. "Thanks, but I'd better head back. Peggy has a list of jobs a mile long I need to finish before we fly out to Francine's."

"I imagine Francine's excited you're coming."

He nodded, his soft blue eyes sweet reminders of Mark.

"She said Todd and the kids want to build a go-cart when we're there."

"I hope you have a good time."

When he drove away, Hailey surveyed the front yard. Santino had mowed it a week ago, but the grass was bushy again. Might as well mow the lawn before the day got too hot. She turned the key and smiled at the engine's smooth hum.

By eleven o'clock, the pollen blurred her vision, and she couldn't stop sneezing. She pushed the mower to the backyard and went inside. The rest of the mowing could wait while she took a break.

In the bathroom, Hailey grimaced at her reflection in the mirror. She took an antihistamine for her puffy eyes, then she strode into the kitchen.

After she ate a ham sandwich and leftover macaroni and cheese, her eyelids drooped. Her chest felt heavy, and she struggled to take deep breaths. When she made her way upstairs to the bedroom, the room began spinning. Her body tensed while she held onto the dresser. *Why is this happening again?* A high-pitched noise buzzed inside her head, and she shuffled in small steps, hanging onto the dresser until she reached the bed. Her entire body ached. Was this what heat stroke felt like? She leaned back onto a soft pillow and drifted to sleep.

She ran on the trail behind the house, past the neighboring houses to the cul-de-sac where Joyce and her girls lived. She looped back toward the house; the path was longer than she remembered. She leaped over a fallen tree. The tree hadn't been there before. Did she pass her house already?

Hailey peered through the woods. A small brick house was on the other side of the woods. Odd. She slowed when a man wearing a hooded sweatshirt stepped onto the path. Mark? *Her heart sped as he smiled and waved. Oh my God! He's here! She raced toward him, his outstretched arms waiting.*

Thud! A tall tree fell in front of her. She jumped over it and continued running, but another tree fell. And another. She slowed her steps, veering her way around the trees as they collapsed like dominos. As she got closer, Mark faded into a tiny cloud. Mark! Wait! *Another tree fell, barely missing her feet.*

Boom!

She woke, blinking hard at the alarm clock. 1:58 PM. *Why am I in bed?*

Hailey rubbed her forehead. Oh yeah, she'd been dizzy.

Another noise. Not a tree.

She listened more intently. A door was shutting. She brought her feet to the floor; phew, the dizziness had subsided.

Ethan and Anna would still be in school—or did she forget about another early dismissal?

A clunk came from below. Perhaps the garage? With her ear implants, she picked up even the smallest sounds. *Dammit! Someone's in the house.*

Rushing to the closet, she yanked out the bottom shoebox and opened the lid. The metal end of a gun chilled her hands.

She padded softly down the stairs toward the kitchen. Every few steps, she stopped and tilted her head. How many intruders were there?

At the garage door, she halted. The intruder was still moving around. Who would have the nerve to rob a house in broad daylight? Maybe those punks Ethan hung out with. Chase and Zac. Hailey gripped the gun tighter. She should've called 9-1-1 first. Darn. Her cell phone was in the bedroom. Should she go back upstairs and call the police? No time. She knew how to handle a gun. Besides, whoever was out there might try to break into the house. Surprise attacks were better.

Taking a deep breath, she turned the doorknob, swung open the door, and pointed the gun.

The overhead garage light illuminated a man hunkered over in the front seat of Mark's car.

"Freeze!"

"Don't shoot! It's me, Parker."

She lowered her arm a little. "Parker?"

He pushed the door open and got out of the car. "When did you get a gun?"

"It's none of your business. How did you get in here?"

"I punched in the code."

"You don't know the code."

"Anna told it to me yesterday when we took out the trash. I thought I'd check out the car while you were working today and see if I could find anything to lead us to Mark."

She scowled. "Why didn't you call me? I almost blew your brains out."

"Check your cell phone. I texted I was coming."

"It's upstairs. I was sleeping."

His eyes narrowed. "Sleeping?"

"I mowed the grass earlier and got dizzy, so I lay down. Then I heard you in the garage."

"How are you feeling now?"

"Better. I took an antihistamine for my allergies. They always make me sleepy."

"Did you take an antihistamine last week when you fainted?"

Had she? Santino had mowed the grass that day. "I think so."

Parker frowned. "You shouldn't be mixing antihistamines with your anxiety medication."

Hailey slapped her forehead. How could she be so careless?

"Keep track of what you're taking. Mixing meds isn't good."

"I know. I should've known better."

"Can you put the gun down so we can talk? You're making me nervous."

"I think I'll keep the gun raised until I know if you're telling the truth."

"Why are you so stubborn?" He lowered his arm.

"Watch it!"

He lifted his arms in the air again. "Let me get out my cell—I'll show you my text."

She waited as he retrieved his messages.

He extended his arm. "See? It's right here."

Hailey read the screen. —*Hi. I found out some info from Stefan. I'll stop by this afternoon. I want to check Mark's car for clues. Anna told me the code yesterday. I'll keep you posted.*—

Her face heated, and she laid the gun on a shelf. "I'm sorry."

"I thought you knew by now I'd never hurt you." The sadness in his voice stung.

"What did you find out from Stefan?"

"The files you copied from Mendoza's mansion were also encrypted with links to underground drug routes and sex trafficking networks. The SCA didn't decode all the details until last fall. José de Mendoza is a hundred times more dangerous than Manuel."

Her heart pounded harder. Let's hope he never finds out I opened the files. "Why would Stefan tell you this?"

"I'm investigating drug networks around Maryland, Virginia, and D.C. for him."

"Wait a minute." She scratched her head. "You're working with the SCA again?"

He nodded, lowering his gaze. "I started in January."

"You're not working at the police station?"

"I'm undercover. The police chief told his men I transferred from Chicago on special assignment."

His betrayal hurt worse than his lies. "You kept this from me? Even after I told you I had found Mendoza's files? How dare you!"

"I didn't know the files you opened were connected to my investigation. Besides, Stefan didn't want you involved. He thought you'd go off on your own and muck up the inquiry."

Hailey opened her mouth, but quickly closed it. Stefan had a point, but still, she didn't like the deceit. "Well, I am involved."

"I know. That's why I'm telling you this. For months, the SCA has concentrated on tracking drugs shipping into the country. This year alone, we've seized a dozen cocaine shipments. Most of them were Mendoza's."

"How do you know he's involved?"

"It's funny how sleazebags talk when they feel threatened. José and Manuel are raising capital for another revolution. The DEA has men working with the Colombian government to confiscate the drugs once it leaves port. Unfortunately, Mendoza and his father made new connections in the U.S. to launder money and traffic drugs, so we haven't been able to stop all the shipments."

"What does this have to do with Mark?"

"I'm not sure how his death ties in yet. Maybe Mendoza wanted to punish him for putting Colleen in jail?"

She scoffed. "Mendoza would have gone after us first. This might not have anything to do with Mark."

"There's something else. Euphoria was mentioned in some of the recent busts around town."

The hair on her neck bristled. "That's impossible."

"The name is getting around, but we haven't confiscated the drug itself on the streets yet. Mendoza's got to be shipping it here somehow."

"How could he have the drug? He doesn't have a plant."

Parker shrugged. "You ask some excellent questions, but I don't have any answers."

She groaned. "Bruce has a plant. You're not thinking—"

"No. I checked him out. He got his plant from Charles Moulin when they were in med school. Bruce told Stefan that Moulin's father also grew one. When the father died five years ago, Bruce searched the house after the funeral, but the plant was gone. I think someone broke into the man's house and stole it."

Hailey's head throbbed. "That plant could've been dead for years. Don't you remember how fatal Euphoria was? If it were here, we'd see a rise in drug deaths."

"Maybe Mendoza figured out how to process it so the drug isn't as lethal. Something suspicious is going on. You have to be cautious of everyone you meet."

Like you. "That's why you said yesterday to trust no one." She pointed to the car. "The DTA searched the car before they brought it back. Did you find anything?"

"Just a chewed piece of gum and a photo jammed under the seat." He reached in his pocket and handed her the picture. "Do you know who this is?"

A lump lodged in her throat as she studied the photograph. The baby with wavy black hair couldn't have been more than a year old. She steadied her voice. "It's Mark's niece. The picture must have fallen out of his wallet."

Parker reached for the picture.

Hailey tucked it into her jeans pocket. "Mark's family has nothing to do with this case. I'll put it back in the album."

He scratched his chin. "I'd hoped it had some meaning for us."

"For us? Or for you?"

"I wish you'd believe me." Frowning, he leaned against the car. "I texted I was coming. Anna told me it upsets you to look at Mark's car, so I figured I'd save you the unhappy memories."

The dejected expression on his face softened her heart. "I'm a big girl. I can handle it. Promise you won't keep anything else from me."

"I won't." His voice brightened. "I have news about the Maryland Correctional Facility where Colleen is staying."

"You mean West Virginia?"

"No. She was transferred to Maryland four years ago."

"Why?"

He shrugged. "Security reasons, maybe."

Mark died in Maryland. Was there a connection? "Can we see her?"

"We have to fill out an application. The approval takes one to six weeks."

"One to six weeks!"

"There's more."

Nothing could be worse than waiting six weeks. "What?"

"Colleen needs to add us on her visiting list."

Fat chance of her ever inviting them. "Can't you do something? Pull some strings. Ask Stefan to get us in."

"I'll ask him. Maybe he can convince the warden this is top secret. I'm sure Colleen will want her lawyer there."

"Can't hurt to ask." This would take a miracle.

When Parker drove away, Hailey stepped back into the house and poured a glass of ice water. Parker's conversation the previous day echoed in her mind. *Trust no one.*

Could she trust him? She closed her eyes, collecting her thoughts.

The passion in his kiss the previous night wasn't pretend. He was her partner at the Special Crimes Agency. Obviously, she could trust him. Or maybe she couldn't. Damn. She wouldn't give her heart to someone unless she could trust him completely. Mark would never lie to her.

An eerie feeling came over her. Would Mendoza and his father come after her for opening the files? By now, they had to have discovered what she did. Determination hardened inside her. With Mark gone, she had to protect her family.

She pulled the baby picture from the jeans. The girl in the photo was a beautiful child, but she definitely wasn't Mark's niece. And she had a darker complexion than Laura or Francine.

Who are you, and why were you in Mark's car?

The picture had to be a clue to Mark's death.

Parker's warning rang in her head. Could she trust David? He was a good go-to guy. Santino? She didn't know him well enough yet. She rubbed her head. Another tension headache was starting.

Chapter Twenty-Five

Peggy opened the kitchen door, a smile spreading across her face. "Hailey! What a nice surprise."

"Sorry I didn't call. I have an hour while the kids are at counseling." Hailey passed her mother-in-law a layered chocolate cake. "Anna and I made this for Dad. I forgot to give it to him last night when he dropped off the car."

The older woman set the dessert on the countertop. The fifteen pounds she lost after Mark's death exacerbated her fragile appearance. "You shouldn't have gone to all the trouble. But Adam will love it. He's picking up a pair of brake rotors. How's the counseling going?"

Hailey shrugged off her sweater. "I think Anna and Ethan are opening up more."

"Is Anna still biting her nails?"

"Yes." Hailey dragged out a chair from the wooden farmhouse table. "The habit has gotten worse. I hope she stops once school's over."

"How many more weeks?"

"The kids have four. My classes end this week."

Peggy poured two glasses of lemonade and handed one to Hailey. "Laura and her kids can't stop talking about this summer."

Hailey drained her drink. "Ethan and Anna are excited."

"The visit will be good for Laura, too. She needs a distraction from Jack and his new girlfriend." Peggy sipped her lemonade. "Someday Laura will find someone who will treat her with the respect she deserves."

"She will." Jack's infidelity had been heartbreaking for the entire family. "I wonder if Laura and David would hit it off."

"I've known Davey since he and Mark were young kids. I think Laura had a crush on him at one time."

"That reminds me." Hailey opened her purse. "I came across a picture yesterday." She handed Peggy the photo. "Do you recognize this child?"

Peggy studied it. "No…I don't."

Hailey did her best to hide any disappointment. "Would it be Laura? Francine?"

"No. My girls had russet-colored hair."

"Could it be one of your grandchildren?"

Peggy placed the photograph on the table. "No. This child's hair is darker, and the other grandkids have brown or green eyes. Where did you find this?"

"In some old papers." Hailey's throat tightened as she returned the picture to her purse. She'd been certain Peggy would recognize the child. "It's no big deal. I'll add it in the family album."

Peggy squeezed her hand. "Are you doing okay, honey? Is it getting any easier?" Wrinkles etched deep in her forehead.

Hailey caught her breath. The last thing her mother-in-law needed was a blubbering crybaby. She had to stay strong for Mark's parents. "Yeah. I have good days and bad days…I know you and Dad miss Mark, too."

"We do. I don't know how we'd get through this without you and the kids." Sadness darkened Peggy's eyes.

"I feel the same." Why had she assumed the pain was easier for them? Losing a child was just as difficult as losing a spouse. Memories of Justin's death still stung.

Peggy patted her hand. "Promise me you won't be afraid to move on."

Hailey stared. "Where's this coming from?"

"Please hear me out." Peggy's voice was brittle. "You're still young. If you get a chance at happiness again, go for it. Adam and I don't expect you to mourn Mark forever."

Her vision blurred. Why did she feel the deepest loss around Mark's parents? "But I loved him."

Peggy's lip quivered. "We all did."

"I don't want to lose you and Adam."

"You won't. Ethan and Anna are our grandchildren, and you'll always be our daughter-in-law. But Mark would want you to be happy."

Hailey squeezed her hands into a ball, trying to stop the itching sensation. Parker had said the same thing. Had she been forbidding herself from moving on? "I'm so sad now that Mark's gone."

Peggy reached over and hugged her. "I know, dear. But one day, your feelings might change. And when you're ready, don't be afraid to love again."

****

Manuel ignored his father's scowl and studied the others in the meeting room. Two comrades were from Venezuela, but the majority of the coalition lived in Colombia.

Papà's efforts to revitalize cocaine production and overthrow the government elicited keen interest among rebels from distant territories. The latest government tactic of using drones to spray the coca plants had wiped out acres of crops. So far, the spray hadn't affected *Bixa aparra.*

Manuel could think of a million other places he'd rather be than in the room, plotting drug shipments and attacks.

José glared at him and dismissed the men.

Manuel pretended not to notice. As the group shuffled toward the door, his phone pinged. He moved to the far end of the room and read the message.

—Nothing in Child Welfare files.—

A muscle in his neck tensed. *Asshole!* He had checked messages a hundred times today for this nonsense? A two-year-old could do better.

"*Hijueputa!* Stop fixating on your American *puta* and focus." José's voice boomed behind him.

Heat spread down Manuel's neck, and he shoved the phone into his pocket. "What the hell do you want from me?"

"Go with Luis. Start transporting supplies for the revolt."

"Open your eyes, old man! No one cares about overthrowing the government anymore, except you and those other crazy-ass fanatics you hang with. You're living in the past."

José pointed a gnarled finger at him. "Watch your tone with me, boy. Cocaine is our livelihood. The government is trying to crush us."

"There has to be a better way. We don't need more bloodshed."

"And you don't need to obsess over your damn daughter."

Manuel flinched. "What did you say?"

José's eyes were blazing swords preparing for battle. "You heard me."

"You know about my daughter?"

"I do."

"How did you find out?"

"I make it my business to know everything. I have eyes and ears in many places—and your whore's prison is one of them."

Manuel's heart pounded against his chest. "Where's my daughter?"

"Why are you consumed with finding her? *Ella es una puta*—just like her mother."

Grabbing José's shirt, Manuel lifted his father in the air and lobbed a hard punch in his gut. "My daughter is not a whore, and neither is her mother."

José swung his arm, landing a solid blow on Manuel's jaw.

"What's going on?" Camila rushed into the room and eyed the two men.

Manuel reluctantly lowered his father to the floor.

José stepped backward, putting distance between them.

Manuel rubbed his chin. "Mamà, I have something to tell you."

"What is it?"

"I have a child. A little girl." His tension dissolved.

Camila clapped her hands together and stepped closer. "I have a granddaughter? I had given up hope." She hugged him. "Can we see her? Who is the mother?"

"Bella."

"The woman in the States? You were going to bring her here, but you never did."

"I wish I had. She was arrested for helping me manufacture Euphoria."

Camila nodded. "The drug you're working on here."

"Yes. Bella had a baby while she was in prison. A little girl."

"Where is your daughter now?"

"I don't know." Manuel glared at his father. "But Papà does."

Camila gaped. "José? Is this true?"

José stomped his foot. "I will not have that wretched child in my house!"

"Why?" She gasped. "She's Mano's daughter—our granddaughter."

José bared his teeth, spitting venom. "She's an American!"

"She's half-Colombian." Camila shook her fists. "And so was my grandmother! Tata didn't care when he married her."

Manuel stepped closer to José. How could this vile man be his father? "Where's my daughter?"

José's lips tightened in a fine line. "I'll never tell you."

Camila grabbed Manuel's sleeve, her face ablaze. "Find her. This is your daughter's home."

He glared at José. "What if Papà hurts her?"

"Your father will not lay a hand on her."

"But—"

"*I* will handle your father."

"Woman! Stop." José glowered.

C. Becker

Camila's eyes spit venom as she gave him a withering stare. "José de Mendoza, you will not harm our granddaughter."

José's nostrils flared. "You can't control me."

She remained unperturbed. "For forty-four years, I've lived with you. I've seen the shameful things you've done, and I've gathered evidence. Tons of it. So don't tempt me."

He sneered. "You have nothing on me."

"I have evidence you headed the assassinations on the former FARC leaders."

Manuel flinched. His father turned on his own cohorts?

Like a lion preparing to attack, Camila circled her husband. "I have spies, too. If our grandchild gets harmed in any way, I will kill you the same way you murdered your allies. Do you understand me?"

"*Mierda*! You can't threaten me, Camila." He lunged toward her.

She slapped his face. "Oh yes, I can. I've given all the damning evidence to friends. If I die, your crimes will be on everyone's lips. I suggest you look around. All of this property you pretend is yours is going directly to Mano and his child. That was Tata's final wish. His lawyer still has the deed with the provisions." She waved her fist in the air. "If you undermine the search for his daughter, Mano will leave you nothing. Do you hear me? You will have nothing!"

José's face turned crimson. "I won't help Manuel find his *puta*'s illegitimate child."

Tightening his hand, Manuel swung hard, and his fist landed on the side of José's face. "Don't you call Bella a whore again."

Blood dripped from his father's nose. José charged at him, delivering three hard punches in the gut.

Manuel buckled over, but garnered strength, and he struck back.

Camila gripped Manuel's arm. "Go! Bring your daughter home. Bella is welcome, too."

Manuel's confidence strengthened; never had he felt so empowered. He stormed out of the room. He didn't need his father's help. He'd find Katia in the States and bring her home.

Chapter Twenty-Six

Hailey drove into the courthouse lot, turned to Ethan sitting in the passenger seat, and gave his hand a reassuring squeeze. "It'll be okay."

They walked to David's car where he was already waiting.

She gave a shaky wave. "Thanks for coming."

David's buoyant grin calmed her nerves.

"Some guys like football. I like to spend my free time in Juvenile Court proceedings." He walked beside Ethan and clasped his shoulder. "Are you ready, buddy?"

Ethan's face paled as they set foot in the building.

Hailey adjusted his tie and brushed lint off the suit coat he had worn for homecoming last fall. "No matter what happens, I love you."

Inside the front entrance, Ethan gave his name to the receptionist.

Hailey remained silent, her stomach knotted like a set of tangled Christmas tree lights.

They followed the directions to the designated chamber.

Mr. Greene waited outside the room and reviewed the process with them. "This should go quickly." He glanced at his watch. "The judge should come in a few minutes. I have the video that shows Ethan was not directly involved in the vandalism."

Hailey tucked a strand of hair behind her ear. "And the store owner's sworn affidavit?"

The lawyer closed his briefcase. "He confirmed Ethan and Jake paid for damages and repaired the store window."

His self-assuredness didn't stop her heart from racing. If only she could be as easily convinced. "Will it be enough evidence to convince the judge?"

Mr. Greene nodded. "I think so. The judge will speak with Ethan and make a decision."

****

"So it's finally over?" Mark sat in his chair and exhaled as he listened to David's recount of Ethan's hearing.

David leaned back in the sofa. "Ethan has to continue counseling for the rest of the school year, but it's over."

"This is the best news I've heard all month. Hailey must be relieved."

David nodded. "They both are. Ethan's mood already did a complete turnaround."

Relief flooded Mark. At least the chains binding his son were broken. He rested his head in his palms. "Hailey shouldn't have to deal with this. Or you."

"Don't worry about me. Hailey's a strong woman. I'm glad she's discovering that part of herself again."

Mark raised his head. "She's always been my rock."

"While we were waiting for the judge this morning, she mentioned Parker came over for dinner Sunday afternoon."

Mark's fingers tightened in his compression gloves. "Did you warn her about him?"

David shook his head. "I didn't have to. She said they're just friends. She's not ready to get involved with anyone yet. Not Parker or Santino."

Mark rose and paced the floor. "I hope she can forgive me one day."

"Have faith in her." David rubbed his chin. "Your gait improves every time I see you."

Mark jutted his jaw. He had noticed the progress, but a relapse could still happen. "Dr. Costello said I'm getting stronger. The cane is easier than a walker." He pointed to his legs. "Wish they didn't look so bad."

"Considering what you've been through, you're coming along just fine. The compression garments will minimize the scarring."

Mark gazed out the window. Would he be able to live in this limbo while he healed?

"By the way, Hailey asked more questions about the fire."

He turned. "What kind of questions?"

"She wants to know about the case you were working on. Why you were in Maryland. Who owned the building that caught fire. Why your partner wasn't with you."

It was only a matter of time.

Mark stepped into the kitchen and pulled out a water bottle from the fridge. "Hailey's starting to piece things together. I bet Parker is putting her up to this."

"Could be. I dropped some subtle comments about Parker leaving Chicago."

Mark guzzled some water. "What did Hailey say?"

"She didn't say anything. I made a few calls after the hearing. Parker's back at the SCA." David extended his arms along the couch. "The big question is why?"

"It's not a coincidence he showed up in town after I died." Mark drained the water bottle.

He made his way into the living room, sat in his chair, and extended his arm. The stretching was a constant exercise. Four months ago, he couldn't get off the bed.

"Parker better not interfere with our investigation. We can't jeopardize Colleen's release."

Mark continued stretching therapy on his fingers. The routine had taken over his entire life. This recovery was the hardest job he'd ever had. His fingers cramped, and he stopped. "Any sighting of Mendoza?"

"The surveillance team hasn't notified me. Here, I'll help you." David reached over and massaged the scar on Mark's arm.

An image of a thug beating him flashed through Mark's mind. He jerked his arm, almost hitting David. "He's running out of time. Colleen's release is in three weeks."

"Calm down." David lowered Mark's arm and continued the therapy. "Maybe Manuel won't come."

"Where's the girl?" Mark broke out in a cold sweat at the memory of the attackers' question. "Oh, he'll come. I wish I could remember what the thugs looked like."

David stopped the massage. "If Mendoza leaves Colombia, Owen and I will post security at your house. Don't worry. This case will be over soon. Then you can focus on your future."

Mark stiffened. The future was even scarier. When the ordeal was over, he'd face the most crucial fight of his life—getting Hailey back.

****

The biochemistry final concluded at three o'clock, and Hailey ignored the students' moans as they handed in their exams. She walked back to the office.

Her office mate sat at her desk, crying.

Hailey handed her a tissue. "Liz, what's wrong?"

The woman dabbed her eyes. "George is up to his old ways again. The bank called. Our account is overdrawn."

Hailey slid a chair closer. "I'm sorry. Are they sure it isn't a mistake?"

Liz nodded. "George flew the boys to Vegas last month. He has a favorite place he goes to because one of the pit bosses extends him credit. I don't know if I can go through this again. He's ruining our family—and his career. If the city council discovers what's going on, they'll ask him to step down. We need his income."

"Can I do anything?"

"Thanks, but this is my mess. I'll figure it out. I always do." Liz wiped her nose. "How did the hearing go?"

Hailey related the main points of Ethan's hearing.

Liz shook her head. "Oh, the trials of parenting. Children are the biggest cause of gray hair."

"I doubt Ethan will do anything reckless like that again." Hailey pointed to the small stack of papers on Liz's desk. "Grading finals?"

"I'm almost caught up. I'll enter grades in the portal over the weekend. What about you?"

"I still have four finals to give." Hailey glanced at the stack of exams. "I had planned to stay and grade papers, but from the looks on the students' faces when they turned in the exams, I think it will ruin my day."

Liz threw the used tissues in the trash. "Any plans for the weekend?"

Hailey groaned. "I don't even have plans for dinner tonight. What about you?"

"I'm not sure." With a pinched expression, Liz tidied her desk. "George and I need to have a long talk."

Frustration coated Liz's angry voice. Over the past year, George frequented casinos more often. Sometimes he bragged about small winnings, but more often, he returned home empty-handed and owing.

Could Hailey turn the other way if Mark gambled away their savings?

When she arrived home in the afternoon, Anna was lying on the sofa talking on the phone. Hailey tried not to eavesdrop on Anna's conversation with Samantha about a cute boy at school, but her implant made it too easy.

Anna glanced at Hailey. "Sam, I gotta go. Call you back later."

Hailey sank onto the cushion beside Anna. "How was school?"

"Good."

"Is Ethan home?"

"Santino picked him up. They need to mow yards before it rains tomorrow. Ethan wants you to save him dinner. He'll be back in time for counseling."

"Did he tell you about the hearing?"

Anna nodded. "He said he has to stay in counseling."

Counseling was a gift in many ways. The judge could've been a lot tougher on Ethan. "I'm glad it's over."

"Me, too." Anna unzipped her backpack and pulled out a notebook. "When we came home, the front door was unlocked."

Hailey tensed. "What?"

Anna's eyebrow arched. "Ethan took the key from the brick, but the door opened without it. We thought you must have forgotten to lock the door this morning."

Had she forgotten? Ethan grabbed breakfast, and they walked out together. She used her car remote to unlock the doors, and then realized she had forgotten her cell phone. When she went back to the kitchen to retrieve it, Ethan was already in the car. "I guess I forgot. Humph…I never forget to lock up."

"You forget a lot lately." Anna opened her notebook and began solving math problems.

A cold chill ran down her spine as Hailey surveyed the area. Nothing looked out of place. "I'll be back in a jiffy. After I change my clothes, we can make dinner."

Upstairs, Hailey hurried down the hallway, checking each room. In her bedroom, the hairbrush was still on the dresser, next to the earrings she had worn the previous day. Everything seemed in its place. She almost wished it wasn't. That would have made it easier to know if someone had broken in. *My gun!* She sprinted to the closet and opened the bottom shoebox. Relief settled over her as she held the weapon. A faint smell of musky cologne floated through the air. Or was she being paranoid?

Had Parker come into the house? She fished her cell from her purse and dialed.

"Hailey. Hello. What's going on?"

"Did you come in my house today?"

"What? No."

"You didn't come inside to look for more clues?"

"For crying out loud, no. You said you had exams today. What's going on?"

"Anna said the front door was unlocked when she came home."

"Did Ethan come home before her?"

"No. They get off the bus the same time."

"Did you lock it this morning?"

Tension spread across her temples. "I don't know. It's possible I forgot. But I've checked and double checked my locks my whole life. You know I'm OCD about that."

"Do you want me to come over and look around?"

What *did* she want? "No, I'm okay. I just freaked out for a minute. Sorry I bothered you."

"You're not a bother. I'll call you tonight."

Hailey turned off her cell and picked up a frame from the nightstand. Had she placed it in that position? Touching a finger to her lips, she kissed Mark's face and lowered the frame. With Mark gone, it was her responsibility to protect the kids.

Chapter Twenty-Seven

Hailey toweled off after her morning shower and checked her phone.

A message from Parker lit the screen. —*You owe me.*—

He had her attention. —*Why?*—

—*Stefan got us in. We're on Colleen's approved-visitors list.*—

She danced a little jig. —*No way! When can we go?*—

This was nothing short of a miracle. She fell onto the bed and waited for his reply.

Parker texted a minute later. —*Visiting hours are Fri 4-8pm, Sat & Sun 12-8*—

Darn. Why couldn't there be visiting hours tonight? The kids had counseling anyway. She texted back. —*I vote Friday*—

Downstairs, Anna and Ethan were chatting at the table as she stepped into the kitchen.

The sweet scent of waffles greeted Hailey. "Morning. It smells wonderful in here. Who made the waffles?"

Anna opened a jar of grape jelly. "I did."

"Thanks, Anna. You're becoming quite the cook." She grabbed a plate from the cupboard. "Ethan, did you clean your bedroom? I'm stripping sheets this morning."

"I forgot." Ethan forked a giant serving of waffle in his mouth.

Anna smeared peanut butter over a slice of bread. "Mom, are you wearing that to work?"

Hailey glanced down at her faded denim shorts. "No. I plan to clean this morning. I'm not going in until noon."

Anna wedged her sandwich in a plastic bag. "Can I play at Sam's after school?"

"As long as you take the path behind our house and text me when you get there."

"When will you let me walk on the main road?"

"Never. The road has a wide curve. Cars zoom around way too fast, and drivers can't see you walking."

Anna chewed on her nail.

The habit was occurring more often. Why would she be anxious about a playdate? "Is everything all right with you and Samantha?"

"Everything's fine." Anna packed a banana into her lunchbox.

Hailey's gaze followed her daughter's movements. Anna didn't act fine. "Are you sure?"

Anna hesitated. "Sam asked me to sleep over Friday night."

"And—you don't want to go?"

"No. I do…but I don't want to leave you alone."

Guilt swept over Hailey. Since Mark had died, the kids hadn't had any sleepovers. "You should go."

"But—"

"I'll be okay. Ethan's here."

Her son pushed back his plate and poured a bowl of corn flakes. "About that…Jake asked me to go fishing with him and Santino this weekend. Can I go, Mom? He's been inviting me for a while."

"Will you be gone overnight?"

Ethan nodded. "Until Sunday. We'll sleep on Santino's boat."

Hailey nibbled on a piece of waffle. Their plans could be a blessing in disguise, especially since she might not get back from the prison until late. "You both can go. You deserve to have some fun."

When Ethan and Anna left the house, Hailey cleared the table and stuck her phone into her purse. The photo from Mark's car was still beside her wallet.

Who are you?

Studying it again, she stepped to the living room and opened the most recent photo album, securing the picture in the plastic covering.

Next, she cleaned Anna's bedroom, putting on fresh bedsheets and collecting stray socks hidden under the bed. She moved to Ethan's room; a trail of musky cologne still lingered in the air. After she gagged at the sweaty clothes beside the hamper, she swept the carpet and pushed the vacuum cleaner into the hall. Outside Ethan's room, a small white pill lay on the carpet.

Hailey switched off the vacuum and held the translucent pill between her fingers. Her chest tightened as anger overtook her. Was Ethan using? Dammit! What did she have to do to convince him?

She searched the carpet for more and found none. Could it be Anna's? Maybe Jake's? He played video games upstairs with Ethan. Should she mention it to Santino? Better not to involve him until she knew more.

"I wonder." She went downstairs and grabbed her phone.

Bruce answered on the third ring. "Hailey? Is something wrong?"

"I hope not. Can you do a favor for me?"

"Shoot."

"I found a strange pill on the floor. It's not one of my anti-anxiety pills. I'm worried it belongs to Ethan or Anna, but I don't want to accuse them until I know for sure. If I send it to you, can you analyze it?"

"Absolutely."

"Thanks. I knew I could count on you." She fetched a mailing envelope from the study. "Any progress on your research? Last time we talked, you said *Bixa aparra* wasn't thriving."

"It's wilting like a flower in a Texas drought. I've been in contact with a museum in South America. The director is trying to put me in touch with a shaman. Are you sure you can't help me with my research? The company has corporate housing available in a private wing of the facility."

"Bruce, I can barely handle my own life. I have two teens." She glanced at her watch. "I've got to go. I'll ship the pill overnight delivery. Let me know what you find."

Chapter Twenty-Eight

"Are you feeling all right?" Liz's question broke the silence in the office. "You've been scratching your hands, staring at the paper for ten minutes."

Hailey glanced up from the final she was grading. The urge to scratch had been constant since Parker's text the previous day. "I have a lot on my mind." *Like visiting Mark's former girlfriend.*

"Want to talk about it?"

"Not really." Colleen Toole had been implicated in kidnapping, murder, and drug manufacturing; the woman's unscrupulous activities were as speckled as a contaminated petri dish.

"Are you going to the meeting tonight? I know I need the support."

Hailey leaned back in her chair. That's right, Rita had moved the meeting date to Friday. "Did something else happen?"

Liz primped her hair. "Hunter let it slip George blew a lot of money during a poker game last night."

"Ouch." Hailey struggled to say something reassuring. How long could Liz stand by and watch her husband spiral downward? A gambling addiction was as painful as drugs.

"I'm talking to the dean this afternoon about picking up some summer classes. I need to get us out of this black hole."

"What did George say?"

Liz's lips quivered. "He insists gambling is no different than blowing money at an amusement park or fancy vacation."

Hailey gave a sympathetic smile. "I can't make the meeting tonight, but call me if you want to talk."

"Thank you. You've been a good friend." Liz wiped her eyes and rushed to the door. "I'll be in the ladies' room. I don't know why I'm so emotional today."

Should she check on her? No, better to give Liz some time alone. Thank goodness Mark had never put Hailey through anything like this. She and Mark had conserved finances carefully, discussing all major expenditures together. They had dream vacations they planned to take after Mark's retirement. An image of the Hawaii brochure crossed her mind. A deep sadness wrapped its arms around her. *Life cheated me.*

An hour later, Hailey met Parker in the university parking lot. She regarded the dark clouds thundering in the distance, and she fetched an umbrella from her car. "Remind me to thank Stefan for getting us in to see Colleen."

Parker programmed the phone's GPS. "It helps to have friends in high places."

As they neared the correctional facility, the GPS's silvery voice interrupted. "In one mile, turn right."

Parker signaled and switched lanes.

Hailey leaned forward and rubbed the knots in her neck. "How long before Colleen is released?"

"Three weeks."

She shuddered. "It doesn't seem fair she's getting out soon. She almost killed us."

"She might not be the same vindictive woman you remember. The associate warden spoke of Colleen in a positive light."

Hailey scowled. "She's in prison. How remarkable can she be?"

"She's tutoring inmates to help them get their GEDs."

"Really?"

Parker nodded. "Colleen's a bright woman. I didn't realize she has a degree from Harvard. She's been drawing pictures for the Prison Foundation to raise money for the women prisoners. Her pieces are listed on the Internet."

Hailey quieted. Colleen was a nasty, self-centered woman; this didn't conform to the narrative. "I wonder what Colleen will do when she gets out."

"She's probably set for life. I imagine her father willed her a hefty inheritance."

Hailey remained silent. There was no inheritance when her parents died. How ironic she and Colleen, both only children, led such diametrically opposite lives.

A small sign pointed to the facility. Parker steered a hard left onto the designated roadway and parked the car in the lot. "We'll need our ID."

She plucked her driver's license from her wallet and stashed her purse beneath the seat.

Through a light drizzle, Parker and Hailey trotted to the security entrance and cleared the metal detector and drug and weapon searches. They entered a large room filled with cubicles.

Hailey studied the canvas paintings on the walls. Some were quite good. Had Colleen drawn any?

Each compartment had a window into another room; two phones hung on the walls in the visitor cubicle. The setup was just like the ones she'd seen in the movies.

A soft hum of the air conditioner provided white noise as they waited.

Nearby, a small boy held a homemade card as he fidgeted beside an elderly couple.

She caught her breath at the scene. *This must be so difficult for children.*

Parker stopped at station ten and dragged out a chair from under a counter. "This is our spot."

Across the thick pane of glass, a bell buzzed, and a female guard led a small group of prisoners into the other room.

Hailey sat next to Parker. She recognized Colleen instantly; the woman looked the same as the newspaper photos from six years ago.

Colleen tugged at her slate-gray shirt as she neared.

No, Hailey's first impression was wrong. Wrinkles set around the inmate's eyes, mouth, and forehead. Gray strands peppered her thick blonde hair. A memory flashed of Colleen hovering while holding Hailey hostage. Did the woman still wear magnolia-scented perfume?

The place was cold and isolated, not the warm, fuzzy home she'd want to live out her years. She almost felt sorry for Colleen.

Colleen sat and held the phone next to her ear.

Parker spoke first. "Thank you for seeing us."

"When the guard said I had visitors, I was intrigued." She turned to Hailey. "I'm sorry about Mark. My lawyer told me what happened."

Her sultry voice pummeled Hailey like a wrecking ball.

Hailey's brain screamed, "Fraud!" Colleen couldn't be "sorry" after everything she'd done. "Thank you." Her voice quavered as she fought to maintain control. "Do you know my friend, Tom Parker?"

Colleen shook her head.

Parker gave a small nod. "I don't believe we've met."

Hailey leaned forward. "We won't keep you long. We have a few questions."

"I'm not saying anything without my lawyer." Colleen's polished words would make any attorney proud.

"Please. It's about Mark."

Colleen glanced at the officer standing behind her.

Was she always so jumpy around security or was there a reason behind her distrust?

"Please."

Colleen crossed her arms. "Two minutes—for Mark." Her voice broke on the last two words.

My God. She still has feelings for him. Hailey clenched her hands. "Have you spoken to Mendoza recently?"

Colleen scowled. "I thought this had something to do with Mark."

"It does." *Sort of.* Hailey switched the handset to her other ear. "We think Mark was investigating something that involved Euphoria before he died. Has Mendoza contacted you about producing more of the drug?"

In defiance, Colleen lowered her head and picked at her unpolished nails.

Parker leaned closer. "There's been talk about Euphoria circulating around D.C."

Colleen stared at him for a moment. "I told you I'm not talking about this."

"Do you want to be associated with Euphoria resurfacing and being blamed for more deaths? Do you want to spend another six years in here?" Parker threatened.

"No." Her voice came out as a whisper. "Are you sure it's Euphoria?"

"We haven't confiscated any yet, but we're certain the claim's legit." Parker lowered his voice. "We know Charles Moulin's father grew *Bixa aparra*. Did Manuel get his hands on it?"

In an almost hidden movement, she nodded. "Six years ago, Manuel's bodyguard shipped the plant to Colombia."

Parker scrubbed a hand over his chin. "Would Manuel be able to propagate enough Euphoria by now for mass distribution?"

Colleen gave another small nod. She glanced again at the guard. "I didn't know he was making Euphoria again. I swear."

Hailey turned to Parker. His suspicions had been right. Gripping her phone, she leaned closer to the window. "Why should we believe you? For all we know you're scheming with him."

"I'm not." Colleen's cheeks flushed. "I promised Mark—"

"You've talked to Mark since you've been here?" She studied Colleen's reaction. Just how good was this liar?

"No." Colleen's eye twitched.

Hailey slapped her hand on the table. "Liar! Did you lure him here so Mendoza could kill him?"

"What?" Colleen leaned backward, as if she'd been hit. "No, I swear—"

"Did he visit you the night he died?" Hailey lurched to within inches of the glass. "Answer me!"

"I don't remember."

"Did Mark visit you sometimes?"

The inmate was like a frozen rabbit on the highway. "Sometimes—" Colleen stammered.

"Why would he contact *you*? You tried to kill him."

"Mark forgave me for that."

"Then he's a better person than me."

"I hope you can, too."

"I'll never forgive you."

"I was talking about Mark." Colleen formed a swaggering grin. "You're angry with him."

Hailey didn't need the psychoanalysis. "Why wouldn't I be? Mark never told me he was seeing *you*. His death is your fault. Yours. Do you know what it's like to have a child never see their parent again?"

Colleen's smug expression faded.

Determination drove Hailey to continue. "Just tell me why he was here. You owe me that much." Would the woman give her the closure she desperately needed?

Colleen's lips tightened. "I don't owe you anything."

Hailey turned to Parker. "Why did I think she'd give a damn about my husband?" She began to hang up the phone.

"Wait!" Colleen's voice squawked through the handset. "Mark was trying to help me."

"Help?" Hailey fell back in her seat. "Why would he do that?"

"Mark and I were once lovers. We became close again after I came here."

The officer behind Colleen tilted her head toward them.

Colleen lowered her voice. "We thought Hawaii would be a fresh start after I got released."

"Stop." Did Colleen actually believe these lies?

Colleen gave an impish grin. "Mark was looking for a place in Kauai. I swear to God. A realtor was searching for a house. Zoe Dixon." She raised a hand in the air, as if swearing in for court.

The brochure of the Hawaii trip flashed in her memory. *Buy two tickets.* Hailey's hands trembled. "You're lying. Mark was taking *me* to Hawaii."

Colleen shifted her back away from the officer and whispered into the phone. "I was going to Kauai. Not you, you spoiled bitch." She hung up the phone. "Guard."

Hailey shouted into the handset. "Wait. You can't leave."

Parker grabbed her arm. "Let's go."

"Come back, you lying whore!" Hailey pounded her fist against the glass.

Parker clasped his arms around her shoulders and dragged her away.

"Let me go. She's lying!"

Hailey kept it together until Parker unlocked the car. She buckled the seatbelt and dragged her purse from under the seat. Then she removed the bottle of pills.

The driver's door opened.

Parker reached over and grabbed the bottle from her hands. "You don't need those."

Rage blinded her as she grabbed for them. "Yes, I do. Give them to me."

"When something goes wrong in your life, you pop one. Where's the woman who worked through every adversity that hit her? She's still inside you."

"I need the pills." She smacked his arm. "If you don't give them to me, I swear I'll—"

"You'll what? Whack me again? Go ahead, Hailey. Punch me all you want. It's not going to change anything. Mark's not coming back."

"Stop it!"

"He's never coming back."

She hit him again and covered her ears. "Leave me alone. Just leave me alone."

Parker leaned over and wrapped his arms around her. "I'm sorry. I didn't mean to say that."

She jerked away, tears streaming down her face. "Just take me home."

He turned the ignition and drove.

Hailey cried until she had no tears left, and then she sat in silence, unable to stop the conversation with Colleen replaying in her mind. *"I was going to Kauai. Not you."*

Colleen had to be lying. But how would she know about Kauai?

Hailey breathed in, letting the heavy rain dull her senses.

Parker glanced at her several times during the drive. After maneuvering through heavy road construction, he tapped his fingers on the steering wheel. "Are you okay?"

Hailey glowered at her hands. She was a hypocrite for wearing the wedding ring on her finger. Mark had minimized their marriage into a pathetic joke. They had made love the night before he died. Was that a lie, too?

"Why would Mark leave me and the kids?"

He signaled, steering into the left lane. "I don't know. Did you notice how jumpy Colleen was around the guard? It was obvious the officer was spying on her."

Hailey leaned her head against the window and stared at the cars whizzing past. Her tears merged with the rain streaming down the glass. *Mark. How could you?*

When they merged off the Capital Beltway, Parker turned on the radio and listened to the traffic report. "Can I take you to Moe's for a cup of coffee? Give you time to regroup before the kids see you."

She sniffled and blew her nose. "The kids are at sleepovers tonight. I just want to get my car and go home."

Ten minutes later, Parker steered the car into the faculty lot. "This place is a ghost town. Where is everyone?"

"Most kids have taken their finals and moved out. Damn."

He glanced at her. "What's wrong?"

"My G.A.'s graduating next weekend. I forgot to buy a gift. What do you get a twenty-five-year-old man ready to start a career?"

"Money to help pay off his student loans?"

She shook her head. "I'm serious."

Parker gave her a hurt look. "So am I." His phone beeped as he parked next to Hailey's car.

She touched his sleeve. "Answer your phone. I can let myself out."

Parker yanked on his door handle. "It can wait a minute. When are you going to accept my help?"

Hailey kept her lip from trembling as he opened the car door. She had accepted Parker's help once when she had no one. It wasn't fair to lean on him again. He wasn't a replacement—that's what scared her. Was it wrong to move on with Parker?

He offered his hand.

She accepted it. The strong grip felt good. "Thank you for getting us in and coming with me."

He gazed at her for a long moment and handed her the bottle of pills. "Promise me you won't use these anymore."

"Parker—"

"Promise me. You're acting differently."

"I am not." She snatched the bottle from him.

"You're forgetful. You sleep a lot. You're moody. You're—"

"All right. I'll cut back." Were they really affecting her? The dizziness ended when she stopped taking antihistamines, but the chest pain and numbness persisted. "You worry too much."

"I'm worried about you. Are you sure you're okay?"

She lost herself for a moment in his gray eyes. They still mesmerized her like they had years ago.

He pulled her into a hug.

The warmth and earthy scent reminded her of Mark. When was the last time she had felt this vulnerable? Could she trust Parker? She'd thought she could trust Mark.

Parker laid his chin against her head and kissed her crown, his warm breath drifting across her skin. "Let me know if you need anything." He kissed her forehead and brushed his lips lightly to hers. "I'll call you in the morning."

Hailey gave a small wave as Parker drove out of the lot. The security he exuded scared—and stunned—her at the same time. She opened her hand and fingered the bottle, pouring three pills in her palm. Her hands shook as she clenched her fist. Should she take them? God, her life was a mess. Resting her head on the steering wheel, she dropped the pills and wept.

Hailey gazed at the dusk until she could breathe again, and then she checked her text messages. The screen was full. Life moved on whether she was ready or not.

Anna's message appeared first. *—Sam and I took the path back to her house. Love you. Good night.—*

Ethan had texted around six o'clock. *—Santino's here. See you Sunday.—*

Liz's text was next. *—Some faculty from the department are going out to The Lazy Den tonight if you're interested. I plan on going after the meeting.—*

A text from David pinged and appeared on the screen. *—Sorry, I missed pizza night. I was finishing a case. Is it too late to stop by?—*

Her fingers skated around the keypad. *—It's not too late.—*

Hope filled her as a plan formed. David could give her answers. She dropped the phone in her purse and started the engine. She may not have Mark, but she could question his best friend.

****

245

Mark leaned his weight on the walking cane as he shuffled across the floor. That's odd. The pain wasn't as intense. Smiling, he took longer strides into his bedroom. His mobility had improved a lot over the past days. At least walking was one aspect in life he could control.

He'd breathe easier after Colleen's release. If she left town before Mendoza contacted her, she might have a decent chance at a new life. Colleen deserved that, and her daughter deserved a life without violence and drugs.

Outside, a siren from a fire engine blared from down the street.

He froze, remembering the crackling flames surrounding him. The heat scorching his skin. He stifled a sob and focused on his breathing. *Don't lose control.* Brittany was in the other room. She'd report his breakdown to David.

When he calmed down, Mark bowed his head. What was wrong with him lately? His volatile temper scared even him.

Resting his cane, he settled into the lounge chair by the bed and dimmed the lamp, allowing his cautious excitement to build. After all this time, he might restore his life with Hailey and the kids. He stared at the snug garment around his arms—hiding the scars. He opened and closed his fist. *Hang in there, Hailey.*

Mark closed his eyes, cherishing the memory of their last night together.

He had lain in bed, pretending to sleep, while Hailey bathed and brushed her teeth. When the bathroom door opened, the room filled with the coconut scent of her body wash. Most nights, his work preoccupied him. The realtor had helped narrow down Colleen's housing choices to three possibilities. Soon, she'd be out of his—and Hailey's—life forever.

Desire flowed through his loins as his wife slipped the nightgown over her head, the nipples on her breasts erect. His body stiffened. God, he wanted her. She had a magic touch that made him lose control. He faked a snore as she flipped the light switch. If she didn't hurry, he'd grab and make love to her on the floor. She tugged back the comforter and slid under the sheets.

Rolling over, he placed his arm around her narrow waist. "Babe, you look hot."

She laughed. "You can't even see me. It's dark."

"It wasn't dark a minute ago." He pecked gentle kisses along her neck. "Hmm. You smell delicious."

She moved beneath him. "Mark." The lighthearted laughter in her soft voice was unmistakable. She wanted him, too.

His fingers caressed her warm satiny skin. "I thought you'd never come to bed." Even his voice signaled his deep longing.

Hailey rolled over and moved closer. "If I knew you were planning this, I would have come upstairs as soon as the kids went to bed." She wrapped her arms around his back and probed his mouth with her tongue.

He captured her tongue and lingered in a long drugging kiss. "Better late than never, I always say."

"Since when?"

Mark brushed the stray hair off her face and kissed her again in a hungry urgency. How did he get so lucky? "Since now."

He moved his lips over her swollen breasts, adoring. her sexy gasps. Teasingly he pinched the hard tips, tightening his hand on her buttocks as she pressed closer toward him. Damn. The mere movement aroused him. He was like a sex-starved teenager.

Heat flowed through him like lava as his erection grew against her legs. He waited for her touch.

As if she could sense his need, she delayed his pleasure by stroking his arms. "You've been working your biceps. This is impressive."

The gold flecks in her eyes captured his gaze in the dim light. "Check a little lower." He pressed tighter against her as her fingers teased below his abdomen.

She reached lower and held his swollen flesh. "You've been building muscles all over."

Mark lifted her hips over him and held his breath. He was going to die before the night was over.

She pressed her breasts against his skin and planted a delicious kiss on his lips.

After they made love, Hailey nuzzled closer, toying with the hair covering his chest with tender tugs. "What time do you work tomorrow?"

"Work?" He had cleared his throat. Work was the last thing on his mind.

A door slammed, sounding like a bomb exploding.

He jumped. The memory of Hailey dissolved into graphic flashes of his brutal beating.

"Mark? You awake?"

David. Why was he here?

"Brittany. Is Mark in bed?" There was urgency in David's voice.

Mark adjusted the lamp. "I'm in here."

The bedroom door opened, and David strode inside. "I know it's late, but I just saw Hailey."

"Is she okay?" He grabbed his cane.

"No. She and Parker went to the Correction Center this evening."

"What?" Mark blinked. "Why?"

"Why do you think?"

"Nothing you're saying is making sense. How did they get in to see Colleen?"

"Hailey's former boss pulled some strings."

"Shit! Did Colleen talk to them?"

"Oh, she talked. She's a spiteful troublemaker."

"What did she say?"

When David finished telling him what happened, Mark banged his cane. "Dammit!"

"I told you not to trust the bitch." Red streaks ran down David's neck. "Hailey thinks you were leaving her to run off with Colleen. She's a wreck."

Mark sank his face into his hands. "Couldn't you convince Hailey she was lying?"

"I tried. I told her Colleen was a partying sorority girl, but Hailey said she has proof Colleen is telling the truth."

Mark flinched. "What proof?"

"The morning of the fire, when you were in the shower, she searched your briefcase and saw a Hawaii brochure. Hailey said you had been acting strangely so she snooped. She thought the trip was an anniversary gift."

"Dammit." He was a fool for keeping this from Hailey. The pain he caused was unforgivable. "This is a fucking mess."

"There's more."

What more could David say? "What?"

"She found a note in your handwriting to buy two plane tickets."

Mark collapsed on the bed. He remembered writing the note. "The tickets were for Colleen and her daughter—not Colleen and me." He tunneled a hand through his hair. "Can you meet Colleen—ask her to tell Hailey the truth?"

"Are you kidding me? Colleen's not going to risk revealing her secret." David sat beside Mark. "I don't know how long I can stand by and watch Hailey hurt like this."

This debacle was his fault. Mark started to shake again. "I hate this too."

"She doesn't deserve this." David's voice cracked. "Hell, no one deserves this type of pain. She has a broken heart, and we're gutting it."

Mark squeezed his eyes. "This is torturing her *and* me."

"And me."

Mark had never seen his best friend look so lost.

David shook his head. "I'm going to be real with you. I've had some tough assignments, but this one is taking me to the edge."

Chapter Twenty-Nine

Turning on her side, Hailey kicked the bedsheets. How could Mark have lied?

A memory of their lovemaking the night before he died flashed through her mind.

That wasn't a lie. Her life with Mark wasn't a sham. They had two beautiful children. She had to keep those memories foremost in her mind.

"I was going to Kauai. Not you." She shut her eyes, blocking out Colleen's taunt.

Joyce mentioned she had met Mark at *True Living Realty*. Maybe a realtor would remember Mark. Tomorrow, she'd call the company. She'd prove Colleen was lying. Zoe Dixon probably wasn't even a realtor.

She jerked the comforter over her shoulder and glanced at the clock. 11:47 PM. If she had taken her pills, she'd be asleep right now. Why did Parker make her feel guilty for wanting them?

As she counted sheep, lightning flashed outside the window, illuminating the room.

The tree limbs scratched the pane as if wanting to escape the storm. A loud crack followed, and rain pounded hard on the rooftop.

Hailey rolled onto her back.

The house was quiet without the kids. Was this pit of loneliness an indication of how empty her world would become? Dammit. She was only forty-one. Her head had only a few gray hairs. She had a lot of life to live.

12:35 AM.

"It's now or never."

She tossed off the covers, slid into the jeans and blouse she had worn earlier, and hurried downstairs. A surprise attack on Parker might work to her advantage.

At the door, she tied the laces on her sneakers and plucked the car keys from her purse. Hailey rushed out the front door, locking the deadbolt, and she raced to the car.

Butterflies flitted in her stomach the entire ride to Parker's apartment complex. As Hailey drove around the parking lot in search of an empty space, the rain became a heavy downpour. She'd lose her nerve if she delayed seeing him any longer.

Dashing across the lot, she climbed the stairs to the second floor and stopped at the first apartment on the left. Excitement steeled her resolve as she pounded on the door. "Parker? Are you in there?"

A gust of wind whipped through the open space as she struck the door again. She was ready to take a chance again. "Parker! Wake up!"

She shivered in the cold rain, looking around the packed lot for his car. Was he home?

The outside light turned on next door.

Would the neighbors call the police? *Oh, let them come. Maybe the 9-1-1 operator will dispatch Parker.*

She struck the door harder. *"Open the—"*

The door squeaked and opened.

Parker stood in a white undershirt and boxers, rubbing his eyes like a sleepy child. "Hailey?"

A clap of thunder echoed in the sky.

In a flash, he yanked her inside and shut the door. "What are you doing here? You're drenched."

Hailey dropped her purse and kissed him.

****

The kiss was more passionate than she'd anticipated, but when her lips touched his, desire fired shock waves through her veins. The attraction she carried for him as a young woman surfaced.

Parker broke the kiss. "Are you sure?"

She nodded, loving how his eyes sparkled in the dim light as he wrapped an arm around her. Any doubts about moving on with her life evaporated. "I trust you, Parker. I know you'd never hurt me."

Pulling her closer, Parker held her tightly, capturing her mouth with his.

Hailey met his hungry urgency, trailing her fingers through his thick hair. She lowered her hands, touching his broad shoulders, taking in the contours of his warm chest muscles. Never had she felt the freedom to touch him so openly.

Parker caressed her back and tugged her blouse loose from her jeans. He pushed against her mouth and slid his tongue between her lips in a sweet invasion.

She shivered.

He moved back. "You're soaking wet."

She stood shamelessly as he lifted the top over her head. Would he want her like Mark had?

His fingers traced the lining of her lacy bra. "God, you're beautiful."

Beautiful. It felt flattering to hear the candid desire in his husky voice.

Emboldened, she unbuttoned her jeans.

Parker's wide-eyed smile faded. "No, Hailey."

She crossed her arm over her breasts. "What's wrong?"

Parker must have realized her humiliation; he reached out and crushed her against him. "It's not you—it's me."

The rejection hit her like a two-ton weight. How could she have mixed up all his signals? "What do you mean?" She searched his face. Why hadn't she recognized the sadness in his smoky eyes?

"We need to talk." Parker grabbed a throw blanket from the sofa and wrapped it around her. "Let me get you some dry clothes." He hurried down the hallway.

The faint smell of leather filled the air as she waited in the living room. An L-shaped sofa gave the place a contemporary feel. She stepped to the accent table next to the sofa and switched on a rustic metal lamp. She picked up two empty beer cans from the floor and set them next to the lamp, knocking over a photo. As she set the frame upright, she paused, touching Justin's face in the picture. He looked around Ethan's age; both boys shared her hazel eyes. Hailey sighed. She'd never get past the guilt of not knowing her son.

Parker rushed in the room and handed her some dry clothes. "This should warm you up." He stepped into the kitchen. "Can I make you some coffee?"

"Coffee sounds good, thanks." She pulled the oversized sweatshirt over her head and then removed her wet jeans. She slid her legs through the baggy sweatpants.

In a few minutes, he returned with two mugs. "Let's sit." He led her to the sofa and sat beside her.

Hailey savored a long sip, taking the chill from her body, and lowered her cup on her lap. "What's wrong? I thought you wanted this."

Laying his cup on the end table, Parker cleared his throat. "I do—but not this way."

"I...I don't understand."

"I haven't been honest with you." His shoulders slumped. "I didn't quit the force." Parker sunk his head in his hands. "I was terminated."

She gaped at him. He couldn't be serious. "What are you talking about?"

He raised his head. "Two years ago, a new team of rookies joined the force. One was assigned to me—Ben Gerome."

An image of the teenager flashed in her mind. "Justin's friend?"

"How do you know Ben?"

"We met after Justin died. At the cemetery. When Mark and I visited the gravesite."

"They were best friends." His face paled, and he managed a wan smile. "I hadn't realized how badly the boy was grieving over Justin's death."

"What do you mean?"

"One evening, we were patrolling the West Side when a call came in on a drug deal going down. We were close by and answered the call. When we arrived, the dealer was selling drugs to a group of teenagers. I recognized him immediately. Wendell Hautz."

She waited. "Should I recognize the name?"

"He was the dealer who sold Justin Euphoria."

She loathed the man already. "Go on."

"Hautz took off down the street. I ran after him while Ben called for backup. I chased Hautz a few blocks, and we ended up in an alleyway. Hautz caught me off guard. Knocked me over the head with something hard. I fought from passing out, and we struggled. Then Wendell drew a gun and aimed it at my head."

Hailey covered her mouth. "Parker. No."

His eyes became distant. "I thought I was a dead man. But Ben came from out of nowhere and pulled him away. Slammed him against a brick wall. His head cracked." A vessel in Parker's neck pulsated. "Somehow, Hautz had enough strength to lurch forward and fire his gun. The first shot went astray, but then Hautz pointed the firearm straight at me. Ben knocked it out of his hand and charged at him, ramming Hautz against the wall...over and over...for God knows how long, until I dragged him off. By the time backup arrived, Hautz was unconscious." Parker unclenched his fists. "The paramedics took Hautz to the hospital, but he was already gone. His brain was pulverized. He was in a coma for a day before he died."

"Oh my God, Parker! The man could have killed you."

"I had some bad bruises. The lowlife deserved to die. He'd been dealing drugs for years. Every time he went to prison, he'd serve a few months and get out. Who knows how many lives he ruined selling drugs."

Hailey squeezed his hand. "How is this related to you losing your job?"

"Turns out, Hautz had some politically influential relatives. They wanted someone to pay for his death."

She tilted her head. "But it was self-defense."

"Didn't matter. His family wanted revenge. They said I had it out for him."

"But Ben was the one who killed him."

"We both wanted him dead. The scum was lower than rat shit."

"Surely the body cams—"

"Hautz ripped off my camera in the attack." Parker scratched his head. "Just as well no one saw what happened. The chief put us on administrative leave while he examined the case. It was all over the news."

"What about Ben's camera?"

"In the commotion, Ben forgot to turn his on. He was new. You know how nervous rookies get when they start this type of work."

Hailey nodded. Her first few cases with the SCA were prime examples. "Did they reinstate you once you explained what happened?"

"No." His jaw tensed. "And that's the way it has to be."

"What do you mean, 'the way it has to be'? You lost your job." She gasped when he lowered his gaze. "Oh, Parker. You didn't. You *wanted* to take the blame for killing him?"

"Ben was going through a rough time. His mother was battling cancer, and he was financially supporting the family." Parker paced the floor, pausing as he repositioned the framed photo of Justin. "His career was only beginning. If the chief had kept digging, he would have figured out Ben despised Hautz as much as I did. The boy didn't need a mark on his record. It was easier if I admitted I had lost control."

"You ruined your career for him."

"Ben was there when Justin was dying. He practically lived at the hospital with Grace when I was tracking down Euphoria. I owed him."

"What did Ben say?"

"He was against it until I convinced him he could honor Justin's memory by continuing his career, arresting other scumbags like Wendell Hautz."

In her heart, Hailey had to agree. Justin deserved to have something positive come from his death.

"So you quit the force?"

"I took some time off. Wandered around for a while. Drank a little too much, feeling sorry for myself. I was living, but not really living. You know how it is."

She had felt that way the last seven months.

"One day I was hungover, drinking a six-pack in bed, and Stefan called. He asked if I'd come back to the agency."

"Did you tell him about Hautz?"

Parker sat beside her. "He already knew. Word had gotten around about the investigation. Stefan guessed I was covering for Ben. He thought I'd appreciate a new start and some income." Parker rubbed a hand against his whiskers. "And that's how I ended up here. I'm not sorry for what I did, but I want you to know. If you and I are going to have a chance, I want us to be honest."

"Thank you. It means a lot." She leaned over and kissed him.

"I don't want pity."

"I'm not pitying you. I admire you—not just for going after Wendell Hautz, but for protecting Ben."

His mouth curved upward in a coy smile. "Where do you suggest we go from here?"

Hailey covered a yawn. The clock on the DVD player read 4:30 AM. "I'd like to see where life takes us—but we need to go slow. Can you hold me tonight? I want to lie in your arms and feel you next to me."

Parker leaned back against the sofa and drew her against him, covering them both with the blanket. "I think I can manage that." He nestled against her neck. "How do you expect me to get any sleep tonight?"

When was the last time she felt happy? "We're not getting any younger. I bet you won't have any problem sleeping." She curved her head, and he kissed her.

He stroked a finger under her lips. "We'll see."

****

Parker's soft snores disturbed the silence of the night. They had talked into the morning hours before drifting off. Goosebumps ran along Hailey's arms at the memory of Parker kissing and holding her like a delicate toy. Now reality was setting in.

His strong arms tightened around her, and she breathed in his woodsy scent. Mark had a mossy scent. Hailey closed her eyes. What was she doing here? She wasn't over her husband. Even if Colleen's remark was true, she wasn't ready to start a relationship. Not when she felt like she was cheating on Mark.

Mark's dead.

She still missed him. Would there ever be a time she didn't? Was she pushing herself too fast? Hailey gazed at Parker. She had made a mess of her life. He didn't deserve to be hurt.

With careful effort, she rolled under his arm and slid off the sofa. In the kitchen, she rummaged through a desk drawer and found a pen and paper. She sat at the table and started writing.

Parker,

Tonight was wonderful. It's been a long time since I've felt this type of closeness. I thought I was ready to move on, but I'm not. Not yet. My heart is torn between loving Mark and allowing myself to love you. Our pasts go deep, and sometimes I think you know me better than I know myself. I'm gambling you'll understand I need to find closure with Mark's death. Though Mark hurt me, I'm not ready to give you my heart. I appreciate your honesty tonight. I need to give you the same courtesy if we are ever going to move ahead in a relationship.

Love, Hailey

She folded the paper and laid it on the table.

As Hailey crept past the living room toward the entrance, she collected the damp clothes tossed on the floor and slipped on her shoes.

Parker's clothes felt unsuitable on her now. He deserved more, but she couldn't give him more—not yet.

With a heavy heart, she clutched her purse, blew a kiss, and hurried to the car.

Chapter Thirty

"Mom?" Anna tapped on Hailey's bedroom door. "The delivery guy brought flowers again. Do you want the card?"

Hailey stationed herself next to the window and waited as the florist's van backed down the driveway.

Parker had sent the flowers.

She knew without even opening the envelope. Probably another dozen roses to match the two dozen he sent yesterday. For two days, he had been flooding her with flowers, texts, and voicemails.

She picked up a photo from the dresser. The family picture taken at the beach two years earlier was one of her favorites. Sadness stirred inside her. She didn't want flowers from Parker. Roses were for Mark to give.

Saturday morning, she had returned home ready to crash, but too many issues weighed on her mind. The mysterious pill she had found three days earlier baffled her, and Bruce still hadn't called with the results. She had left a message with the realty company and asked Zoe Dixon to return her call. Then there was Parker's kiss, and his revelation about losing his job.

Justin's death had affected Parker in ways Hailey hadn't considered. Parker had always been the strong one. Determined. In control. And yes, selfish. Learning he had given up his career for Justin's best friend, well, that was too much.

Parker had changed—for the better—and it attracted her. But this tender side also scared her. Should she let their relationship blossom or cut it off now? Was it worth the risk to love again? Her heart might not recover. Hailey clutched her head to keep it from spinning.

"Mom? Are you sleeping?"

Hailey swept a brush through her hair and faked a yawn as she opened the door. "Sorry, honey. I must have fallen asleep."

Anna handed her a small envelope and eyed her suspiciously. "Did you and Parker have a fight?"

When had her daughter become so perceptive? Hailey opened the card.

Please. Don't shut me out.

She could hear the desperation in his voice.

"No, we didn't have a fight. I told Parker I wanted to spend more time with you and Ethan." She laid the note on her dresser. "Did you recover yet from your sleepover?"

Anna reddened. "Mom, it's been two days. I'm fine. No one's supposed to sleep on sleepovers."

Despite promising to go to bed early at Samantha's house, Anna had come home Saturday at noon and crashed on the sofa.

Unable to sleep before, between the florist deliveries and phone calls, Hailey had curled up beside Anna and slept, too.

By the time they woke and ate dinner, it was late. They had made popcorn, snuggled together in their pajamas, and watched a comedy on TV.

The deadline for grading finals nagged at her conscience, but Anna was little for only a short time. "I have an idea. Let's get a manicure before Ethan comes home. We haven't done that for ages. The mall opens at ten on Sundays."

"No, it's okay." Anna shifted her hands in her pocket.

"Come on. It'll be fun. What colors do you want this time—" Hailey stopped as her daughter lowered her head. "What's wrong?"

Anna held up a hand, revealing her bitten-down fingernails.

"Honey, why are you biting your nails?"

"I don't know." Anna's voice came out as a squeak.

Please don't let her be like me. Hailey had been a few years older than Anna when she obsessively scratched her skin until it bled. Could Anna be experiencing some type of anxiety? "Tell me what's wrong." She guided her daughter to the bed and brushed back the wisps of hair covering Anna's face. "Are you upset because of Dad?"

Anna bit her lip. "What will happen if you leave me too?"

"Oh, honey. I'm not going anywhere."

"But sometimes parents can't help it." Anna wrapped her arms around Hailey.

"What happened to Daddy was different. I'm working at the college, and it's safe there."

Anna buried her face in Hailey's chest. "Why do bad things happen to good people?"

"I don't know." Hailey held Anna, pained she hadn't concentrated more on Ethan and Anna's well-being. "Since we can't do a manicure, let's get our toes done. Pedicures are just as much fun."

****

When Hailey pulled into the driveway, she couldn't remember having a better outing with Anna. After the pedicure, they spent the day shopping, browsing around a pet shop, and eating lunch at the mall.

Anna seemed happier, acting more relaxed as she claimed her purchases from the trunk.

On the way to the porch, Hailey mused over the orange-and-blue colors swirled on her toenails. "That woman was the most creative nail technician I've ever seen. I've never had tie-dye nails before."

Anna looked down at her flip-flops and wiggled her toes. "I like how she gave us matching rhinestones on our big toes." Her freckles danced in the sunlight as a wide smile revealed her braces. "Thanks for spending the day with me, Mom."

Hailey gestured at the porch rocker. "Want to hang out here for a while?"

Anna frowned. "I'd better finish my homework first. When I'm done, do you want to draw? Rose has been teaching Sam and me how to draw people. She draws better than we do."

"Sounds like fun. Bring your drawing stuff outside when you're ready." Hailey fished the keys from her purse.

Anna stooped over and plucked the spare key from the brick receptacle. "I got it." She planted her hand on the knob, and the door opened. She gaped at the key still in her hand and replaced it in the hiding spot. "Didn't you lock the door, Mom?"

Twice in one week? She mentally smacked her forehead. "I guess I forgot." Surely, she hadn't overlooked locking the door again. Was someone breaking into the house?

Hailey peered through the foyer. From outside on the porch, the place looked fine, but she'd better inspect it. She spun and browsed in her purse, handing Anna the car key. "Can you check in the car for my wallet? It must have dropped out of my purse."

Anna seemed oblivious to Hailey's motives.

While her daughter meandered back to the car, Hailey rushed through the living room, study, and kitchen. At a glance, everything was in place. Panic followed her as she hurried upstairs and inspected the rooms. She should hide her gun behind the nightstand drawer in case she needed it at night.

A few moments later, Anna stepped into the bedroom and gave back the car key. "I couldn't find your wallet."

"Thanks for looking. I'll check my purse again."

Satisfied nothing seemed amiss, Hailey stepped into the hallway. The musky cologne scent was there again.

Anna placed a hand on her hips. "Mom, are you feeling okay?"

"I'm fine."

"If you say so." Anna stepped down the hall. "I'll be in my room. Let me know when Ethan comes home. I can't wait to hear if he got seasick."

Straightaway, Hailey marched out to the porch and loosened the brick. Maybe she was being paranoid, but she didn't trust hiding the house key there anymore.

Santino's truck came up the driveway as she retrieved the key.

Ethan opened the passenger door. "Hi, Mom."

He'd only been away two days, but he seemed taller, older. Even his voice sounded deeper.

Jake tagged behind as Ethan dropped his duffel bag on the porch.

She grabbed a quick hug from Ethan; a strong whiff of sweat assaulted her nostrils. "How was the trip?"

"Good. Do we have anything to eat? We're starved!" He hurried into the house with Jake.

Hailey held back a grin and waved at the brawny tatted man trudging behind the boys. "I guess the boys didn't eat much fish?"

Santino flashed a brilliant smile that balanced his rugged appearance and three-day beard.

"Ethan wouldn't eat anything we reeled in." He stepped to the porch step and tucked his wrinkled shirt in his jeans. "Never saw a boy who didn't like flounder and sea bass. The boys wiped me out of snacks the first evening."

"I should have warned you Ethan's a picky eater."

He pointed to the brick on the porch floor. "Have a loose brick?"

"No." Hailey inserted the brick back in the hole. "I'm moving the spare key. When I came home earlier, the door was unlocked. I'm not taking any chances."

"Unlocked? Are you sure?"

"Anna thinks I forgot to lock up, so I can't be certain." She thumbed the key. "I've been really forgetful lately, but this is the second time in a week I've found the door unlocked."

"Did you call the police?"

"No. I'm not positive anyone broke in. Nothing looked out of place."

"Do you want me to check?"

She warmed at his concern. "Thank you, but I'm being overly suspicious. What do I have that someone would steal?"

He scratched a hand against his whiskers. "Is it possible your husband was hiding something?"

"What do you mean?"

"Mark worked a dangerous job. Would he have hidden something?"

"He kept everything at the office." *Except a Hawaii brochure.*

"You have to be careful, Hailey."

He sounded like Parker.

"I will." She pointed inside. "Can I make you a sandwich?" When he hesitated, she persisted. "It's the least I can do since you fed Ethan this weekend."

"I don't want to impose…in case your police friend comes."

"Parker?" So that was his concern. Hailey shook her head. "He isn't coming around anymore."

"I'm sorry." The corner of his mouth curved.

How easy it was to read Santino's thoughts.

"Okay, but I can't stay long. I still have to unload the fish from the coolers."

She led him to the kitchen.

Ethan had stacked three peanut butter and jelly sandwiches on a tray and was pouring milk into glasses.

Jake balanced a bag of chocolate chip cookies on his plate. "We'll be upstairs playing *Random Quest.*"

"You have ten minutes." Santino covered a yawn and pulled out a seat at the table.

When the boys departed, she laid a paper plate in front of Santino. "Did you get any sleep this weekend?"

He exhaled. "Not too much. Friday night it rained so we kept the boat docked until Saturday morning. Last night, I kept lookout while the boys slept, but I dozed for three hours before we weighed anchor today."

"I hope you can sleep when you get home." Hailey placed a generous spread of rolls, lunchmeat, and condiments on the table. "Do you want some coffee?"

Santino stacked cold cuts on a roll. "Hot coffee if you have it, thanks."

Hailey poured two cups of coffee and sat across from him.

He squirted mustard on the roll. "Aren't you eating?"

"Anna and I ate lunch earlier."

He sank his teeth into the sandwich. "Are you and your officer friend over for good?"

The sound of hope in his voice was unmistakable. She shouldn't lead him on. Hailey sipped her coffee, uncertain where to begin. "I told him I'm not ready to see anyone."

"When Janet took off, it took a while before I felt like dating."

She fidgeted with her hands. "I'm having a hard time accepting Mark's death. I know his work was dangerous, but I can't get over him dying in that horrible fire."

"That's the type of job your husband worked. My wife's work was dangerous, too. I fought with her all the time about quitting."

"You did?"

Santino nodded and sipped his coffee. "You wouldn't think a nursing job would be hazardous—

other than catching diseases. Janet used to come home and tell me wild stories about her patients. She was a traveling nurse. The agency sent her everywhere. She filled in at hospitals, nursing homes, prisons, rehab clinics—anywhere." He took a gulp and wiped his mouth with the back of his hand. "Some nights she'd come home, shaken up because a gang member had shot a round of ammo in the ER, or she'd come home with bruises on her face from a drunk throwing punches."

"Did you worry about her?"

"Hell, yeah. But I had to let go. Trust me. You can't beat yourself up thinking you should've done something differently."

She patted her heart. "I still miss Mark."

The lines on his forehead softened. "I can tell. Give it time. There's no rush."

"Time is about the only thing I have left."

"You're too hard on yourself. You have two great kids." Santino finished eating. "Ethan's a hard worker. He's been a positive influence on Jake."

She finished her coffee. "Thanks. You've done a good job with Jake, too."

"That was his mother's doing. He was ten when I married Janet."

Santino still seemed fond of his ex-wife. Would Hailey forgive Mark so readily if she learned Colleen had spoken the truth? "Did Janet give any indication she was having an affair?"

He frowned. "No. She was real clever at keeping secrets."

Hailey understood the pain in his voice. Mark kept secrets, too.

Jake and Ethan shuffled into the kitchen, carrying their empty plates. Ethan grabbed a bag of potato chips from the pantry. "Can Jake stay a little longer?"

Santino tousled Ethan's hair. "Some other time, son. We have to drop off the fishing gear and unpack the cooler. Monday morning comes fast."

Hailey walked them to the door. "Thanks again for taking Ethan. He'll talk about this trip for weeks."

"My pleasure. Next time, you and Anna can join us."

When Santino and Jake left, Anna came downstairs with her backpack, wrinkling her nose. "Ew, Ethan, you smell like fish."

Hailey grinned at Anna's sarcastic laugh, enjoying her daughter's payback for the times Ethan had teased her.

Ethan's eyes sparkled as he gave details of baiting hooks, casting the line into the water, and reeling in fish. "You wouldn't believe how many fish we caught."

Anna slumped backward on the sofa. "I wish I could've gone."

Hailey wrapped her arm around Anna's shoulders. "Santino invited us to come next time." The invite was growing on Hailey. As long as Santino understood this would be a platonic outing. "I imagine Santino could use an extra set of eyes when everyone's sleeping."

Ethan scratched his head. "That was the strangest thing about the trip."

"What?"

"I heard voices last night when I woke up in the cabin. Speaking Spanish. In the middle of the ocean."

Hailey rubbed her cheek. "Was someone else on the boat?"

"No."

"Was it Jake?"

"No. He was sleeping next to me in the cabin."

"Did you ask Santino about it?"

"I asked him this morning. He said he was watching a movie to stay awake."

Anna's eyes narrowed. "Why would he watch a Spanish movie?"

Ethan shrugged. "Santino used to live in Puerto Rico."

"Does he talk to you in Spanish?"

Ethan shook his head. "No, but sometimes he yells at Jake in Spanish."

"Can you understand what he's saying? I bet he uses swear words." Anna chuckled.

Ethan propped his feet on the coffee table. "All I know from Spanish is how to count to ten and conjugate verbs."

Hailey tousled his hair. "You probably should study harder." She tapped her chin. Watching a Spanish movie at night in the Atlantic Ocean? Ethan was right. It did seem strange.

Chapter Thirty-One

The alarm sounded like a chainsaw buzzing.

Manuel woke from a deep sleep and slapped the snooze button. 5 PM. He burrowed farther under the threadbare bedspread and plumped the flattened pillow.

The motel room lacked the luxuries he was accustomed to when he traveled, and it had a claustrophobic feel. It barely fit a double bed.

He'd flown into Canada two days earlier, deciding it was easier to enter the U.S. from the north. He shaved his head and kept a beard, matching the photo on one of his fake passports. When the border service officer detained him an hour for questioning, Manuel remained composed, confident no one would discover his real identity.

Security into New York was even tighter. A comrade from Toronto, who partnered with him on his first Canadian drug deal, provided Manuel with a flashy disguise of a music manager and papers that convinced border patrol the pair was traveling on essential business. When Manuel conversed in both French and English, the border guard didn't blink twice. The hours he had spent learning to speak English without a dialect was worth it to outwit the guard.

Once they were west of New York City, the Canadian cohort leased a car for Manuel and headed back to Toronto.

Traveling alone at night, Manuel stayed vigilant. No doubt his name and picture had spread all over INTERPOL. The bastards would climb over each other to apprehend him, and if they succeeded, he'd never see his daughter or his homeland again.

As he drove around the District, he saw new roadways and housing developments under construction. It was foolish to expect everything would look the same. What had become of his mansion after the government repossessed it? He had made love to Bella in the California king bed many nights. Had time changed how she felt about him?

The time he spent in the States felt like three lifetimes ago. He missed taking Bella to shows and concerts around the city. Spending time with the woman he loved was…damn, what was the word he wanted…*estimulante*. Bella had changed his life.

Her research enabled him to continue Euphoria's production. The Euphoria he smuggled with his shipments would someday be as profitable as cocaine. Border Patrol might have slowed the influx of drugs at the border in Mexico and Florida, but they weren't able to stop the eastern coastline trade. Drugs flowed in like water seeping from a cupped palm.

When Manuel flew from Colombia, he notified his U.S. connection. The contact booked a hotel south of Washington, D.C. At a rest stop along the interstate, Manuel texted his ETA. If he didn't hit traffic, he'd have time to nap before the man arrived.

The alarm beeped again.

Manuel rubbed his neck and headed to the bathroom. He blinked at the stranger in the mirror. God, he looked rough. The beard itched and irritated his skin.

It would take time to adjust to his new look, but the shaved head and dark plastic-framed glasses would prove useful in helping him remain incognito while he continued activities in the States. The road to get here had been treacherous. He removed his ear clip and red silk shirt, and he wrinkled his nose. He needed another shower. His Canadian friend's cheap cologne and pungent cigar smoke fused with the sweat on Manuel's skin.

He turned on the faucet and stepped back as a roach scurried across the mildew-stained shower pan. What a shithole. A different vibe from the room he would have reserved. He unwrapped the bar of cedar soap and lathered his hair, letting the stream of hot water splash over him.

The last argument with his father played in a continuous loop in his head. Why did he still seek Papà's love? The man was incapable of loving.

Manuel leaned against the shower wall. Would he really inherit his grandfather's estate? If what Mamà said was true, he could afford to hire the best nannies. He would have to shield Katia from José, but Mamà would help take care of her.

Would Katia ask about Bella? *Bella.* The name still tasted like sweet wine on his lips. But poison tasted good, too. Did Bella still have the sparkle in her eye? Was she still alluring or did prison harden her? He frowned. Damaged goods might not be worth trying to refurbish.

He toweled dry and dressed in casual slacks and a polo. As Manuel scratched his long, bushy beard, he studied his reflection. The disguise was holding up well.

He passed time watching TV. As dusk settled across town, he checked his phone. It was growing late. The man had better not double-cross him. Manuel had invested too much money into this search to come home empty-handed. He lifted a rolled shirt from his suitcase and unwrapped the gun his Toronto cohort had smuggled across the border.

A soft tap drummed a rhythmic pattern at the door.

Clutching the gun, Manuel checked the peephole and cracked open the door. His contact hadn't mentioned a partner.

"Yes?"

"Butterfly."

Manuel opened the door to two men. The older one, dressed in faded jeans and a ball cap, looked around Manuel's age. Muscles bulged beneath the man's sleeves, and his tanned arms were marked with tattoos. He had the weathered body of a hard laborer.

This man must be the contact. From the texts, Santino Ruiz was a resourceful man, but he'd probably had his share of run-ins with the law.

Standing beside Ruiz was a younger man, no more than twenty-five. He was rough-looking, with gauges in his ears and eyebrow piercings, and smelled of a strong musky cologne.

Manuel blocked his arm across the opening. "I told you to come alone."

Ruiz waved away the comment. "He's harmless. He helped distribute a shipment."

Manuel glared and lowered his arm. "Next time, follow my instructions."

The younger man carried in two plastic grocery bags and tossed them onto the desk.

Manuel closed the door and shoved the gun in his pants. "Were you followed?"

"No." Santino peered out the window blinds, and turning, he extended his hand. "We finally meet. Santino Ruiz."

He shook Ruiz's hand. At least the man was respectful. Manuel would hold judgement on the other guy. "You're late."

Santino removed his cap and glanced around the room. "Couldn't help it. I was on the boat last night, picking up the delivery. I had to make a stop this afternoon before I unloaded it."

The narco sub. How could he have forgotten? "Did the men have any trouble?"

"No. The Coast Guard patrolled the waters, but our system is working well. The shipments are easier to deliver at night. Your men were gone in no time. The hidden compartments in the cooler work perfectly."

At least one burden was lifted. Manuel switched his attention to the delinquent with dilated pupils and bloodshot eyes standing next to Santino. Cocaine eyes. What was Santino thinking, hooking up with an addict? "Who's he?"

"Name's Chase." The punk pulled out a vaping device from his pocket and inhaled.

Santino grabbed it from Chase's hand. "He's been helping with the case."

"Looks like he helped himself to some of the product. Make sure you deduct it when you give him a share of your payment." Manuel glowered, but the kid didn't seem to care—or notice. He turned to Santino. "I didn't tell you to involve a punk. Now tell me about my daughter."

"There's nothing new to report."

"That's not the answer I wanted to hear." He considered Ruiz. Was the man a yes-man or did Santino know a lot more than he had led Manuel to believe? "I want to know how you found out about my daughter."

Santino sat on the sofa. "My ex-wife was your girlfriend's nurse during the delivery. Janet spent eight hours holding her hand, getting her through labor. Colleen told my ex all about you and how she ended up in prison."

Manuel raised an eyebrow. "But apparently not everything, or you'd know where my daughter is."

"Colleen begged Janet to contact Mark Langley when the baby was born. She gave Janet his info and said he'd know what to do."

"Mark Langley? The DTA agent?"

Ruiz nodded. "Do you know him?"

"We met. His wife is a government agent, too. Did your ex call him?"

"That night."

"Did you question Langley?"

"Yes, but he died in a fire before we got any info."

"He's the one you roughed up and killed? Why didn't you tell me it was him?" Manuel massaged his neck. "Dammit! The whole DTA is probably searching for you."

Ruiz seemed confident. "No one knows what happened, not even his wife."

"Someone has to know where Katia is staying." Manuel paced the carpet. "Where would Langley have hidden her?"

"Chase broke into Langley's house a few times, but he hasn't found any leads." Ruiz fidgeted with his cap.

"He hacked into West Virginia's juvenile database, but the files are sealed."

"You were foolish to kill Langley before you got the info." Manuel scoffed. "Maybe you're looking in the wrong place. What if the girl's not even in foster care? Bella could have given her to a friend."

Santino nodded. "Or relative."

"Her father died six years ago. She had no other family." A pang of regret haunted Manuel for deserting Colleen during her saddest time. "Who are her friends?"

Chase snickered. "It's lit you banged her and don't know anything about her."

Manuel shoved him. "Why don't you shut the fuck up?"

Chase backed away, raising his hands. "Okay, dude. Don't pop a button."

Santino stepped between them. "He's only a boy. He has some issues going on."

"The punk doesn't know respect. You shut him up or I will." Manuel resisted shooting the dumbass right there. "What about private investigators? Assign one of them to dig up her friends. Get old addresses."

Santino shook his head. "The PIs contacted her high school friends, but Colleen hasn't kept in contact with them. Now they're checking the faculty and roommates from the University of Maryland, too. So far, no one remembers what happened to her."

"Try Harvard, too. She transferred there her sophomore year."

"They'll hunt down those contacts next."

Manuel scratched his neck. "Give me all the information you have on Langley's widow. Who she hangs out with. Where she goes. What she does in her free time."

"I'll do it now." Santino reached for the tablet on the desk.

"Can you hack into Maryland's juvenile records? Maybe custody records were filed when Bella was transferred there. Find out her release date." Manuel tilted his head at Chase. "Put him on it since he knows computers."

"We'll get on it." Santino pointed to the bags. "We brought food. Figured you'd be hungry."

"Thank you." Manuel opened the bag and took out a sub and water bottle. He'd leave the chips and beef jerky for later.

Santino laid down the pen and handed over Hailey's schedule. Manuel slipped the paper in his pocket. "I'll find a way to get her to talk."

Chase chuckled. "Not if she don't know anything. Besides, the fuckin' Parker cop is constantly with her."

In an instant, Manuel pressed the gun on Chase's temple. "You listen here, you piece of shit. Why don't you try passing seventh grade English before you shoot fucking comments out your mouth." Satisfied when the blood drained from Chase's face, Manuel lowered the gun. "Now get the hell out of here before I have some target practice."

Chase tripped as he scrambled to the door.

Santino donned his cap. "I'll be in touch."

Manuel pointed the gun at Santino. "I expect results. I've paid you over half a mil, and all you have to show for it is a dead DTA agent. If you can't come up with info on my daughter soon, you and your buddy are going to wish you had died in that fire."

279

When they left, Manuel sat on the bed and finished his sandwich. He was within an hour's drive from Bella, but traveling to the prison would be reckless. Dammit! How could Santino and the PIs come up empty-handed?

A text pinged, and Manuel checked his phone.

Santino had sent a message. *—Toole Release 20 days—*

An image of Bella in her prison uniform holding their bundled baby floated through his mind. When he found Katia, Bella could come along, too, but Manuel didn't need her. He'd have his prize.

He tugged Hailey Langley's schedule from his pocket. She had to know something. One way or another, he'd get the *puta* to talk.

Chapter Thirty-Two

Hailey sat at the kitchen table, pouring honey into her tea as she read the dean's email on her cell phone.

Faculty Reminder—Grades for the spring semester need to be submitted by 3:00 PM today.

She groaned. If she hadn't forgotten to pack the finals in her tote bag Friday when she and Parker visited Colleen, she wouldn't be behind.

Lowering the phone into her purse, Hailey took out the anti-anxiety pills. She hadn't taken any since Friday. She'd prove to Parker that she didn't need them.

The phone rang.

Parker. She massaged her temples. *Third time this morning. I can't talk. Not yet.*

She was packing a light snack when the phone vibrated again. *True Living Realty* flashed on the screen. Hailey picked up. "Hello?"

"This is Zoe Dixon from *True Living Realty*. Is Hailey Langley there? I'm returning her call."

"This is Hailey. Thank you for calling me back."

"Sure. What can I do for you?"

"Seven months ago, I believe you were helping my husband Mark look for houses in Hawaii."

"Yes, I remember. I'm glad he finally told you. He said no one was to know."

Hailey blinked. The realtor hadn't read about Mark's death in the newspaper? She could wing it.

"He's a sweetie, but he can't keep a secret. Mark tells me all my birthday and anniversary gifts before the day comes."

Zoe laughed. "Lucky you. So how can I help you?"

"Mark's been busy with work, so he asked me to contact you to resume the search."

"Sure thing. Does he still want a place in Kauai?"

"We think so. What kind of criteria did he give you?"

"He wanted something small and remote, which is easier to find in Kauai than the other islands. Let me look up my notes." Hailey waited as the agent clicked on the keyboard. "We don't get many requests to find homes in Hawaii. Mark was very specific about his requirements...Ah, here it is. He wanted something small for two people. A one bathroom, one- to two-bedroom place. Secluded. He stressed secluded. Is this still what you want?"

"Yes, it's fine." If only they had gone on vacation before he died. "I forget what Mark said about the plane tickets."

"We're a realty company, not a travel agency. We handle home sales and rentals. You would have to buy the airfare yourself. When do you plan to move?"

"Move?"

"Well, yes. He gave the impression he needed the place late spring."

"Are you sure he wasn't looking for a vacation rental?"

"Yes, ma'am. Mark wanted to buy, not rent. I had a few houses lined up to show him, but he never called back. I can start researching availabilities again on the MLS and have a list ready in a few days."

Hailey picked up the bottle of anti-anxiety medication. She could use a couple pills. "Let me check and get back to you. We might want something bigger."

"Sure thing. You have my number when you're ready."

When the call ended, Hailey fell back in her chair.

They would need more than two bedrooms in Hawaii. How could they pick up and leave Virginia? She and Mark had jobs here. His parents lived nearby.

What exactly had Colleen said about Hawaii? *"I was going to Kauai. Not you."* Would Mark really leave her for Colleen? *"We became close again…"*

Hailey collected the tote bag.

On the counter, a petal had fallen from one of the roses Parker sent. Her finger lingered over the soft petal. Roses were only special when they came from Mark. A connection like theirs didn't just go away. Whatever Mark was doing, he wouldn't leave her and the kids.

What case was Mark working on before he died?

He'd been masterful at keeping work at the office.

Who would know? Owen would never share top-secret information. Stefan already said Mark's cases were off-limits. Parker might be able to—

She scraped a fingernail across her hand. It was wrong to use him to get information. Maybe David could dig around.

****

Hailey parked her car in the faculty lot next to the Life Sciences building. The once-lively campus was empty. Like her soul.

When the automatic glass door opened, she stepped inside the building and walked toward the elevator. The spring semester was finally over. The year had been the worst in her life, but she had grappled through it.

The immunology teacher with a long braid stopped chatting with a secretary from the biology department, and he nodded.

Guess I'm not the only one still finishing work.

Upstairs, dimmed lights and a soft hush of empty halls welcomed her. She unlocked the office door and flipped the light switch.

Liz's desk was bare, with all pens neatly in a pencil holder. *Liz probably submitted her grades before the weekend.*

Hailey dropped the tote bag on her desk and pulled out Zhang's graduation card. He messaged earlier he'd swing by within the hour. She was eager to show him the favorable student comments on the course surveys.

She switched on the computer and settled in her chair, grabbing a stack of ungraded Biology II finals. An hour passed, and Zhang texted.

—My landlord still hasn't come to inspect my apartment. He has my security deposit.—

Satisfied money was the perfect gift, she texted back. *—Don't worry. I'll be here for at least another hour.—*

As she entered the last student's grade in the computer and hit the submit button, her cell rang. Relief settled in her when she read Bruce's name on the screen. For reasons she couldn't explain, she felt better after speaking with him. "Hi, Bruce."

"Hailey. I've been meanin' to call you sooner, but I keep getting sidetracked with research."

She considered the piles of graded exams on her desk. "I know the feeling. Did you get the pill I sent?"

"Sure did. It's Euphoria."

She blinked. "Wait, what?"

"Euphoria. Where did you say you found the pill?"

"By Ethan's bedroom."

"How did Euphoria get into your house?"

Hailey shook her head. "I don't have a clue. Are you sure it's Euphoria?"

"Positive." He coughed. "This isn't good, Hailey. You know what happened last time Euphoria was on the streets."

"Was it made from the plant or synthetically?"

"I haven't had time to research it yet."

"Thanks for letting me know. By the way, how's your shrub doing?"

"Not good. The leaves are spotted and brown. Some of them have started dropping."

Hailey frowned. "Have you checked for fungus?"

"Yes. And for mites and insects. I can't explain it."

If the decision were up to her, she'd say good riddance. "Are the roots rotted?"

"Part of the root ball was slimy. I trimmed the roots and replanted the bush in new soil. It will take years until I harvest a bush large enough to do meaningful research. I wish I had studied the flowers earlier."

"Did you hear back from the shaman?"

"No, but I contacted a curator from Peru who knows a shaman. I'm waiting for more information."

"Would you actually fly to Peru?"

"I would if a shaman can help me save *Bixa aparra.*"

The more he talked, the stronger the connection she sensed between Bruce and the plant. What was it about Euphoria he couldn't let go?

She glanced at her desk. So much for tidying her office. "I should go. If I think of any ideas, I'll let you know."

"I appreciate it." A timer beeped as Bruce spoke. "Can you let Stefan know about Euphoria? He should know it's back in circulation."

"I will." Hailey slipped the phone in her purse.

Please don't let the pill belong to Ethan.

The memory of standing at Justin's grave made her quiver. She couldn't go through another child dying. She'd have a long talk with Ethan. If the pill belonged to Jake, she'd tell Santino. Where were kids getting these drugs?

Ethan said Santino was speaking Spanish on the boat. *I wonder...*

Hailey shook her head. She was being ridiculous. Santino wasn't trafficking drugs. He had family in Puerto Rico. Of course, he spoke Spanish. She checked her email and became absorbed in reading directives about the summer sessions she'd be teaching.

As Hailey typed a question to the department head, the door squeaked. She kept her attention on the screen and continued typing. "Zhang, give me a minute to finish this email. Did you get your deposit back?"

When he didn't respond, Hailey raised her head and jumped.

Manuel de Mendoza stood in the doorway, his intimidating dark black eyes centered on her.

He looked different with a shaved head and beard, but she'd recognize his weather-beaten face anywhere. His icy stare chilled her with fear.

He wasn't holding a weapon, but his posture was like a poisonous snake poised to strike.

Think, Hailey. Think.

She clutched the red pen on top of the finals. If she pushed hard enough, she could jam it in his eye. Or jugular.

"What do you want?" Her voice came out as a high-pitched squeak.

Manuel closed the door. "You need better security around this place."

She swallowed hard. "You need to leave."

He strode closer, stopping at the rolling cart near the left corner of the desk.

Hailey pushed the chair and stood behind it, pointing the pen at him. "Don't come any closer."

Mendoza reached across the desk and grabbed at the pen.

She moved it from his reach.

Gnashing his teeth, he stepped around the desk. "I didn't come here to hurt you."

"Then leave before I call security." With her free hand, she slid the chair between her and the desk. Clamping her hand around the back of the seat, she used the chair as a shield and steered to the front of the room.

With a smirk, he backtracked three steps, and paralleled her movements, keeping a yard between them. From his pocket, he withdrew a long switchblade. "Sit down. We need to talk. I didn't come here to hurt you."

Eyeing the knife, she tightened her grip on the pen. The door was ten feet away. If she could beat him to the hall, she'd outrun him.

Hailey sidestepped right, inching toward the door. "Then why did you bring a knife?"

"Sit down."

She surveyed the door. Five feet away. *Get ready.*

As if he could read her mind, he lurched forward, blocking her path. "You have something I need."

"I *need* you to leave." She searched her memory. What would she have that belonged to him? The flash drive with the computer files? She didn't have it anymore.

The door was within reach.

Now!

She heaved the chair.

Mendoza lunged, aiming the knife at her chest.

She shoved the pen toward his eye.

Seizing the pen, he tossed it on the floor and attacked again, directing the blade at her abdomen.

With her right arm, she grabbed his elbow and spun behind him, blocking her shoulder against his neck as he twisted around. Keeping one hand on his wrist, she wrapped her arm under his weapon arm and applied pressure, immobilizing him.

He dropped the knife. As Hailey reached for it, Manuel kicked her legs, knocking her to the ground. He grabbed the knife and leaned forward, pressing it against her throat.

The cold blade stung when she swallowed.

He snickered. "*Puta.* I should have killed you six years ago."

"What do you want?"

"Where is she?"

"Who?" The knife pressed deeper. Was warm blood running down her throat?

Manuel yanked her hair. "Don't play dumb."

Her mind reeled. "I'm not—"

"*Hijueputa*! Where did your husband hide—"

The door creaked.

Hailey rotated her head toward the door.

Zhang stood in the hall. "Sorry, I'm late— Oh fuck." His eyes were as wide as a petri dish.

As Mendoza looked at Zhang, the blade's pressure against her neck eased. Hailey mustered all the breath she could. "Run!"

Zhang spun around, disappearing into the hallway. "Active shooter!"

Hailey twisted her torso and brought her foot against Mendoza's face, kicking him.

He slashed the knife across her arm as she wrenched free from his hold. He grabbed her hair and yanked her to the floor.

Blood ran down her arm as she elbowed him in the face.

He leapt to his feet, pulling her with him.

Hailey lifted her leg and kneed his groin.

Groaning, Mendoza buckled forward and plunged the knife in her chest.

Frozen, she stared as the pain shot through her like lightning.

For a moment, neither of them moved.

Her breathing grew labored, and her skin became cold and clammy. She stumbled, struggling for air as she fell. A buzzing resonated inside her head. Was he going to watch her die?

Fire alarms blared.

Mendoza wheeled around and disappeared.

The buzzing inside her head grew as loud as the fire alarm. Everything around her blurred and turned dark.

****

A hot sting throbbed through her chest. Pain gripped her in waves.

Voices shouted above her. "Hailey!"

Was that Parker? Her head pounded like a sledgehammer was clobbering it.

The commands continued in a string of fragmented words. "Stabbed. University. Crossmatch. Chest tube."

Gathering strength, she lifted her eyelids. Masked faces blurred with bright lights. What was happening? *Don't let me die. Please, God. I can't leave Anna and Ethan.*

"Transfer two more units of O neg."

She tried to decipher the orders, but the pain was overwhelming…

Chapter Thirty-Three

"You seem tense today." Kit eyed Mark as she finished his morning stretches. "Are you feeling okay?"

Mark nodded. "I'm fine. Just distracted." It was hard to focus on the exercises when Colleen's release monopolized his thoughts. Until she left town with her daughter, he'd worry.

"You're making remarkable progress. Keep up the good work." Kit helped him into a sitting position on his bed. "Faith called out sick today. Before I leave for my next appointment, I can make lunch, if you'd like. Brittany will be here this evening."

Mark stood and followed her into the kitchen. "That would be great. Thank you." The morning workout had been demanding and strenuous, but the results were worth it. He walked with a cane today. Never had he thought this day would come. Every step forward brought him closer to the day he'd reunite with Hailey.

Kit gestured to the chair. "Go ahead and rest."

Within minutes, the smell of grilled cheese filled the room.

Mark grabbed a napkin. "This is wonderful. Thank you."

She placed two sandwiches and a bowl of tomato soup on the table. "*Bon appetit!*"

Loneliness nipped at him. "Can you stay and eat?"

"Maybe another time." She picked up her sweater and travel bag. "I have a therapy session downtown in thirty minutes."

When she left, he powered on the TV. A soap opera he'd become hooked on was beginning. He was biting into the second sandwich when a local news reporter appeared on the screen.

We interrupt this show to report a stabbing incident at Greenway University in Fairfax.

Mark spit out his sandwich. Hailey's workplace.

One professor was seriously injured and taken to the hospital. The whereabouts of the attacker are not known at this time. A graduate student alerted university security of the attack. The incident prompted a lockdown on the campus. A spokesperson said semester classes had ended and no students were injured. Stay tuned as more information unfolds.

His skin turned cold. "Oh my God. It's Hailey."

Bolting from the chair, he rushed into the living room and picked up his phone on the end table. He fought to keep from heaving his lunch as his shaky hands pressed in David's number. *Please let her live.*

"Mark." David's voice was somber.

"I watched the news. It's Hailey, isn't it?"

"Calm down."

"Don't tell me to calm down." He kicked a hole in the drywall. "Was she the one attacked?"

"Yes, but—"

"Dammit! I need to be with her."

"You can't."

"Like hell I can't."

"Owen's already posted security at your door in case you try to leave."

"She's my wife!"

"I know that, but you're supposed to be dead. Owen won't jeopardize the plan."

A sick realization punched him. "You think Mendoza attacked her, don't you?"

"We don't know anything yet. The police are questioning the grad student."

Mark stifled a moan as he maintained some sense of control. Through the phone, a siren screeched in the background. "Where are you?"

"I'm in the hospital parking lot. I'll call as soon as I hear anything."

Mark brushed the sweat beading on his forehead and kicked his chair. *Dammit! This was not part of the plan.*

Chapter Thirty-Four

"Mom." A soft voice stirred Hailey into consciousness.

A ton of bricks pressed on Hailey's chest, suffocating her.

"Mom."

Anna? She struggled to overcome the weights sealing her eyelids. Finally, light penetrated the opening. Hailey blinked as blurry images came into focus. Ethan sat beside his sister, and Parker leaned against the bedrail beside him. With great effort, Hailey tried, but couldn't raise her arm.

"Mommy." Anna wiped the tears streaming down her face. "You're awake."

Monitors beeped beside Hailey. She was in the hospital. Her parched mouth felt like gritty sandpaper rubbing against her throat. "Hi." The word came out in a raspy whisper.

Ethan patted her arm. "Hi, Mom." She blinked twice. He looked so much like Mark. The kids were all she had left of him.

"Where…happen…what?" She swallowed and tried speaking, but her words were garbled.

"You were stabbed." Ethan's voice quavered.

Hailey coughed. The room swayed, and she held her head. Bile inched up her throat. Breathing was impossible.

Parker moved closer and adjusted the pillow. "Hailey, are you okay?"

She coughed again, an irritating bark. "My chest…I can't breathe."

The blood pressure monitor next to the bed shrilled.

Clutching the remote, Parker turned as a nurse ran into the room. "Get a doctor in here—now! She can't breathe."

Hailey fought for air as the nurse loomed over her and more staff dashed inside.

"Her blood pressure's dropping." Parker pointed and backed away.

"What are they doing to my mom?" Anna squealed.

"Let the doctor examine her." Parker rushed Anna and Ethan through the doorway. "Don't worry. Everything's going to be all right."

Hailey stretched out her hand. *Anna!* Her chest was expanding, but she was suffocating.

The doctor lowered the bed and opened her gown. His sputtered orders registered in fragments. "14 gauge needle. Decompression."

Hailey's mind receded into darkness again.

****

When Hailey woke, her entire chest felt like a hammer had mashed it. She blinked, trying to sort through muddled memories. Why couldn't she remember anything?

A chair screeched, and she turned her head.

Parker.

"Hey." His voice was a husky whisper. He held her hand, caressing a thumb over her fingers, and with his other hand, he brushed the damp hair from her forehead. "Welcome back."

As she breathed in, soreness spread across her right side. "Am I going to live?"

"God, I hope so." His eyes shone through the dimmed light. "You had complications with the chest tube the paramedics inserted. The doctor stabilized you."

Tension pneumothorax. She had read about it in a graduate class. It felt a lot worse than what the textbook described. "I'm so groggy."

"Shh. Try to rest." He continued to caress her hand. "Don't worry about the kids. They're okay. A counselor talked to them this afternoon, and David drove them home afterward. He'll bring them here tomorrow. I've been texting them updates."

She moved her shoulders and groaned at the pain shooting through her chest.

"Do you want me to get a nurse?" Parker started to rise.

"No...don't go."

Even after how she had treated him, he still cared for her. Deep down she had always felt something for him, too. She shouldn't have walked out on him the way she did. "I need...to talk to you."

"Okay..." His voice sounded tentative.

"It's about...the other night." Hailey blinked back tears, and when she coughed, her parched throat felt raw.

He swept a strand of hair off her cheek. "Shh. We can talk about it later."

"No, now." She struggled for the right words to form. "Sorry...I left..."

"You don't have to—"

"I was wrong…" Time was so short. Hadn't she learned that from Mark's death? "I don't want to waste…the time we have."

He wiped a tear from his cheek. "Neither do I."

She squinted at the wall clock. "What time is it?"

"A little after ten." He gazed at her. "You've had quite an eventful day."

She drew comfort in the tenderness of his eyes. "Can you…stay with me tonight?"

He gently kissed her hand. "I wouldn't be anywhere else."

****

Mark surfed the news channels, growing more agitated with each passing minute. The entire evening, he had listened to one TV station after another, gaining as much information as he could. Each reporter gave a brief report on the attack. 'Stabbing update' flashed on the bottom of the screen, and he increased the volume on his remote as a news reporter spoke.

…Professor Hailey Langley is in critical condition at Fairfax General Hospital. No information is known about the attacker at this time. Police are still searching for the man responsible for the attack.

Mark chucked the remote on the sofa. "This is bullshit!"

Awkwardly, he paced the floor. He had grumbled at Brittany tonight and sent her home. The therapists and nurses had no clue about his real identity. As far as they knew, he was Mark Smith, ranch owner in Colorado. That's all the information anyone needed.

It was strange the police hadn't apprehended the attacker. Did they access the security cameras? The grad assistant had to have given a description. An uncanny feeling came over him. The authorities knew more than they were letting on. Dammit! Where was David?

At eleven o'clock, a hard knock rapped on the door.

In a rush, Mark moved without his cane, taking unsteady steps to the entranceway. He opened the door. "Owen?"

A short man, standing around five and a half feet tall, charged into the room. "David asked me to stop by."

Mark nodded at his sixty-year-old supervisor. "Come in." He led Owen to the living room. "How's Hailey?"

Owen hesitated. "She's stabilized. She was stabbed in the chest, and her lung collapsed. Fortunately, the knife missed her heart."

Mark grabbed a chair for support. "Is she going to be okay?"

"She's in ICU. I don't know much more. David's staying with the kids tonight."

"Why aren't my parents watching them?"

"They're in Arizona visiting your sister. David will stop by tomorrow and fill you in on the rest."

"Did he see Hailey?"

"Just for a few minutes, but she was sleeping."

"I need to see her."

"No."

Mark slammed his fist against the wall. "Dammit! I have a right to see my wife."

"Calm down. You'd blow your cover, and we'll all be in deep shit. We have less than three weeks until

Toole is released." Owen's eyes gleamed. "Our plan's working."

"Mendoza's here? He was the attacker?"

Owen nodded. "Hailey's grad assistant could only give the sketch artist a brief description of the man, but it might be him. The authorities will question Hailey tomorrow if she's up to it."

"I want Hailey under twenty-four-hour protection—her and the kids."

"I already have a guard parked at your house."

"What about the hospital room?"

"We posted one there, too."

Owen's stare made Mark self-conscious. "What's wrong?"

"Nothing. It's been a while since I've seen you. You talk strategy as if you've never left." Owen's cranky demeanor softened. "You're looking well, Mark. I'm glad to see you out of the wheelchair."

A sadness cloaked Mark. Since the fire, Owen had visited twice. Mark chalked it up to his boss feeling awkward. If Mark's supervisor couldn't see past his appearance, how did he expect others to see him as more than a hideous mutant?

Owen smoothed his combover. "When David carried you out of the fire, I thought you were a goner. You're one hell of a fighter." Extending his arm, he regarded Mark's gloved hand and awkwardly lowered his hand into the coat pocket. He mumbled, "Good night," and took off.

Chapter Thirty-Five

Sunlight warmed Hailey's face, blanketing her in comfort. A strong odor of disinfectant assaulted her senses, and she blinked as the room came into focus.

A tube passed from underneath the sheet to a drainage container on the side. Machines beeped a steady rhythm beside a tiny dresser.

Anna, Ethan, and David sat in a row of chairs beside the bed, like ducklings eagerly waiting instruction.

When she swallowed, her throat was like sandpaper. "Hi."

"Mom. You're awake." Anna's angelic face was a welcome sight. "Are you feeling better?"

A bandage adhered to her neck restricted movement. "Just sore."

"Parker said you've been sleeping a lot."

She dipped her chin. Maybe the anesthesia was affecting her. Fatigue haunted her through the morning hours while Parker made phone calls. The last thing she remembered was him speaking with Stefan about the stabbing.

Anna's eyes glistened. "I was so scared. You could have...I don't want to lose you, too. The nurses said we couldn't see you. Then Parker made a big scene."

"Don't cry." Hailey squeezed Anna's hand. "How did Parker know I was here?"

Ethan leaned forward in his chair. "He was at the police station when the 9-1-1 call came in. He picked us up when we got home from school." He glanced at the doorway. "Your nurse should be back soon. The police want to question you, but Parker told them to wait."

"Is Parker still here?"

Anna gnawed at her fingernail. "He's in the waiting room. You're only allowed to have two visitors, but the nurse let David come in with us."

Giving a sly smile, David leaned closer and propped his arms on the bedrail. "If you wanted a break from teaching, you could have resigned. Getting stabbed is a little dramatic, don't you think?"

She chuckled, wincing as a sharp pain rippled through her chest.

David poured water into a glass and brought a straw next to her lips. "Drink this. It should help."

Hailey sipped the water and leaned into the pillow. "How long have I been asleep?"

"Most of the afternoon." David set the glass on the overbed table. "Don't worry about the kids. I can take care of them."

A young nurse came in the room and checked Hailey's vitals. The cheerful woman surveyed the supplies on the bedside table. "I'll be back with some tape to change the dressing."

David grimaced. "That's our cue to leave, kids."

Anna pouted. "But Mom just woke up."

He stood. "We don't need to see your mom's stitches. If I pass out on the floor, you'll need a hospital bed for me. Besides, it's dinnertime." He tousled Anna's hair. "Say good-bye. You can see your mom tomorrow."

Ethan and Anna leaned over and hugged her. "Love you, Mom."

"I love you, too." Hailey took in their familiar teen scent. It didn't matter that they needed a shower. She had almost lost them. "Ethan, would you mind calling Grandma and Grandpa and tell them what happened? Aunt Francine's number is in the address book."

He squared his shoulders. "I already did. They got tickets to fly back tomorrow."

Anna slid a backpack over a shoulder and held up Hailey's cell phone. "Parker got your purse from the office yesterday and gave it to me to take home." She handed Hailey the phone. "Do you want to keep your phone here so we can text?"

"What a great idea." Girl talk. Feeling giddy, Hailey set the phone on the bed table.

David waited as the kids said good-bye. "Can you kiddos wait outside and give me a minute alone with your mom?" He waited until Ethan and Anna left the room, and then he stepped closer. "I know this isn't the best time, but the police need to question you. Did you know your attacker?"

She closed her eyes. All morning the stabbing was a blur. An image of the attack flashed in her mind, catching her breath. "Mendoza…Oh my God. He's here."

"Are you sure?"

She nodded. "He was angry."

"Did he say why?"

"He asked, 'Where is she?' "

David arched a brow. "He said that?"

"He must want Colleen, but surely he knows she's in prison."

He was quiet for a moment. "I'll let the police know. They posted a guard outside the door in case he shows up."

"Do you think he will?"

"I doubt it. He has to know you'd identify him. Mendoza's not stupid." David patted her arm. "Don't worry about anything. I'll have the kids call you tonight."

"Thanks. Can you ask Parker to come in after the nurse changes my bandage?"

David nodded. "He hasn't left since you got here."

He seemed to be studying her. Was he judging her for moving on without Mark? She wouldn't get into that argument today.

She closed her eyes and waited for Parker.

****

The room was as cold as an icebox. Shivering, Hailey tugged the blanket over her arms. The IV taped to her hand restricted her movement. She touched the thick bandage under her right breast; the covering extended to her armpit. Soreness rippled through her chest, but she refused to ask the nurse for more pain medication.

The moonlight cast shadows in the dimmed room, and the memories of the attack flashed in her mind. She was lucky to be alive.

She turned to Parker, asleep in a chair, his head down.

The door opened and dark shadows elongated on the wall as a young female nurse tugged back the curtain. "Time for your antibiotic." She checked the bandage and made adjustments on the monitors. "How would you rate your pain?"

Hailey tried to sit, but pain streaked across her ribcage. Wincing, she closed her eyes until the soreness subsided. "A five."

The nurse nodded. "I'll bring your pain meds."

"I'd rather not have them. They might interfere with my anti-anxiety medication."

"It won't. Mr. Parker showed your medication to the nurses when you came in. The lab tested your bloodwork in the ER and the values came back undetected. It's in your chart. The nurse even called your doctor to verify the prescription."

"That's strange. The metabolites should've shown up on the bloodwork."

"When was the last time you took any pills?"

"A few days ago."

"Several factors can affect how fast medication metabolizes in your body—your age, your weight. Depending on the type, medications are long-acting, short-acting, or intermediate."

"Dr.Thomkin switched me off the long-acting because I had problems with brain fog. He's been trying different medications, but nothing has helped."

"Are you experiencing any problems now?"

The answer surprised her. "Actually, I haven't noticed any issues."

"Make sure you talk to your doctor about it. I need to check your pulse." The nurse placed her fingers on Hailey's wrist. "Your hands are cold. I'll get you another blanket." She nodded at Parker snoring softly. "Your friend was questioning everything we did. I'm glad he's finally resting."

Hailey gazed at him, eager to talk. "Did the surgeon come in today?"

"Dr. Trevor came earlier, but you were asleep. He'll make rounds again in the morning." The nurse stepped to the door. "I'll be back with a blanket and your pain medicine."

Hailey glanced at Parker. Since Mark passed away, she was afraid to get close to anyone again. She loved Mark. Thought she had a lifetime with him. Now, she was at an impasse—unable to move forward until she found out what happened. Why was she making things difficult? Life was too short. She had a chance to be happy again—with Parker.

Was she capable of giving her heart to another man? Smiling, she pulled the sheet under her chin. *Yes, I think I am.*

Chapter Thirty-Six

When a newscaster reported the delayed baseball game, Mark flung the remote on the bed. *Why don't they talk about Hailey?* Two days ago, his wife's attack had been the main story. Today, she was old news. Where were the updates? Even the hospital operator wouldn't give out any information.

The hairs prickled on the back of his neck at the thought of Mendoza lurking around Hailey. He picked up his cane and paced the floor. His steps were still too slow, too clumsy.

After the weatherman instructed the viewers to enjoy the only sunny day in the forecast, the newscast anchor appeared on the screen. Mark tilted his head toward the television as the anchor spoke. At the end of the update, he powered off the TV. The news was worthless!

At the familiar rhythmic tapping on the door, Mark moved his cane forward and hobbled toward the foyer as quickly as he could. Did David have news about Hailey?

The caller unlocked the door and stepped inside the apartment.

Mark snarled. "It's about time."

David scowled, holding up two bags and a drink carrier. "If you're going to bite my head off, I'll eat this myself."

Tempted by the aroma of coffee, sausage, and eggs, he refrained from antagonizing his friend further and led the way into the kitchen.

David set the bags on the table. "You're walking a lot better."

"The therapist suggested moving off the walker." The small victory was the furthest from his mind. "How's Hailey?"

David gestured at the chair. "Why don't we sit?"

Mark leaned his weight on the cane. "I'll stand."

"Then I'll sit." David slid out a chair from the table. "We have a big problem."

A lump lodged in Mark's throat. "Oh my God. What happened to Hailey?"

David removed a coffee from the carrier. "Nothing. She's a trooper."

"Is it the kids?"

"No. They're fine."

Mark paced to the living room. "Dammit! Why do you scare me like that?"

"Sorry. I wasn't thinking. So much has gone on the past two days."

No kidding. "Tell me about Hailey. How is she? How are Ethan and Anna?"

"She's doing better. The kids were scared, but they're hanging in there."

"Did someone tell my parents? They'd want to help."

"Ethan and I called them. They were visiting Francine, but they're flying back."

"I need to see Hailey."

David blew on the coffee and swallowed. "It's too risky."

307

C. Becker

"There *has* to be a way." He gritted his teeth. "Talk to Owen."

"And say what?"

Mark kicked a trash can out of his path. "Dammit! I want to see my wife for a few minutes. To see with my own eyes she's okay. I've called the hospital, but no one will tell me anything."

David set the trash can upright and handed Mark the other coffee cup. "You shouldn't call the hospital."

"I'm not telling them who I am."

"Doesn't matter. Even if you *did* tell them you were her husband, they have privacy rules."

"What am I supposed to do?" Dejected, Mark sat and reached for the coffee. "You didn't call last night."

David pounded his fist on the table. "Fuck! I can't do everything. I have a life too, or have you forgotten?"

Mark rubbed his temples. Shit. He *had* forgotten. He was a selfish asshole. "I'm sorry. You're right. Go back to work—"

"Dammit! That's not what I'm saying."

Mark raised a hand in the air. "What the hell is wrong with you today? You're jumping all over me. All I asked was why you didn't call last night."

"You didn't ask. You accused. There's a difference." David took a long sip, and his temper seemed to mellow. "I can't text around your kids. Anna and Ethan watch me like a hawk, thinking someone might be texting about Hailey. I can't risk them getting suspicious." Tears pooled under his eyes. "Anna was up most of the night crying her eyes out because she thought Hailey was going to die like her dad did." He choked. "I love your kids, but I don't know if I can keep doing this."

"Don't say that. You're the one who's always kept me centered."

"I don't know what we were thinking. Hailey almost died yesterday. She's been through hell and back, and now we're putting her through this? And the kids. This is fucking cruel."

"What do you suggest we do?" Mark tightened his grip around the disposable cup.

"I don't know. But I'm done." David raised his hands. "After Colleen leaves town, I'm finished. If you want to stay in hiding away from your family, it's on you. You'll have to live with the repercussions. I'm warning you, though, you're going to lose your wife to Parker if you don't tell her you're alive."

"Has Parker been hanging around?"

David nodded. "Looks like they're back together."

Mark slammed the cup on the table, spilling coffee from the lid. "Damn. We are so close."

"Are you ready to tell Hailey you're alive once Colleen leaves town?"

He felt his burn mask. "Not yet."

David shook his head.

Mark loathed himself even more. "What do you want me to do?"

A muscle in David's neck twitched. "Tell her the truth."

"I thought you were my friend."

"I am."

"Then act like it." Mark snapped. "I never expected you to give me a hard time."

"A friend tells a friend when he screws up. Why are you putting Colleen's happiness above Hailey's? Colleen doesn't care about you."

"I promised to help her."

"Promises don't mean anything."

"To me they do." They did to Hailey, too.

David withdrew two breakfast sandwiches from the bag and pushed them toward Mark. "Better eat these before they get cold."

Mark opened an egg sandwich and took a bite. "Is there still security on Hailey's room?"

David nodded. "Since yesterday. Owen posted guards at your house, too."

"Can you call the warden and make sure Mendoza doesn't try sending Colleen a message?"

"I called this morning."

"Can we get Colleen's release date moved up? Catch Mendoza off guard?"

David drew his phone from his pocket. "We can try, but I doubt the judge will concur."

Mark finished eating the sandwich. "How close were Hailey and Parker?"

"Pretty close." David met Mark's gaze. "It's obvious how much he cares for her."

Mark's neck muscles tensed. "Parker's always loved her. He helped her when her parents died, and after her assault. I can't compete with their friendship."

David sipped the coffee. "I have a terrible feeling you may lose her if you wait too long."

"I'd rather lose everything than force Hailey to stay in a marriage where she'd be unhappy." Mark opened the second wrapper, shot it at the garbage can, and missed. "Have the authorities found any leads?"

"The police have an APB out on Mendoza. They don't expect him to stay in the area."

"Do the police know about Colleen's daughter?"

"No. Owen called this morning. He warned if Mendoza finds out you're alive, Hailey and the kids will be targets to make you talk. We need to be careful."

Mark surveyed the apartment. "This place is secure. The nurses and therapists all have top security clearances."

David picked up the wrapper from the floor and threw it in the trash. "Still, we need to be careful."

"Will you take me to see Hailey tonight?"

The lines deepened on David's forehead. "Not this again."

Mark tried in vain to control his emotions. Why didn't David understand he was at his breaking point? The dam of tears he'd blocked was breaking fast. "Just for a half hour. Please. I have to see my wife. I'm going crazy worrying about her."

"You're beginning to sound like a broken record."

"I don't care how I sound!" Mark grabbed the tabletop and tipped the table onto the floor. "I want my wife! Can't you understand?" He swiped his arm across the counter of pill containers, creams, and dressings. "I have nothing without my family. Nothing…Argh!" Moaning, he grabbed his burn mask and ripped it off. "I am so damn sick…of being…cooped up…in this shithole." He slumped on the carpet, sobbing. "Why did this happen to me? Why couldn't I die?" Never had he felt so helpless, so worthless. When he finished crying, he wiped his face with his sleeve. Body aches camouflaged the emptiness. "I'm sorry."

"Don't be." David fell beside him and sniffled, his eyes moist and red. He wiped a napkin over his cheeks and handed one to Mark. "I know this is hard, but you've got to find a way to deal with your emotions. One minute you're angry, the next minute you're falling apart. I don't know how to help."

"I don't expect you to."

They sat in silence a few minutes.

Then helplessness clouded David's face. "You win. I'll get you in to see Hailey."

Chapter Thirty-Seven

Between the overheated room and the carts rattling across the floor, sleep was impossible. Even the quiet lulls brought new worries about the kids. Hailey rolled on her side, only to lie back when the chest tube blocked a comfortable position.

Parker sensed her frustration, and he called the nurse twice during the night, asking for ways to ease her discomfort.

It felt right having him stay with her. Like she was his awestruck patient again, enamored of his presence. Parker still had a knack for calming her, and the realization brought her peace.

In the morning, the surgeon strode into the room and checked Hailey's wound. "You're a lucky woman. Another inch and the knife would have cut your heart." Dr. Trevor repositioned the gauze dressing he had removed. "The stitches are healing nicely."

Hailey tugged the hospital gown higher over her breast. "When can I go home?"

The thirty-something doctor chuckled, and he inspected the lacerations on her neck and arm where Mendoza's blade had penetrated her. "Let's get you out of ICU first. I'll move you to the surgical wing this afternoon. See how you feel. If you're doing okay tomorrow, I'll take out the chest tube. You might be able to go home by the end of the week."

She tugged at her ear. Her implant couldn't be working correctly. "The end of the week?"

"Is there a problem?" Dr. Trevor gave her a look that dared her to object. "I could have you stay longer if you aren't feeling well."

She glanced at Parker and sulked. Didn't the doctor understand she had kids at home? "No. Thursday or Friday will be fine."

When the surgeon departed, she pulled the bed table closer and gripped her cell phone. "The battery's almost dead."

Parker inspected the charging port. "We use the same charger. I'll bring mine when I come back this afternoon."

Hailey checked her messages filling the screen and set the phone aside. It would take hours to read them. "Are you going to work today?"

He kissed her. "I called off. I'm not going anywhere until I know you're okay."

"Thank you." She could get used to his attention.

He gently rubbed her hand. "For what?"

"For not giving up on us."

His gray eyes sparkled. "I've waited too long to be this happy. I'm not going to lose you." Parker pointed to her plate. "You should eat something. I don't want you to fade away."

"I have a headache. And my chest is still sore."

"Food might help." He pushed the tray in front of her, buttered an English muffin, and passed it over. "Do you remember anything more about the stabbing?"

She nibbled on the muffin. "My memory's coming back in pieces. I forgot Bruce called before I was stabbed." Hailey told Parker about the mysterious pill.

"Why didn't you tell me sooner?"

"I was worried you'd report it. Besides I don't know if it was Ethan's pill."

"I didn't think Justin was using drugs either, but kids do stupid things sometimes. They follow whatever their friends do."

She frowned. "I know. But the pill could be Jake's. He's been to the house a few times."

He nudged a bowl of mixed fruit toward her. "You should talk to Ethan."

"I will." She picked up a fork and stabbed the cantaloupe. "Bruce said the pill was Euphoria."

"Are you sure?"

She nodded, repulsed to hear the word Euphoria again.

"How would Ethan get his hands on Euphoria?"

Heat rose up her neck. "It might not be his."

"Stefan stationed me here because of rumors Euphoria hit the East Coast. Mendoza must have found a route to traffic the drug."

"I thought about that, but how did the pill get into my house?" She dropped the fork. "Oh my God, Parker. What if Mendoza broke into my house and dropped it?"

"We can't jump to conclusions."

"I know, but the front door was unlocked at least twice. Maybe three times."

"Have you found more than one pill?"

"No."

"Ask Ethan. He might shed light on things."

Around noon, Hailey and Parker were watching TV when her phone rang.

"Hailey, oh my God. Are you okay?" Liz's high-pitched voice reverberated through the speaker. "The

315

department chair and I have been calling the hospital since Monday. No one will talk to us."

She tightened her grip on Parker's hand. "I'm going to be fine. I'm sorry I haven't had time to return your call."

"Never mind about that. Is there anything I can do? Do you need help with your kids?"

"Thanks, but Ethan and Anna are self-sufficient." She fingered a tulip from the bouquet Peggy and Adam had sent. "Mark's parents will take care of Ethan and Anna when they get back from Arizona."

"Do you need anything?"

Hailey gazed at Parker. She had everything she needed. "Sleep."

"Sleep is impossible to get in hospitals. I can visit tomorrow if you're feeling up to it."

Liz's energy was hard to turn down. "Yes, that's fine."

"The dean has been sending out memos about updated security. I'll fill you in tomorrow."

Next, Santino called.

Hailey chatted a few minutes until transportation arrived and moved her to the surgical unit.

Satisfied with her new room, Parker talked to the guard outside the door and went home to shower.

Cherishing the quiet time, Hailey closed her eyes and slept.

At three, David strolled inside the room, towing Ethan, Anna, and a stuffed teddy bear dressed in green scrubs.

She stretched her arms and yawned. "I wasn't expecting you until later."

Ethan grinned. "David signed us out early."

What a sneak. Maybe putting him on the approved contact list at school wasn't such a smart idea.

David avoided her stare. "We would have gotten here sooner, but we didn't know you moved rooms."

Anna hugged Hailey and handed her three homemade cards.

She opened the first card, and her heart warmed at the sentimental poem Anna had penned. Misty-eyed, Hailey placed the card on the bed table. "Honey, this is beautiful."

Anna beamed. "Sam and Rose made the other cards."

Hailey opened the two cards and paused at Rose's artistry. No wonder Anna had picked up an interest in drawing. "They're beautiful. Tell the girls thank you."

After they had chatted for a time, David pointed at the empty chairs. "Why don't you two start your homework while I talk to your mom?" He dragged a chair nearer to the bed as the kids opened their backpacks. "Where's the guard?"

"I sent him away."

"Why?"

She caught Ethan's furtive glance, and she lowered her voice. "I don't want to worry the kids. Besides, Parker's been staying with me at night."

Soon Parker returned, freshly shaven and showered. He gazed at Hailey with a longing that made heat spread through her chest.

Flustered, she glanced at the clock. "It's dinnertime. If anyone's hungry, there's food in the cafeteria."

Ethan crinkled his nose. "I'm not eating hospital food. David's getting us fast food on the way home."

Anna nudged her brother. "Shhh."

"Busted." Hailey shook her head.

David stammered. "What? I said I'd watch the kids. I never said I would cook."

Hailey turned to Anna. "Would you mind taking Parker and David to the cafeteria and get a snack for everyone? Ethan can stay and keep me company."

Parker led the way, and Anna and David followed him out the door.

Hailey smiled at Ethan and patted the bed. "Come closer. I need a hug." When she gave him a tight squeeze, she was half-afraid he'd pull away, but he didn't move. Did Ethan miss their closeness, too? "How's school going?"

"Okay. I got a C-plus on my geometry test."

"Great job!"

He blushed and opened his history book. "It's no big deal. It's not an A or a B."

She had never felt prouder. "That's okay, you're working on it. You need good grades if you're going to college."

"I'm not sure what I want to do. Jake's going to tech next year to learn bricklaying, but I know Dad expected me to go to college."

Guilty as charged. She and Mark had spent many nights talking about the kids' futures. "We wanted you to choose something that made you happy so you'd have a rewarding profession. What's more important is you are an honorable young man. You have another year to decide." She paused. "Can I ask you a question?"

"Sure, Mom." He laid the history book on his lap.

"Have you ever seen Jake use drugs?"

"No." Was it her or did he answer too quickly?

"Are you certain?"

He squirmed in his chair. "He vapes, but it's all I've seen."

"What about Jake's cousin?"

He nodded. "Zac and Chase do drugs."

"Have they ever offered you any?" She paused at his uneasiness. "I'm not going to judge you. I just want to know the truth."

Ethan shuffled his feet. "Chase gave me marijuana once."

Oh God. Her fears were real. "Did you tell him no?"

His gaze lowered, and he shook his head.

"You smoked marijuana?" With effort, she kept her voice calm.

"It was only one time. I swear, Mom."

"Do they use any other drugs?"

Ethan shrugged. "Usually marijuana. Chase said it was legal when he lived in California, so it can't be bad. Sometimes he uses cocaine and meth."

"Have you seen this?"

He crossed his arms over his chest. "Why are you asking me all these questions? I only used weed, I promise."

"No reason." She scratched her hands. "Does Santino use drugs?"

"I've never seen him use anything."

"I don't want you hanging around Jake anymore. You'll have to tell Santino you quit."

Ethan slammed his book. "Mom, drugs are everywhere. I know they're bad. You can't shelter me from them. Besides, since Zac left, Santino needs me.

Don't make me stop working. I like making money. I almost have enough saved up to buy the sneakers I want."

Maybe she was acting irrational. "Do Zac and Chase use anything else?"

"Like what?"

"Euphoria."

He nodded. "Chase talks about it. He said it's as strong as coke."

"Where did he buy it?"

Ethan's face puckered in a strange expression. "I'll ask Jake."

Better not make Jake suspicious. "I was just wondering. Don't mention it."

"Can I keep working for Santino?" Ethan pleaded. "Jake's my friend."

"No. Tell Santino you need to stop working because you have too much homework."

"Mom, that's lying. There's no homework. School's out next week." Disappointment covered his face.

Was she being unreasonable? Was this what Parker and Grace went through with Justin?

Anna's laughter echoed through the hall. In the next moment, she stepped into the room with Parker and David.

Anna handed Hailey a small bakery bag. "The cafeteria was crowded, so we went to the kiosk by the gift shop. They had your favorite. Oatmeal raisin cookies."

As the group chose their seats, Hailey tore open the bag and munched on a sugary cookie. "These are scrumptious, Anna. What did you get?"

Anna held up a larger white bag. "Chocolate chip."

David's cell phone chimed. He read the screen and stood. "Hailey, I have to go. It's an emergency at work." He turned to Parker. "This is probably going to take a while. Can you watch the kids until I can cover? They have counseling tonight. Ethan's not supposed to miss it."

Hailey brushed the cookie crumbs from the overbed table. "Anna might need help studying for finals, too."

Parker shook David's hand. "Sure. I don't mind. I'll take the kids out for dinner on the way. I don't cook either."

"Thanks." David slipped the phone into his pocket. "I'll text when it's over. I hope to be done before ten."

When he left, Hailey patted the bed, and invited Anna to jump on. "Tell me about your day."

Anna chewed on a nail. "It was good. Mrs. Rogers asked about you at the bus stop this morning. She offered to let Ethan and me stay with them."

"That's sweet she offered, but Grandma and Grandpa should be home anytime. They called before boarding this afternoon."

Parker folded the newspaper he'd been skimming. "Well kiddos, if you want to eat before counseling, we should head out. Traffic gets backed up around here. What do you want for dinner?"

Ethan picked up his book and stood. "Burgers."

After Hailey hugged them good-bye, Parker removed his wallet and pulled out some bills. "Anna and Ethan, can you two go to the gift shop and buy us each a water bottle? I'll meet you there in a few minutes."

Parker waited until they left, and then he leaned down and kissed her. "I didn't want to upset the kids, but I've been dying to do this all afternoon."

Hailey grinned. "I like how you think."

He kissed her again, a playful single lip kiss.

Her stomach fluttered at the novelty of their budding relationship. "I won't break."

Parker leaned closer, kissing her with a fierceness that made her lips tremble. "I'll drive back here tonight after David comes to watch the kids."

She contemplated the dark circles under his eyes. "It's okay if you'd rather stay home. We're both exhausted. Besides, counseling lasts until eight. By the time you get the kids home and help with their schoolwork, it'll be late."

His breath warmed her lips as he kissed her again. "I don't care if it's after midnight. I want to stay with you tonight."

She was losing her wits at his carefree side. "You want to sneak in another kiss."

He winked. "Maybe a few."

****

"Nervous?" David grinned as the car stopped in the hospital parking lot.

"You could say that." Mark wiped his sweaty hands against his pants. "Are you sure Parker's not here?"

"He's watching the kids until I can relieve him tonight. Go ahead. I'll be here when you come back." David helped Mark out of the car. "I wish you'd taken your pain medicine."

Mark pressed the elevator button. "It makes me sleepy. I need to remember every moment tonight."

David handed him a map of the surgical wing. "I outlined the path to Hailey's room. Good luck. I'll be in the car." He waved as Mark stepped into the elevator and the doors closed.

On the surgical floor, Mark plucked a scarlet rose from a floral bouquet in the nurse's station and hid in the shadows of the supply closet.

A nurse came out of Hailey's room and disappeared down the hallway.

He wouldn't have much time. Seeing Hailey tonight was risky, but he had to see her with his own eyes. He lumbered across the hall to the darkened room.

The place was quiet except for intermittent beeps of the monitor. An IV dripped solution from the stand beside the bed. The light from the screens lit her sleeping face.

She looked like an angel of peace. His heart raced. Oh God, how he had missed her.

He inched closer and studied her delicate form. She seemed so fragile lying there. Hailey was the reason he continued living in his dismal abyss.

Mesmerized by her breathing, he exhaled, not realizing until that moment that he was holding his breath. For a few minutes, he stood, watching her.

He breathed in the flower in his hand. The scent brought back memories of when he'd surprise her with a rose, a sign of their enduring love. He kissed the top petals, lowering the flower onto the bed table next to a bouquet of daisies with a card nestled among the leaves—*Love, Parker*.

A mixture of jealousy and frustration surged through him. Why couldn't there be another way to keep his family safe from Mendoza?

Touching his transparent face mask, he fingered his cheek, now a bed of lumpy scars. Would Hailey recognize him if she woke? Mark hesitated to touch her; his scarred fingers would feel rough. He had ached for this moment for so long. Unable to resist, he lightly touched her bruised hand, something akin to his own imperfections. Mark slumped, gripping his hands on the bedrail.

Why wasn't I there? I'm supposed to keep Hailey safe. Touching her hair, he whispered, "I love you, babe."

With painful steps, he tiptoed to the door, waiting until the voices outside faded. He opened the door and checked the hallway. Lowering his baseball cap over his burn mask, he moved toward the elevator, passing a nurse typing on the computer in the center station.

The elevator chimed as he approached. With effort, he pushed to walk more balanced, without drawing attention to his gait, and he hurried inside.

As the doors began closing, Parker appeared, walking down the hall. He cast a glance toward the elevator and halted.

Oh shit. Mark twisted to the side and pressed the ground floor button. *Close!*

"Wait!" Parker's voice broke the silence as he raced toward the elevator.

Mark slapped his palm against the button again.

"Hold it!"

The elevator slid shut as Parker's hand thwacked the door.

Mark's heart pounded as each floor flashed and descended. The doors opened, and he exited, hurrying past the stairwell where footfalls echoed. He wrestled through excruciating leg pain as he peered through the harsh glow of the fluorescent lights in the parking garage. *Why didn't I bring the cane?*

David's car was in the lane across from the elevator, the engine already running.

In agony, Mark rushed as quickly as his legs could move. His fingers fumbled, trying to open the door.

David unlatched it from inside.

Mark opened the door and fell in the passenger seat.

"What happened?"

He kept his gaze on the stairs. "Step on it. I'll fill you in after we get out of here."

As the car veered around the corner to the lower level, Parker appeared from the stairwell.

David sped out of the garage and merged onto the interstate. "Why the hurry?"

"Parker came."

"What?"

"I thought you said he was watching the kids." Mark latched the seatbelt and massaged his legs.

"He was."

"Well, he must have cut out early. I was getting onto the elevator when he was walking down the hall."

"Damn." David rammed his hand against the steering wheel. "Did he see you?"

"Not close up."

David hit the steering wheel again. "You should have worn one of the disguises I brought for you."

Mark lifted a paper bag from the floor and opened it. "Yeah, that's a great idea. Let's see…I could have worn your black facemask leftover from the pandemic. Or I could have worn this SWAT helmet." He lowered the covering onto his head. "Looks good, eh? Wouldn't create any suspicion with the nurses?" Satisfied he proved how absurd David's comment was, Mark removed the helmet and placed it back into the bag. "I don't know why you even brought this. It's ridiculous."

"I wanted to calm your nerves. Thought I'd give you a laugh." David's eyebrow arched. "I guess it wasn't very funny."

"No, it wasn't." A moment passed, and Mark chuckled. "Actually, it was."

David joined in the laughter. "Maybe Parker didn't even recognize you. He wouldn't know what you look like anyway." He checked the rearview mirror and signaled a lane change. "Other than Parker, how did it go?"

"It was hard. God, I miss Hailey." Mark wiped his eyes. "She could have died. Why did I think Mendoza would leave Hailey alone if I played dead? I should've told her about Colleen."

David remained silent until he drove through a patch of night construction. "You okay?"

Mark nodded. He grabbed a tissue from his pocket and wiped his nose. "We have to up our game."

"I agree. Mendoza's desperate. Who knows what he'll do next time."

Mark clenched his jaw. "There'd better not be a next time."

Chapter Thirty-Eight

Hailey woke to a series of chimes from the cell phone. She glanced over at Parker snoring, sprawled on the recliner chair, and she picked up the phone.

Anna's text was first on the screen. *—Grandma and Grandpa slept here last night. They're taking us to c u after school. I luv u.—*

Ethan: *—Talked to the counselor. We had a good talk.—*

Peggy: *—Adam and I flew in and stayed with the kids. I'll call later this morning. Can I bring you anything?—*

A food service worker tapped softly on the door. He placed a breakfast tray on the bed table and went out.

Hailey dropped her phone and gasped at the single rose lying beside the cards. She picked it up and twirled the stem between her fingers. It was like the kind Mark used to send her. There was no note. How odd. She could have sworn she heard Mark's voice while she slept. *Now I'm really dreaming.*

Parker stirred, knocking the pillow to the floor as he stretched his arms. "Morning."

"What time did you get here last night? I must've fallen asleep waiting."

"Around ten-thirty." He adjusted the chair upright and picked up the pillow. "Your in-laws came straight

C. Becker

from the airport and offered to watch Ethan and Anna. They seem nice."

"They're great."

He leaned over and kissed her. "So are you." He kissed her again and pointed to the rose. "Who sent you a flower?"

"I don't know. It was here when I woke up. Maybe the nurse will know."

"It was here last night when I came."

"You should have woken me."

"You needed rest." Parker folded the blanket. "Did David call you last night?"

"No. Why?"

"Your father-in-law was going to call and tell him they would watch the kids." Parker laid the blanket on the chair. "How long did David and Mark know each other?"

Hailey breathed in the rose's sweet fragrance. "Since kindergarten. Why do you ask?"

"I'm wondering if David actually had a work meeting last night."

"You think he was on a date?" She laid the rose on the bed table.

"Something like that."

"Parker, don't. It was bad enough you didn't trust Santino. Now you're acting like David can't be trusted."

"How long have you known him?"

"I've gotten to know him more since Mark died. David doesn't like Colleen either, so he's all right in my book." Hailey lifted the breakfast lid from the plate. Scrambled eggs, toast, grapefruit, and black coffee. Hmm. This was more than she usually ate at home.

"How did Mark and Colleen meet?"

"I'm not sure exactly. They dated in high school and then in college for a while."

"Did Colleen go to the same college as you and Mark?"

She sampled the toast and passed a piece to Parker. "Yes, but by the time I started, Colleen had already transferred to another university."

A quick series of knocks rapped on the door. "Hailey? Good morning." Dr. Trevor lowered his pager into his jacket. "How are you feeling?"

She pushed the tray to the side and propped a pillow behind her back. "Much better than yesterday."

"That's what I like to hear."

Parker stood. "Let me text Stefan and give you some privacy. I'll be back when the doctor is finished." He tucked his shirt into his jeans and stepped into the hallway.

Dr. Trevor pulled the curtain. "Let me take a look to check for any swelling or redness. Any chills? Stabbing pain? Foul odor?"

She shook her head as he peeled back the bandage on her chest. "No."

"Have you had any headaches? Nausea? Dizziness?"

"That's gone, too. When will I get to go home?"

"You're running a low-grade fever. I'd like to keep you another day or two to watch for infection."

Hailey resisted voicing her objections.

After Dr. Trevor left, Parker returned and slid his chair closer. "I know you want to leave, but the doctor needs to make sure you're okay."

She sipped some coffee. "But I feel fine."

"Even the brain fog and dizziness you had?"

"I haven't had any issues lately."

Parker chewed on the last slice of toast. "What about your shortness of breath and numbness?"

She extended her fingers. "It's gone."

He was quiet for a moment. "When was the last time you took your pills?"

"Friday night. When you gave me a hard time about using them."

"You actually listened to me?" Navy flecks teased in his eyes. "It's a miracle!"

Hailey sighed. "I don't understand. Dr. Thomkin prescribed three different medicines, and I've had the same side effects each time." She picked up her phone and opened her contacts. "I'll call Bruce. Would you mind going to the house to get my pills?"

Parker gave her a blank look. "Why? You said you were feeling better without them."

"I'm not going to take them. I want you to go to the post office and mail some pills overnight delivery. Maybe Bruce can tell me if there's something strange going on."

****

At eleven o'clock, Liz knocked on the door. "Hailey?" She entered the room carrying a shopping bag. "Oh my God! How are you feeling?"

Hailey smoothed her hair and raised the bed to a sitting position. For once, she didn't focus on Liz's outfit. What was the point when even a country mouse dressed better than the thin hospital gown Hailey wore? "I'm doing better, thanks."

"You look frail. You must have lost a lot of blood." Liz lowered the shopping bag on the overbed table. "I brought you some magazines and toiletries. Figured you'd want to pass the time with crossword puzzles. Oh, and I brought some slippers." She fished them out of the bag and whispered, "Who knows how many germs are on this floor."

Hailey grinned and accepted the slippers, making a mental note to never invite Liz camping. "I'm not worried about any microbes. I'm sure the custodians use a strong disinfectant when they clean, but thank you. You're very thoughtful."

Liz waved her hand with a dismissive gesture. "It's the least I could do. You could have been killed. After the shooting, the dean ordered the entire wing sealed. The university established new safety protocols for active shooter incidents. We're also getting new locks on the doors."

"You're lucky you weren't there when the shooting happened. You might've been hurt, too."

"That's what George said."

Hailey slid on the slippers; the smooth velour wrapped her feet like a cozy blanket. "How are things going with you two?"

"Not good." Liz's hand trembled as she picked at her nail polish. "He opened a new credit card."

"Oh, no. Another card?" This had to be the fifth or sixth credit card he owned.

Liz chewed her lip. "I broke down after I saw the balance. I told George I was going to leave him unless he got help. I can't keep covering for him."

Hailey applauded Liz's assertiveness. "What did he say?"

"He agreed to see someone about his gambling problem."

"That's a positive sign. Do your sons know the extent of his problem?"

"I had to tell them." Liz wiped a tear from her cheek. "I can't do this alone any longer. They can help keep George on the right track."

****

Hailey laid the half-eaten sandwich on the plate and gazed again at the mysterious rose. One of the nurses had dropped the flower into a vase, and each time Hailey inhaled the scent, it brought back warm memories of Mark. She mused over it during late-morning phone calls from Peggy, Santino, and Zhang. Even the nurses and gift shop manager didn't know the source.

Parker walked into the room as she dipped a spoon into her tomato soup. The amber cologne he wore sparked her senses when he leaned over and kissed her. His tender affections were becoming more natural, but she didn't feel comfortable initiating anything herself. "Did you mail the package?"

"Yep. It'll be delivered tomorrow morning." He sat on the bed and accepted the ham sandwich she offered. "Why are you eating so late?"

"Liz came to visit—"

"Liz?"

"Elizabeth Shoemaker. My officemate at the university. Her husband's on the city council." Hailey pointed to the climate control vent. "She brought over slippers, hand creams, and some other necessities. After she left, Mark's mom called." She opened a pack of crackers and crumbled them into the soup. "The department chair called from the college to check on me, too. She said if I needed time off this summer to recover, she'd hire someone else to teach. I told her I'd think about it."

"It's a good idea. You'll need to take it easy for a few weeks."

"I'm sure Dr. Trevor will be extremely careful." She swallowed some soup and dipped her spoon in again. "Santino and Zhang called afterward, and then David stopped by."

"David?"

"Yes. I'm surprised you didn't see him. He was heading to the cafeteria to get a sandwich—where are you going?" Hailey stopped eating her soup.

Parker turned from the doorway and stepped closer. "I forgot to do something. I'll be back later." His kiss grazed her lips, and he rushed out the door.

Hailey slurped the soup and chuckled. Parker was wasting his energy if he was trying to spy on David. Next to Mark, the guy was as honest as they came.

****

"How could I be so damn stupid?" Manuel peered out the hotel blinds. Because of the ill-advised attack, he was a prisoner in a land he abhorred.

He held a fist to his stomach as it growled. He hadn't eaten since the fiasco. The food Santino brought tasted like cardboard. He craved fresh *cuajada* and tamales covered in banana leaves. That was real food. And it tasted so much better than the greasy American-Mexican fast food.

After the stabbing, the blaring fire alarms caused mayhem in the building and worked to his advantage. No one noticed as he bolted past onlookers. The news on TV hadn't given a detailed description of him. Did the *puta* identify him as the attacker?

He rubbed a hand over his clean-shaven chin. The beard was gone. His hair was growing back.

A knock sounded on the door and a voice said the password.

Manuel opened the door. "Where have you been?"

Santino rushed inside, carrying a grocery bag. "Here's more food. We have to be careful in case someone followed me." He pointed to the TV. "Did they identify you yet?"

"No."

"Maybe the Langley dame didn't recognize you? I've tried visiting her, but that troublemaker Parker keeps hanging around her hospital room. He's ruining everything."

Manuel grabbed a burger and soda from the bag. The greasy burgers made his insides convulse, but it was food. "She knew who I was. The police must be keeping a lid on the investigation." He sank his teeth into the burger, yearning for the ground maize flavor of an *arepa*. "What have you learned about my daughter?"

"One of the PIs dug up Colleen's activities at Harvard. She was involved in student government, research, and a sorority. We're tracking down her classmates."

"Bella was close with one of her sorority sisters. Someone from Boston."

"The PI's trying to locate the lady, but she moved around a lot after she married."

"How difficult can it be to find a five-year-old girl without a mother?" Manuel clenched his hands.

"We should know something soon." Santino pulled out his phone. "Chase is searching school databases. I'll have him help the PI."

Manuel withdrew his gun from his back pocket, and he took pleasure at the fear glowing in Santino's eyes. He never met a man who wasn't afraid of getting his brains blown apart. "If we don't find my daughter, your days are numbered."

Chapter Thirty-Nine

Hailey woke early and planned her debate with Dr. Trevor. Once she convinced the overly cautious doctor she could recuperate at home, she'd get her life back to normal. Whatever that was. Life without Mark. Life with Parker.

She gazed at Parker, who was snoring in the lounge chair with his head half off the pillow. Each time she woke, he was there. Sharing subtle intimacies with him was exciting. He'd hold her hand or sneak a kiss when Ethan and Anna weren't watching.

When the doctor discharged her, she'd miss Parker's presence at night, but the kids weren't ready to have him overnight at the house. She wasn't ready to open her bedroom to him yet, especially while she convalesced. Undoubtedly, though, the emotional attachment was growing. Hailey could see waking next to him—someday. How long would Mark's ghost hover by her pillow? *It's time to move on.* She'd expended too much energy to learn the circumstances behind Mark's death.

Her cell phone beeped. Santino sent an emoji waving hello.

She texted back. —*Good morning*—
—*How are you feeling?*—
—*Better*—
—*Ethan said he can't work anymore?*—

How should she respond? *—I don't want his grades to fall—*

—This is my busy season. What if he only works weekends?—

Was she being overprotective? *—Okay. Weekends will work—*

Hailey slouched back on the pillow. She made the right decision. Santino was her friend.

A few minutes passed, and her phone pinged again. A message from David appeared on the screen.

—Any word on your release today?—

She was lucky to have him as her friend. *—I'm waiting to talk to the doctor—*

—Don't twist his arm too badly. LOL—

Parker woke, stretching his arms over his head, like a little child rousing. "Morning."

She smiled, taking in his handsome face. "How did you sleep?"

"I should ask *you* that question." He stepped closer and sat on the bed, capturing her lips in a lingering kiss. "Hmm. I missed you."

Her cheeks warmed. "You're only three feet away."

"It's too far." He pointed to her phone. "Are the kids texting already?"

She shook her head. "David."

"What does he want?"

Hailey considered her reply. Although Parker never admitted it, he had taken off in a rush the previous day to follow David. She felt it in her bones. She didn't want any tension between the two men. "He wanted to say hello."

Parker frowned. "He keeps a close eye on you."

"He's concerned. That's all."

A food service worker tapped on the door and brought a breakfast tray.

Raising the bed to a sitting position, Hailey mumbled, "Perfect timing." Food would distract Parker. She buttered a muffin and gave him half.

When she'd finished eating the scrambled eggs, the phone rang. Hailey held up her cell. "It's Bruce."

Parker swallowed his last bite of muffin. "Put him on speaker."

She pressed the screen. "Hi, Bruce."

"I hope you're sitting down, Hailey."

"I am. Parker's here with me, too."

"Good. He should hear this."

"What did you find?" She laid the phone on the bed table and gulped some coffee.

"The pills you mailed are from *Bixa aparra*. Land sakes, Hailey. What's going on?"

She spit out the drink. "Wait. I've been taking Euphoria?"

"No. Bixine."

Hailey shook her head. "You're losing me."

"Euphoria came from aparistine—found in *Bixa aparra's* leaves and bark. These pills are made of a different chemical—bixine, found in the plant's roots."

She gasped. "Are you sure?"

"Yes." Insult welded to his scoff. "When the results came out negative for the panel of anti-anxiety drugs, something told me to compare it against *Bixa aparra*. I still had the roots I clipped last week. It was an exact match."

Parker leaned forward. "Are you saying someone added bixine to Hailey's medicine?"

"Not added. The pills are one hundred percent pure bixine."

Hailey held the phone. "How were you aware of bixine? I've never heard of it."

"When I was researching shamans, I came across a 1965 medical journal article about a drug made from the root of an Amazon shrub. The researchers identified bixine and showed it had the ability to affect cognitive functions. The shrub was *Bixa aparra*."

"Oh my God." Hailey covered her mouth with her hand.

Parker rubbed her shoulder. "Bruce, what symptoms did the subjects experience?"

"Rapid heartbeat, shortness of breath, poor circulation. Twenty percent of the study participants died from a heart attack."

Hailey gasped. "I've been experiencing the same thing."

Parker wrapped his arm around her. "Would antihistamines exacerbate the symptoms?"

"I'd have to do my own research, but my guess is yes. Hailey, I'm assuming you ordered the pills from a pharmacy?"

"Yes. But I've used this pharmacy for years. There's no way the pharmacists would sabotage my prescriptions."

Parker's face was crimson. "Have you gotten all your prescriptions through mail order?"

"Yes. It's easier."

"Maybe someone got to your mail before you."

Hailey scratched her hands. "Sometimes the medicine comes a day later than the text messages tell me. I assumed the post office was running behind."

Parker frowned. "We can deal with that later. Bruce, were other studies done on bixine?"

"No. Peru was in a civil war at the time. Scientists were testing it as a potential mind-control drug, but it wasn't very strong."

Hailey snickered. "Not very strong?"

"Believe it or not, there are more powerful drugs out there. Shamans are meticulous about which shrubs they grind down to make brews for their villages. You might compare the brain fog from bixine to a mild date-rape drug. In low levels, it caused confusion and dizziness. Higher concentrations elicited even more dangerous side effects."

Parker scratched his head. "The million-dollar question is who put these pills in Hailey's bottle."

"I reckon you and Hailey can figure it out." An alarm sounded from Bruce's connection. "I'm sorry to run, but I need to pack."

Hailey blinked. "Wait. Where are you going?"

"Peru. A curator is taking me to the Mayantuyacu sanctuary to meet the shaman whose grandfather used the *Bixa aparra* plant. I leave Monday."

"How long will you be gone?"

"Maybe a month. It will take at least a week to fly down and hike to the village."

"What about your other projects?"

"Another researcher will monitor my work until I return." Bruce paused. "I could really use you this summer if you're available."

When the call ended, Parker loosened his arm around her. "Should I be concerned about his offer?"

Her heart melted at his concern. "No. I'd rather stay here with you and the kids."

Exhaling, Parker reached into his jeans and withdrew his phone.

Hailey's smile faded. "What are you doing?"

"Stefan needs to know about the pills. This must be connected to Mendoza."

"Why would someone switch my anti-depressants with bixine? This whole matter doesn't make sense."

"You said the medicine usually arrived a day late." Parker massaged his temples. "What exactly did Mendoza say when he attacked you?"

Hailey rubbed the bandage on her throat where Mendoza's knife had cut her skin. She shivered, remembering his bristly beard scratching her skin, his disgusting breath blowing across her cheek. "He was looking for Colleen. He asked where I was hiding something."

"Hiding what?"

"I don't know. Zhang came before Mendoza finished the question."

Parker paced the floor. "You thought someone was breaking into your house. I bet Mendoza's looking for something."

"Like what?"

"I don't know. But Colleen might." He powered on his phone. "I'll head out to the prison now. If I need to, I'll ask Stefan to pull some strings again."

Hailey tossed aside the covers. "Can you wait until I get out of here? I'll go, too."

He shook his head. "You shouldn't be near Colleen, especially after last time. Text me if the doctor discharges you. I should be back in time to take you home." He leaned over and kissed her. "I still have your pills in my car. I'll drop off the container to the crime lab on my way. See if the analyst can run some fingerprints."

"That's a long shot. My prints are on the container. And yours. And the pharmacist's."

Parker shrugged. "It's worth a try."

****

Hailey stepped out of the bathroom when Dr. Trevor tapped on the door. She eased back onto the bed and crossed her arms. "I was beginning to think you were avoiding me."

The surgeon gave her a cunning smile. "The idea crossed my mind. I wanted to wait until the labs were completed." He lifted the bandage on her chest and inspected the wound. "The stitches look good. There's no sign of infection, and your temperature is back to normal."

"Does this mean I can go home?" She scratched her hands, waiting.

"Only if you promise to take it easy."

Hailey clapped. "Trust me. The last thing I want to do is look for trouble."

When Parker returned two hours later, Hailey was gathering the items Liz had brought. She lowered the slippers into the bag. "Did you see Colleen? What did she say?"

"Nothing at first. When I told her you were stabbed, she didn't show any reaction—until I said Mendoza did it. Then she got nervous."

"Did you tell her Mendoza is looking for her?" She handed Parker her bag.

"I did. Colleen cursed and ranted, saying she shouldn't have trusted Mark. Then she sprang up and shouted for the guard."

A nurse stepped inside the room with Hailey's discharge papers and explained the after-care instructions.

Parker adjusted the bag in his arm and dug the keys from his pocket. "I'll get the car and wait in the pick-up spot while they wheel you outside. I can fill you in about the rest on the way home."

****

When Hailey opened the front door, a coterie of family and friends shouted, "Surprise!"

Ethan and Jake were hanging a "Welcome Home" banner across the living room wall, while Adam held three helium balloons in his hand.

The aroma of cinnamon and apples signaled one of Peggy's famous pies was baking. The scent of roasted chicken wafted from the kitchen.

Anna rushed through the crowd with her arms extended. "Welcome home, Mom."

Hailey eased into a chair and chatted with everyone. The day had been long, and it was only late afternoon.

The doorbell rang.

Peggy smoothed her apron and opened the door.

Joyce followed her to the living room and set a tuna casserole on the end table. "Thought Hailey could use some dinner for her first night home. I didn't realize you were having a party. The dish can be saved for tomorrow."

Hailey thanked her. "Please, stay."

"I wish I could, but Rose will be waking from a nap soon, and I have to start organizing the house. The packers are coming."

"Packers?"

"Oliver leaves with his unit in three weeks. We sold our house. Didn't Anna tell you?"

Hailey shook her head. "She didn't mention it, but congratulations."

"Thank you. You've had a lot going on. Anna mentioned Ethan's working for a landscaper. Can you give me the man's contact info? I need to hire someone to trim the bushes and mow the yard until we go to settlement."

"Sure. I think Santino's here somewhere." Hailey rotated her head and pointed to the kitchen. "He's the dark-haired man talking to Ethan."

"I don't want to interrupt your party. If you text me his info, I can call him later. We thought our house would be on the market longer. Three years ago, when we went to Germany, the house sat for four months."

"I'll text you this evening. Where are you moving to?"

"Boston. I grew up and went to college there. My dad still lives in his house. We'll stay with him until Oliver returns. Dad can use the company. He's been alone since my mom died."

Hailey nodded. "I'm sure he's looking forward to seeing you."

Ten minutes later, Santino and Jake moved toward Hailey. "We have to head out."

She did a quick study of Jake. His eyes weren't dilated, and he acted normal. If the pill wasn't his, where did it come from? "Can you stay and eat?"

Santino shook his head. "This is your first day back home. You need some quiet time. Ethan said he could work this weekend. With all the rain we've had, I might need him tomorrow and Sunday. He'll be home early enough to do his schoolwork." He waved and followed Jake out the front door.

Her father-in-law shuffled over. "Dinner's ready anytime you are."

As she rose from her chair, the doorbell rang again.

"I'll get it." Anna sped past her and welcomed David and the container of potato salad he bought from Logan's Diner.

Hailey inhaled, taking in the love surrounding her. The day would be complete if Mark were here, too.

Parker slid an arm around her waist. "Are you doing okay?"

Was she? It was time to move on. She gazed into his compassionate gray eyes. How lucky to have found love twice in a lifetime. "Yes. Let's eat."

****

When Adam ate the last crumbs of apple pie, Peggy picked up the empty pie pan. "The kids and I will take care of the dishes. Why don't you go and rest on the sofa?"

With her father-in-law in the room, Parker and David kept the conversation light, circumventing Adam's questions about the stabbing.

Soon Peggy followed Ethan and Anna to the living room. She untied the apron around her waist. "The dishes are put away. You should have plenty of leftovers. Can I do anything else?"

Hailey stood. "No, Mom. Thanks for your help."

"We're glad you're home. Adam and I have been worried sick over you."

"Please don't be." Hailey had never felt happier to have Mark's parents in her life. "I'm going to be fine. I love you both."

"We love you, too." Peggy handed Adam his sweater. "Ready, dear?" She hugged Hailey, and they stepped onto the porch. "I saw the unmarked patrol car beside the road. David told us you have security while they search for your attacker. Do you want to stay with us?"

Hailey shook her head. "We'll be okay."

Peggy waved good-bye. "Let us know if you need anything."

After they drove away, David met Hailey at the door. "I should go, too. It's getting late." He lowered his voice. "I still have surveillance posted by the road."

Hailey glanced at the patrol car near the driveway. "I doubt Mendoza will risk doing anything stupid."

"It can't hurt to wait another day or two." He shoved his hands in his pocket, hesitating. Was that sadness in his eyes or regret? "I'm glad you're okay."

"Thank you for everything, David. You're a good friend." Hailey hugged him and waved as he backed his car to the street. Why was he acting awkward around her tonight?

When she turned, Parker was standing at the door. "I have to leave, too."

"What? Why?"

"I need to do something." He kissed her and tucked a strand of hair behind her ear. "I'll come back in an hour or two. You can spend time with your kids."

He's following David. Hailey sighed. What was it about men needing to protect her?

"Don't be too late, or I'll be in bed."

Parker grinned. "I don't mind."

She strolled into the house and sat next to Anna on the sofa.

Ethan rocked on the recliner, watching TV.

Being home with the kids settled her soul. "How was school today, Ethan?"

He pressed the remote and switched the channel. "It was okay. I ate lunch with Jim and Rex."

"I'm glad your old friends want to hang out again."

"They wanted to all along."

"Why didn't you?"

He shrugged. "I don't know. After Dad died, everything changed. All my friends had a dad and I didn't. Santino's not Jake's real dad. We had more in common."

Next to her, Anna colored in her book. She was still biting her nails. Hailey chose a green-colored pencil and filled in a section. "How's my little girl?"

Anna snuggled closer. "Good. I missed you."

"I missed you, too."

At nine o'clock, Ethan stood and powered off the TV. "I'm heading to bed. Santino's coming at seven tomorrow."

Hailey hugged him. "That reminds me. Joyce asked for Santino's number. You might have work at her house soon."

When he went upstairs, Anna collected her coloring supplies. "Can I go to Sam's tomorrow night?"

Another sleepover. "I thought we would order Chinese and have a movie night."

Anna's lips pursed. "I'm not allowed to go?"

Hailey brushed the bangs from her daughter's eyes. "Honey, I just got home. We need to start getting back to normal—doing things together."

"We can get back to normal Sunday. Please, Mom? Just this one time. They're moving soon."

"I'll think about it."

An hour later, Hailey texted Joyce the contact info for Santino and powered on the TV. She was watching the news when the phone rang. "Parker?"

"Good. You're still awake."

"Did you find David?"

"Ah…How did you know?"

"I know you."

"Are you mad?"

"Just irritated. He's a good friend. I wish you'd trust my judgment."

"I trust you. I don't trust him."

Hailey shook her head. He was so stubborn sometimes. "Did you find anything?"

"No—don't say I told you so."

I told you so. "I won't."

"I know you think I'm crazy, but I think he's hiding something. After dinner, your father-in-law asked him what he did in his free time, and David got all flustered. I followed him to an apartment complex in Arlington."

"That sounds suspicious. You should arrest him." She laughed. "Who did he see?"

"I don't know. It was a gated community. By the time I got through the gate and spotted his car, he was already gone. I waited two hours and left."

Hmm. So David had a companion after all. Good for him. "Would you like to come over, or is it too late?"

"It's never too late. Besides, we have a lot to talk about."

Her cheeks warmed. "I hope you're referring to *us.*"

"Yes..." Parker paused. "But there's something else. The crime lab called with the fingerprint results. They found a useable partial print."

Chapter Forty

Mid-morning, the doorbell rang. Hailey wiped her sweaty palms on her capris and opened the door.

Liz stood on the porch holding a plastic grocery bag. "I brought your milk."

"Thanks for picking it up." Hailey gripped the carton. "Want to come in?"

"I can visit a few minutes." Liz followed her to the kitchen and sat at the table.

Hailey set the milk in the fridge. "Would you like some coffee?"

Liz loosened the floral-print designer scarf around her neck. "Sure, thanks."

Hailey poured coffee in two mugs and set out creamer. "How much do I owe you for the milk?"

"Don't worry about it." Liz waved off the offer. "After everything you've been through, this is the least I can do." She poured creamer in the mug. "Where are the kids?"

"Ethan's cutting grass, and Anna's playing with friends." Hailey sat and pointed to the banner in the living room. "They had a welcome-home party for me last night."

"They must be happy you're home. How are you feeling?"

"Better—as long as I don't look at the stitches." Hailey grimaced.

"Did the police find the attacker?"

Hailey shook her head. "Not yet."

"Well, I hope we get more protection in the building before summer sessions begin." Liz sipped the coffee. "Security is putting new locks on our office door."

"I'd like new locks for my desk, too."

Liz gripped the mug. "Why?"

Hailey inhaled. She'd need to tread lightly. "Remember when I was experiencing brain fog this spring and my doctor kept prescribing new medicine?"

"Yes."

"When I was in the hospital, the doctor ordered bloodwork. The lab didn't detect any drugs or metabolites from the anti-anxiety pills. I thought it was strange, so I had the pills tested in a private lab. The pills weren't even anti-anxiety pills."

Liz's hand trembled as she sipped the coffee. "Maybe the lab tested for the wrong drug. There are dozens of anti-anxiety medications on the market."

"The ER nurse wrote down the prescription on my pill bottle. My purse is with me all the time, except when I lock it in the desk to teach. The only explanation I can come up with is someone switched my medicine when I was in class." She studied Liz's movements. *Please let Parker be wrong.* "The police checked the container for fingerprints."

Liz glanced at her watch and stood. "Gosh, look at the time. I forgot about my hair appointment."

"Don't you want to know whose prints are on the container?"

Liz looped her purse around her shoulder and turned. "Another time. I'm late."

The woman was a piece of work. Hailey moved behind her. "Yours."

Liz halted. "You think I did something to your pills?"

"A partial print under the lid matched yours."

Liz's face turned scarlet. "This is a sham. You're trying to throw the blame on me. How dare you!" She marched into the living room and collided with Parker.

Hailey stepped beside him. "Liz, meet my friend *Officer* Tom Parker."

The accused woman's eyes lit. "How dare you try to implicate me in this...in this...I thought we were friends."

"So did I." *Boy was I wrong.*

"I bet Zhang switched your medicine. He's always in the office."

"It wasn't Zhang." Hailey chose her words carefully. "I thought you were my friend. For months, you knew I haven't felt well. How could you do this to me?"

Liz's lips quivered. "I haven't committed any crime."

"That remains to be seen." Parker crossed his arms over his chest. "Either way, I don't think the university will tolerate more bad publicity. They might even link you to her stabbing."

"Stop." Tears pooled in Liz's eyes. "It wasn't like that... Please...I need my job."

"Why did you switch my prescription?" As Hailey waited, anger turned to disappointment.

Liz fidgeted with her purse handle. At last, she closed her eyes. "George's gambling was taking us deeper in debt. The bank was going to foreclose on our assets. George asked me to help switch your pills. He said it would keep us out of bankruptcy."

Hailey gasped. "How?"

"Someone associated with the casino contacted him, offering to erase his obligation if he'd switch the pills."

Disgust filled Hailey. "You could have killed me."

Liz shook her head. "The pills were supposed to make you forgetful. I tried one before I let him swap the medicine. The brain fog lasted only a few hours."

How could Liz be so irresponsible? "I had toxicity effects from accumulating too much of the drug. I could have fallen down the steps or killed someone while driving."

Liz's face crumpled. "The man promised George it wasn't deadly."

"What man?"

"The man involved with the casinos...José Mendoza."

The hair on Hailey's arm bristled. "José? Are you sure it wasn't Manuel?" She turned to Parker. A heavy anchor pressed inside her as the memory of copying the files from the flash drive ran through her mind. José must have discovered she'd opened them. Dammit!

"His name was José." Liz wiped a tear from her cheek. "He said it was payback for something you did...I couldn't let my marriage fall apart." She collapsed on the floor and wept. "I'm so sorry, Hailey. I never wanted to hurt you. The bank was going to take our house. Our boat. Our vacation homes. Our reputation would be ruined. I didn't know what else to do..."

****

"Mom, I'm home. What's for lunch?"

Hailey jumped. Liz's sinister caper had preoccupied her thoughts since Parker took the woman to the police station an hour earlier.

Anna stepped closer to the sink. "Why are you dumping a carton of milk down the drain?"

"It smelled sour." Hailey wrinkled her nose and stepped to the refrigerator. "I don't want to get sick." She opened the door and handed Anna a plate of leftover chicken salad sandwiches and a bowl of pasta salad from the welcome-home party. Then she filled two glasses with lemonade.

Anna placed a sandwich on her plate and sat at the table. "Did you decide if I can go to Sam's tonight? Please? We want to have a sleepover together before they move." She chewed on a fingernail.

Hailey sat next to her daughter. "Why are you still biting your nails? I thought you were doing better."

"I was."

"Then what's bothering you?"

Anna lowered her gaze. "I don't want you to leave me."

Hailey stared. Leave? "Why do you think I'd leave you?"

"Dad did." The pain in Anna's voice was unmistakable.

"He couldn't help it."

"Sometimes parents don't die, and they still leave their kids."

Hailey cringed. The number of students living in alternative home-life situations had increased drastically in the county. "Do you know of anyone living without their parents?"

Anna slowly nodded, her eyes misty. "Nevaeh lives with her grandparents. Logan lives in the shelter with his mom and brother. Rose lives with Mrs. Rogers."

"Rose?"

Anna nodded again. "Mrs. Rogers is taking care of her while her mom's away."

"I didn't realize that. Is Rose's mom in the military like Mr. Rogers?"

Anna shrugged. "I don't know. She's been gone for a long time. Sam's not supposed to talk about it."

"Do you know when her mom is coming back?"

"I think she's coming next week. I overheard Mrs. Rogers tell Mr. Rogers."

"Rose must be excited."

Anna sulked. "I'm going to miss them."

"You can always write letters, or text, or video chat—" Hailey sighed. Who was she fooling? It wasn't the same. Friendships were treasured relationships. Joyce's kids probably needed Anna as much as Anna needed them. "Okay. You can sleep over tonight. But I want to spend time with you this afternoon."

Anna clapped. "Can we go shopping? I want to get a going-away present for Sam and Rose."

"Sounds like fun." Especially after the stressful week. "Shucks. I'm not supposed to drive until next week."

"Let's ask Grandma to take us. It'll be fun." Anna brightened at the plan.

The afternoon flew. After Anna bought two photo frames with the words 'Forever Friends,' Hailey treated her and Peggy to ice cream.

Peggy drove them home, then Anna raced into the living room and ripped open the packaging around the frames. "Sam and Rose will love these. I took a selfie of us last weekend. I'll print copies in the study and wrap them."

"Good idea. Why don't you print one off to keep for yourself?"

While Anna worked on the going-away gift, Hailey stepped onto the porch and relaxed into a rocker.

At four-thirty, Santino pulled into the driveway.

Ethan leapt out of the truck and ran past her into the house. "Hi, Mom. Do we have any cookies left?"

She waved to Santino plodding across the yard.

In the breeze, his hair blew to the side. Grime and sweat streaked his T-shirt; his tattooed arms were tanned a deep copper.

He stopped at the top step. "You're getting back some color."

Hailey smiled. "I'm feeling better. It's amazing what a good night's rest in your own bed will do."

"I bet."

"Is something wrong? You seem frustrated."

He shook his head. "I'm just tired. There's a lot going on."

"Where's Jake?"

"He took his truck to pick up a load of mulch. Your neighbor called for an estimate on yardwork. Thanks for the referral. I plan to stop by there tomorrow." Santino leaned his back against the porch post. "I saw your police friend—Officer Parker—at your party yesterday. Ethan tells me you two are back together."

With his grass-stained shoe, he kicked the concrete floor like a shy schoolboy.

So that's why he's upset. The moment couldn't get any more awkward. It hadn't been long since Hailey told Santino she wasn't ready for any relationship. "I'm sorry—"

"Don't be." He shoved his hands into his jeans' pockets. "You deserve to find someone who can make you happy."

"Thanks. I hope someday you will, too."

He pointed to the unmarked patrol car on the side of the road. "Do you know that car's been here since yesterday?"

"The police are staked out in case the attacker comes."

"They haven't located him yet?" When she shook her head, Santino rubbed his neck. "I've been thinking about the attack. Maybe it's connected to your husband's death."

"Why do you say that?"

"You have suspicions about your husband's death. What if the person who killed your husband wanted information, and now he's going after you?"

Parker alluded to the same thing. But Mendoza wanted Colleen. Her court records were public. Hailey shrugged. "I don't know what the attacker would want."

"Then I guess you're back to square one." He tipped his baseball cap. "Heavy rain is forecasted for Monday. I have Ethan and Jake mowing yards in the area tomorrow. Jake or I will come by at eight and pick up Ethan."

Hailey waited as he backed out of the driveway, and she opened the door. Santino's words lingered in her mind. Was it possible Mendoza wanted something other than Colleen?

In the living room, the phone on the table had a lit screen.

Parker texted. *—I'm heading over. Pizza for dinner? My treat.—*

Thirty minutes later, she opened the door and welcomed him with a kiss. "What happened? You were gone all afternoon."

Parker glanced around the room. "Where are the kids?"

"Upstairs."

"Let's go into the kitchen. I'll fill you in after I order the pizza." He brought his two fingertips together and made a light kiss, touching the air. "Tonight, you'll have a dinner that is *deliziosa*."

Parker placed the order, then he sat in a chair next to Hailey. "I spoke to Stefan. He'll alert the agents about José. The CIA has José's drug routes with his former contacts under tight surveillance. He hasn't been able to ship out any drugs. He's ripe for revenge."

She nodded, aware of the implications. "Is José in the U.S.?"

Parker shook his head. "Don't worry. According to our intelligence sources, he's still in Colombia."

Hailey arched her brow. "That's what you said about Manuel before he attacked me."

"Manuel left Colombia last week. The sources didn't relay the news in time. That mistake won't happen again. Stefan's already assigned agents to investigate José Mendoza's networks in Canada and the U.S. We learned José has ties to a casino in Vegas. We think the pit manager was approving additional gambling markers for Liz's husband. When he couldn't pay the money back, José must have offered to pay off the debt in exchange for swapping pills."

"How did he know to target George?"

"Who knows? José's a resourceful man. Once he found out you copied his files, he probably made a list of your acquaintances and targeted their Achilles' heel. In this case, it was George's gambling addiction."

"How did Liz know when my prescription was mailed?"

"She used a track phone and added the phone number as a second contact. Apparently, you left your cell on the desk one day. Liz went through your messages, saw the pharmacy you used, and made the request."

"What will happen to her?"

"Probably nothing. She's cooperating with the police. She claims she didn't know the pills would cause any harm. There was no malicious intent. It will be hard to charge her."

In an odd way, Hailey took comfort in the news. "Liz has been through a lot. I'm glad she came clean. At least we know to watch for José."

"You're a very empathetic woman. That's one of the many reasons I love you." Parker tightened his arms around her and claimed her lips in a sweet kiss. "But you may want to get a different office mate."

She winked and parted her lips for another kiss. "I already submitted a request."

The doorbell rang, and Parker peered out the window. "Pizza's here. Call the kids. I'll get everything ready. This is my kind of dinner—no dishes." He donned a white chef's hat and answered the door.

Hailey smiled. He was growing on Ethan and Anna. In fact, he was growing on her, too. She had always found him charming, but now she could see Parker as an important part of their family dynamic.

Chapter Forty-One

The bathroom door creaked shut, stirring Hailey from peaceful sleep.

She glanced at the alarm clock. 7:30 AM. Ethan must be getting ready for work. Satisfaction filled her as she stretched her arms over her head; she'd slept eight solid hours without any medication.

She grabbed her phone from the nightstand and read a midnight text from Anna.

—*Going to bed now. I'll be home for lunch.*—

Hailey texted Parker. —*Morning! Interested in breakfast?*—

Parker called her within seconds. "I wish I could."

"Are you working?"

"Not exactly."

"Where are you?"

"In a parking lot."

"Where?"

"North of here."

"Stakeout?"

"You could say that."

"Don't lie to me, Parker. You're spying on David again, aren't you?"

"Yes." His sheepish voice was barely audible.

"You're being ridiculous. Be happy he's finally found someone." Hailey sighed. "You're going to miss a delicious breakfast."

"Rain check?"

"Sure. I owe you for driving Anna to Samantha's last night."

"Glad to help. It was only a two-minute drive down the block."

"I know, but it was too dark for Anna to walk the path. Ethan enjoyed chatting last night." She had forgotten how slick Parker's interrogation tactics were. Not only had he quizzed her about David, Parker also grilled Ethan about Santino.

"Ethan seems to like his job."

"Santino's been a good role model. He's not as shady as you think."

"I'm more interested in his boat."

"You're hopeless. I'll call you back. Ethan's leaving soon."

She dressed in a tank top, oversized sweatshirt, and jeans, and then she hurried downstairs.

In the kitchen, Ethan was packing water bottles into his insulated lunchbox.

She flashed a warm smile. "Morning. Do you have time for breakfast with your mother?"

The last slice of French toast landed on Ethan's plate just as the doorbell rang.

"Tell Santino I'll be right down." He shoved the toast into his mouth and darted upstairs.

Hailey carried his lunchbox into the foyer and opened the door.

Santino stood, rubbing his eyes. His jeans had the same stains as the previous day, but he wore a fresh, wrinkled T-shirt.

"Come in. Ethan will be down after he brushes his teeth."

Santino removed his hat and stepped inside. "How are you feeling today?"

"I'm doing a lot better."

"I thought you'd be in bed." His expression was kind, but his voice was gruff.

"I'll sleep after Ethan leaves. The house will be empty for a few hours. Anna's on another sleepover."

His brow raised. "Another one?"

"Her best friend is moving to Massachusetts. The girl's mother is my neighbor who called you yesterday to clean her property. Anna's taking it hard."

"I imagine Anna was afraid of losing you, too, when you were stabbed." Santino scratched his head. "Jake was upset after Janet ran off. He still misses her."

Hailey nodded. "It's a shame how many kids deal with difficult home life situations. Ethan and Anna. Jake and Zac. Even the little girl where Anna stayed overnight has issues. The poor child is only five years old and has separation anxiety."

"Five years old, really?"

She nodded. The disheartening news still tugged at her heart. "Her real mother has been gone a while, but she should be returning any day."

Santino's mood perked up. "Where's the mother?"

Hailey shrugged. "I assume she's overseas. The family taking care of her is in the military."

"Your neighbor mentioned her husband was being deployed. Where is the family moving?"

"Boston. Joyce grew up there."

Ethan ran down the stairs and picked up the lunchbox. "Sorry I'm late, Santino."

Santino fished his keys from his pocket. "It's okay. Tell Jake to start the truck." He waited until Ethan left, and then he adjusted the baseball cap on his head. "We might be late coming back. Jake will drive Ethan in his truck, and they'll mow in the area while I take care of some business. It was good talking to you."

****

Manuel glanced at the screen. 8:27 AM. How long had he lain in bed, trembling? Dreams of Selena and Bella tormented his sleep during the night. Both had called to him, desperate to escape José's executions, but Manuel ran away like a whimpering coward. He lost his first love years ago. He couldn't lose Bella.

Could he convince her to live in Colombia? He'd spoil Bella with the extravagant family jewels his grandmother had bequeathed him. Indulge her with the lavish lifestyle to which she'd been accustomed. They would travel throughout Colombia, swimming in the beautiful Marinka waterfalls, watching the stars in the Tatacoa Desert, and relaxing on the Caribbean beaches, where he'd leisurely pleasure every centimeter of her body until she begged him to stop. He'd give Bella complete control of the lab. He'd give her—and Katia—the world.

His phone vibrated. Manuel opened a text from Santino.

—*I think we found her.*—

Manuel gripped his burner phone. —*Where?*—

—*I'll text within the hour. Need to verify.*—

Chapter Forty-Two

Hailey changed the dressing over her wound and climbed back into bed, her thoughts juggling between Mark, Mendoza, and Parker. Her soul shattered when Mark had died, but it was time to rebuild her spirit and mend her tattered heart. The kids deserved a mother who was happy.

Mendoza robbed her of that happiness. His name burnt like acid on her tongue. Her chest wound ached, but her spine turned to steel. Had she ever met another clan as dangerous, malevolent, and vengeful as the Mendoza family?

Parker made her laugh again, and they shared an intimate bond. He'd raised her first child. Years ago—long before Mark—he had brought her out of a depression when she had no hope. And now he was saving her again. Her heart fluttered. She could see a life with Parker. They finally had a chance at love.

Too distracted to sleep, Hailey walked downstairs. She sat on the sofa, grabbed the TV remote, and surfed the channels. When nothing interested her, she perused Ethan's video games and Anna's coloring supplies scattered across the carpet. *Parker was a good sport playing with the kids yesterday.*

Anna would be home in a few hours. Might as well tidy the room. When she fluffed the pillows, a photo on the end table flitted to the carpet. Hailey leaned over and grabbed it. The snapshot was a group selfie of Anna, Samantha, and Rose—a copy of the pics Anna wrapped as gifts. Hailey hadn't seen it until now. The camaraderie of the three giggling girls brightened her soul.

Stepping to the bookcase, she hauled out the most recent photo album, opened the cover, and flipped through the pages of Anna's birthday party. The next page was full of Anna's dance recital photos. She paused at the photograph found in Mark's car. The toddler's mysterious eyes seemed sad in a way. *Who are you?*

Hailey opened the plastic covering and inserted the picture of Anna and her two friends. Rose's dark-blue eyes were similar to the girl's eyes in the other picture. The left eye in both prints turned upward. She held the photographs side by side. She hadn't seen Rose up close in a while. How odd….

Rose definitely *looked* like the girl in the picture. Anna had said Rose's mother was coming home any day…Colleen was in jail and due to be released next week. Hailey gasped. Could the child be Rose?

The album slipped through her hands, and a chill ran down her spine. What had Mendoza said before he stabbed her? *"Where is she?"* Hailey covered her mouth. *Oh my God! Colleen gave birth to Mendoza's child, and now he's trying to find his daughter.* It had to be.

She paced as a flood of memories began to organize into puzzle pieces.

Someone was breaking into her house to find clues.

Was it possible Joyce was taking care of Colleen's baby? How would they know each other? Anna said

Joyce went to Harvard. On the way to the prison, Parker said Colleen had a degree from Harvard. Joyce was tight with her sorority sisters. David mentioned Colleen was a sorority girl. Joyce and Colleen were around the same age. They could have known each other.

Hailey picked up her cell. Parker would never believe this.

****

Mark brushed his teeth in the bathroom and studied his reflection. Most days he didn't have the courage to look. From a distance, the transparent burn mask he wore twenty hours each day might fool an unsuspecting viewer, but up close, the plastic covering compressing his scars was quite noticeable. If he contacted Hailey, would she take him back?

He studied his eyes and lips peeking through the openings. Would she recognize him in this shell?

"Mark?"

He stepped back from the sink. David must have come to assist with the therapy. "Just a minute."

Mark dabbed his eyes with a washcloth and finished buttoning his shirt. Satisfied, he pushed back his shoulders. At least he could dress himself when the nurses were off for the weekend. Although walking was his most noticeable improvement, he'd made a lot of progress with the occupational therapy. His fine motor skills had improved to the point he could eat without creating too much of a mess. He still couldn't write his name legibly without using a keyboard, but his handwriting hadn't been exemplary before the fire.

He opened the door and crashed into David. "Shit. Why are you standing here?"

"I was worried about you."

Mark scowled. "Can't a man piss in private?"

David gave an impish smile. "Obviously not." He followed Mark to the living room. "Damn. You're walking even better."

Mark tried not to let the compliment swell his ego; he had more progress to make. "I guess the therapy is working."

David pointed to the kitchen table a few feet away. "I brought you some bagels—oh, and something else." He emptied his pocket and spilled his keys, receipts, and coins onto the end table. He sorted through the pile and held up a small paper. "I bought you a lotto ticket. Figured you were past due for some good luck."

"Thanks." Mark stepped into the kitchen and opened a brown paper bag. He removed a blueberry bagel and spread cream cheese over a half. "It would be my luck to win the lottery and not be able to claim the prize because I'm *dead*."

"I'd spend the money for you."

"Funny." Mark chewed on the bagel and picked up a pamphlet under the bag. "What's this?" As he skimmed the contents, rage churned through him. "You think I have PTSD?"

David nodded. "I read up on post-traumatic stress disorder. You have a lot of the symptoms."

Mark flung the pamphlet on the floor. "Name one."

"I'll name more than one. You have nightmares. You're edgy. Your mood fluctuates between anger—"

"Then ask the doctor to prescribe more anti-depressants." Mark's voice grew more agitated.

David shook his head. "The medicine's not working. I think we should consider psychotherapies. You can't go home if you're going to blow up at Hailey and the kids." He gave Mark a sympathetic look. "Just think about it. We don't have to do anything today."

Mark's appetite vanished, and he laid the bagel on the table. With a heavy heart, he trudged into the living room and sat in his chair. He didn't have a damn anger problem. "Any word on Mendoza?"

David sat on the sofa. "No, but Owen assigned agents to follow Colleen in case Mendoza contacts her."

"He will. I can feel it."

"Then you can concentrate on Hailey."

Mark scowled. "Don't start this again."

"You have to face it sooner or later." David stared a moment and shook his head. "How did you sleep last night?"

"I had another nightmare."

"About the fire?"

Mark nodded. "I remembered more about the man who led the attack. He had a tattoo on his arm. A maple leaf."

David leaned forward. "Where on the arm?"

"The forearm. Right here." Mark pointed with his finger.

David snapped his fingers. "Holy shit. That's—"

A loud pounding banged on the door.

Mark shrieked as images of the thugs flashed before his eyes.

"Wait here. We need to talk about this." David stepped toward the entrance and opened the door. "What the hell?" His voice bellowed in a mixture of surprise and anger.

"Who's there?" Mark turned and stared at the caller standing behind David. *Parker.* "Son of a bitch."

"Mark?" Parker gaped. "You're alive?" Eyes blazing, he lunged at Mark. "You selfish bastard! Why aren't you with your family?" He grabbed Mark's shirt, and then shrank back, instantly dropping his fists.

Mark lowered his head. Parker's reaction was exactly how his family would react. Dammit! How could he ever compete with Parker to win back Hailey?

David gently squeezed Mark's shoulder. "How did you find us?"

"I followed you for days, but I couldn't track which apartment you were going into...until now." Parker stepped back, studying Mark. "The fire. How did you survive?"

Mark's vision blurred. Never had he felt so pitiful.

"Have a seat." David gestured at an empty chair and waited as everyone sat. "Mark's been recovering here for the past few months."

Parker's brow furrowed. "Why are you keeping this from Hailey?"

Mark shook his head. "I couldn't hurt her that way. If I had died during my recovery, she would have mourned twice."

"Do you have any idea the pain she's in? Hailey's a mess. The kids are a wreck. Your house feels like a funeral home."

"I know."

Parker glared. "How could you know?"

Mark bowed his head. "Because David tells me everything. Their pain is my pain."

"Then stop their pain, man. Tell them you're alive!" Parker pleaded.

"And then what? Watch them shrink in horror when they see what I've become?"

"They love you."

"Look at me." Mark pointed at his head. He raised his shirt, baring more scars covering his chest. "My arms. My legs." He swallowed the lump swelling in his throat. "How can I expect them to accept me when I can't even look at myself?"

"So you're going to hide here the rest of your life? What's your plan?"

Mark shrugged. "I wish I had one."

"What do your doctors say?"

"Scarring is part of the healing. My compression garments and mask will hopefully minimize the disfigurement, but I'll never look the way I used to."

"There's got to be someone who can help you. What about Bruce Hanover? He does remarkable work with his research."

Mark pointed to his face. "*This* would take a miracle." He rubbed his head and winced. The pain was worse today. "Don't worry. I won't come between you and Hailey. I know you're seeing her."

"That was before I knew—"

Mark lifted his hand. Losing Hailey was so hard. "It's okay. I want her to be happy."

Parker's jaw clenched. "Hailey has a right to know."

"And I have a right not to tell her. It's my hell I'm living, not hers."

Parker shook his head. "Who did this to you?"

David cracked his knuckles. "Santino."

Mark flinched. "Santino?"

David nodded. "Before Parker charged in here, you remembered seeing a maple leaf tattoo on the attacker's forearm."

"Oh shit! Santino's tatted up." Parker squeezed his eyes. "I've seen his leaf. Dammit! Ethan's with him today."

David bolted from the sofa. "Parker, we need to go."

Parker darted toward the door. "I'll drive."

Mark reached for his cane. "I'm going, too."

David shook his head. "Parker and I will warn Hailey."

Mark slammed the cane to the floor. "Ethan's my son. He's my responsibility."

Parker's phone rang, and he glanced at the screen. "It's Hailey." He swiped the keypad and held the phone to his ear. "I was about to call."

"I learned something that will shock you." Hailey's voice was agitated.

Parker glanced at Mark. "Too late."

Mark tilted his head toward the phone. It would be easier to listen in if Parker put Hailey on the damn speakerphone.

She continued. "I know what Mark was hiding. Colleen had a baby."

Mark froze, powerless to move away from Parker's icy glare.

****

"Parker? Can you hear me?" Hailey trembled as she gripped the photo. Why did he sound distracted?

"Slow down. What are you talking about?"

"The photo in Mark's car. I thought the baby was one of Mark's sisters, but this girl has curly black hair, and her left eye is different from the right. I think the baby is Rose."

"Anna's friend?"

C. Becker

"Yes. Where you drove Anna for her sleepover. I think Joyce has been watching Rose while Colleen is in prison. Rose has Colleen's eyes. Parker, it all makes sense. Colleen must have had Mendoza's baby while she was in jail."

"Hailey—"

She slammed her foot on the floor. "Dammit! Listen to me. I don't have time to debate this. Anna told me Joyce isn't Rose's mother. Rose's real mother is coming to get her next week. I bet Colleen is taking Rose back when she gets out of prison."

"Where's Anna now?"

"She's still at the sleepover."

"Hailey, you have to warn Joyce. If Mendoza finds out where Rose is staying, there's no telling what he might do."

"I'll pick up Anna now and talk to Joyce."

"Don't go anywhere yourself. You're still recuperating. Ask the guards securing your house to drive you. I'll leave now and meet you at Joyce's house."

"Okay. Where are you? Are you still spying on David?"

"No. I suspended that. I'll be there soon."

Hailey ended the call and hurried down the driveway to the guards' car. She tapped on the window.

The two security guards in the front seats ignored her.

"I need help!" She banged the window harder. "Open the door."

When they didn't respond, she unlatched the door.

A powerful metallic odor emanated from the car's interior. Two bullet holes penetrated the front windshield. The male officer sat, slumped to the side, blood oozing from his neck. In the driver's seat, a female officer stared as blood dripped from her forehead.

Hailey turned and retched. Ice filled her veins. *Mendoza! Oh God. He knows!*

She sprinted into the house and dashed upstairs, ignoring the stitches pulling her skin. Opening the nightstand drawer, she grabbed her gun, loaded it, and shoved it in her jeans. As she landed the bottom stair, her cell phone vibrated in her front pocket.

Anna texted. —*Mommy. Help. A man has a gun.*—

Mendoza. She clamped her hand around the phone. —*Where are you?*—

—*The secret playroom.*—

Her hands wouldn't stop shaking. —*Don't move. I'm coming.*—

Should she call Parker? He was already on his way, and every minute counted. She considered her car keys and tossed them. If she drove, she'd lose the element of surprise. She raced out the back door to the wooded path.

****

Nervously, Mark paced the floor. Dammit! David and Parker should have let him tag along. This was his mess. It was the second time in a week his family was in danger. The whole purpose of the ruse was to keep them safe. He should be there.

Why didn't I remember the tattoo sooner?

Cold sweat beaded across his back at the memory of Santino beating him. Mendoza and Santino could be anywhere. What if they discovered where Rose was staying? He should have warned Joyce and Oliver about

373

Mendoza. They thought Rose's father wasn't in the picture. Colleen had insisted the less Joyce knew, the smaller the risk. Besides, even sorority sisters had limits on their charity.

He picked up the remote and switched to a news station. Would the reporters know anything yet? After a minute, he hurled the remote at the TV, wincing at the crash. Mark stared at the shattered screen. What was happening? Never had his anger been this unbridled.

He eyed the pile of junk on the table David had left. Mixed in the receipts and loose change were David's car keys. *Oh my God. I* won *the jackpot!* Pocketing them, Mark grabbed his cane and rushed out the door.

Chapter Forty-Three

Hailey raced through the wooded path to the narrow opening behind the Rogers' house. She crept along the garage wall, the prickly junipers and thorny barberry bushes scratching her arms.

Hearing voices, she crouched under a window, risking a look.

Mendoza was harassing Joyce, pointing a gun at her.

Another man moved into view, brandishing a second gun.

Hailey's gut clenched. *Santino?* She ducked, letting her implants pick up the conversation.

"Where's my daughter?" Mendoza demanded.

"I...I...don't know what you're talking about."

At Joyce's shaky denial, Hailey chanced another peek.

Mendoza grabbed Joyce's arm and twisted it behind her back.

"Ow! Stop. Please, stop."

"I know she's here." Mendoza jerked Joyce's arm harder.

Hailey's heart pounded. Would Joyce break under pressure?

"She...she's at the movies."

With his free hand, Santino removed a knife from a wooden knife block on the counter. "No one drove in or out of here today. Start talking or I cut off your fingers."

Hailey buckled over and gagged. How did she ever believe Santino was a good man?

She gripped the gun from her jeans. If she fired at either man, the other might shoot before she took a second shot. She'd get the girls out first. *Parker should be coming any time. I'll text—*

Hailey patted her front pocket. Damn! The phone must have fallen out when she was running.

Past the garage, she inched her way to the front door and took in the smashed doorjamb.

"*Mentirosa*! Where are you hiding my daughter?" Mendoza's voice bellowed from the kitchen. Slap!

She winced as Joyce cried out. Gripping the gun, Hailey crouched below their line of sight and crawled into the house.

Santino and Mendoza put the pressure on Joyce, their backs toward the foyer.

Hailey aimed her gun at Santino, but he shifted and yanked Joyce beside him. *Damn!*

Stooping lower, she crawled up the stairs, plotting her movements. Based on Anna's recaps of the floorplan, Rose and Anna had the same room. Hailey slinked to the left into a bedroom where pink pajamas strewed the crumpled comforter. Rotating her head toward the closet door, she concentrated a moment and exhaled. *The girls are in there. Thank God!*

Sliding the weapon into her front pocket, she opened the closet and pushed the hangers across the wooden clothing rod, exposing a three-by-three-foot access door. Hailey unfastened the panel door and peered inside the secret room. The space was dark, except for a nightlight casting shadows on the three children huddled in the corner.

Rose sobbed softly while Samantha and Anna soothed her.

Hailey placed a finger over her lips. "Shh." It was just a matter of time before Santino or Mendoza came upstairs to look for them.

Turning, she shut the closet door, spread out the clothes hanging on the rod, and secured the panel.

Anna crawled over and squeezed Hailey in a tight hug. "I knew you'd come."

She breathed in Anna's sweet scent. "Thank God you're safe. Are you okay?"

Anna nodded. "Mrs. Rogers was outside watering the grass. All of a sudden, she ran in the house and told us to hide. Then there was a loud bang, and we hid in here and texted you."

Hailey kissed Anna's head. "You did the right thing. Did any of you see how many people there were?"

Samantha and Anna shook their heads.

"Anna, do you have your phone? I'll call Parker."

Anna stammered. "We played games on my phone last night, and I forgot to bring a charger. I used the flashlight in here until the battery died. I'm sorry."

"It's okay. Where's your phone, Samantha?"

Samantha bit her lip. "Downstairs. We were putting on our shoes to go outside."

Hailey hugged the girls. "Everything's going to be okay. Don't be scared." She turned to Samantha. "Your mom is downstairs. Once I get you out, I'll help her."

Through the walls, noises echoed as doors banged, glass shattered, and furniture crashed on the floor.

Hailey raised her finger to her lips again. "Shhh." The gun was ready in her pocket.

The footsteps became louder. Someone tramped into Rose's bedroom.

Hailey tightened her fingers around the gun and listened. She had forgotten how sensitive her implants were.

The closet door creaked as it opened.

No one moved. The girls' hearts pounded against her.

Finally, the footfalls faded.

That was too close. Next time the lurker might look harder. She considered the space, no larger than six by eight feet in area, filled with baby dolls, a two-story dollhouse, and accessories.

Hailey pointed to an access door on the rear wall. "Samantha, does this door open to the garage attic?"

Samantha nodded. "Mom stores decorations in there."

Hailey whispered, "Follow me." She unfastened the latch and opened the door.

Heat smashed her chest as heavy stale air choked her lungs. Sunlight shone through a window, lighting the roof tresses, which framed the attic. Across the rafters were tubs of Christmas decorations on sheets of plywood.

With one foot, then another, Hailey tested the plywood's strength, and then she helped Rose step onto the platform. Anna and Samantha followed.

When everyone was inside, Hailey moved the dollhouse over the opening and closed the access door. She led them across the plywood flooring to the window on the far side of the room.

Samantha nudged Hailey, pointing to a box. "Mom keeps the escape ladder over there. She has one in every upstairs room."

Making a mental note to do the same, Hailey retrieved the ladder from the box and unlocked the window. She hooked the chain ladder over the wooden sill, taking extra care to minimize any noise.

The distance from the base of the ladder to the wooded path seemed close, about ten yards. Hailey scanned the grounds and turned. "Anna, climb down first. Hold on tight as you step down. Samantha, you'll go next. I want you two to run on the path to Mrs. Peterson's house and tell her to call 9-1-1. I'll be right behind you after I get Rose down."

Anna and Samantha quickly climbed down. When they reached the ground, the girls gave her a thumbs-up and sped into the woods.

"Our turn." Hailey squeezed Rose's shaky hand. "It's going to be okay. I won't let anything happen to you."

Rose choked back a sob. "Promise?"

Hailey's heart broke for the girl. Rose had no idea this break-in was because of her. What kind of life would she have growing up as Mendoza's daughter? "I promise. I'll keep you safe."

Rose sniffled. "Okay."

Using her shirt, Hailey wiped Rose's nose. The little girl acted like Anna had when she was younger. "You're a brave girl."

She started down the ladder, guiding Rose as they stepped down each rung. When Hailey reached the ground, she lifted Rose from the ladder and clutched her hand. "Now it's our turn."

Click. "Don't move."

Hailey closed her eyes at the sound of a round being chambered. *Damn.* She'd be shot before she could reach her gun.

A strapping man with a ratty beard stepped in front of her and aimed the gun at her head. He looked no older than twenty-five. Her nose twitched at the trail of his cologne.

"Zac, look who I found."

Zac? Was this Chase?

A younger man with long straggly hair came from behind the garage. "Well, well. If it isn't Ethan's mom."

"Frisk her." Chase jerked Rose from Hailey and waited as Zac patted Hailey's legs and sides. That cologne scent was familiar, but from where?

Zac removed the gun from her pocket and shoved the weapon into his pants. He gripped Hailey's arm. "Where are the others?"

"What others?"

"Bitch." Zac slapped her face.

Chase lifted Rose with his free arm and glared at Hailey. "Start walking. If you run, I'll kill the girl."

Fearlessly, Rose thrashed her legs as they trekked across the yard. Chase smacked Rose's head, but she kicked him harder.

Hailey glanced at the woods. *The girls should be calling for help soon.* What was taking Parker so long?

When Zac reached the front door, he tightened his grip on Hailey's arm and pushed her through the living room to the kitchen. "We have company."

Santino turned, his expression a mixture of bewilderment, anger, and surprise.

Beside him, Joyce sat in the chair, trembling; a mixture of tears and blood trickled down her chin.

Hailey tried to shrug free from Zac's grasp. "Still finding people to do your dirty work, Mendoza? Let them go."

Mendoza's neck muscle twitched. "I may need some hostages." He turned to Rose, still captive in Chase's arms. Mendoza stroked her cheek, his face brightening. "Katia."

Rose raised her leg and she kicked Mendoza in the chin. "Go away, you bad man." She writhed away from Chase's grasp, slid to the floor, and scrambled onto Joyce's lap.

Joyce clutched Rose against her chest. "Hush now, Rose. It's going to be all right."

"Enough." Mendoza shoved his gun into his jeans and wrenched the child from Joyce's arms. "We've searched everywhere for you."

Bewildered, Rose spun around to Hailey. "Help me. You promised!"

Joyce stood, straining to grab Rose. "She doesn't belong to you."

With a hard shove, Santino pushed Joyce to the floor.

Mendoza's teeth gnashed. "I'm her father."

Chase helped Mendoza secure Rose's arms as sirens echoed in the distance.

Santino pulled out a syringe from his pocket and pricked Rose's upper arm.

Within seconds, she became limp.

Mendoza nodded at Santino. "Kill them both after I leave." Holding Rose in his arms, he marched through the living room and out the door.

Soon, a car engine revved and sped away.

Hailey jerked free from Zac, and she slapped Santino's face "You're an asshole."

Santino's hand clamped down on her arm. "I never said I wasn't. Let's go."

Zac led the way to a commercial van parked in the driveway and opened the rear door.

Santino gripped Hailey's arm so tightly she lost feeling. "Where are you taking us?"

"Chase's grandfather has a farm." Santino's eyes turned cold. "Tonight, we'll load your bodies into my boat and dump them in the ocean."

Her heartbeat raced. Parker still hadn't come. Could Santino and Chase actually get away with this? She hadn't come this far to die.

The sound of an engine rattling became louder as Jake drove his truck into the driveway and parked beside them.

Ethan leaped out first. "Mom?" His gazed darted between Hailey and Santino. "What's going on?"

"Stay out of this, Ethan." Santino's face tensed. "Jake, I told you not to come until I texted."

Jake seemed as dumbfounded as Ethan. "But we finished mowing all the yards. You said you'd be trimming bushes here today."

Ethan took a tentative step toward them. "Someone tell me what the hell is going on."

Hailey held her breath. *Please God, don't let Santino kill Ethan.*

A car with its siren blaring stopped at the bottom of the driveway.

Chase positioned Joyce as his shield, pressed his gun against her temple, and cowered behind the van.

Santino hooked his arm around Hailey's neck and rushed to the rear.

Thirty feet from Santino's truck, Parker pulled his car into the driveway.

David opened the passenger door and hunkered behind it. "Drop your weapons."

Hailey blinked. Why was David with Parker?

Opening his door, Parker pointed his gun at them and squatted. "Let them go, Santino."

Chase turned to Zac. "Give Ethan his mom's gun. Make him kill Parker. Teach the cop to mind his own fucking business."

Sneering, Zac passed the gun. "Kill him."

When Ethan hesitated, Chase raised his weapon to Joyce's head. "Do it, or your mom and this bitch die."

Hailey's heart pounded hard against her chest. How could she stop him?

Ethan glanced at her, and the color drained from his face as he reluctantly took the weapon.

She stood, frozen. Her son didn't know how to shoot a gun—or did he?

"Time's up." Chase sneered. "Shoot the fucking prick!"

"Ethan, don't do it!" Hailey tried to pull free, but Santino tightened his grip.

Arms shaking, Ethan raised the gun.

"Shoot him or I'll kill you too!" Chase released his hold on Joyce and aimed his weapon at Ethan.

First Justin, now Ethan? Hailey wrestled harder. "No!"

Santino lowered his gun. "Just shoot the fucking son of a bitch. This cop's been nothing but a pain in the ass."

Sweat beaded on Ethan's forehead as his gaze shifted between Parker and Santino. In a swift movement, he hurled the gun into the woods.

"You fucking idiot." Chase fired his gun and missed.

Ethan bolted across the open yard.

Scrambling, Jake took cover behind Santino's truck.

Hailey elbowed Santino in the chest, and he dropped his gun.

She shouted, "Joyce, get down!"

As Joyce plunged to the ground, Hailey dove for the gun. Santino reached for it, but she grabbed it first, and she fired, hitting Santino's leg. She glanced up at Ethan, sprinting across the yard, an open target. *Oh God! He's going to get shot!* "Parker, cover me!"

She raced toward her son, moving in an unpredictable path, turning, and firing shots as a fusillade of gunshots echoed from all directions. When Hailey spun around again, Joyce was running inside the house.

David and Parker exchanged shots with Santino's group.

Zac stooped at the rear of the van, shooting at Hailey and Ethan, and a bullet shattered the van's windshield, as Chase moved closer with Santino.

A round struck Jake, and he fell backward.

Amidst the mayhem, Hailey ran harder, the stitches burning against her skin. She fired at Zac.

Parker darted after her as the volley of gunshots continued. "Hailey!"

Hailey spun around again.

More shots blasted near the van.

Parker closed in from behind, but Ethan was still a good ten yards ahead. "Ethan, get down!"

David took a shot at Chase and missed.

Chase rose from behind the van and fired.

The blast was close—too close. She returned fire, striking Chase in the chest, but Santino scrambled along the ground, grabbed Chase's weapon, and fired at David.

From the trees on the side yard, an officer wearing a black SWAT helmet charged toward them.

She couldn't see his face, but he had a lumbering gait. Was he with the police?

Zac emerged from behind the van's rear door and fired.

The shot echoed through the air as the SWAT officer pounced on Ethan and pushed him to the ground.

A yard away, Parker fired twice and brought Zac down. "Hailey, get down!"

She scanned the area. Only Santino remained.

Boldly, he stepped from behind the van and aimed.

Boom. Boom.

Her ears rang. The shot just missed her.

David fired and another window shattered.

Parker hooked his arm around her waist and, turning, he fired as Santino blasted another shot. Parker fell on her as she toppled to the ground.

A loud crack sounded from David's direction, and then there was silence.

After a few moments, a heavy stream of sirens deafened the air.

Hailey's heart thumped. *It's over. Did David shoot Santino, or had Santino killed David?*

"Stay down, son, until your mom gets you."

"Dad?"

Hailey opened her eyes. *Ethan? Mark?*

She crooked her head and peered at the man three feet away. The SWAT helmet was dark, and she couldn't make out his face, but the man's gaze lingered on her for a moment. Could it be? She breathed the name softly. "Mark?" Then he limped away before she could make sense of everything.

"Mom?" Ethan's voice shook as he crawled closer.

"Ethan?" She struggled to move from under Parker's weight.

"I'm sorry, Mom. I didn't know..."

She nudged Parker. "You can get off now."

When he didn't move, she rolled him onto the ground.

He moaned.

The pain in his voice stunned her. "Parker?" She stared at the slippery blood on her hand. "Oh my God, Parker, no!" She leaned over him.

His face paled as his eyelids fluttered.

"Don't move, I'll get help." Hailey lifted her gaze to Ethan standing there openmouthed. "Call 9-1-1 and get David. Go!"

Without delay, he sprinted across the grass.

Hailey brushed back Parker's hair. "Stay still. You were hit. Help's on the way."

"There's...no time." He was shaking. Bright-red blood gushed from his chest.

"Don't give up on me, Parker." She wrenched off her sweatshirt and pressed it against his wound.

Dribbles of blood spurted when he coughed. "I need...to tell you something."

His skin was cold. God, why did he have to get shot? "Save your energy. We'll talk later."

He winced, his hand lightly grasping her fingers. "You're the only woman…I ever loved."

"I love you, too." Her voice choked. "Hang on—for us." Tears ran down her cheek. He couldn't be saying good-bye, not when they just started hello.

He coughed again and grimaced. "You made me… the happiest man alive."

She kissed him. "Stop talking like you're going to die. I won't let you. Do you hear me? Do not die, dammit!"

She glanced up at David and Ethan standing in the distance, directing the paramedics toward her and Parker.

"I want…you…to do something…for me." His strained voice was barely audible.

Wiping her eyes, Hailey leaned closer. "What?"

"Find Mark."

He was talking nonsense. "Mark's gone."

"No…he needs…you."

She whimpered. "What are you talking about?"

"David." He gurgled. "Ask Dav—" His body became limp, and the life faded from his eyes.

In desperation, she gripped his shirt. "Parker! No!"

As the ambulance attendants kneeled beside them, David bent over beside her and whispered in a gentle voice. "The paramedics need room."

Her knees wouldn't move. She stared at the warm blood on her hands as David guided her back.

"Mom?"

"Ethan?" Her vision blurred as she clung to him in hope.

Chapter Forty-Four

The shaking wouldn't stop. She was trapped in another cruel nightmare.

Parker was gone.

Already she missed his strength. His deep voice. His compassionate gray eyes. Grabbing a handful of tissues, Hailey sat on her living room sofa and released a new wave of tears.

The doorbell chimed.

She glanced at the wall clock. Eight o'clock. The day was never going to end. She made her way to the foyer and opened the door. *David.* She had no energy for him. Or anyone for that matter.

He gave a tentative smile. "I would've come sooner, but I waited for the officer to give me a ride. Feeling any better?"

She shook her head, afraid to speak, and walked back into the living room.

He followed her and pulled out a phone from his shirt pocket. "The police found your phone when they searched the area. It was on the path behind the house."

She managed a smile. Already she missed Parker's texts. "Thank you."

"Where's your neighbor? She said she'd stay until I came."

Hailey curled up on the sofa and wrapped her arms around her knees. "Joyce had a hard day, too. When her husband arrived, I told her to leave so they could check in at their hotel."

David sat beside her, putting his hand on hers; he looked as exhausted as she felt.

"Their property will be sealed off for a while. You must have a lot of questions. I'll do my best to answer them when you feel up to it."

The only question she had was how to get Parker back. "I appreciate it."

"Did Joyce tell you about Rose?"

She nodded. Rose's guardianship had surprised her. And the fact Joyce and Colleen were college friends. "She said Colleen planned to petition the courts to regain permanent custody of Rose. Mark was finding a home for them in Kauai." The travel brochures in Mark's briefcase were for Colleen after all. Hailey scratched her arm. "I wish Mark had told me."

"He was trying to protect you." David scrubbed a hand over his jaw. "How's Anna?"

Hailey wiped her cheek. "She's a wreck. Anna and Samantha cried all afternoon. I can't even imagine how scared Rose must be." The memory of her promise to Rose as they stood at the garage window flashed through her mind. "*I won't let anything happen to you.*" Why did she make a promise she couldn't keep?

"And Ethan?"

"He blames himself for Parker's death."

"I'll talk to him." David wrapped his arm around her. "It's not his fault. Santino used him to get close to you. The police searched Santino's warehouse this evening. They found cocaine packed between bags of mulch. They also found other pills. We sent them to the lab for ID."

"Probably Euphoria." Chase's cologne. The mysterious musky scent in her house. She shook her head, connecting the pieces together. "Chase must have broken into the house searching for info on Rose. I bet he dropped the pill I found outside of Ethan's room."

Hailey laid her head against David's chest. "Parker suspected Santino was trafficking drugs in his boat. I should've listened."

"Santino had us all fooled."

"Is there any sign of Rose?"

David shook his head. "An Amber Alert was issued, but nothing yet. Police in Pennsylvania found Chase's car in a mall-parking garage where an SUV was reported stolen."

Mendoza was fleeing the country. Every passing hour increased the likelihood he would succeed. What kind of life would Rose have with him? "Does Colleen know?"

"Her lawyer will tell her. She'll be released next week. We were so close to getting Colleen and Rose out of town."

Her animosity toward Colleen softened. Hailey would never wish this pain on anyone. She pulled out another tissue and dabbed her eyes. "Did Jake make it?"

David shook his head. "He died at the hospital. Zac's in critical condition. Last I heard, he might live to see prison."

Such terrible loss of young lives. "I'll let Ethan know. Peggy and Adam took the kids to their house tonight."

"You shouldn't be here alone."

"I told Peggy I'd drive over later."

"Are you allowed to drive? With your stitches?"

Was he serious? "After what I went through today, my stitches are the last thing I'm worried about." She bowed her head as another wave of tears crashed.

David passed her another tissue. "I wish I could make you feel better."

He couldn't. No one could. "Why is this happening? First, Mark. Now, Parker. My heart can't take anymore." She shook uncontrollably.

"I know." He held her until she stopped crying. "Parker was a good man."

"He saved my life. I loved him."

"I know you did." He handed her the near-empty tissue box. "Do you need help with the arrangements for Parker's funeral?"

"I called Grace…his ex-wife." She wiped her nose and raised her head. "Parker wanted to be buried in Chicago next to his son." *My son, too.* "I'm sorry. I thought I was done crying."

"It's okay."

"It's not fair. I was finally happy again. After Mark—" She massaged her temples. *What had Parker said about Mark?*

He waited, as though studying her. "Are you all right?"

Something about David. "Ask David." She leaned back. "Parker said something strange before he died."

His brow pinched. "What did he say?"

"He told me to find Mark." She watched his reaction. "He said Mark needs me."

A muscle twitched on David's neck. "What else did he say?"

Hailey leaned back. Could she be right? "Dammit, David. Is Mark alive?" The red rose from the hospital flashed through her mind. "He *is* alive. Damn you. Why didn't you tell me?"

He looked so miserable she had to be right. She smacked his chest and stood. "What's wrong with you? Why would you lie to me?"

"It's not what it seems."

"What kind of sick game are you two playing?"

"It isn't a game."

"What would you call it? For eight months you let me believe my husband was dead." She slapped his face. "Damn you!"

"Mark wanted it this way. He was trying to keep you safe."

Lies. "Get out of my house—now!"

He stood. "Can I at least explain?"

"And make up more lies? If you cared about us, you wouldn't have let us grieve all this time."

"I do care about you." David's face was crimson. "Mark's my best friend. We thought he was dying—"

"We?"

"Owen—"

She raised her hands in the air. "Owen! That explains everything!"

"You have it all wrong! Listen to me. When I dragged Mark from the fire, he was severely burned. He wanted to spare you the pain of seeing him, and then grieving twice if he died. He's still in recovery."

Recovery? A thickness in her throat suffocated her. Mark was wearing a dark helmet when he saved Ethan. He didn't want to be seen. "How bad is he?"

"His left side has most of the scarring." David rubbed his forehead. "He's had skin grafts, but he's disfigured. He's afraid you'll reject him."

How could she reject him? She loved the man beneath the skin. "Where is he?" She raised her fist. "Dammit! Tell me. I want to be with him."

David closed his eyes. "He's staying in a government apartment in Arlington."

Hailey squared her shoulders. "Take me to him."

"I don't have a car. I rode with Parker this morning."

She grabbed her purse. "We'll take mine. Let's go."

"Now?"

She started toward the door. "Yes, now. Before you have time to warn him."

The corners of his mouth curved up. "I hope Mark will forgive me."

"I'll tell him you didn't have a choice."

"Do I?"

"No." She locked the deadbolt and followed him to the car.

****

"Buckle up!"

Manuel peered from beneath the blankets and dirty clothes and waited as the truck driver merged onto the interstate. Ignoring the stench of diesel fumes, he uncovered Katia, sleeping on the twin bed behind the cab's front, and he slid into the passenger seat.

It had taken ten hours of solid driving to travel through Canada's border security. The worst part of the trip was getting out of Virginia; police cars swarmed the interstate. Taking the back roads to Pennsylvania was a good decision. He was lucky to find a car to swap at a mall in Harrisburg. Americans were careless, leaving keys and purses in their vehicles.

Manuel gave Katia another sedative as she stirred during the switch.

He avoided the interstates, heeding Santino's advice regarding Amber Alert signs on the highway warning boards. When Manuel drove into Maryland, he phoned the Canadian contact. At the designated meeting place in New York, he transferred Katia to a tractor-trailer where the contact's son, Felix, waited. Out of caution, Manuel injected his daughter with another tranquilizer. Was he giving her too many sedatives? What choice did he have? Katia would need time to become accustomed to him.

"You can relax now. We'll be in Ottawa in two hours." Felix lit a cigarette and passed it over. "Looks like you need this more than me." He searched his radio and chose a channel without static.

Leaning back in his seat, Manuel took a drag and half-listened to the music. He could barely keep his eyes open. The next few days would be challenging. What had the Rogers woman called Katia? *Rose.*

The girl looked like Bella, with her charming blue eyes, but with darker flowing hair. She seemed like a feisty little child. Strong-willed. Just like her mother. Katia was probably intelligent like Bella, too. No doubt, she'd be hungry and cranky as hell when she woke in the morning.

He would need Mamá to help raise her. His responsibilities in Colombia still demanded his attention. Manuel needed to establish new contacts and review the drug shipments. Papà had placed too much trust in Luis and the other men. Now that he'd found Katia, he could focus on the business and his inheritance. Euphoria was his to control.

He'd keep his father from meddling with bixine. Papà was right. Power was everything. It was time to take a larger interest in the business. The Mendoza legacy would be Katia's one day.

Pride swelled in him as he watched her sleep. *What will Mamá say when she sees her* nieta*?* Reaching into his pocket, he ran his fingers over the passport he had transported from Colombia that would need Katia's photo inserted. He took another drag, crushed the butt on an empty soda can in the door, and rested his head.

At one time, Manuel dreamt of a family with Selena. Now he had a second chance with Colleen. She must still love him if she didn't turn state's evidence for a reduced sentence. Would Colleen come to Colombia once she got out of prison? Kidnapping Katia might be the only way to lure Colleen to his homeland and rekindle their love. Time would tell.

****

Questions circled through her mind. Hailey waited until David merged onto the interstate. "Tell me more."

He peered out the windshield through the thick fog. "About what?"

"Mark. Anything. Everything. Does he ask about us?"

David signaled left and maneuvered behind a car. "You're all he talks about. I give him updates every week."

Friday pizza nights. "So you spied on us?"

"If Mark had died, I still would've checked on you. He's like a brother to me."

"Did he suffer other injuries from the fire?"

"Mendoza's men broke his legs." He glanced at her when she gasped. "He's getting stronger each day.

Hobbles well without a cane. He's determined to get better so he can see you again."

Despite everything he'd been through, Mark was still centered on her and the kids. "He must have been in a lot of pain."

"He still is. We have to be careful with his recovery. I think he's suffering from PTSD. Certain sounds and loud noises cause him to freak out." As the fog dissipated, David leaned back against the seat. "Some nights, he wakes up screaming. Santino and his goons poured gas on him after they broke his legs."

She moaned. "Oh God."

"The asshole who poured the gas splashed some on his own clothes. He was the one the coroner couldn't identify—the one we used to cover Mark's disappearance. I stormed into the room just as he lit the match." David choked up. "I carried Mark out. If I'd reached him sooner, I could've prevented all this."

She shuddered in the darkness. "It's not your fault."

"He asked me to take care of you. It was his only request."

"How did you pull this off?"

"Owen used his government connections. A medical helicopter took Mark to a military hospital in Maryland that specialized in burns. The doctors didn't think he'd pull through. The first couple of weeks were so rough, I prayed Mark would die. As soon as he was stabilized, Owen flew him to the SCA in Austin. Mark moved back in the spring."

How fitting he had recuperated in the same place that saved her life when she was seventeen. "Mark had skin grafts?"

"His left side. He wears a compression mask and has compression garments for his hands and torso. He uses a splint for his leg and arm."

"To prevent contractures?"

"Yeah. He's had a lot of rehab, too. The therapists work with him 24/7."

"How did he afford all this? I never got bills from the insurance."

"Owen's agency took care of the hospital bills, therapies, and the apartment."

"And you flew back and forth from Texas to Virginia?" Hailey sank in the seat. "Why didn't you tell me the truth when he started getting better?"

"Mark didn't want anyone to see him. For a while, he didn't even want to see me."

She sat in silence for a few minutes. "Did you tell him about Parker and me?"

"Yes." David slowed the car as they approached road construction.

Damn. He had to be heartbroken. "Does Colleen know?" It would be the mother of all betrayals if Colleen knew Mark was alive.

"No. Only Owen and I know."

Strangely, the information soothed her.

David merged off an exit and drove a mile through town, passing through a secured gate. In the lot, he parked Hailey's sedan next to his SUV. "Mark must have taken my car. It's parked in a different spot from this morning."

Outside the building, David flashed his ID at the door attendant.

Hailey scratched her hands as they stepped down the long hallway.

At the last door, David halted. "Mark's going to be pissed I brought you here. If he gets agitated, I want you to leave. The guy's gone through hell and back."

Chapter Forty-Five

Mark regarded the broken chairs and smashed lamps he had hurled around the room. Sitting in his chair, he sank his head into his hands, unable to stop the helplessness.

What was happening to him? Another violent outburst. Worse, the shattered TV screen made watching the news impossible. What had he planned to accomplish, going to Joyce's house today? Like a coward, he'd parked David's car on the side of the road and hid in the woods. When Mendoza carried Rose out of the house, Mark watched, powerless to stop the kidnapping. He didn't even carry a gun. Preoccupied with Hailey and Anna's safety, he hadn't strategized a plan. Never had he been so reckless. He was a trained agent, for God's sake. Only through some miracle had he saved Ethan. *My boy. My beautiful boy.*

A familiar tap knocked on the door. Mark braced for a stern lecture, and he stared down at the duffel bag beside his feet as the door creaked open. He owed David the decency of a thank you before heading out. It was the least he could do.

Mark turned. "How are the kids and Hail—"

Holy. Shit. His throat tightened as he gazed at his wife standing next to David.

"Ethan and Anna are shaken up, but they're going to be okay. They're with your mom and dad." David cleared his throat. "I think I left something in the car." He stepped out and closed the door.

Mark stared at Hailey for what seemed like years. She had lost weight, especially in her face. A few gray hairs lined her face, and there were dark circles under her eyes, but she was more stunning now than when they had married. If he could only kiss her. Let her know he was sorry. What was going through her mind right now? Did she regret she came?

Tears blurred her eyes. "So it's true."

Standing, Mark searched for the right words, but shock and guilt governed his emotions. He bowed his head, concealing his face mask. "I know you must be angry." Was she horrified at his face?

He risked a peek, his body trembling.

Hailey's lips tightened in a fine line and for a moment, he thought she was going to cry. Then her frown softened, and her shoulders relaxed.

"Angry? More like hurt. Do you have any idea how devastated I was? And Ethan and Anna. Their life has turned upside down."

"I wanted to protect you." His response sounded rehearsed and cold, even to him.

She shook her head. "I should've been there for you. We promised to be there for each other 'in sickness and in health.' Didn't our wedding vows mean anything?"

"You have no idea how dangerous Mendoza can be."

Scarlet streaked across her cheeks. "Oh, I think I know. The son of a bitch stabbed me."

The news coverage of the stabbing raced through his mind. "I'm sorry I wasn't there for you."

Her expression hardened. "Why did you stay away?"

"I didn't want to." How could he convince her? "Have a seat. I'll tell you what happened." He inched closer, careful not to scare her.

"David told me about the fire and the different therapies." A tear ran down Hailey's cheek. "The kids and I could've helped you."

"I'm sorry." Taking a small step, he stood in front of her. She was so damn beautiful. God, he ached to hold her in his arms and promise her everything was going to be okay. "I was wrong. I should've trusted us more."

Her jaw quivered. "I wish you had." Staring, she extended her arm and smoothed his hair.

Did she pity him? He didn't want her pity. Mark tensed, preparing for her rejection.

Instead, she rested her head against his chest. "Oh, Mark. Why didn't you tell me? You didn't have to go through this alone."

He held her as she sobbed in his arms, her body shaking so hard he caught his breath. Oh God. She was crying for him, not out of pity, but love.

"Why did you let us go for months thinking we lost you?"

"I didn't want you and the kids to see me like this." Mark moaned. Would he ever find a way to make this up to her—to Ethan and Anna? "I'm a monster. I can't even look in a mirror." His shoulders slumped, and he wept, too.

Hailey wrapped her arms around him, and they cried together. "You're not a monster. You're my husband, and I love you." Finally, she held his hand.

"Let's go home." Her voice cracked. "We can talk about it there."

Home. His heart began pounding. "I can't go."

****

Hailey stared. "What do you mean?" She caught sight of the packed duffel bag next to the sofa. "Are you going somewhere?"

"Owen's driving me to the bus depot. He's giving me enough cash to get by for a few months while I find another place to finish my therapy."

"You don't want to come home?" She stepped back. What was he saying? "We need you!"

"I want nothing more." Tears shimmering in his eyes, Mark unfastened his face mask.

Hailey's heart wrung at his uneasiness at revealing the mottled blotches of red skin extending from the sides of his neck to his forehead.

"I'm not ready to go back. Look at me."

"I *am* looking at you." Hailey held his hand, protectively caressing the raised skin. Life was so unfair. "You listen to me, Mark Langley. You're the same man I fell in love with twenty years ago. Your scars don't change anything."

His shoulders dropped, and Mark bowed his head. Tears rolled down his cheek. "I'm not the same man anymore."

"When I look at you, I see what's inside. A man who loved his family so much he risked his whole life—and happiness—so we could be safe." She gently squeezed his hand. "This is the most profound testament of love I know."

Mark wiped his nose with his sleeve. "I didn't want this for us."

"I didn't either, but we'll get through this together." She leaned her head against his chest and embraced him, letting their hearts beat in synchrony.

"There's something else I need to tell you. I'm having a lot of nightmares, and now violent outbursts, too." He gestured at the broken TV screen. "I lose control."

The PTSD. "David mentioned that."

"I've got to do something. Any loud noise makes me break out in a cold sweat." He raked a hand through his uneven hair. "If I'm having post-traumatic stress, I need help, so I don't hurt you and the kids."

She blinked back another wave of tears. Even now, he was trying to protect them. "Don't do this to us again. I'll go with you."

Mark shook his head. "The kids need you here. I have to do this on my own." He caressed her cheek with his thumb. "I promise I won't abandon you again. I'll text you every day. I just need time to heal."

She considered Mark's torn expression. He needed to do this. Memories of her own brutal assault as a young woman flashed through her mind. It had taken her years to deal with the pain. Now her husband was suffering similar long-term trauma. "I needed time once, too." Hailey sighed. She was going to lose him again. "Promise me you'll come back."

Sadness clouded his face. "Are you sure you want me to come back?"

"What's that supposed to mean? You know I do."

"What about Parker?" Mark arched an eyebrow. "David told me you were seeing him."

She gasped. "You don't know."

"Know what?"

403

"Parker died."

Mark blinked. "He was just with you earlier today."

"Santino shot Parker." Her vision blurred. "The round was meant for me."

When she had explained what had happened, he shut his eyes. "Damn…I'm sorry."

Was the memory of Parker lying on the ground only this morning? She shuddered. "Parker was a dear friend—a very dear friend. I'm going to miss him. Before he died, he told me you needed me. He was right." Hailey scratched her hand; the realization of Mark leaving again stung. "Promise me you'll come back."

Mark tilted his head to the side, his dreamy blue eyes mesmerizing her, erasing the terrible burns and allowing passage to his soul. "I promise."

His husky voice gave her goosebumps. "I'm going to hold you to it."

Holding her tighter, he lowered his head, his breath warm on her lips. "I love you." With a hungry urgency, Mark captured her mouth, and in response, she parted her lips.

Chapter Forty-Six

Sunlight shone through the window, warming Mark's face. He trembled. How would his life change now that the world knew he was alive?

A group of rowdy teens stepped off the bus. They didn't seem concerned with his appearance, or if any of the passengers did, they didn't stare.

He stretched his arms; his muscles ached something awful. Running through the Rogers' yard had taken an enormous toll on him.

The rest of yesterday was a blur—except last night. He moaned, remembering his powerful kiss with Hailey. Heated passion had seared his lips. He touched them. The longing was still there.

Hailey had molded perfectly in his arms. And her hair. He could breathe in that coconut-scent all day. God, he had missed her. She was his rock. If Owen hadn't arrived with a bus ticket and stayed with him at Union Station, Mark would've taken a taxi home.

During the night, Mark had slept with his head against the window. The bus stopped in several cities, and every pothole the tires landed on jolted him out of his seat. He had considered renting a car instead of taking the bus, but his reactions had been slow when he drove David's car the previous day.

Fatigue and sadness weighed on him. He was alone now, but leaving was the right thing to do. Hailey and the kids needed to continue living life while he focused on getting better.

Even David needed to return to a normal life. Mark would miss him, too.

David brought the notion of a best friend to a whole new level. He had seen Mark at his absolute worst and hadn't abandoned him. David had sacrificed his career and his integrity.

Mark blinked away tears. God, he loved the man like a brother. He checked the phone he'd bought before he left town. No reply yet. His one hope rested on the response. If his idea worked, he'd have Parker to thank.

He glanced at the time on the front of the bus. 8:17 AM. His stomach rumbled. When was the last time he'd eaten? He unzipped Owen's timeworn duffel bag, opened a breakfast bar, and perused the PTSD pamphlet David had given him.

As the bus started moving, his phone pinged, and he read the message.

—Good to hear from you, Mark. I think I can help you. I'll make the arrangements.—

Mark clutched the phone. A tear splattered on the screen. There was hope.

****

Hailey opened the passenger door of David's car and walked alongside David on the gravel driveway to Adam and Peggy's house.

She'd spoken only a few words during the ride, her mind processing all that had ensued during the past twenty-four hours. Dizziness whipped at her from the ups and downs, twists and turns. Now more than ever, she appreciated how precious life was. Twice, Parker had saved her and brought joy back into her life. The season Hailey shared with him may have been short, but she'd treasure it for a lifetime. Hopefully she wouldn't lose much more time with Mark.

She turned as they stepped onto the porch. "Ready?"

"No." David grimaced. He'd followed her home after leaving Mark's apartment, and he'd been quiet since he woke up in her guest room an hour earlier. "Mark's parents will be angry I kept this from them."

She also wondered how her in-laws would react to David's secret. "They'll get over it once they find out Mark's alive." She knocked on the screen door.

The aroma of fresh-brewed coffee escaped from the kitchen when Peggy opened the door. "Come in, dear. The kids are still sleeping. Did you get any sleep last night?"

"A little." Hailey stifled a yawn. There was no point in divulging she and David had killed a bottle of Chablis as they talked until dawn. "How were Ethan and Anna last night?"

"They took a while to settle down. I'm glad they're sleeping in." She turned to David and pinched his cheek. "It's always good to see you, Davey."

The honorary member of the Langley family stepped to the table, his face reddening. "You, too, Mrs. Langley. Morning, Mr. Langley."

Adam gripped David's hand. "Davey, my boy. This is a surprise. Have a seat. Peggy was starting to make pancakes."

Hailey dragged out a seat. "I asked David to come with me this morning because I have some news we need to discuss before the kids wake up."

"Okay." Peggy removed her apron and sat in a chair next to Adam.

Hailey exhaled, glancing at David for support. She was about to deliver the happiest news in the world, but what if the shock was too much on Adam's heart? "There's no easy way to tell you this, but I learned something yesterday about Mark."

Adam's brow furrowed. "What is it?"

Hailey inhaled. She shouldn't just blurt it out. "Mark's alive."

Mark's parents gazed at each other, and for a moment, the room was quiet.

Peggy gave a sympathetic smile and patted Hailey's hand. "Dear, have you seen Dr. Thomkin lately?"

She shook her head. "What does he have to do with Mark?"

Adam hesitated. "We're worried about you. You've been through a lot. Losing Mark. The stabbing. And now Parker's death. We think you should talk to someone."

Hailey turned to David. "Please tell them I'm not crazy."

David cleared his throat. "Hailey's right. Mark's alive."

As he explained the events from the past eight months, the reaction from her in-laws shifted from confusion to euphoria, sadness, anger, and then euphoria again. When David concluded, Adam embraced his wife.

Peggy dried her eyes. "Our son's alive."

They reacted exactly how Hailey had hoped. She'd made the right decision to tell them.

Peggy poured coffee and passed Hailey a cup. "Are you telling the kids?"

Hailey scratched her hand. "I want to, but I wonder if it's the right time. Anna and Ethan will need a lot of counseling after yesterday. I don't want to add to their burden thinking Mark deserted them again."

"Nonsense." Adam shook his head. "They need some happiness in their life."

Peggy sipped her coffee. "I understand Hailey's concern. If the kids know Mark's alive, and he left town without seeing them, they might resent him."

"Mom. You're here!" With puffy eyes, Anna softly padded into the kitchen, making a beeline to Hailey's open arms.

Hailey gave her a bighearted hug. "My brave girl. Sorry, I didn't come over last night. I was too tired to drive." She smoothed Anna's tangled hair and paused when Anna bit her nail. "What's wrong?"

Anna glared as her brother followed her in the room. "Ethan's making up stories again."

Ethan stomped his foot. "I am not. I know what I saw."

"You're lying."

Hailey motioned Ethan closer. Was it too much to ask her children to stop arguing for one day? "What did you say to your sister?"

"Nothing. I was trying to cheer her up."

"Liar." Anna settled closer against Hailey's chest. "He said Dad's alive."

Ethan stammered. "I saw him. During the shooting, when I ran across the yard. Dad ran after me and pushed me to the ground so I wouldn't get shot. He wore a black SWAT helmet. I heard his voice, too."

Ethan's jaw clamped, as if he dared her to disagree. "I didn't want to say anything at first, but I thought about it all night. I know the man was Dad."

Hailey swallowed some coffee. She'd wondered if Ethan had processed Mark's presence in the tumult. "So much for finding the perfect time."

While Peggy made pancakes and sausage, Hailey and David relayed the details of Mark's absence, filling in specifics about Mendoza and Santino's search for Rose.

Ethan and Anna sat quietly, asking a few questions as David told them about the fire and Mark's rehab.

Anna lowered her juice glass. "Why did Dad hide from us?"

David gave a warm smile. "He wanted to get stronger. Your dad knew he was too weak to protect you, and he was worried the bad guys who took Rose would try to hurt you."

Anna nodded at his reasoning. "Will Dad get better?"

Ethan straightened his shoulders. "He will. Dad's a fighter."

Anna brightened. "Are you sure he's coming back, Mom?"

Hailey tightened her arm around Anna. "He will when he's ready."

When breakfast was over, Adam clamped his hand on David's shoulder. "Let's take a walk. I'll show you the engine I rebuilt in the garage. You remember hanging out in my shop when you and Mark were younger?"

David gave Hailey an uneasy look and muttered, "Here comes the scolding."

Peggy collected the dishes. "I'll handle the cleanup. Why don't you and the kids get some fresh air on the deck? Adam hung a new swing from the ceiling this week."

Outside, Hailey admired Adam's handiwork. As a child, she had loved porch swings. Sitting between the kids, she draped her arms around their shoulders.

Anna cuddled closer. "Do you think the police will find Rose?"

Hailey kissed Anna's crown, breathing in the strawberry-scented hair. "I hope so. People all over the world are searching for her."

Anna wiped a tear from her cheek. "Will Rose remember me?"

"Of course she will. You and Samantha are her best buddies." Hailey closed her eyes and shuddered. During the night, the scene with Rose had haunted her dreams. *I promise. I'll keep you safe...* Hailey had tried so hard to keep the promise.

Ethan's cell phone pinged, and he glanced at the screen. "When's Parker's funeral?"

"Next Wednesday. Who's texting you?"

"Jim and Rex. They want to know if I'm doing okay." His fingers skated across the keyboard. "Are you going to the funeral?"

Hailey nodded. "I plan to."

Ethan jammed the phone back in his pocket. "Can I go? Parker was a cool guy."

"I'm sure he would like that. We should pay our respects."

Anna twirled a finger around her hair. "I want to come. Parker was really nice to us."

Hailey warmed at her children's empathy.

"Don't you have to teach this summer?" Ethan planted his feet on the deck planks. Then he leaned the swing backward and raised his legs, letting the swing glide through the air.

"The department chair said she'd hire someone else. I'll recover quicker from the stabbing if I stay home and rest. I'd like to try family counseling, too." She steeled her voice as uncertainty struck Ethan and Anna's faces. "No quibbling. We can all benefit from counseling."

Ethan leaped off the swing and leaned over the deck rail as a cardinal flew past. "Are we still going to Aunt Laura's this summer?"

"If you want to."

Anna entwined her fingers with Hailey's. "Will you be okay by yourself?"

Hailey thought for a minute. For the first time, she'd be on her own. David wouldn't need to continue his Friday visits. Parker was gone. Joyce was moving. A chill ran down Hailey's spine. Would José find someone else to exact his revenge on her? If he did, she'd deal with it. She wouldn't live in fear. Hailey nodded. "I'll be fine. I might visit my friend Bruce Hanover for a few days. He wants to show me his research."

"Who's he?"

"An old friend who lives in Georgia. He knew my father." Hailey suddenly ached to learn more about her family. She imagined Bruce's surprise if she knocked on his office door. The white-haired man would open the door and adjust his wire spectacles. Then he'd greet her with a "Howdy, Hailey!" in his Texas accent, and grip his chest in a panic attack.

"I think you should see him." Anna spoke as though the idea was hers. "He might have some pictures of your dad for our photo album."

Ethan pushed the swing again and jumped on.

Excitement stirred inside her as she floated through the air, holding Anna and Ethan in the crook of her arms. Their future was a blank slate, and somehow, they'd draw their own map.

If Parker hadn't pulled her through a terrible ordeal when she was younger, she might not have recovered and realized her own strength. Now, Mark needed to get over his trauma. He deserved the chance.

A new determination flowed through Hailey. After she supported Ethan and Anna with counseling, she'd convince Stefan to let her work one last case and rescue Rose. Then she'd find Mark and bring him home— where he belonged. Those were promises she intended to keep.

A word about the author…

A native from western Pennsylvania, C. Becker earned a B.S. degree in Medical Technology and MT (ASCP) certification. C. Becker has worked in clinical settings testing drugs of abuse, among various lab responsibilities. The author has published multiple stories in different genres.